Mi Vida Loca

Trust

Carter Reynolds

BOOKS BY J.L. PERRY

Destiny Series

My Destiny
My Forever
Damaged – Jacinta's Story
Against All Odds – Angel's Story

Standalone Reads

Bastard
Luckiest Bastard
Hooker
Jax (coming soon)
Nineteen Letters (coming soon)

BASTARD

J.L. PERRY

hachette
AUSTRALIA

> **WARNING**: This book contains sexual content, coarse language and some violence. It is recommended for persons over the age of 18.

hachette
AUSTRALIA

First published in Australia and New Zealand in 2015 by J. L. Perry
This edition published in 2016 by Hachette Australia
(an imprint of Hachette Australia Pty Limited)
Level 17, 207 Kent Street, Sydney NSW 2000
www.hachette.com.au

10 9 8 7 6 5 4 3 2 1

Copyright © J. L. Perry 2015, 2016

National Library of Australia
Cataloguing-in-Publication data

Perry, J. L., 1972– author.
Bastard/JL Perry.

ISBN 978 0 7336 3582 3 (pbk)

Romance fiction, Australian.

A823.4

Cover design by Soxsational Cover Art, www.facebook.com/SoxsationalCoverArt
Cover and internal images courtesy of Dollar Photo Club
Illustration of Carter by Melissa McDonald
Edited by Nicola Rhead Editing, www.nicolarheadediting.com
Formatted by Max Effect, www.formaxeffect.com
Printed in Australia by Griffin Press, Adelaide, an Accredited ISO AS/NZS 4001:2004
Environmental Management Systems printer

This book is dedicated to my best friend, my sister,

Kylie

Thank you for always having my back,
always being there for me when I need you,
and for loving me unconditionally.
I love you more than words could ever convey.
I'd be lost without you.

PROLOGUE

CARTER

the past ...

REACHING OUT, MY MUM WRAPS HER LONG, DAINTY FINGERS around my small hand. "Jump, baby." She smiles as I launch from the bottom step off the bus, landing on the sidewalk. We both laugh. I love my mum. She's fun.

"Brrrrrr, it's cold today," she says.

Looking up, I find her shivering. I smile at her as she zips up her coat to keep warm. Digging through her bag, she takes out my favourite Spiderman beanie and scarf, holding them up for me to see.

"Put these on, sweetie," she says smiling as she crouches down in front of me, placing my beanie on my head and wrapping the scarf around my neck. "Let me get your gloves," she adds, reaching into her bag again. "I can't have my little man getting sick." I stand and watch as she pushes my small fingers into my blue gloves, one by one. "There, all snug."

"Snug as a bug in a rug," I add. This is something she says to me every night when she tucks me into bed.

"That's right, baby," she says leaning forward, giving me a soft kiss on my nose. Rising to her feet she reaches for my hand. "Come on."

As we walk down the street, my eyes take everything in. I don't think I've ever been here before. There are shops on one side of the street, and big houses on the other. "Where are we, Mummy?" I ask while looking around. The loud roar of a motorbike passing makes me jump.

"This is my hometown. I grew up here." I look up at her. Wow. Mummy lived somewhere else before our home?

She gazes down at me, but she looks sad. "You lived here when you were little, like me?" I ask.

"Uh huh. This is where your grandparents live."

"I have a grandma and grandpa?" I didn't know that either. I feel my eyes widen and I smile. I hear the kids at school talk about their grandparents all the time. I've always wondered why I didn't have any of my own.

I've never asked my mum why. Once I asked her how come I didn't have a daddy like the other kids, and it made her cry. I don't like seeing my mummy cry.

"I'm taking you to meet them now. They've never met you before." I'm getting so excited, like I did a few weeks ago when I turned five, and my mummy bought me a big chocolate cake. My friend, Josh, was allowed to come over. He even bought me a present. Nobody but my mummy has ever bought me a present before. I met Josh's grandparents once, when I was playing at his house. They were really nice. I hope my grandparents are like his.

I start jumping along because I'm so happy. Mummy stops in front of a big, white house. It's really, really big, like the houses you see in movies. It's so much bigger than where mummy and me live.

My mum's hand starts shaking as she holds mine. I look at her. She looks mad, like the time I drew on the wall at home. Her eyes are doing funny things.

"Your hands are shaking, Mummy."

"I'm okay little man, I'm just cold." She looks down at me and smiles. Her eyes look happy when she looks at me.

"Do you want to borrow my gloves?"

"No, baby," she says as her smile widens. She crouches down, placing her hands on either side of my face. "No matter what happens when we go in here, just remember how much I love you, and how special you are."

"Okay," I say. I love my mummy. I know I'm going to love my grandparents too.

"Good boy." She leans forward and kisses my cheek before standing up and reaching for my hand again. "Let's do this."

As we walk down the long driveway, my mum's hand continues to shake. I wish she'd put my gloves on. I hate how she's cold.

"One ... two ... three ... four ... five." I count the stairs in my head as we climb them before we stop in front of the big yellow door. I hear my mum let out a big breath. Letting go of my hand, she makes a fist as she raises her arm, but she stops mid-air. Looking down at me, her lips turn up before finally knocking on the door. I can't wait to see my grandparents. I hope they have chocolate. I love chocolate.

Reaching for my hand, she gives it a squeeze. When the door opens, I look up at the man who stands there. He doesn't look happy when he sees mummy.

"Elizabeth," he says sternly.

"Hi, Daddy," she replies nervously. He relaxes when mummy says that. The corners of his mouth turn up slightly. I feel my own big smile. Wow, this must be my grandpa. He looks so strong.

"What are you doing here?" he asks.

My mum doesn't say anything for what feels like one hundred years. "I wanted to see you. I ... ummm, wanted you to meet your grandson, Carter." She gives my hand another squeeze as she looks down at me.

"Hello, Grandpa," I say. I'm seeing my very own grandpa. I want to hug him.

He looks angry again as he stares down at me. Then his head snaps back up to look at my mummy. "Why did you bring that little *bastard* here?" he asks really, really meanly. "Get him out of here. Don't you ever bring him here again." Stepping back, he slams the door in our faces.

My mum makes a strange sound and I feel like crying. I'm sad because my mummy is sad. She only makes that noise when she's upset. I don't like my grandpa. He's mean. "Come on, baby," she says. When her eyes meet mine, I see her tears are already falling. I don't like seeing my mummy cry.

I'm almost running behind her as she tugs on my hand. She hurries down the driveway and back out into the street. "What's a bastard?" I ask. I've never heard that word before. The way my grandpa said it, it doesn't sound like a nice word.

My question stops her walking. Wiping her eyes with the back of her hand, she squats down in front of me. "You're not a bastard," she says sadly. "Pay no attention to what he said. You're a beautiful boy." She gives me a kiss on my forehead. "I'm sorry I brought you here."

"It's okay, Mummy," I say trying real hard to be brave. When my bottom lip starts to quiver and the first tears fall, I know I've failed. I'm not brave.

"Oh, baby." She opens her arms, pulling me tightly against her as I cry into her chest. "You're not a bastard," she whispers.

I want to believe her, I do, but why would grandpa say it if it's not true? *I hate that I'm a bastard.* Even though I don't know what it means, I know that this moment and that horrible word are going to stick with me for a long time. Maybe even the rest of my life.

••••

bas·tard
1. *Offensive* A person born to parents not married to each other.
2. *Slang*
   a. A person considered to be mean or contemptible.
   b. A person, especially one considered to be unfortunate.
3. Something that is of irregular, inferior, or dubious origin.

It's funny how one fleeting moment in time can change you. One stupid, crazy, fucked-up word can define you. I didn't know it at the time, but after that day things changed—I changed. I was only five years old the day I learnt I was a bastard, and sadly as the years progressed, that's exactly what I became.

PART
ONE

CARTER

present ...

PACKING THE LAST OF THE BOXES INTO THE TRUNK OF THE CAR, I turn and take one final look at the only place I've ever called home. The place I've lived for the last seventeen years of my life. Sure it's just a shitty old apartment block, but it's my home. It's all I've ever known. I'm fucking pissed they're forcing me to leave here. I've been dreading this day. I hate that I'm going to have to live with that *fuckwit* my mum now calls her husband.

Thank God it's only for six months. That's when I'll be turning eighteen; finally becoming a legal adult. You can be sure as hell the first thing I do, is blow this godforsaken place. My mum has that cock-sucker to look after her now. She doesn't need me anymore.

She started dating John Shepard six months ago. It was a whirlwind romance you could say. I guess she's been alone since I was born, so I can't really blame her for wanting a companion. It's always been just the two of us. At first I kind of liked the idea of having a father figure around, but my hopes were soon dashed when I got to know Fuckwit.

That's my pet name for him. It suits him perfectly.

I saw the difference in her when she'd come home from being out with him. She was happier. Lighter. Like she was floating or some shit. I liked seeing her like that. She deserved happiness.

They'd been seeing each other for a few months before she brought him to the house to meet me. I was on my best behaviour the first time we met. I did it for her. He was very pleasant until she left the room for a few minutes to get us some drinks. The way he looked me up and down with disdain instantly had my suspicions rising. As time wore on, those looks turned into hateful remarks. In the beginning I'd done nothing to provoke them. I guess he just took a disliking to me for some reason. Maybe because I was a bastard. Who knows? I was used to rejection. I'd faced it my whole life.

My mum's love has always been unconditional. Even when I acted up, she still loved me, still cared. I'll be forever grateful for that. She's been through a lot with me over the years, but her feelings for me never wavered. *Not once.* I was nothing to Fuckwit, I guess. Just a thorn in his side. Someone standing in the way of him being with my mother.

I was shattered when he proposed and she accepted, but I didn't let her know that's how I felt. I wasn't about to burst her bubble. She deserved happiness after all the sacrifices she'd made for me over the years. I wasn't about to stand in her way.

The day he finally put the ring on her finger was the same day he made his true feelings for me be known. They had some lame-arse civil ceremony at the registry office. It was my mum's first marriage. She deserved so much more than that. I didn't even want to attend, but she wanted me there, so for her sake I had to grin and bear it.

Afterwards, the three of us were heading to a nice restaurant for a celebratory lunch. Well, they were celebrating. I sure as hell wasn't. My mum asked Fuckwit to stop off at the local patisserie so she could buy a nice cake to take with us. The minute she was out of the car he gave me a hateful look through the revision mirror.

"I love your mother," he told me. "But don't think for a minute that any of that affection extends to you, because it doesn't. In my eyes, you're the unwelcomed part of the package." I hate to admit it, but his hurtful words stung. It only served to make me feel even lower about myself.

Why was I such a hard person to love?

Before I get a chance to close the trunk, my stepfather leans out of the driver's side window. "Hurry up, *son*. I haven't got all day," he sneers in a sarcastic tone. I swear he does shit like this to bait me. My head snaps in his direction.

"I'm not your son. You best remember that, old man," I retort, my eyes narrowing. "If you got off your arse and helped instead of sitting there barking orders at me all afternoon, we would've finished hours ago."

Throwing back his head, he laughs at my comment. He acts so sweet in front of my mum. She falls for his pathetic shit all the time. Truth is, he's a fake-arse prick. As soon as my mum's back is turned he treats me like dirt. She might love him, but I don't. *I fucking hate him.* This is going to be the longest six months of my life.

Slamming the trunk shut, I make my way around to the passenger side of the car. "Wipe your damn feet before you get in the car," he barks. I swear if there were some dog shit nearby right now, I'd tread in it just to spite him.

Sighing, I do as he asks before seating myself in the passenger side. *"Prick,"* I mumble under my breath.

"Watch that smart mouth of yours, boy. I won't tolerate you speaking like that in *my* house, and especially in front of your mother." *I'd never speak like that to my mum.* Him though, that's a whole other story.

Ignoring him I turn my head, gazing out the window, taking one last look at *my* home as he backs out of the drive. Christ, it hasn't even been twenty-four hours and I already want to punch him.

Not a word is spoken on the drive to his place. I'm thankful for that. My stomach is in knots. Living with this arsehole is going to be pure fucking hell. I have no idea what my mother sees in him, but surprisingly he makes her happy. That's the only reason I'm going along with this bullshit. I'm doing it for her, no other reason. After everything she has sacrificed for me she deserves to be happy.

It's about an hour's drive from my old neighbourhood to the gates of *hell*. Fuck, I need a cigarette. As soon as we pull into the street I'll now be calling home, my heart rate picks up. The street is lined with perfect houses, with perfect lawns and fancy manicured gardens.

I hate it here already.

"This is your new home, *my* home. Remember that," Fuckwit says when we pull into the driveway.

"Whoop-de-fucking-do," I reply as I exit the car before he has a chance to say another word. I make my way around to the back of the vehicle to unpack the boxes. Of course that lazy fucker heads straight inside. I guess I'll be doing all the work again.

Figures.

As I go to open the trunk, I'm stopped when I hear laughter. Pure, sweet, sickening laughter. My head snaps in the direction it came from, and that's when I see her. Well actually, the first thing I see is her tight little arse. She's bending over patting a dog, wearing these sexy little shorts. Tearing my eyes away from her, they land on the dog. It's a long-haired German Shepherd.

The perfect dog.

Growing up I always wanted a dog like that, but living in an apartment building that didn't allow animals made it impossible.

When the girl stands up straight my eyes move up to her long, dark hair that now cascades down her lean back. The sun's beaming down on it, illuminating its shine. I find myself wishing she'd turn around so I can see her face. She doesn't, so my gaze moves back down to her arse. Fuck me, what an arse.

Images of me wrapping her hair around my wrist as I bend her over, pounding her from behind enter my mind. It makes my dick stir. Jesus, why did I let my thoughts go there? Her body might be rockin', but that doesn't mean her face is. I guess, if I was giving it to her from behind, that wouldn't really be a problem anyway.

I watch as she raises her arm, throwing the ball across the yard. She's got a pretty good throw for a girl. The dog turns, galloping towards it. When he makes his way back he almost bowls her over in his excitement. She starts to laugh again, and I feel the corners of my lips turn up in a smile as I watch them.

"Good boy," she says in a sweet voice as she scratches him behind the ears. "Who's a good boy?" When the dog notices me standing there watching, he drops the ball from his mouth and trots in my direction.

"Hey boy," I say holding my hand out for him to sniff. He seems friendly so I reach down, running my fingers through his long mane. I can feel my smile widen. Smiling is something I don't usually do.

"Lassie," I hear her call out, making my smile instantly turn into a scowl. She's got to be fucking kidding. *Lassie?* She had the audacity to name this cool dog Lassie. What in the hell was she thinking? He looks more like a Rambo or Butch, definitely not a fucking Lassie.

"You poor thing," I whisper as I scratch him behind the ears. "She'll probably be cutting your balls off next and putting a fucking bow in your hair."

My head snaps up and my brow furrows as she makes her way towards us. Fuck me if her face isn't as beautiful as that luscious body of hers. I swear my jaw goes lax as she approaches. *She's a fucking babe.* Her long dark hair frames her angelic face. Her large eyes are surrounded by thick, dark lashes. Her creamy skin is flawless, just making me itch to touch it. My eyes drift down to her tits. They're kind of small, but more than a mouthful's a waste, I suppose. She has a cute little button nose that makes me want to throw up in my mouth.

Okay, maybe that last comment was a bit over the top. That's just my bastardry rearing its ugly head. It's a defence mechanism I've developed and mastered over the years. A barrier I've put in place. I hate that she's already making me feel things I don't want to feel. I've learnt over the years if you can't feel, you can't hurt. If I'm going to be seeing her daily, I need to nip this shit in the bud right now before it gets out of hand.

"Hey, you must be Carter. Your mum told me you'd be moving in today." Her beauty has rendered me speechless. *What the hell?*

Pulling myself together I straighten up to full height, towering over her tiny frame. Her sexy-as-fuck plump lips curve up into a smile as her beautiful green eyes meet mine. "I'm Indiana. Your new neighbour," she says sweetly, extending her hand to me.

Game on.

It's time to push her away before she gets too close. It's called self-preservation. I learnt a long time ago, it lessens the sting if I reject someone before they get a chance to do that to me.

My gaze moves down to her extended hand then back up to her face. "You called your dog Lassie?" I snarl. "What were you fucking thinking? That's a pussy name for a dog like this. You do realise he's a boy, right?"

Her sweet mouth opens in shock and her pretty green eyes widen before narrowing into slits. "The dog that played Lassie in the movies was a boy too, you know," she retorts, folding her arms over her chest. If she's trying to look tough she's failing miserably. Crossing her arms only manages to push her perky little tits up further. I feel my cock grow at the sight, and that pisses me the hell off. I hate how she's having this effect on me.

Opening the trunk, I reach in to retrieve a box and place it in front of me. The last thing I want her to see is the damn hard-on she's just given me.

"What's your problem anyway?" she asks, her eyes meeting mine again. "You're not exactly making a great first impression."

I almost want to smile at her fucking attitude, but there's no way in hell I'll be giving her that satisfaction. "I don't give a fuck what you think of me, *kid.* Why don't you run along and go play with your dolls like a good little girl?"

I'm really struggling not to smile now as her eyes widen in disbelief at the way I'm speaking to her. When her lips open, forming a perfect little O, all I can think is she has the most fuckable mouth I've ever seen. That thought only makes my cock even harder.

Sweet Jesus, what is she doing to me?

I'm surprised I almost feel bad for the way I'm treating her, but riling her up is way too much fun. I'm not about to stop now.

"Well that's just plain rude. Something pretty shitty must've happened in your life to give you such a bad attitude." She hit the nail right on the head. It sure did I want to say, but I don't. My brow furrows. Why does her saying that piss me off even more?

I hate that in less than a minute she has already seen through my facade. What is she, some kind of crazy clairvoyant or something? My eyes lock with hers again, and the sympathetic look I see on her face makes me dislike her even more.

"Nope. I'm just a bastard, and stop fucking looking at me like that. You're creeping me the hell out."

"Like what?" she huffs, placing her hands on her hips.

"Like you feel sorry for me. I don't want or need your sympathy. The sooner you learn that the better off we'll all be, Princess. Do yourself a favour *kid*, stay the fuck away from me." She gasps at my words and a satisfied smile crosses my face.

Mission accomplished.

"Later, Larry," I say to the dog, giving him one last scratch behind the ears before walking away.

"His name's Lassie, arsehole," she snaps to my retreating back.

"Not to me it isn't," I chuckle as I walk towards the house. "You won't catch me calling him that pansy-arse name." Maybe living here isn't going to be as bad as I thought.

"Come on boy," I hear her say, exhaling an exasperated breath.

As I walk up the porch stairs to my new hell, I hear her front door slam shut. Surprisingly, this makes the smile instantly drop from my face. I actually feel shitty for the way I just treated her. I don't often feel remorseful for my actions.

Why am I such a bastard? That's right, I was born one.

TWO

INDIANA

SLAMMING THE FRONT DOOR, I STOMP DOWN THE HALLWAY towards the back of the house. "Out you go, boy," I say to Lassie once I slide open the glass door. I feel so let down. I can't believe I was actually looking forward to meeting that douche. Nobody has ever been so rude to me. *Ever.*

He's nothing like I expected. Well, I don't really know what I was expecting. Certainly not what I got. He's a prick, plain and simple. A rude, egotistical arse. And as much as I hate to admit it, a sinfully hot one. *Why does he have to be so good looking?*

He's so tall, and so built. Every stinking inch of him. His dark hair and haunting chocolate eyes just add to his attractiveness. His cute little dimple on his left cheek. His perfectly straight white teeth add to his illuminating smile. Well they do when he smiles. I hate to admit that he's gorgeous even when he frowns. To top all that off, he has this perfectly chiselled face, which I'd seriously like to slap right now, by the way.

That part definitely took me off guard. Sure I've met a lot of hot guys before. Nothing that could compare to him though. He towers over my tiny five-foot-one inch frame. His dark hair and eyes suit his equally dark persona. It's a shame he doesn't have the personality to accompany his looks. If he did, he'd be perfect.

Unexpectedly, I felt an instant attraction to him. That was until he opened his damn mouth. God I'm so mad right now. How could I let him get under my skin like that? *Jackass.* I almost feel sorry for him. I did say almost. Crazy I know. I swear I saw something in him. I can't explain what. It was almost like his bastardry was an act, a front. I could be wrong. Surely no one could be naturally so rude and mean. His mother seems so sweet.

I'm glad my dad isn't home at the moment. I'd hate to have to explain my sudden bad mood to him. He'd be furious if he knew how Carter just spoke to me.

I make my way towards my bedroom. I need my iPod. Music may be the only thing that can calm me down. At the very least, it can help occupy my mind so I don't have to think about my new neighbour from hell. I thought Mr. Shepard held that title, but his new stepson has just taken the prize.

After placing my earplugs in my ears I turn the volume up to full. I also grab my iPad off my desk and move to my favourite spot in my room—the window seat my dad built for me. This is my happy place. I sit here for hours some days. Even though my bedroom window is at the side of the house, it's towards the back, so I get a glimpse of the lake that backs onto our property.

Logging onto my Facebook account, I send a private message to my bestie, Meg. If anyone can cheer me up, it's her.

> **Me:** You around?
>
> **Meg:** Of course. You know I live on here. LOL. What's up pretty girl?
>
> **Me:** I just met my new neighbour.
>
> **Meg:** What? Mr. Don't-let-your-dog-poop-on-my-lawn-

again moved out?

Me: LOL. No. His new wife and stepson moved in.

Meg: WHAT! Someone married the fucktard? OMFG!

Me: I know. Crazy! She's actually really nice. I have no idea what she sees in him. Her son on the other hand ...

Meg: How old is her son?

Me: A year older than us.

Meg: Is he hot?

Me: Meh. He's okay.

Total lie. He's more than okay. If I tell her the truth she'll be over here in a flash. I'm not sure why the thought of her crushing on him doesn't sit well with me, but it doesn't. Maybe because today he just became my enemy. Maybe it's something else. My bestie is boy crazy. She has a new boyfriend practically every week. I swear I can't keep up with them.

Meg: What's the deal with him then?

Me: Ugh! He's a douche. A rude prick.

Meg: Oh. Did he upset you? You need me to come over and teach him some manners?

Me: No. I can handle him. Thanks for the offer though.

If I told her what he said to me she'd be straight over. She's very protective when it comes to me for some reason. We've always had each other's back.

Meg: Wanna come over to my place? I'm still in prison for sneaking out the other night. My parents suck.

She makes me laugh. Meg is grounded because she got busted sneaking out to meet her boyfriend in the middle of the night. If my sixteen year old did half the things she has done, I think I'd lock her up permanently.

Me: Sure, I'll be over soon. x

I have a quick browse through my newsfeed before I log off. Looking out my bedroom window, my eyes move towards my neighbour's house. Imagine my surprise when I see Carter standing at the window directly opposite mine. He's looking straight at me. *Great.* Don't tell me that's going to be his bedroom.

My eyes narrow at him. What is he staring at? A small, smug smile plays on his lips. God he infuriates me. Standing up, I reach for the cord of my blinds. I don't think I've ever closed them before. I love the sunlight the window provides. There goes my sanctuary, my happy place. Could this day get any worse?

When my eyes reluctantly move back to his, I find him laughing. Fuck him. I can already tell he gets pleasure out of pissing me off. Flipping him off only makes him throw his head back and laugh harder. *Arsehole.*

I tug on the cord, hard, in frustration. Dreary darkness fills my room when the blinds are down. I have a feeling this is what my life is going to be like now that I have that douche as my neighbour.

Grabbing my phone off my desk, I storm out of the house. I end up staying at Meg's place until late. Her parents treat me like one of their own. My dad's working the night shift for the next two weeks, so there's no need for me to be home. The further I'm away from that arsehole, *Carter*, the better. His room is so close to mine we're practically damn roommates. What a nightmare.

••••

My dad's still asleep when I get up Monday morning. It was around 3:00am when he finally got home. I hate the hours he works sometimes, but he loves his job. He's been working in the Police Force since he was eighteen years old. That's all he knows, he'll never give it up.

After I eat my breakfast and wash my dishes, I set about getting things ready for my dad when he wakes. I pour his cereal into a bowl and cover it with plastic wrap. I put two slices of bread in the toaster. All he'll need to do is pop it down. I fill the kettle with water and place two sugars and a tea bag in a mug, leaving it on the benchtop.

When he's doing day shift we always eat together. When he's not, I usually get things prepared for him. Not that he expects it, but I like doing it for him. I'm sure being a single parent for the past ten years hasn't been easy for him.

I was around two years old when my mum's headaches first started. She would spend days, sometimes weeks in bed because of them. My dad tried to get her to go to the doctor, but she refused, saying they were just migraines. My dad said she was stubborn like that. It's a trait I've inherited I'm afraid.

By the time she finally did go for tests, the tumour on her brain was so large it was inoperable. They tried chemo. It was her only option. It wasn't successful. It made her so sick. She spent the last six months of her life bedbound. She died when I was six. Her death broke my dad's heart. They were teenage sweethearts. I'm not sure if he'll ever completely get over it.

••••

I open the blinds in my bedroom before leaving for school. I'm not going to be home all day, so I don't need to worry about stupid Carter taunting me. I don't even bother to look in the direction of his house. I'm not going to let him ruin my day again.

Heading out back, I give Lassie a quick pat before I feed him and replenish his water dish. "I'll see you this afternoon, boy," I say as I leave. He's too busy eating to even notice me disappear through the side gate.

Just my luck as I walk down the drive, Carter and his mother come out of their front door. "Morning, Indiana," she says to me. "This is my son, Carter. The one I was telling you about."

"We met yesterday," I reply, plastering a fake smile on my face.

"Oh, you didn't tell me that," she says turning her attention back to her son. I use that time to narrow my eyes at him. I have a good mind to tell his mother how rude her son is. Maybe he's adopted. How else could someone so lovely have such a prick for a kid?

Now that he's standing by his mother, I see they have the same eyes. That's pretty much it though. He must get his looks from his father. I bet he's good looking. His mother is extremely attractive, but her features are fairer than Carter's.

"Slipped my mind, I guess," he says, looking my way and winking. Ugh!

"Why don't you give Indiana a lift to school, since you're both heading the same way? It'll give you a chance to get to know each other better." *What little I know about him is enough.*

"No," we both say in unison.

"Carter," she scolds, causing him to frown at me. "It will do you good to have a friend on your first day." I almost want to laugh at her comment. Friends is something I doubt we'll ever be.

"Thanks anyway, Mrs. Shepard. I usually get the bus to school."

"Don't be silly. Carter will drive you. Won't you?" she says nudging him.

"Fine," he exhales while rolling his eyes in frustration. Even when he's angry he still looks sexy. That just pisses me off even more. Getting in the car with him is the last thing I want to do. If giving me a lift is going to annoy him though, then I'm all in. I'll take pleasure out of giving him a taste of his own medicine.

"Okay. That'll be great," I say smiling at his mother. When she turns to look at her son, I wink at him. I grin when his eyes narrow. Two can play at this game buddy.

"Have a nice day you two," she says sweetly. How she could've produced such a monster is beyond me.

"Bye, Mum." I'm surprised when he bends down and gently kisses her cheek. She smiles up at him. He's so tall he towers over her petite frame.

"Nice car," I say once I'm seated in the passenger seat. He grunts at my comment. I roll my eyes. I should've known better than to give him a compliment.

I have no idea what type of car it is. It's an oldish type, I know that much. It looks like it's in the process of being done up. A muscle car I think they're called. Don't quote me on that. My dad will know. He loves anything to do with cars.

It's a ten-minute drive to school. I decide to keep my mouth shut for the rest of the journey. Well, that was my plan until he leans over when we're stopped at a red light, and retrieves a packet of cigarettes from the glove compartment.

After he lights one up, he throws the packet in the centre console. "You shouldn't smoke you know," I say. "It's not good for you. Don't you read the warning labels on the packet?" I pick up his cigarette packet and point to the words **'SMOKING KILLS'** that's written in large bold font.

He blows a puff of smoke in my face before snatching the packet out of my hand. "Mind your own fucking business, *kid.* You really think I give a shit if I die?"

"Why would you say that?" I ask, horrified. Hearing him say that upsets me. I know firsthand how devastating cancer can be. "Carter?" I add when he doesn't answer me.

"What?" he sighs, looking over at me.

"You want to die?" I see what looks like sadness briefly cross his features before he recovers. Returning back to that hard-arse look he always seems to wear.

"I didn't say I *want* to die. I just said I don't care if I do."

"Well that's just sad."

"Listen, stop with all the damn questions. I'm only giving you a lift because my mum made me. We're not friends. Got it."

"Got it." Loud and clear you stupid jerk. I turn my head to look out the window. "Word of advice. If you want to make any friends here, I suggest you lose the bad attitude. This is a small town. You don't want to get a bad reputation on your first day." He doesn't bother replying to my comment.

We travel the rest of the way in silence. When we reach the street the school is situated on, he pulls over to the curb. "Get out," he barks.

"What? The school is further down the road."

"I know," he says smirking. "If you're so worried about my reputation, you'll understand why I don't want to be seen travelling to school with a kid in my car."

"I'm not a damn kid," I snap. "I'm one year younger than you."

"Huh. You could've fooled me. You look like you're twelve." Abruptly removing my seatbelt, I get out of the car.

"Fuck you," I say as I slam the car door shut. So much for not letting him ruin my day again.

THREE

CARTER

I SIT AND WATCH HER WALK DOWN THE STREET TOWARDS THE school. Why does she make me feel bad for being mean to her? I *almost* want to drive up beside her and tell her to get her sweet arse back in the car. Fuck that. Not happening.

Damn her arse is fine. My eyes are glued to it. Today she's wearing these sexy as hell skin-tight jeans. Why does she have to be such a babe? Why can't she be an ugly fucking troll or something? I feel my dick stir in my pants. *Hell no.* I need to get some action today—anything to get her face, those lips, and that sinful arse of hers out of my head.

I lose sight of her when I pull into the car park. That's probably a good thing. Having her living next door is bad enough. Knowing how she affects me, and having to see her around school every day, isn't going to be fun.

Parking the car, I grab my backpack and head towards the school office. My mum said I have to go there to pick up my schedule.

••••

By the time lunch rolls around, I'm feeling pretty good. I've managed to avoid Indiana all day. I've even managed to organise my first hook-up with a pretty blonde. Don't ask me what her name is. I've forgotten it already. The name's not important anyway. I'm only up for a bit of fun, nothing more.

After I grab something to eat, I make my way towards a table. "Carter," one of the guys from my math class calls out. "Come sit with us." He seems like a cool enough guy so I head over to him and his friends.

"Thanks," I say when I take a seat at the end of the table. He proceeds to introduce me to his mates. There are at least ten of them. I'll never remember all their names.

Brad, the guy sitting opposite me sizes me up. I hate it when people do shit like that. I feel like I'm being judged. "You're a pretty big dude," he says flicking his head my way. "Have you ever played football? We could use a guy like you on our team." He's one of those pretty boys. The kind the girls seem to fall all over. Smug bastard. I don't usually associate with his type.

"Nope. Not a fan of sports. Running around the field with a ball seems like a waste of fucking time if you ask me. The only physical exercise I like to do is the bedroom kind." The other guys at the table laugh. He doesn't seem impressed though. Fucker.

"You don't just run around the field with a ball, you dick. It takes skill."

"Whatever you say, man," I shrug, like I don't give a shit. He's obviously offended by my comment. I choose to ignore the fact he just called me a dick. I've already made one enemy today, Indiana. That's enough for one day.

The table goes quiet. I'm sure they're waiting to see where this goes. I'm guessing nowhere unless he decides to call me another name.

I pick up my food and start eating. When I look up and make eye contact with him he's glaring at me. If he thinks that's going to intimidate me, he's seriously mistaken. I don't scare easy. I stare him down.

"Hey Brad, here comes Indi," I hear one of the guys say. My head snaps towards the entry. *What's it to him?* She's walking towards our table. She has a friend with her. She's not bad. I might need to add her to my list of conquests. I'm sure that would piss Indiana off.

"You tapped that yet?" one of them asks. I'm presuming he's asking if he and Indiana have got it on. Why that pisses me off I have no idea. That cocksucker better not say yes.

"Not yet, but this weekend my parents are going away. I'm gonna invite her over," he chuckles. The cock sitting next to him gives him a high five. I'd like to high five his fucking face.

"I bet you can't get her to go all the way," another one adds. Fuck. Am I going to have to take on this whole damn table?

"How much?" Brad asks.

"Fifty bucks."

"You're on," Brad answers reaching over the table to shake his hand. Seriously, they're making bets on her now? "It won't be the first cherry I've popped and your fifty will make it all the sweeter." He rubs his hands together when he says that. *Like hell will he be having her over this weekend.* I have no idea how I'm going to put a stop to this, but I will.

As the girls walk past, Brad reaches out and pulls Indiana onto his lap. "Hey, beautiful," he whispers in her ear. It instantly gets my back up. Why do I care that his hands are on her? But fuck me, I do.

"Brad," she giggles, trying to get up off his lap. I want to tell him to let her go, but I keep my mouth shut.

"Don't make any plans for Saturday night, okay?" he murmurs in the crook of her neck. She pulls her head back and smiles at him. She has a pretty smile. When she's around me, all I seem to get is a scowl. I guess with the way I treat her I deserve it.

"What's on Saturday night?" she asks.

"You and me. We're going to do something. Just the two of us," Brad answers.

"Like a date?" she asks. When he looks around at the other guys sitting at the table and smirks, it takes everything in me not to lunge at him. My blood has reached boiling point. I try to act unaffected when the guy next to me mumbles, "A date with his bed." I swear I want to knock him out.

"Yeah, a date. I'll call you, okay?" Brad replies, smiling at her sweetly. Fucker. There's nothing sweet about him. He's a fucking snake.

"Okay." He lets her go and she rises from his lap. Her eyes quickly scan the table before landing on me. The smile drops from her face and her eyes narrow. That makes my lips turn up for some reason. Sure I'd prefer one of the smiles she gave that fucker, but I like that my presence affects her.

"Hi. You must be new here," I hear her friend ask. Tearing my eyes away from Indiana, I find her friend smiling down at me. She's even prettier up close, but has nothing on Indiana.

I can feel Indiana's eyes boring into the side of my head, so I decide to turn on the charm. "Carter," I say, plastering a huge grin on my face. I extend my hand to her friend and she takes hold.

"I'm Megan," she giggles, batting her eyelashes at me. That shit pisses me off. I hate it when girls act this way. Like the rest, she's putty in my hands.

"Let's go," Indiana snaps grabbing her elbow and dragging her away. I chuckle. If talking to her friend pisses her off, I may have to do it more often.

INDIANA

"I think I'm in love," Meg says as I drag her away from that arsehole. He can put on the charm for her. Why didn't I get that kind of greeting when I met him? God, he gets on my nerves. I hate that seeing the way he was with Meg just now made me jealous.

"You need to stay away from him," I demand as we weave our way through the other students, making our way towards our table.

"What? Why? Have you heard something about him?" she asks.

"That's my new neighbour. The one I was telling you about."

"Shut the fuck up," she says looking over her shoulder in his direction. "No way. That hottie is your new neighbour? Damn girl, you get all the luck."

"Don't let his good looks fool you. That's all he has going for him," I say.

"With a face like his that's all he needs," she laughs.

"Meg," I exhale, frustrated. "Please."

"Okay. Don't get your panties in a knot. Anyway, I think he has the hots for you." Her comment makes me laugh. That's the most ridiculous thing I've ever heard.

"Trust me. He doesn't have the hots for me. He can't stand me," I admit as we take our seats. Maybe I should've sat on the other side. I have a clear view of my infuriating neighbour from here. Pulling my lunch out of my bag, I realise I suddenly have no appetite. *That smug bastard is eating his food like he doesn't have a care in the world.*

"Oh, I beg to differ. I saw the way he was looking at you when you were on Brad's lap. If I'm not mistaken, those gorgeous brown eyes of his turned green."

I ignore her observation. She must be seeing things. I know how a guy acts when he's interested. Carter's definitely not interested. "What do you think I should do about Brad?" I ask, trying to change the subject.

"Are you seriously asking me that? He's been chasing you forever. Go out with him. He's a babe. Anyone else would kill to be asked out by him."

"Well I'm not just anyone. I'm not sure if I want to be serious with a guy yet. You know what his reputation is like. He's going to expect sex."

"So give it to him. You're nearly seventeen Indi. You can't hold onto your virginity forever." She's right. I know that, but I don't want to give it up to just anyone. I was hoping to give it to someone special.

Brad and I have hung out a bit. Mainly in a group. Never on our own. Well, except last weekend when he walked me home from a party. He kissed me goodnight. Technically it was more than a goodnight kiss, but it never went any further.

It's not like I haven't made out with guys before. I have. But, now we're getting older, the guys expect more than kissing. I know I'm ready. I'm just not sure if Brad is the one.

"Stop overthinking this," she says reaching for my hand when she sees the worried look on my face. "We've been over this a thousand times."

"I know. It's just ..."

"Just what? At least he's had experience. He should know how to please you. My first time was horrible." I laugh at her comment. She was fifteen when she lost her virginity. It was the first time for both of them. Going by what she's told me, it was a disaster.

I try to put it out of my mind for now. I only manage to pick at my lunch. My gaze keeps wandering towards the boys' table. Damn my traitorous eyes. Instead of looking at Brad, they're focused on Carter. I can't help but notice all the pathetic girls that walk past his table whispering and giggling like a bunch of morons when they see him. It infuriates me no end.

••••

After fifth period, Meg and I run into Carter in the corridor. "Hi, Carter," Meg purrs. *Bitch.*

"Megan," he says nodding his head. At least he uses her name. That makes me jealous too. I shouldn't let it worry me, but it does. "If you want a lift home, meet me in the car park," he adds turning his attention to me. I choose to ignore him. After the way he acted this morning, he's delusional if he thinks I'll get in the car with him again.

"He doesn't seem as bad as you're making out," Meg says on the way to our next class.

"Don't let him fool you. He's a monster." She laughs at my observation.

"He was nice enough to offer you a lift home. That's got to count for something."

"Yeah, and he gave me a lift to school as well. Trouble is, he stopped at the end of the street and told me to get out of the car. He was worried if people saw us together it would ruin his reputation."

"He said that?" she asks, shock clearly evident in her voice.

"Yep."

"What a bastard," she says pursing her lips.

"I know right. Now do you see where I'm coming from?"

••••

I steer clear of the car park after school and opt for the bus instead. Sure it will take me longer to get home, but it's worth not having to put up with Carter's rudeness and insults. I'm surprised he even offered. It was probably a ruse to fool Meg into thinking he's actually a nice guy, which he's not.

FOUR

CARTER

I WAITED TEN MINUTES, BUT WHEN SHE DIDN'T SHOW I MADE my way home. I kind of figured after the way I treated her this morning she wouldn't show up. Her loss. Even though I'll admit I'm disappointed, I'm not going to dwell on it.

When I pull into the driveway at home, I reach over and stow my cigarettes in the glove compartment. My mum hates it when I smoke. I don't do it often. I only started back up when I found out she was marrying Fuckwit. Smoking calms me, and lord knows I need it when I'm around him.

I don't think I'll ever get used to living here, in this house, or this neighbourhood. It's too fucking perfect. *I hate perfect.* People like me will never belong in a place like this. I'm flawed. The families that live in these kinds of areas are usually showy, pretentious and fake. Too good to be fucking true. Just like my stepfather. *Fuck I hate him.*

I exit the car just as someone pulls into the driveway next door. My first thought is it's probably *pretty boy* dropping Indi off, but I'm surprised when an older man gets out.

"Afternoon," he says making his way towards me.

"Hey," I reply, flicking my head in his direction. I wonder if this is her father. He may want to kick my arse if she's told him how I've been treating her.

"You must be Elizabeth's boy. She told me you were moving in over the weekend."

"Yes. Carter. Carter Reynolds," I say as I offer my hand to him.

"Nice to meet you, son. I'm Ross. Ross Montgomery."

"It's nice to meet you too, Sir." I'm surprised that him calling me son doesn't piss me off. I hate it when my stepfather says it. I suppose he only does it to antagonise me. *Arsehole.*

"Nice set of wheels. A 1975 Holden HJ GTS Monaro."

"It is. You know your cars," I say in a surprised tone.

"I'm a petrol-head from way back," he chuckles. "My old man used to have one of these. Are you doing it up yourself?"

"Yeah. I've done a bit to it. Some of the parts are hard to find, and a little pricy for a seventeen year old," I laugh. "I'll get it finished one day."

"I used to spend hours helping my dad work on his car when I was a teenager. If you ever need a hand with anything, I'd love to help out." His offer makes me smile. Why couldn't my mum have married someone like Ross Montgomery?

"I'd like that," I tell him honestly, because I would. With my track record, I usually have my guard up around strangers, especially older males, but for some reason with him I don't. After all, my father never wanted me, my grandfather rejected me, and my stepfather hates me with a passion. Ross seems like a genuine guy though.

I like him already.

"Can I have a look under the hood?" he asks.

"Sure." I reach inside and pull the lever and follow him around to the front of the car.

"Do you know much about the mechanics of the car?" he asks as he waits for me to open the hood. I watch as he runs his hand over the paintwork. A small smile plays on his lips. I love that he appreciates this car as much as I do.

"I was lucky the guy I bought the car off still had the manual, but no, not much. I'm learning fast though."

"Well, when you've got some spare time, I'd be happy to show you what I know."

"I'm free now," I say way too eagerly. The thought of working on the car with him excites me for some reason. Not sure why. Maybe it's because no one has ever taken time out to help me in the past. Except my mum of course, but she knows shit about cars.

"Okay. I'm working the night shift later, but I can spare an hour or so. Give me a few minutes to change and we can get started."

Stepping away from the car, I reach for his hand again. "Thank you, Mr. Montgomery. I really appreciate your offer."

"Don't sweat it, son. I'm happy to help. And please, call me Ross. I'm going to enjoy this," he says smoothing his hand over the hood when I close it. "I haven't worked on a car for years. These days they're all computerised."

As we stand there chatting, Indi walks across the front lawn. She must have caught the bus home. "Pumpkin," her father says when she wraps her tiny arms around his waist. He leans down and kisses the top of her head. "How was school, baby girl?"

"School was okay." She looks my way and narrows her eyes. I feel the smile on my face grow. I may not think much of her, but I like her spunk. I love that my antics get under her skin. I also admire the fact she gives as good as she gets. Most girls in her position would cry.

"Have you met Carter yet?" her father asks.

"Yes, we've met," she replies dryly. "I'm gonna go and do my homework. Did you get the meat out of the freezer?"

"I sure did," he says.

"Okay, I'll get started on dinner soon." When she walks away we both stare after her. My eyes are glued to her arse. I'm pretty sure her father's aren't.

"She's such a good kid," he says. "I'm lucky to have her." I don't reply. How can I? My feelings for her are all over the place. I hate and lust over her all at the same time. It's totally fucking with my head.

••••

After I've changed I head back to the car where Ross is already waiting. He's laid out some tools on the ground. Apparently they belonged to his father. He seems really keen to help me. I can already tell I'm going to enjoy spending time with him. I hope he will feel the same about me too.

He reminisces while we work and has some funny stories. Time goes by pretty fast. I'm really enjoying hanging with him. He's not only a nice guy, but he's taught me a lot already.

"What do you think about your daughter dating?" I ask out of the blue.

"Why?" he answers frowning at me. "Do you want to date her?"

"Me? Fu ... Ummm no." I can't believe I almost drop the F bomb in front of him.

Cocking his head he asks, "Why wouldn't you want to date her?" He says it like he's offended I don't want to. Jesus. Why did I even bring this up?

"I just heard something today at school." I know that it's low of me to tell her father what Brad said, but there's no way I'm letting her go to that cocksucker's place on the weekend. Especially now I know what his intentions are. I'm not jealous or anything. Well that's what I'm telling myself. It just doesn't sit well with me.

"What did you hear?" he asks turning his head in my direction while we're both bent over the hood of the car. I see his grip tighten around the wrench in his hand. His knuckles have turned white. Maybe pissing him off while he's holding that bludgeoning tool in his hand wasn't my smartest move.

"One of the guys I was having lunch with today ... Brad."

"Brad Cartwright?"

"I don't know his last name," I state.

"Tall. Blonde. Footy Captain. Cocky bastard."

"Yeah, that's him," I chuckle.

"Can't stand that kid. I went to school with his old man. He was exactly the same," he says. "What did he say about my girl?"

"Look. I don't want to cause any trouble for Indi." Because I don't, I just don't want her going near Brad.

"I want to know what he said. If someone is saying shit about my little girl ..."

"It's not like that. It's just ..."

"Just what, Carter?" he snaps. I can tell his patience is wearing thin.

"He was bragging to his mates that his parents are going away over the weekend. He plans on inviting her over."

"He fucking what?" he screams, standing to full height and bumping his head on the raised hood in the process. I feel like a prick for saying something. Snitching's not my thing, but the idea of her going over there and being taken advantage of by that douche makes my blood boil for some reason.

His face turns bright red as he stands there rubbing his injured head. "I'm sorry. I just thought you'd like to know." *I feel like such a hypocrite.* I invite girls over with the sole purpose of fucking them all the time.

My hope is now that he knows he'll put a stop to it. At least I didn't mention the side bet he made with his mate. "Don't be sorry," he says gripping my shoulder. "I appreciate you looking out for my girl. She's alone a lot of the time with these crazy hours I work. I worry about her. Knowing she has you living next door now makes me feel better."

Now he's making me feel like a fraud. Not only have I thought about doing exactly what Brad wants to, I treat his daughter like a piece of shit. Why am I suddenly consumed with guilt?

••••

Later that night, I sit in my room in complete darkness watching Indiana sitting at her window seat. I don't usually do this kind of thing, so I feel like a stalker. She's on her iPad again. I presume she's messaging with someone because occasionally she throws her head back and laughs before typing a reply. I find myself smiling as I watch her. *What the hell is she doing to me?*

A few times she gazes towards my bedroom window. Logically I know she can't see me. It's pitch black. It did make me wonder. When my phone dings, alerting me I have a text message, my heart starts to race thinking it's her. Of course it couldn't be. She doesn't have my number.

It's my hook-up, Jen. I only know her name because she includes it in her message. She's on her way over. I told her to come down the side of the house. I'm gonna sneak her in my bedroom window. Luckily my bedroom is on the ground floor.

Why Fuckwit chose to live in a house so large is beyond me. It's way too big for one person. Well technically there's three of us now, but before we moved in it was just him. You only have to look at his fancy-arse clothes and the ridiculously expensive European car he drives to know he's a showy prick.

It's not like I can bring her in through the front door. Fuckwit has already informed me, while living here I'm forbidden to have girls in my room. Screw him. His demands only make me want to defy him.

Ten minutes later I hear a tap at my window. "Carter. You in there?" Flicking my bedroom light on, I make my way towards the window. "Carter," she says again. Thankfully, my mum and Fuckwit are sleeping in an upstairs room at the front of the house.

"Keep it down," I tell her when I open the window.

"Sorry," she says smiling up at me. I'd forgotten how pretty she is. Why does the image of a certain beautiful, annoying *kid* pop into my head as I help pull her through the window?

My head snaps up looking over towards Indiana's bedroom. I'm surprised to see her staring straight back at me, a frown on her face. Being the bastard I am, I flip her off before closing the blinds. I don't need her penetrating gaze putting me off my game.

I'm going to fuck blondie with everything I have, hoping to get Indiana out of my mind once and for all.

FIVE

INDIANA

I DON'T KNOW WHY SEEING THAT SKANK, JENNIFER, SNEAKING into Carter's bedroom upsets me, but it does. A lot. I'm already pissed off with him for ratting me out to my father. Seeing this just sends me over the edge. Tears burn my eyes, but I manage to hold them in. Fuck him. I refuse to give him the satisfaction of making me cry.

Feeling deflated, I say goodbye to Meg and I log off Facebook before climbing into bed. The fact that I'm actually upset only makes me angrier. Why does he get under my skin so much? The way I'm feeling right now, I know sleep isn't going to come easy.

When my dad finally came in for dinner earlier tonight, he forbid me to have anything to do with Brad Cartwright. It shocked me. Not only have I not told him anything about Brad, he's never forbid me to do anything.

I know Carter must've said something to him while they were working on that stupid car of his. He had to have. Why else would my dad say what he did? Why is Carter so hell bent on making my life so miserable? I was happy until he moved in next door. *Arsehole.*

Lying in bed, I try not to think about what they're getting up to over there. I know it's not homework that's for sure. Not where Jennifer Darcy is concerned. *Dirty slapper.* She'd have to be one of the biggest sluts at our school. She's really pretty, in that overly made up kind of way. I'm sure she could get the guys without spreading her legs, but she seems to revel in the fact that she's known as the school whore. Meg calls her a human mattress.

She's got that one right.

••••

I'm feeling like shit when I wake the next morning. I tossed and turned for hours before finally falling asleep. I can't believe how much it ate at me knowing that skank was in his bedroom. If you'd asked me last week if I was the jealous type I would've said no. I guess I would've been wrong.

I can't stand him so it shouldn't worry me. I heard her leave a few hours later. She was giggling like an idiot when he helped her out the window. Yes, I'm ashamed to admit I got up and peaked through my blinds.

I wish I could change rooms so I don't have to witness this crap. I get the impression Jen is going to be just one of many in his long line of conquests. I know what some of the girls in this town are like. They'll be lining up for a chance to be with that douchebag. Yuk.

I hope his dick falls off.

Unfortunately, we only have three bedrooms in this house. So moving rooms isn't an option. The room my mum and dad shared when she was still alive is off limits. My dad couldn't bear to sleep in there without her once she passed. He's been sleeping in the spare room ever since.

Compared to the other houses in the street ours is quite small. Don't get me wrong, it's a nice house, just not as grand as the others. My dad was adamant when he married my mum that he wanted his family to live in a nice area. I guess he's seen a lot of bad things being a police officer. My mum being a schoolteacher and my dad working on the force meant there wasn't a lot of money coming in. They managed to secure this block of land, but could only afford to build a smaller house. I love it though. It's perfect for us.

I'm sure Mr. Shepard next door has heaps of bedrooms in his huge house. Why he chose to give Carter the bedroom facing mine, I'll never know. With Carter's attitude though, he probably wanted to stuff him away at the back of the house, away from them. I don't blame him.

After I eat breakfast and rinse my bowl and cup, I set about getting things ready for my dad when he wakes. I feed Lassie before heading to the bus stop. I made sure I left earlier this morning. I didn't want to risk running into that arsehole again.

As I wait for the bus I scan my newsfeed on my phone. I'm not in the mood for dreary Facebook this morning, but I need something to pass the time since the bus won't be here for another twenty minutes. I hate how Carter has only been here a few days, and is already disrupting my life.

My head snaps up when I hear the loud rev of a car. I must admit I'm surprised when Carter pulls over to the curb in front of where I'm standing. "Get in the car, *kid*," he snarls. His ridiculous command makes me laugh. He's fucking kidding, right? His eyebrows rise as he waits for me to do as he's asked. *I don't think so buddy.*

Looking back down at my phone, I continue to scan through my page. He's got a nerve after the way he's been treating me. I'd never admit it, but I'm a tiny bit thrilled he came looking for me. How dumb is that?

"I'm going to give you to the count of three to get in this car," he says annoyed. I roll my eyes as I continue to ignore him. I hear him growl and I have to fight back the smile that threatens to come. I like that my defiance is getting to him.

"One ... two ..." I can't believe he's actually counting. I feel the corners of my lips turn up in a grin. When I hear his car door open, my head snaps up. "Three. I warned you," is all he says as he grabs hold of me and throws me over his shoulder.

"Carter," I scream. "Put me down." He ignores my order as he marches around to the passenger side of the car. His hand is sitting at the base of my arse, holding me in place. I shouldn't like the feel of his hands on me, but I do. It makes me wonder what it would be like if he held me properly. Not like a bag that's just been thrown over his shoulder. Ugh! I hate that I'm thinking about how it would feel to be held in his arms. I'm sure it would feel amazing.

No it wouldn't, I'd absolutely hate it. Liar.

Opening the door, he plonks me down on the seat. "Put your seatbelt on," he growls as he stands over me like a thug. I just look up at him in horror. I can't believe he just did that to me. Leaning forward, he grabs hold of the seatbelt.

"Give me that," I snap as I narrow my eyes at him. "I can put my own damn belt on. I'm not a child."

"Could've fooled me," he says giving me a smug, gorgeous smile. God, he annoys the hell out of me. Why does he have to be so ridiculously handsome?

He waits until my seatbelt is fastened before making his way around to the driver's side. I have a good mind to make my escape, but going by his antics just now, he'll probably come after me.

No words are spoken on the drive to school. Unlike yesterday when he dropped me off down the road, today he heads straight to the car park. I want to make a smart remark about his reputation, but I don't.

"Make sure you're here this afternoon, or I'll come to the bus stop and get you again," he warns. Ignoring him, I get out of the car and slam the door. I hear him laughing as I walk away. I could seriously slap him right now.

••••

"What's up your arse?" Meg asks when we leave our first class. "It's unusual to see you in a bad mood."

"One guess," I reply as we make our way towards the lockers.

"Your hot neighbour?"

"Yes. And he's not hot. He's an arse." She nudges me with her shoulder and chuckles. This isn't funny. Doesn't she realise he's ruining my life?

"He may be an arse, but you can't tell me you don't think he's good looking."

"I hadn't noticed," I snap. I hear her scoff at my words. She obviously doesn't believe me. In all honesty, who wouldn't notice him? He's very noticeable—for a prick that is.

"You fucking liar," she laughs.

"He's okay," I shrug like I'm not affected by his looks. It's a lame shrug too. I'm not even fooling myself.

"He's more than okay."

"Alright he's hot," I admit, rolling my eyes, "but that's all he's got going for him."

"What has he done today to put you in such a fabulous mood?" she asks sarcastically.

"What hasn't he done is more like it." When we reach my locker she stops, turning me to face her.

"Well spill," she demands.

"For starters, just being in his presence annoys me," I reply. It kind of turns me on too, but I'd never admit it.

"And? There has to be more than that. Your mood is nasty." She raises an eyebrow impatiently as she waits for my reply. I want to say none of your damn business, but I know that's just my mood talking. She's only concerned for me. I can't remember the last time I was this riled up.

I turn and place the key in the padlock. I'm feeling bad for being so snappy with her now. I'm lucky to have a friend that cares so much. I hate that Carter Reynolds gets under my skin like he does.

"My mood is that bad huh?" I ask with a sigh as I place my books in my locker and get out what I need for my next class.

"Yep."

"I'm sorry. I don't mean to take it out on you," I apologise as I hook my arm through hers as we walk down the corridor towards her locker.

"Tell me what he did to upset you, Indi."

"He told my dad about Brad. I've now been forbidden to see him."

"What? No way. See, I told you he had the hots for you." Of course she'd see it like that. It has nothing to do with how he feels about me. He's a prick, plain and simple.

"He doesn't have the hots for me," I state.

"Yes he does. You didn't see what I saw yesterday. He was definitely cut when you were on Brad's lap."

"If he has the hots for me, which I don't believe for a minute, why did he have that skank, Jennifer Darcy, sneaking in his bedroom window last night?" She stops walking and pulls me over towards the wall so we don't get bowled over by the other students rushing to get to their next class. Facing me, the first thing I notice is her eyes. They're almost bugging out of her head from shock. Even in my mood, it brings a smile to my face.

"What? No fucking way. Really? God she's a whore. Didn't take her long. I can't stand that human mattress."

"I know right. Can you believe it? She was there for hours too. I know exactly what they were up to," I say angrier than intended.

"Oh. My. God. You like him," she screeches, slapping my arm in disbelief.

"What? I do not." I try my best to act unaffected by her comment, but I fail miserably.

"Bullshit. Look me in the eye and tell me you don't have the hots for him."

"I don't," I answer looking down at the ground. Fuck.

"Holy crap. You do," she says slapping my arm again. Ouch. I hate that she knows me so well. We've been best friends since kindergarten. Inseparable you could say. I guess being in each other's pockets for the past twelve years will do that.

"Stop hitting me," I whine as I rub my arm.

"Well admit it then." She raises her hand likes she's going to hit me again. I have to hold back my smile. *Bitch.*

"Fine. I like him, and hate him if that's even possible," I admit, finally making eye contact with her. Of course she's beaming when I do.

"I knew it," she says smugly. She's such a know-it-all sometimes.

••••

God I wish she hadn't figured out this thing, whatever it is, that I have for Carter. She hasn't shut up about it all day. I'm surprised she isn't talking weddings and babies, that's how bad she's been. At lunch I even threatened to move to another table if she didn't let up. Thankfully that was enough to get her to stop.

She's boy crazy. Always has been. She's not only pretty, but has huge knockers so the guys love her. What is it with them and boobs? Me on the other hand, I like boys, but I'm not obsessed. I guess that's why she's so excited now that she knows how I feel about Carter.

Once school's out, I'm in two minds on what to do. Part of me wants to catch the bus to defy him. How dare he order me around like that? The crazy part of me wants to be near him. Don't ask me why. It's not like he's pleasant to be around.

As I stand here contemplating what to do, two arms slide around my waist from behind. "Hey there, beautiful," he whispers in my ear. I know straight away that it's Brad.

"Hey," I reply, turning in his arms.

"We still on for Saturday?" Before I have a chance to answer, Carter appears beside us.

"You ready?" he asks. His voice is calm, but I can tell by his facial expression he's anything but.

"Ready for what?" Brad says looking between the two of us.

"We're going for a drive," Carter replies all smug.

"You're what?" Brad snaps glaring at me.

"He's giving me a lift home. That's all. We live next door to each other." My gaze moves to Carter. I shoot daggers at him. *Troublemaker.*

"Actually, that's not entirely true. We are going for a drive. I have to get a few parts for my car on the way home. I told your dad I'd be taking you with me."

"Whatever," Brad says to Carter, dismissing him before turning his attention back to me. I can tell he's not impressed. "You gonna be online tonight?"

"Probably," I reply, shrugging.

"Okay. I'll message you later. I've got to get to football training." I find his question and answer a little strange. We're friends on Facebook, but he's never messaged me on there before. He's liked a few of my posts in the past and commented on some pictures I've put up, but that's it.

When he leans forward and places his lips on mine, I'm taken aback. He's never kissed me at school before. Well apart from the goodnight kiss I got when he walked me home from the party, he's never kissed me. I'm sure it's only for Carter's benefit. *Men.* I'm surprised they don't flop out their dicks and compare sizes.

SIX

CARTER

I DON'T KNOW WHY SEEING HIS LIPS ON HER RIGHT NOW
bothered me, but fuck me it did. I thought after my hook-up last night
I'd get this thing with her out of my system. *Wrong.* If anything it's
only cemented the fact that I have feelings for her. Which surprises
me. I thought I was incapable of shit like that.

Whilst banging the blonde's brains out, I hate to admit that her
long, dark, silky hair, big green eyes and lips that I'm dying to taste
crossed my mind more than it should have. It not only scared me, it
pissed me the hell off.

What is it with her? I hate that she's so easily drawing me in
without even trying. I hate that I can't seem to stay away. I hated it
when that prick's lips were on hers just now. I wished they were mine.

I should just drop her off at home. Better still let her get the damn
bus. I can't even tell you why I demanded she be in the car park this
afternoon. Yes I can. I wanted to be near her. I also promised her dad
I'd keep an eye on her.

That's so fucked up. He thinks I'm protecting her from all these horny teenagers. When, in fact, I want her just as much, if not more than they do. If she's got me this tied up in a matter of days, I hate to see what condition I'm going to be in when I leave here in a few months' time.

The quicker I turn eighteen and get away from this place, the better.

We make our way towards my car. Neither of us speak. Maybe that's a good thing. Christ, I hate this feeling I get when I'm around her. It's foreign to me.

We're not even out of the street before she opens her smart mouth. "What did you say to my father about Brad yesterday?" she snaps. Even though I can feel her eyes boring into the side of my head, I stay focused on the road ahead.

"I have no idea what you're talking about, kid," I lie, trying hard to hold back a smile.

"Bullshit, Carter." I don't know why I like hearing my name coming out of her sexy mouth, but I do. I'd prefer it if she was saying it while I was buried balls deep inside her. Shit. I feel my dick twitch. Why did I let my mind go there? "I demand you tell me what you said." Playing it cool, I shrug. "I mean it ... so help me." I chuckle at her words. What's she going to fucking do?

"So help me what?" I say turning my head to look at her. Of course her eyes are saying everything without a single word leaving her mouth. It only makes me smile. Not the desired affect I'm sure.

"He's forbidden me from seeing him. I want to know why," she seethes.

"Your father's a wise man. I'm sure he has his reasons," I state calmly. Her hand is clenching the door handle so tight her knuckles have turned white. The anger is just rolling off her in waves. Seeing her like this makes my dick stir. She's fucking hot when she's mad. A real little spitfire.

"God you irritate me sometimes," she retorts.

"Ditto, kid."

"I'm not a damn kid. Pull the hell over," she says through gritted teeth.

"What? Why?" I ask surprised.

"Because I'd rather walk than suffer one more minute in this car with you." I laugh at her comment. Things don't usually amuse me, but fuck me, she does.

"It's not funny, arsehole. Why are you so hell bent on ruining my life?" That statement really gets under my skin for some reason.

"Ruining your life. Is that what you think I'm doing?" I snarl. When she folds her hands over her chest, pushing her perky little tits up, I turn my head and focus on the road again. I don't need her tits distracting me.

"Yes," she replies with way too much attitude. It makes my blood boil that she thinks I'm trying to ruin her life, when in fact I was only trying to help her.

"Why, because I told your father Brad was bragging to his mates that he was going to invite you to his house this weekend, to get into your pants?" I practically scream. What I say, and the way I say it, takes her by surprise. Her beautiful green eyes widen and the colour partially drains from her face.

"What?" she asks in a horrified, disbelieving tone.

"Yes. Just before he pulled you onto his lap yesterday, that's exactly what he said." I try to speak a little calmer this time. Even though she's getting on my nerves with her attitude, I don't want to scare her.

"He did not," she barks.

"Believe what you want. You think I'd make that shit up?" I look in her direction as I speak. I can tell by the shocked look on her pretty face she believes me.

"He actually said that?" she whispers. I can clearly hear the sadness in her voice.

"Yep," I answer. Her head turns towards the passenger side window. She doesn't speak another word for the longest time. I kind of feel bad now, but she needed to know. That guy is a snake.

"Where are we going?" she eventually asks when I turn onto the main road that heads towards town. I'm still getting used to navigating my way around this area, but thankfully Ross is good at giving directions.

"I told you. To get parts."

"I thought you were making that up to piss Brad off," she states.

"Why would I do that?" I ask reaching over to grab my cigarettes.

"Because you're an arse." Her comment makes me chuckle. "You do know Jennifer Darcy is the school slut, right?" she informs me. Who the fuck is Jennifer Darcy?

"Who?" I have no idea who she's talking about.

"Jennifer Darcy," she repeats.

"Never heard of her. Might need to look her up though," I joke.

"She's the girl who climbed through your window last night," she says in a disgusted tone.

"Was that her name?" I ask smirking.

"You're a pig."

"You almost sound like your jealous," I tease, because that's exactly how it sounds, and that surprises me.

"Hardly," she scoffs.

"You are, aren't you? I bet you wished it was you sneaking through my window last night instead of her."

"You're delusional," she says when I pull up at a red light. I look in her direction. My eyes lock with hers. I'm shocked by what I see. I was only messing with her, but by the way she's looking at me makes me think there's some truth to what I said. Surely she couldn't wish that. She acts like she can't stand me.

Something passes between us. I'm not sure what, but I almost want to reach out and touch her. Kiss her. Whatever it is, it's quickly broken when the car behind me sounds his horn, alerting me the lights have now turned green. Suddenly, I don't like where this is heading.

I should've let her catch the damn bus.

••••

We travel in silence for the next twenty minutes. When we reach our destination I pull into a parking spot. "You gonna stay in the car? Or do you want to come with me?" She shrugs before answering.

"I guess I'll come," she says removing her seatbelt.

Indi's dad recommended this place to me. Apparently he's been friends with the owner since high school. He deals in new and used parts, but specialises mainly in classics. Ross was going to call him today and let him know I was coming in. He said he'll look after me.

Indi falls in behind me as we head towards the shop front. From the street you can see it's attached to a large factory type building. That's probably where they store all the parts.

The bell chimes above the shop door when we enter. A man in his mid-forties walks out from the back room. "Well if it isn't little Indiana Montgomery," he says as he makes his way around the counter. "Look how much you've grown." She's grown? How fucking small was she? She's only pocket-size now.

"Hi, Mr. Gregory," she says hugging him.

"Let me look at you." He pulls back, studying her face. "You look just like your mum did at this age. God rest her soul." What? Her mum's dead? Looking at her face I see a fleeting moment of sorrow pass, but a smile quickly takes over. I'll admit I did wonder why I hadn't seen her mum around, but it never occurred to me she didn't have one. That makes me feel sad for her. Growing up, I would've been lost without my mother. She's all I have. Here I thought she had the perfect life. I guess I was wrong.

"My dad says that a lot," she replies with a sad smile, and he gives her a sympathetic look.

"You must be Carter," he says, eventually turning his attention to me. "Ross told me you were dropping by."

"Yes. I am," I answer, grabbing hold of his extended hand.

"Warren. Warren Gregory," he says.

"It's nice to meet you, Sir."

"So you're after parts for a '75 Monaro I believe?" he asks.

"That's right."

"You're in luck. Come out the back and I'll show you what I have," he says, turning and heading towards the door over by the far wall. Indiana and I follow.

••••

I'm beaming by the time we leave. That place is like spare parts heaven. I got everything I needed, plus I was able to put a few of the larger, more expensive things aside until I can come up with some more cash. Fuck knows how I'm gonna do that. My cash fund has just about run dry. I may need to find a job.

"Wanna get something to eat while we're here?" I ask as I load the last of the parts into the trunk.

"You want to eat something? With me?" she asks surprised. I guess I don't blame her. I've been an arse. I'm not sure why I even asked. I guess I'm hungry.

"I'm hungry," I say with a shrug. I don't want her to think this is a date, because it isn't.

"Okay." We make our way towards the burger joint a few doors down. I'm already regretting asking her. What the hell am I gonna talk to her about? I don't do shit like this. I don't go out much. I'm definitely not what you'd call sociable.

We sit in silence as we both scan the menu. "The burgers are great," she says. "My dad brings me here sometimes." I make eye contact with her over the top of my menu. A burger sounds good.

"Are you guys ready to order?" the waitress asks when she approaches our table.

"Can I get a burger, fries and a chocolate shake?" I answer before looking in Indi's direction.

"I'll get the same," she says closing her menu. I'm impressed. I thought girls like her ate lettuce or tofu, shit like that. I'll be interested to see if she actually eats it.

When the waitress leaves, silence falls over us again. I watch her as she looks around the restaurant, anywhere but me. She looks nervous and a little uncomfortable. Makes two of us. I'm not a fan of small talk.

"So, tell me about your mum," I ask out of the blue. Fuck me. Why can't I keep my mouth shut? When her eyes meet mine I see sadness. It tugs at me for some reason. She doesn't say anything at first. Now I feel like a dick.

"Oh, you heard Mr Gregory did you? Not much to tell," she eventually says. Her hands are twisting nervously in front of her. I can only gather how hard this subject is for her to talk about. "She died when I was six. She had a brain tumour. I don't remember much. My dad tried to shield me from it. She was in a lot of pain and spent most of her time in bed. My dad struggled with her death. Still does. It couldn't have been easy for him. He had a full-time job, a sick wife and a small child to contend with." I see sorrow cross her face. It's fleeting, but I definitely saw it. I guess that's understandable.

"I'm sorry," is all I say. Lame response I know, but it's the best I've got.

"What about you? Do you still see your father?" Her question instantly gets my back up. See this is why I hate small talk. Fuck, me and my big mouth. I should've kept quiet. Talking about my father, or lack thereof, is something I never do.

"I don't have one," I snap.

"Everyone has a father," she responds. *Not everyone. I don't.* Maybe she just assumes my parents are divorced.

"Well I don't. Can we just drop it?" When I glare at her, she gets the message because she changes the subject.

"How long have you had your car?" she asks. Fuck she's nosy.

"I bought it a few years ago. It needs a lot of work to get it to where I want it, but it's all I could afford at the time."

"Did you have a job before moving here?" she asks.

"Yeah. Kind of."

"What do you mean kind of? You either did or you didn't. Did you buy the car yourself?" I wish she'd stop with all the questions. I hate talking about my personal life.

"Yes I did," I snap. "Not everyone has a privileged life like you, Princess."

"What's that supposed to mean?" she asks defensively. I ignore her. It means just that. My mum struggled to put food on the table most days. Any luxuries I wanted I had to buy myself. When I was twelve, I started to do odd jobs for the people who lived in our apartment building. It all progressed from there.

"How did you get money to buy the car then?" she probes further.

"I have ways," I say, smirking when I see her processing my answer.

"What ways?"

I shake my head and scoff, "Fuck you're nosy." I stare her down hoping she'll get the message to quit it. I'm not comfortable talking about this subject with her. With anyone for that matter.

"What kind of job? I can't imagine how someone your age could afford a car like that." Fuck. Obviously my intimidation didn't work.

"Can we change the subject?" I plead, exhaling.

"No. What's the big secret? What, were you a drug dealer or something?"

"Hell no," I chuckle.

"Well what then?" I may as well tell her the truth. She's not going to let up until I do. At the very least it will shut her up.

I lay my hands on the table between us and lean into her. She mirrors my stance before I whisper, "Sexual favours." Her beautiful green eyes widen with shock.

She puts the distance between us as she leans back. "Bullshit."

"It's true," I tell her. That's exactly how I got the money.

I watch her eyes dart around to make sure no one is able to hear her. "Like a prostitute? Oh. My. God. You're a prostitute? You make those girls that jump through your window, pay you?" she shrieks.

"Fuck no. That's for pleasure," I say frustrated as I look around the restaurant. "Look, it's a long story. Just drop it okay." All these questions are starting to give me a headache.

My eyes snap back to hers as she slaps her hand over mine and leans forward. "Like hell I'm going to drop it."

I stare at the top of her hand while she squeezes mine. "It was one person. That's it. When I lived in the apartment building with my mum, the landlady would pay me to scratch her itch you could say. It's no big deal."

"It is a big deal. That's disgusting." Her judgemental tone is starting to piss me off and I pull my hand out from under hers. Who in the fuck does she think she is?

"Whatever," I snap. "I wouldn't expect you to understand. You've always had everything handed to you on a silver platter. So, until you've walked a day in my shoes, don't fucking judge me, okay, Princess?"

Crossing her arms under her chest, she lets me know she's not happy with my comment. "That goes two ways. Don't judge me either. You have no idea what kind of life I've had," she says with a hurt look on her face. I feel like a prick now.

"Okay. I was out of line." Even though I'm pretty sure her life's been a hell of a lot better than mine. This isn't a competition about who's had the shittier life. We all have struggles that we handle differently, I guess.

"Do you still do it? Like, get paid to have sex I mean?" she asks. I roll my eyes, because I thought this conversation was over. Obviously not.

"No. It stopped the day I moved here." Why do the answers keep coming out of my mouth when I don't want them to? I've always been a private person. It's like my brain and mouth aren't even a part of me today. *I wish I'd shut the fuck up.*

"How old were you when it started?" Jesus, what's with all these damn questions? I should've known she wouldn't understand. "How old Carter?"

"Fifteen, I guess," I answer, rubbing my hands over my face in frustration.

"Fifteen? How old was your landlady?"

I squeeze my eyes tight before taking a deep breath. "Fuck, I don't know, in her early thirties."

"What? You were just a kid. What a sick, twisted bitch," she snaps. "That's child abuse."

"Keep it down! It wasn't fucking child abuse. Jesus. It wasn't like that," I angrily whisper, glancing around as I run my hand through my hair silently willing her to drop it. I look around for the waitress. Where is our damn food?

"Like hell it isn't. The legal age for consensual sex in this country is sixteen. You were a minor and she was an adult. She should've known better. Does your mother know?" Her probing has me exhaling an exasperated breath.

"Fuck no," I answer. Now it's my turn to speak a little too loudly. "She'd have a fit if she knew."

"Of course she would, because what that woman did was wrong on so many levels. How dare she do that to you?" she says in a disgusted tone.

"It was more like me doing her," I chuckle. I watch her shake her head.

"This isn't a joke, Carter."

My eyes lock with hers. I expect to see judgement, but I don't. She looks upset. I sigh. I have no idea why I even told her. I've never confessed that to anyone. It's not something I'm ashamed of, but I'm not proud of it either. I did what I had to do.

It started not long after my fifteenth birthday. I was mowing the lawns for the landlady. Prior to that day, I did things like the lawns, putting out the bins on trash night, changing light bulbs, weeding gardens, painting fences. Shit like that. It was hard work, but she paid me well.

That particular day was hot. When I was done cutting the grass, I removed my shirt and wiped the sweat from my brow. I'm well built, so even at fifteen I looked older than my actual age. That's when I noticed the landlady, Simone, watching me through the window.

She was a lot older than me, but still a total babe. I was a teenage kid with raging hormones. Of course I'd noticed her. Who wouldn't? She had long blonde hair, huge fake tits, and a killer body. She was always wearing skimpy, revealing clothes. A young boy's wet dream you could say.

I later found out she was divorced. She married a sugar daddy for his money and used her payout from the property settlement to buy the block of units. Not cool, but I suppose she was set for life.

Usually she'd just hand me my envelope from the door, but that particular day she invited me in for a cold drink. It was hot, so I didn't think much of it. That's when she propositioned me. Of course I was shocked, but as I said earlier, I was a horny kid. The thought of getting my dick wet actually excited me.

I was hesitant with my answer, so she was quick to up the ante. I guess she was horny too. She not only offered to pay me double what she already was, she offered to cut my mum's rent in half. How could I say no to that? I knew how much my mum was struggling.

My mum never found out what I was up to. I know she wouldn't have liked it. When she'd give me the rent money each week, I'd take half out and gradually feed it back in her purse. I was smart. I'd do small amounts each day. That way she wouldn't notice. Well if she did, she never said anything.

After I agreed, Simone asked me to take a shower with her. I was kind of freaking out, but I did it. She gave me my first blow job. Over the coming days and weeks, she taught me everything I needed to know about pleasing women. She knew exactly what she wanted and wasn't afraid to show me. She'd make me do things over and over until I got them right. I guess she made me into the 'Sex God' I am today. I can't complain about that part. The women love me. Not many guys my age would have the experience I have.

Simone got really pissed off when she found out we were moving. I mean really pissed. She screamed, she cried and she smashed things. At first I couldn't understand why. Looking back now I should've seen the signs. Over time things changed; the way she touched me, kissed me, looked at me. I was just a kid, so I didn't think much of it.

A few nights before we were set to move, she offered me two thousand dollars to spend the night. Of course I said yes, even though I wasn't too keen on the idea. That's when it all came to a head. She was riding me, my eyes were glued to her huge fake-arse tits as they bounced around, when suddenly she started to cry. Like sob her fucking heart out.

"Please don't go," she begged as she collapsed on my chest. At first I thought it was the sex she was going to miss, I was a sex god after all. Then she confessed she had feelings for me. Hell fucking no. It was a business arrangement. That's it. I never signed on for any of that other shit. That's not how I roll. She was a means to an end, nothing more. Not once during our time together did I ever think of her in that way. Needless to say, I lifted her off me and got out of bed. I left the money on the nightstand and hightailed it out of there. It was the last time I saw her.

"You must've done a lot of *sexual favours* if you earned enough money to buy a car," Indi says in a repulsed tone. Her attitude really gets my back up. Why I feel the need to justify my actions to her, I'll never know, but for some reason it's important to me that she understands why I did it.

"I started doing odd jobs for her when I was twelve. I gave half of everything I earned to my mum, the rest I saved. As I said, the sexual favours didn't start until I was fifteen. Despite what you think, I worked hard for that money. There's nothing wrong with working hard for what you want."

"I'm sorry you had to go through that," she says, her hand reaching out to cover mine again. I don't know why she's making such a big deal out of this. My eyes travel down to her hand and back up to her face. She quickly draws it back. For some reason I wish she didn't pull away.

"I'm not sorry," I tell her honestly. "That money helped us out a lot. My mum really struggled over the years."

"I don't condone what happened, but I'm glad it helped, I guess. Promise me you won't let her take advantage of you like that again."

"That part of my life is over," I tell her. I kind of like that she appears to care.

"What a grown woman saw in a fifteen year old ..." she adds shaking her head. I hate all this deep and meaningful crap. It makes me feel uncomfortable.

"I guess I'm irresistible," I say with a shrug. Her eyes narrow at my comment, making me smile.

"You're so full of yourself."

"I bet you'd like to be full of me," I say leaning into her space. The quips just roll off without my brain even engaging.

"You're a pig," she replies with disgust, shaking her head. And just like that all is right again. Things between us are back to the way they used to be. Just the way I like it.

Thankfully a few minutes later the waitress appears with our food. Now we can eat and stop all this damn talking.

SEVEN

INDIANA

I'M STILL CONFUSED ABOUT THE AFTERNOON I SPENT WITH Carter. Once we arrived back home, I left him to work on his car while I took Lassie for a walk. The whole time analysing everything that was said between us at the restaurant.

We're still not what you'd class as friends, far from it. To be honest, I have no idea what we are. At least he let his guard down briefly, allowing me to get a glimpse of the real him. Of course his bastardry was back in full swing on the drive back home, which didn't really surprise me.

To say I was shocked to find out he was paid for sex would be an understatement. His landlady sounds like a monster. A predator. She could go to prison for what she did. No matter what he thinks, a grown woman having sex with an underage boy is wrong on so many levels.

It also broke my heart. I love that he did it to help his mum, but I also hate that he had to do it in the first place. He acts like it was no big deal, but I'm sure there were times it wasn't easy for him.

He shut me down when I asked about his father. There's definitely a story there, but it's his choice if he doesn't wish to disclose it. I'm glad he and his mother no longer have to struggle. Mr. Shepard isn't short of money. In my eyes that's all he has going for him. I have no idea what Carter's mother sees in him. He's a tool.

My father and I say hello to be polite, but neither of us really like him. My dad nearly came to blows with him a few years ago when he verbally abused me and made me cry because Lassie defecated on his lawn. He's a dog. That's what dogs do.

When Lassie and I arrive back at the house, I find my dad and Carter with their heads buried under the hood of his car. I like that my dad is helping him. Since he doesn't have a father and my dad doesn't have a son, I think this will be good for them both. As long as Carter doesn't continue to get me in trouble that is.

I can't believe Brad said what he did. Well actually I can. He does have a bit of a reputation. I knew if we ever got together he'd expect sex. The fact that we're not even dating and he planned to meet up just to get in my pants though, pisses me off. I can assure you he won't be getting anything from me now.

•••

As the days pass, nothing really changes between us. Carter still insists I travel to and from school with him, even though he continues to be an arse ninety-nine percent of the time.

He hasn't had a girl climb through his window since that skank. That's a plus. I'm not sure why it pleases me, but it does. It's not like we're ever going to get it on.

Saturday rolls around fast. I get up early and take Lassie for a walk. When I arrive back home I run into Elizabeth, Carter's mother. "Morning, Indiana," she says as I walk down the driveway.

"Morning. You're out and about early," I say.

"I'm going to visit an old friend today. She lives a few hours away," she replies, smiling pleasantly. I really like her. How she produced such a douche I'll never understand.

"That's nice. Have a nice day," I tell her, returning the smile. "Drive safely."

"Thank you. You too, sweetie." She reaches out and gently grabs my arm as I go to walk away. "I'm glad you and Carter have become friends. He didn't have many friends where we used to live," she confesses. Why does that not surprise me? I just grin in response. I have no words. We're far from friends but I can't bring myself to say that to her.

After I take Lassie off his lead, I leave him to run around the back yard while I head inside for breakfast. Meg has finally been let off her grounding so she's coming over to hang with me later. It's going to be hot today. We'll probably go swimming and do some sunbathing down by the lake.

Once I've eaten, I clean up my mess and head into my room to make my bed. Of course my betraying eyes find their way towards Carter's bedroom window. Suddenly, his bedroom door flies open and he storms into his room. He must be in a mood today. Nothing out of the ordinary.

I'm taken aback when I see Mr. Shepard hot on his heels. He grabs hold of Carter's arm, roughly swinging him around. I watch on in horror. He is right up in his face, screaming. I can't hear what he's saying through the closed window, but he's not happy. I feel sorry for Carter. My father would never treat me like that, no matter how bad my behaviour was.

Ugh! I can't stand that man.

A few minutes later he storms out. Carter slams his bedroom door. His hands clutch either side of his head as he tilts it back, looking up at the ceiling. Poor thing. Seeing him like that tugs at my heart. I'm tempted to go over and see if he's alright, but I don't. He's liable to take it out on me.

He must sense me watching, because his head snaps in my direction. I want to duck down, but it's no use. I'm already busted. I give him a sympathetic smile, but the arsehole flips me off. He takes a few steps towards his window and abruptly closes his blinds. He makes me so mad sometimes.

I get a text from Meg saying she'll be over in an hour, so I decide to go out back and play fetch with Lassie while I wait. I'm only outside a few minutes when I hear Mr. Shepard's angry voice.

"I want the lawns and edges done. You better do a good job too. I'm happy to have your mother living here for free, but you need to earn your keep. I'm not supporting some bastard child that isn't even mine."

My hand comes up to cover my mouth. I'm both appalled and shocked he would say that to him. How dare he? "Yeah, well if I had my way I wouldn't be here either," Carter replies in a deflated tone. The cruel comments bring tears to my eyes. Everything in me wants to go over there and give that dipshit a piece of my mind. He has no right to speak to Carter in that way. I'm appalled.

"Just get it done," Mr. Shepard snaps. "When you're finished you can clean out the garage." I hate him even more now. Poor Carter. I wonder if his mum knows he's being treated this way. I'm going to mention it to my dad when he wakes. Maybe he can talk to him about it next time they're working on his car.

A few minutes later I hear the lawnmower start. I sneak towards the wooden fence that divides our properties and peek through one of the gaps in the paling. A lump rises to my throat when my eyes land on him. His shoulders are slumped and there's a frown on his face. He looks even more miserable than usual.

Our yards are big. It's going to take him forever to do it on his own. My dad at least has a ride-on mower. Carter is doing it with a push one. I wish I could go over there and help, but I know he wouldn't want me to. He's too proud for that.

••••

"Oh. My. God. His body is just as beautiful as his face. It should be a crime to be that hot," Meg says. I turn my head to look at her. Her glasses are pulled low on her nose whilst she stares straight ahead.

My head turns in that direction, following her line of sight. I almost swallow my tongue. Carter is heading our way, shirtless. His abs are so defined. He's wearing black swimming trunks that sit low on his hips, revealing his delicious V. Damn that body. It's even more delectable than I imagined. All I can say is, *'Thank God I'm wearing sunglasses'*. I'm pretty sure my eyes are bugging out of my head right now.

"Hi, Carter," Meg purrs from beside me.

"Megan. *Kid*," he says with a nod when he reaches us. I wish he'd stop calling me that. Just because I'm short doesn't make me a damn kid.

Is that a tattoo across his ribs? It is. It says *Trust*. I don't think I know any other seventeen year old that has a tatt. He's so bad-arse. I don't know why I find that hot, but I do. I like that he doesn't conform to society's ways, unlike me. I've always been a goody-goody. Always done what people expect of me. I like that he's an individual and doesn't seem to care what people think of him.

Meg and I are both laying on our stomachs. When I see his eyes travel the length of my body, I regret putting on this tiny revealing bikini. I feel so exposed. I swear I hear a groan come from him when his eyes land on my arse, but I'm not entirely sure.

"What's the water like?" he asks when his eyes make their way back to my face.

"Nice," Meg cuts in. "I'm sure it will reach boiling point once you get in though."

"Meg," I screech. That girl has no shame.

"Don't tell me you didn't think the same thing, *kid*," he smirks. God he frustrates me. He's so full of himself. I choose to ignore his comment. Instead, I roll over onto my back and pull my sunhat over my face. I hear him chuckle as he walks past me. A few seconds later, I hear the splash when he dives into the lake.

"He was totally checking out your arse and your tits when you rolled over. He wants you bad," Meg chimes. I roll my eyes.

"He does not," I snap.

"He so does. You should go for it. If you don't, I might."

"Don't you dare," I say removing the hat from my face and looking over at her. "Besides, you have a boyfriend, remember?"

"Derek's starting to bore me. I think it's time to find some fresh meat," she admits with a sigh.

"You're such a hussy," I laugh.

"You should try it sometime," she replies, winking at me.

••••

My dad has one of his rare days off today, so tonight we're going to have a barbeque on the back deck. I'm in the kitchen making a salad and potato bake to go with the meat. Dad's in the shower cleaning up. He spent the afternoon working on Carter's car again. He seems to be really enjoying it. Meg has gone home to get changed. She'll be joining us as well.

"Hey, Pumpkin," my dad says when he walks back into the kitchen. "What can I do to help?"

"It's all pretty much organised. When Meg gets back you can heat up the grill. I'm just going to pop the potato bake in the oven now," I reply.

"I invited Carter as well. Hope that's okay." My mouth curves up into a smile. I love that my dad has taken to Carter. He needs a positive male role model in his life.

"Sure. You like him don't you?" I ask.

"He's a good kid." I have to agree with him. I think underneath the front he puts on and all the smart arse remarks he makes, he is too. I think he's just misunderstood.

"Listen, there's something I need to tell you. It's about Carter," I say turning to face my dad.

"I'm all ears," he says grabbing a beer from the fridge.

"I know it's none of my business, but Mr. Shepard was screaming at Carter this morning. He called him a bastard child and said if he wanted to live in his house he needed to earn his keep. He made him mow the lawns with a push mower and then clean out the garage."

"He what? That man is a prick," my dad sneers, anger clearly visible on his handsome face.

"My thoughts exactly, Daddy. I felt so sorry for Carter. I know there probably isn't much you can do, but I thought you'd like to know. Maybe you can have a talk with him or something."

"Leave it with me, Pumpkin," he replies, leaning down to kiss the top of my head. "I'm going to go out back and clean the grill."

"Thanks, Dad." I'm lucky to have such a wonderful father. I love him so much.

I stay in the kitchen preparing things until Meg arrives. I'm secretly thrilled Carter is coming over. I know he won't give me a hard time in front of my father. Well I hope he won't. My dad would kick his arse if he knew how he treats me. Occasionally his nice side shines through, but not very often.

He seems different when he's in my dad's presence. I often hear them laughing while they're working on the car. He has such a great laugh. It's so different to the broody side I see. My dad's a good man. He'll be good for Carter.

Once Meg arrives, she helps me carry out what we need to set the table. We both got a lot of sun today so we look tanned. After I shower, I put on a white sundress. It accentuates my brown skin. "You look hot in that dress," she says as she follows me out onto the deck.

"Thanks. So do you. You always look nice."

"I know," she says, and we both laugh.

I'm stopped in my tracks when I walk out onto the deck. Meg wasn't expecting it and walks straight into my back. Carter's already here. I didn't realise. He must've used the side gate. He's sitting on one of the outdoor sofas. Lassie is laying across his lap. He's laughing at something my dad has said. God he's beautiful when he's happy. Just looking at him takes my breath away and sends my heart into a flutter.

Meg shoves me from behind. "Do I need to get the mop to clean up your drool?" she whispers in my ear. *Bitch.* I ignore her smart remark and keep walking. Thankfully, Carter was too busy to notice me checking him out.

"Here's my two favourites girls," dad says when he notices us. Carter's head snaps in our direction. I watch as his eyes travel the length of my body before resting on my face. The look he gives me does funny things to my girly parts. It's hot. He hasn't even noticed Meg yet. His eyes are glued on me.

My dad clears his throat. I look over at him. His eyes are moving between Carter and I. Crap. "Is the meat nearly ready?" I inquire, trying to distract him from saying something.

"Nearly," he replies giving me a strange look. Knowing my father had witnessed the exchange between us makes me feel awkward.

"Okay, good. After I set the table I'll get the potato bake out of the oven," I say without making eye contact with him.

"Would you like another beer, Mr. Montgomery?" Meg asks my dad. God I love her. She must've noticed the look my father was giving us, so she's trying to smooth things over. I love how she always has my back.

"I'd love one," he answers. Disaster diverted. Meg walks back into the house while I set the table.

"Come on, boy," I say to Lassie when I'm done. Although Carter doesn't seem to mind that Lassie is sprawled out all over him, it's a hot night so he can't possibly be comfortable. The dog ignores me. He never does that. Damn traitor. "Lassie." This time my voice is a little more forceful. He still doesn't come.

"Larry's fine, leave him. Aren't you boy?" Carter says smirking at me as he runs his hand through the dog's long mane.

"It's Lassie," I snap, placing my hands on my hips and pursing my lips. His smile widens. I'm sure he does that to annoy me. I hear my dad chuckle. He obviously thinks it's amusing as well. I leave them both in a huff and head back to the kitchen.

Thankfully the rest of the night goes by without incident. Actually, we all seem to be having a nice time. I can't believe how different Carter is tonight. My father really does bring out the best in him.

"It's getting late, I should be getting home," Meg says. She usually sleeps over, but she has to go to her grandmother's house in the morning so she can't tonight.

"I've been drinking," my father says, standing. "I'll get one of the boys from the station to come and give you a lift home."

"No bother, Mr. Montgomery. I'll walk," Meg replies.

"I'll walk you home," I offer, rising to stand next to her.

"No. I don't like the idea of Megan walking home on her own, and if you go then you'll have to come back alone," my dad says.

"I'll go with them," Carter chimes in. My dad's eyes move to him as he considers his offer.

"Okay. It's fine as long as Carter goes with you." I look at my dad. Is he serious? After the look he gave us before, I'm surprised he's comfortable with us being alone together now.

••••

Once we've walked Meg to her door I hug her goodbye. "Don't do anything I wouldn't do," she whispers in my ear. It earns her a pinch under the arm. There's not much she wouldn't do. "Ouch," she laughs. "Thanks for walking me home, Carter," she adds looking over at him.

"No problem," he replies. His hands are shoved in his pockets looking all cool, calm and sexy.

"Feel free to take advantage of my friend on the way home," she says with a wink. Oh. My. Fucking. God. She did not just say that. Carter just laughs at her comment. I, on the other hand, want to crawl under a rock and die. I'm glad I pinched her now. I should've done it harder. She'll pay for that remark tomorrow. I give her a look letting her know I'm not impressed with what she just said. She just smiles at me sweetly. *Bitch.*

We're both quiet on the walk back. I don't know what to say to him. I'm still dying inside from Meg's words. In a way I hope he takes her advice, in a way I don't.

I know I probably shouldn't pry considering I get the sense that all dad talk is off limits, but I jump straight in. "Does your stepdad speak that way to you often?" I ask, trying to break the awkward silence.

"I guess," he shrugs. "He's a cocksucker. I can't stand him. What my mum sees in him, I'll never know."

"I've thought the same thing. She seems so nice," I tell him as I shake my head trying to make sense of it.

"You don't like him either?" he asks, looking at me surprised.

"No. Neither does my dad. They nearly came to blows a while back."

"Why?" he asks.

"Lassie did his business on his lawn. You know, a poop. Let's just say he wasn't impressed. When he screamed at me and made me cry, my dad lost it."

"Larry's a fucking champion," he chuckles.

"Lassie," I remind him.

"Sorry, kid," he says draping his arm around my shoulder. "He's always gonna be Larry to me. You've gotta admit *Lassie* is a shit name for a kickass dog like that."

As much as his comment gets under my skin, I'm smiling like a fool. I can't believe he has his arm around me. I take a deep breath, inhaling his cologne. It's musky and manly and very him. I could drown in his scent. Ugh! It's official—I'm pathetic.

The nights this time of year in the suburbs of Sydney are quite hot, but his body temperature next to mine feels fine. I'm certainly not complaining. "I used to watch Lassie on television with my dad when I was a kid, which I'm *not* anymore by the way." He throws back his head and laughs. Ignoring him I continue. "After every episode I'd beg him to buy me a dog just like that. One day he came home with Lassie. Of course he wasn't a Collie, but I didn't care. They both had the long hair and similar colouring. My Lassie came from a litter of pups from one of the police dogs on the force. That's how my dad got him."

"Nice story, great dog, but unfortunately still a shit name for my man Larry." I playfully elbow him in the stomach and he laughs again. He's really let his guard down tonight. I wish he was like this more often. He's actually not a bad guy when he's not being an arsehole.

"I like it, so it's staying," I enforce.

"Well, I like Larry, so that's what I'm going to continue to call him," he counters, pulling me closer to his side. I'm so short compared to him that I fit neatly under his arm.

We walk the rest of the block in silence. I'm tempted to wrap my arm around his waist, but I don't. I'm sure that his arm around me is nothing romantic on his part, just a friendly gesture. When we reach my place we stop walking. "Are you going to come in, or head home?" I ask.

"Nah. I think I'll head home. Tell your dad thanks for inviting me over tonight," he replies, dropping his arm from my shoulder and turning to face me.

"I will." I turn to walk away. "Goodnight, Carter," I say looking at him over my shoulder. He reaches out and pulls me back towards him. My body lands flush against his. Turning me to face him, his arms slide around my waist pinning me to him.

"Are you sorry I didn't take your friend's advice?" His voice is low and sexy. His eyes lock with mine, and my heart rate accelerates.

"What?" At first I'm not sure what he's talking about, then it hits me. Meg's comment. "No," I screech screwing up my face.

"Liar," he says smirking. "You were hoping I'd take advantage of you."

"I was not." I try to turn to walk away again, but he holds me tight. He's so full of himself. Sure there was a part of me that hoped he would, but I'm certainly not going to admit that to him. It's puzzling that I'd even want that considering the way he treats me.

He pulls me closer against him while one of his hands tilts my face up towards his, locking his eyes with mine. My heart is beating so fast now. His gaze moves down to my lips before moving back to my eyes. His face inches forward ever so slowly. Oh God. I think he's going to kiss me.

My breath hitches when his lips are mere centimetres from mine. "You want me to kiss you don't you?" he breathes.

"Yes," I whisper without hesitation. Did I just admit that out loud? I kind of expect him to start laughing and hold it over me with a, *"See I told you, you wanted me,"* but surprisingly he doesn't. Instead he groans before his lips gently meet mine. My hands slide up his front, fisting in his shirt, pulling him closer.

When my lips part he slides his tongue into my mouth, deepening the kiss. This is one hot kiss. I moan against his mouth. Nobody has ever kissed me like this before. It's one of those kisses that make your toes curl. Is it possible to have an orgasm from just a kiss because I think I'm close to having one right now?

I clench my thighs together. Nobody has ever turned me on like this. Suddenly, the porch light comes on. Shit, my dad. We both pull away from each other with a start. "Indi, is that you out there?" my father calls through the screen door.

"Yes, it's me," I reply, my eyes still locked on Carter. We're both breathing heavy. "I'm coming inside now." Carter exhales as his hands run through his dark hair. His eyes still haven't left mine. I think he's just as shocked as I am.

I take a few steps backwards. What the hell was that? I can't speak. I have no words for what just happened. No words for how that kiss made me feel. "I have to go," is all I say as I turn and run up the front steps. *Far out.*

EIGHT

CARTER

JESUS CHRIST. WHAT THE FUCK WAS THAT? I DON'T KNOW
what just came over me. Sure, from the moment I saw her, I wanted
those lips on mine, I'll admit that. But, *never* did I think I would act on
those feelings. *Never* did I think it would actually happen. And *never*
did I think it would make me feel what I just did. Fuck.

I'm well and truly screwed.

After she walks into the house I continue to stand there. I can't
seem to get my legs to work. My middle leg is working just fine. That
fucker is standing proud. It's so fucking hard it actually hurts. Why did
I go there? *Why?*

When the blood eventually leaves my cock and flows back into my
legs, I drag my arse towards the house. I don't bother going through
the front door. I head straight for my bedroom window. I can't face my
mum or Fuckwit right now. My head is all over the place. What am I
going to do? As much as I'd like to, I can't go there with her. I just can't.

••••

After a sleepless night, I rise early and head for my car. I have no idea where I'm going, but I can't hang around here today. I can't risk running into Indiana. That kiss is still haunting me. What I need to do is stay the hell away from her. She makes me feel things. Things I don't want to feel.

It's taken me twelve long years to build this barrier around my heart. My protective shield. The one that blocks out all feelings. If you can't feel, you can't hurt. Right? That's my logic anyway.

It has only taken her days to put a crack in the foundation I worked hard at erecting. Fuck her and her sunshine and rainbows. Fuck her and her light that's trying to penetrate my darkness. I don't need it, and I sure as hell don't want it.

I end up at a park, miles from where I now live. I'm not even sure of the suburb. Who fucking cares? It gives me what I need: distance, time to think, time to process. Time to figure out what the hell I'm going to do about Indiana-fucking-Montgomery. Why is she worming her way into my heart?

Stubbing out my cigarette, I light up another. That's not helping either. Reaching across to the passenger seat, I slide my hand underneath and pull out my sketchpad. It's been months since I've drawn anything. Maybe that may calm me the hell down. It's worked in the past.

Flicking through the pages, I study some of my other drawings. They're pretty dark; skulls, demons and snakes, shit like that. It suits my personality I guess. Retrieving a pencil out of the glove compartment, I start to draw. When I'm done, I stare down at my work.

Usually I get into the zone and let my hand draw what it wants. Of course today it chose to draw her. Those big eyes framed with long, thick, dark lashes and those beautiful plump lips that taste like fucking heaven. Christ she's beautiful. *Damn her.*

Tearing the drawing from the sketchpad, I screw it up and toss it on the floor. Grabbing my cigarettes, I get out of the car and walk across the park, eventually settling under a tree.

I open my pad to a fresh page. This time I make sure I control what my hand does. No fucking *kid*. It ends up being a picture of a skull with a snake coming out of the eye sockets and black roses wrapped in its tail. That's more like it. Placing it on my lap, I light another cigarette and I sit back and admire my handiwork.

"Hey, buddy. Got a light?" someone asks. I look up to see a guy approaching covered in tattoos. He has a huge silver spike piercing through his eyebrow and one-inch ear plugs in his lobes. I don't mind the odd piercing, but stretching your earlobe seems extreme to me. It's not like you're gonna be wearing plugs in your ears when you're seventy years old. What are you gonna do with those huge-arse fucking holes then?

"Sure," I say throwing it to him.

"Thanks. I left mine at the shop." He leans forward and passes it back once his cigarette is lit. "Hey, did you draw that?" he asks looking down at my sketchpad.

"Yeah," I answer.

"That's pretty good. Mind if I take a look?"

"Sure. Knock yourself out," I say handing it to him. I've never shown anyone my work before, but I don't know this guy, so who cares what he thinks? I don't.

"That would make a fucking awesome tatt. Ever thought of selling these?" he asks.

"Nah. I just do it for fun."

"I own the tattoo parlour across the road," he says pointing across the park towards the line of shops on the other side of the street. He flicks back through some of the other drawings. "Fuck, these are wicked."

"Thanks man," I answer. I'll admit I'm pretty stoked that he likes my work.

"I'm serious. I'd love to buy some of these. I'm always looking for new designs. You wanna sell them?" I shrug. Do I? I'm not really sure.

It would be kind of cool to know my drawings were inked on someone permanently. I've even considered getting a few myself when I can afford it. Tattoos don't come cheap. "Do ya wanna come check out my shop?"

"Sure, why not," I reply, standing. I've got nothing better to do.

"Jax," he says extending his hand to me.

"Carter."

I walk with him across the street. His shop's pretty cool. It doesn't look like much from out in the street, but inside the setup is wicked. My eyes dart around before landing on the girl behind the desk. She has a full sleeve tattoo on both arms and hot pink hair, but believe it or not it suits her. She's pretty hot. She has a nice rack, too. I'm guessing she's in her early twenties.

"Candice, this is Carter," Jax says as we approach her.

She makes no attempt to hide the fact she's checking me out. "Hi handsome," she winks.

"Hey," I say with a flick of my head.

"Check out these drawings," Jax says giving her my sketchpad. I know my drawings are good, but I'm uncomfortable about her seeing them for some reason.

"Wow, these are amazing. Did you do these?" she asks making eye contact with me. I nod. "They're great. Oh I'd love this one on my arse," she says pointing to the image of a skull laying across a bed of roses. Her comment makes me smile. I bet she's got a nice arse, too.

"I'll give you a hundred and fifty dollars," Jax says suddenly. I shrug.

"I guess." I still can't believe he wants to buy them.

"Alright." He flips through the book and counts how many drawings there are. "Fifteen," he says leaning over to pick up the calculator off the counter. He presses some numbers into it. "That's ... two thousand, two hundred and fifty dollars," he adds. "You happy with that?"

"You're paying me a hundred and fifty dollars per drawing?" I ask in disbelief.

"Yeah. Did you think it was one fifty for the lot?"

"I did." I feel stupid now. Jax laughs and shakes his head at my naivety.

"These are good man. I'll make more than my money back in one sitting. They're going to sell well. I already know a few guys that are gonna love these."

"Shit," I say, smiling as I shake my head. Who knew a few little drawings could make me that much cash? I'll be able to get those parts I put on hold for the car now.

"I've got a client coming in shortly. I've gotta go set up. Candice will fix you up with the cash. It was nice meeting you man," he says shaking my hand. "If you have any more drawings you wanna get rid of, you know where to find me."

"Thanks," I reply. I'm still shocked. This is fucking awesome.

"No, thank you. Catch ya on the flip side," he says walking towards the back rooms. I like him. He's a cool guy.

Candice opens the register and starts counting out the cash onto the counter. "There you go, handsome." She gives me a flirtatious smile when she hands me the money.

"Thanks," I say, taking the money and shoving it into my pocket. I watch as she carefully tears out the pages with the drawings on them before picking up a pen and writing something inside the cover of my pad.

"Here. I wrote my number inside. If you ever want to hook up give me a call. I'd like to see what else you can do with those hands of yours." I chuckle at her comment as I reach for my sketchpad. I like a woman who knows what she wants.

"Sounds like a plan," I say with a wink as I turn to walk out of the shop. Usually I'd be all over that, but I need to sort this shit out with Indiana first. Fuck me.

I decide to get something to eat. Since I left the house so early I haven't even had breakfast. There's a café a few doors down, so I head in that direction.

Once I've eaten I head back to my car. It's not even midday and I have no plans to go home yet. If I can avoid seeing Indiana all day I will. Now that I'm cashed up I guess I can do whatever I want.

••••

It's dark by the time I sneak back into my room. Indi's bedroom light is off. She's probably already asleep. Fuck knows what I'm going to do about school in the morning. I'm not sure if I want to give her a lift. Having her near me isn't a good idea. I need to get these feelings I have, sorted out first.

"Carter, are you in there?" my mum asks knocking on my door.

"Yeah, Mum. Come in."

"Where have you been all day? I've been worried," she asks, concern etched on her face.

"Just went for a drive. That's all."

"Are you okay?" she says, coming to sit beside me on the bed. I recognise that tone. She's worried. I hate making her worry.

"Yes. I'm fine," I reply, forcing out a reassuring smile.

"You're not happy living here, are you, Carter?"

"I'm fine with it, Mum. I just wanted to get out for the day. Honestly." That's such a fucking lie. I hate it here, but the thing is, she doesn't. I can tell she's happy. All I want is to see her happy. That's all I've ever wanted. I'm not going to ruin this for her.

Pretending to be happy here is the least I can do for her. I'm sure I'll be able to stick it out for a few more months. *I hope.*

"You sure? I'd hate to think that you weren't."

"I am, Mum. I like it here." Another lie. I hate lying to her, but I'm doing it to protect her, so I guess that makes it okay.

"Okay. I'm glad," she says placing her hand on my knee, giving it a squeeze before she rises from the bed. Leaning down, she kisses my forehead. "Night, baby. I love you," she adds, gently caressing the side of my face.

"I love you too, Mum."

After a quick shower I jump into bed. A few minutes later my phone dings. I reach for it in the dark. Fucking Jen. She wants to know if she can come over. If I knew losing myself in her pussy would help I'd say yes, but I know it won't. Last time I was with her, all I did was think about Indiana. I place my phone on the bedside table, ignoring her message.

When I open my eyes, I look at the clock beside my bed. It's 7:00am. Fuck I don't feel like going to school today, but I have to. I think I'll head off early so I'll miss Indiana. I'm still not ready to face her after that kiss.

My mum has breakfast ready for me when I walk into the kitchen. I like spending this time with her. Fuckwit has already left for work, so it's just the two of us. Just like old times.

"I've noticed you've been spending a lot of time with Ross next door," she says placing a plate of bacon and eggs in front of me.

"Yeah. He's helping me with my car. He knows all about that kind of thing."

"That's nice. I'm glad he's helping you. I must thank him next time I see him. You know John would help you if he knew about cars, don't you?" she says like she actually believes that bullshit. Who's she fucking kidding? That arse wouldn't help me. Christ he really does have her fooled.

"Yeah," is all I say, struggling to swallow the food in my mouth. I guess I'd rather have her think he's nice to me. The alternative would only upset her.

When I head back to my room to grab my backpack, I see Indi sneaking out the gate and hurrying down the side of her house. She must have the same idea as me. Why does that piss me off? I was willing to sneak off without her, but now I know she's doing the same, I'm not happy about it. Not one fucking bit.

NINE

INDIANA

I HEAR A "HEY," AS I RUSH DOWN THE SIDE OF THE HOUSE. CRAP.
I want to keep walking, but I can't. I guess I'm busted. Stopping, I turn around. Carter is hanging out of his bedroom window frowning. I sigh when I see him. "Where do you think you're going?" he snaps.

Is he serious?

I'm pissed with him and I can't even tell you why. Okay, I can. I laid in bed for hours the other night reeling over that kiss. I didn't know what to think or do about it. Then yesterday morning, I heard his car start up at the crack of dawn. I ran to my window just in time to see him backing out of the driveway.

He didn't come back until after 9:00pm. He was gone for over fifteen hours. Did he stay out all day to avoid seeing me, or was it something else? Or should I say *someone* else? Why that thought bothers me I can't say, but it does. A lot. So many scenarios went through my head as the hours ticked by and he didn't return. The later it got, the more worried I became. Was he with Jen? Or worse, his ex-landlady?

"I'm going to catch the bus," I snap, folding my arms over my chest in annoyance.

"Like hell you are." He jumps out of his window and makes his way towards me. I turn and start heading for the street. "Hey," he says reaching out to grab my arm when he catches up to me. "What's up your arse?"

"Nothing," I say, trying to free my arm from his grip.

"Well why are you sneaking off then?" I can tell by the tone of his voice that he's hurt. Turning around, I face him. Shit. He is hurt. It's written all over his face.

"Where did you go yesterday?" I ask. It's none of my business, but it's been eating at me all night. I'm not his mother, and I know one short, incredible, hot-as-hell kiss certainly doesn't make me his girlfriend, but damn it I want to know.

"Out," is all he says. I'm tempted to say, *I know you went out, dumbass,* but I don't. I narrow my eyes at his evasiveness.

"Where?"

"For a drive." Well that tells me a lot. *Not.* "Is that what's this is about?" he asks.

"No," I answer, because suddenly I'm feeling like a fool for even being upset about this. He doesn't have to answer to me.

"Liar."

"I am not," I snap, placing my hands on my hips.

"Yes you are. You're upset that I went out, aren't you? We share a kiss and now I'm not allowed to go anywhere without you. That's a little unreasonable don't you think?"

"If that's what you think, then you're even more full of yourself than I originally thought." I turn and walk away. Not because I'm angry at what he said, but I'm embarrassed by the way I'm carrying on. He's right. I am being unreasonable. I have no right to be angry with him. *Real smooth Indi.* He's going to think I'm like that crazy bitch in fatal attraction. He probably thinks I'm going to cook his rabbit. Well, he would if he had one.

"Get back here," he demands. Ignoring him, I keep walking. I only make it to the sidewalk before I'm lifted into the air and flung over his shoulder. He doesn't say a word and neither do I. After he fishes out his key from his pocket, he opens the passenger side door and deposits me inside the car.

Somebody kill me now.

Silent. That's how we remain all the way to school. That's a good thing. I'm humiliated for acting like a spoilt child. I guess the name kid suits me now. "Be here this afternoon when it's time to go home, or so help me," he says in a warning tone once he parks the car. His ridiculous command almost makes me want to laugh. Almost. Instead, I'm relieved the car is no longer moving. Time to make my escape and get as far away from him as humanly possible.

••••

"Spill," Meg says as I approach my locker. I avoided her calls all day yesterday. "Nothing to tell," I say, pushing her aside so I can put my bag inside.

"Indiana Isabella Montgomery." She always uses my full name when she's upset with me. Damn her. She's not going to give up until I tell her everything. Closing the door, I lean my head against the locker and exhale an exasperated breath.

"We kissed. That's it. Are you happy now?"

"Oh. My. God. I knew it. I was worried when you didn't take my calls, but then I thought maybe you were spending the day with your hot-as-hell neighbour," she says excitedly.

I wish.

Ignoring her I walk away, heading towards my first class. "Indi," she calls out to my retreating back whilst running to catch up. She reaches for my arm pulling me to a stop. "What has gotten into you today? Are you angry at me or something?"

"No," I reply turning to face her. The worry I see on her face brings tears to my eyes. Maybe everything that's happened since *he* kissed me is the real reason I'm upset. I'm guessing that's what it is.

Without saying a word, she drags me down the corridor into the ladies room. "What's going on?" she asks when we're away from prying eyes. I have no words. Placing my hands over my face, I start to cry. "What the hell?" She pulls me into her arms, holding me tight. "What did that bastard do to you?"

"Nothing," I eventually say. Placing her hands on my shoulders, she pushes me back so she can see my face.

"Bullshit. In the twelve years we've been friends, I can count on one hand how many times I've seen you cry." When a few other girls walk in, she pulls me into a stall, locking us in. I'm grateful for that. The rumour mill is rife in this damn school. If it gets out that I'm crying in the toilets, people are bound to make shit up.

I end up telling her everything. From the kiss, to him going MIA yesterday, and what happened this morning. "Babe, I think you're reading too much into this."

"You think?" I ask, because I really need her thoughts on this. My mind is all over the place.

"Yes. I'm sure there's a logical explanation. I see the way he looks at you. He's crazy about you, Indi. I can't see him hooking up with someone else when he has feelings for you." I shrug. Does he have feelings for me? Or does he just want to get in my pants, like Brad?

Once I've pulled myself together, she lets us out of the stall. I splash some cold water on my face before we leave. I'm going to try and put it out of my mind for now.

Carter Reynolds has messed with my head enough.

I manage to avoid running into Carter for the rest of the day. I did see him from a distance at lunchtime. Well, I saw his back as he stormed out of the lunchroom. Brad decided to come and sit with us today. I'm not sure if that had anything to do with it.

Since I gave Brad the brush-off, he hasn't left me alone. I guess he doesn't like being told 'no'. I'm probably the first girl in history to ever turn him down. He can try all he wants, but I can assure you this is one pair of panties he won't be getting into.

Following orders, after my last class I make my way to the car park. Carter is looking ridiculously hot leaning up against his car as I walk towards him. I try my best not to check him out, but my traitorous eyes seem to have a mind of their own. Ugh!

"Like what you see, *kid*?" he asks. God his cockiness annoys me.

"Whatever," I retort, rolling my eyes as I make my way towards the passenger side. He chuckles as he climbs in. Neither of us speak for the first few minutes of the drive.

"Are you going to continue with the silent treatment?" he asks. I don't answer. "Are you going to tell me what I've done to upset you, or are you just moody because it's that time of the month?"

"What? Ewww. No. I can't believe you just said that." He throws back his head and laughs. It's one of those rare moments. He's absolutely breathtaking when he laughs like that.

"Well, at least I got you to talk to me," he says all smug.

I let out a deep regretful breath. "I'm sorry."

"For what?" he asks glancing over at me.

"For my behaviour. It was uncalled for."

"Are you going to tell me what upset you?"

"No. It was dumb. Just forget it," I confess.

"Already forgotten," he replies smiling as he reaches over and places his hand on my outer thigh. "For what it's worth, if it was me that upset you, I'm sorry, too." *Wow*. Did he just apologise? They're two words I never thought I'd hear come out of his mouth.

Removing his hand from my leg, he places it back on the steering wheel. I find myself wishing he hadn't. "I noticed Brad sniffing around you today," he says a few minutes later.

"Yeah. I think I wounded his pride by telling him I wasn't interested."

"You told him that?"

"I told him last week. I'm guessing by his actions today he didn't take me seriously."

"Want me to have a talk to him?" he offers turning his head in my direction.

"No," I laugh. "I can just imagine what you'd say. I'm a big girl. I can handle him."

"You're a big girl?" he asks sarcastically, raising an eyebrow. He's suppressing a smile though, so I know he's joking. "Do you have mirrors in your house?"

"Ha ha," I reply as I reach over and playfully punch him in the arm. We both start laughing. I still have no idea where this thing is going between us, but I'm glad we're kind of okay again.

When he doesn't take the turn-off leading towards our street, I'm surprised. "Where are we going?" I ask.

"I've got to pick something up. I thought maybe we could grab a burger while we're out."

"I'd like that," I tell him. It both pleases and surprises me that he'd want to hang out with me.

We pull up outside the place we ate at the other day. We even sit in the same booth. "You want the same thing again?" he asks. "I still can't believe you ate all of that last time. Do you have hollow legs or something?"

"No," I shrug. "I've always been a big eater." He smiles and shakes his head.

"I don't know where you put it. There's nothing of you."

While waiting for our food to arrive, we fall into easy conversation. Nothing dreary like last time, thankfully. When he's not being a douche he's actually quite funny. This would have to be the best we've ever gotten on.

"Thanks for bringing me here," I say a while later as we leave the restaurant. "You're actually not that bad when you're being nice," I joke, although I'm deadly serious. He drapes his arm over my shoulder.

"You're pretty alright, too, for an annoying little kid," he laughs. I playfully elbow him in the side. "I'm just messing with you. Hanging with you isn't as painful as I thought it would be." I smile because I know in his twisted sort of way that's a compliment. He leads me towards Mr. Gregory's shop.

"You're not going to put more parts on hold are you? Don't you think you should wait until you can afford the other ones first?" I ask.

"Actually, I'm here to pick them up," he replies.

"I thought you didn't have the money for them." It makes me instantly suspicious.

"I didn't. Let's just say I happened to come into a little bit of money yesterday," he says winking. My heart drops. I was right. He did go and see that whore-bag, his ex-landlady. I feel like I'm going to be sick. He promised me he wouldn't go back there.

"Do you mind if I go and wait in the car?" I ask, trying my best to play it cool.

"Sure. You okay?"

"Yeah. I think I just ate too much," I reply, forcing out a smile. He chuckles.

"You certainly can eat a lot for a squirt."

"Ha ha," I say sarcastically, holding my hand out for his car keys. Tears burn my eyes as I leave the shop. I take a few deep breaths to will the tears away, but a few manage to spill over. I quickly wipe them away with the back of my hand. I can't believe he went back there. At least before he was doing it for his mum, for rent and for food. To sell your body for car parts though, that's shameful.

Once I'm seated in the car, I pull my iPod and earplugs out of my bag. I need a distraction otherwise I might do something incredibly stupid, like burst into tears. I'm hurt. Maybe I have no right to be, but I am.

Flicking through my playlists, I find what I need. Placing the plugs into my ears, I press play. The first song booms to life. This playlist, funnily enough, is called 'Distraction'. Perfect for what I need right now.

It has no sad or sappy songs on it, nothing that would make me sad or possibly cry. I actually made this list up last year. Every year on the anniversary of my mum's death, or her birthday, my dad goes MIA. They're the only two days of the year I cannot count on him for anything. He locks himself in the bedroom he once shared with my mother, with a bottle of scotch, and I don't see him again until the next morning.

That's where my 'Distraction' playlist comes in. As night falls and my dad's bottle of scotch has been consumed, and the heartache of missing my mum settles in, he starts to cry. It breaks my heart. It's the same thing every year. I wish more than anything I could take his pain away.

I'm sure he doesn't realise that I can hear him, but I can. I usually lay in my bed and cry too ... for him, for my mum, for our family. Last year I decided I wasn't going to do it anymore. I can't stand to hear him falling apart. He's usually so strong and put together. I guess he's allowed those two days a year to reflect and be consumed by his loss, hence the playlist. I listen to it until I fall asleep, trying hard not to think of my dad falling to pieces in his room.

A few minutes later there's a tap on the window. Turning my head I find Mr. Gregory standing there, smiling. Pausing the music, I wind down my window. "Hello Indi," he says.

"Hi, Mr. Gregory. How are you?"

"I'm good, and you?" he answers.

"I'm fine thanks." Which is a lie. I'm far from fine.

"Well I just wanted to say hi. Best be getting back to the shop."

"Goodbye," I say, forcing out a smile.

"Bye. Tell your dad I said hello."

"I will." When he walks away I quickly put my earplugs back in and press play. If I continue to listen to the music on the way home, I won't have to talk to Carter.

Leaning my head back on the headrest, I close my eyes. I don't hear Carter get in the car because of the music, but I feel him. I know his eyes are on me, but I don't look in his direction until I feel his hand tap my leg. Removing one of my earplugs, I turn my head to face him. "You feeling okay?" he asks.

"Yes. I'm fine." Before he says another word, I reinsert the earplug and close my eyes again. That's how I stay for the remainder of the drive. I feel his eyes boring into me a number of times on the way home, but I don't dare look his way.

When we pull into his driveway, I remove my earplugs and reach for my bag on the floor. "You sure you're alright? You're acting weird," he says as my hand grasps the door handle.

"Yep. I'm perfectly fine. I'll see you later," I answer glancing at him. Bad move. He looks hurt and that makes me feel like a bitch for the way I'm acting. His pleading eyes search out mine. I know he's probably wondering what's got into me.

"I've gotta go," I say breaking his stare. I hear him sigh, but I ignore him. That makes me feel even worse.

••••

I feel the first tear fall as soon as I walk through the door. Twice in one day he's made me cry. I'm not usually an emotional person. What is he doing to me? My dad's at work at the moment, so I'm all alone. I'm used to it. It doesn't usually bother me, but today it does.

Retrieving my phone out of my pocket, I call Meg. "Can I stay at your place tonight?" I ask as soon as she picks up.

"Are you crying, Indi?" I can hear the concern in her voice.

"Can I stay or not?"

"Of course. What's wrong, babe?"

"I'll talk to you when I get there," I reply wiping my eyes with the back of my hand. I feel stupid for crying.

"I'll get my mum to come and get you. We'll be there in five minutes," she says.

"Thank you."

CARTER

I HAVE NO IDEA WHAT THE FUCK JUST HAPPENED. ONE MINUTE we were actually getting on, the next minute things changed. She changed. Something's going on with her, but I have no clue what. Fuck this shit. This is exactly why I never let my guard down and get close to people.

"How was school, sweetie?" my mum asks when I walk through the door.

"Okay," I reply, kissing her cheek before heading to my room. I'm not in the mood for small talk right now. I'm still trying to figure out what made Indiana shift like she did. I've never seen her act so cold. It's the first time I've ever completely been myself with someone other than my mother. The first time I've actually tried to be normal. Big fucking mistake. These damn walls are up for a reason.

My mum always tells me I need to open up and trust more. I trust her, but that's about it. I know she's right, though. I can't hold what my grandfather did to us, against others. Logic tells me not everyone is like him. It's a hard habit to break. It's something I've been doing since I was five years old. That's why I got my tattoo. As a reminder to *trust*. Well at least try. Look where trusting Indiana got me. Fucking nowhere.

Sitting on my bed, I rest my elbows on my knees and bury my face in my hands. My mind is trying to make sense of it all. I'm trying to remember exactly what I said to her, hoping that will give me the answers I seek.

I hear a car horn sound from next door. Gazing over towards Indi's bedroom, I catch a glimpse of her as she throws a backpack over her shoulder and runs out of her room. Standing, I make my way towards the window. Where the fuck is she going?

INDIANA

As soon as we arrive at Meg's house, she drags me towards her bedroom. "Dinner will be ready in an hour girls," her mum calls out.

"Thanks, Mum," Meg replies.

"Thanks, Mrs. Miller," I add. Meg closes the door once she's pulled me inside her room. She takes my backpack off my back and drops it on the floor before leading me towards her bed with her hand between my shoulder blades.

"What the hell is going on with you?" she asks as soon as we are seated.

"One guess."

"What has he done now?" Her face screws up with disgust.

"Nothing to me. Well kinda … it's just …"

"Just what?"

"He told me something a few days ago. I'm not sure if I should tell you. It's kind of personal and pretty bad," I admit.

"Seriously, you have to tell me now." I chuckle when she rubs her hands together and bounces on the bed with excitement. She thrives on gossip.

"I'm not sure if I should." I'd feel like I'm betraying Carter if I tell her.

"Did he tell you not to tell anyone?" she asks. I know she's saying this to try and get me to spill. She's such a schemer.

"No."

"Well what's the problem then?" she asks, raising her eyebrows hopefully.

"I'd feel like I was betraying his trust. I'm not sure how he'd feel about me repeating it," I tell her.

"That juicy huh?" She rubs her hands together again.

"Yes," I laugh.

"Look, if you don't want to tell me that's fine. I respect that. But, I need you to know that not knowing is probably going to kill me."

"You're such a dork."

"It's up to you, babe. You know you can trust me. We tell each other everything. Maybe I can help if I know exactly what you're dealing with," she says. I trust her with my life. In my heart I know she'd never repeat anything I ever told her, just like she knows I wouldn't do that to her.

"I guess," I reply with a shrug.

"So you're going to tell me?" she squeals. See what I mean, she thrives on this shit. There's nothing funny about what I'm going to say. I know she's going to be just as shocked as I was when he told me.

"Promise me this stays between us." Although I know I don't need to ask.

"Pinky promise," she says holding her little finger up to me. Wrapping my little finger around hers we shake on it. I take a deep breath before I speak.

As I tell her everything Carter told me, her eyes almost bug out of her head. "No fucking way." She's gobsmacked. This is no pissy little thing. It's huge.

"Yes way. See why I was hesitant in telling you?" Her mouth is still open. I'm sure I must've looked the same when Carter confessed it to me. It still upsets me that he had to go through that.

"He got paid to have sex?" she deadpans.

"Uh huh."

"Fuck. He must be good. All the more reason you should jump his bones." Her eyes drift up towards the ceiling and she breaks out into a smile. Oh. My. God. She's thinking about his sexual skills, I know it. I reach out and slap her arm.

"You're disgusting," I laugh.

"So is that why you're upset?" she asks rubbing her arm. Hello. Is she even listening?

"Yes and no."

Meg reaches her hand out, putting it over mine. "You know what guys are like. They think with their dick not their brain, babe."

"I blame his landlady, not him. He was only fifteen. She took advantage of him."

"Does he see it that way?" Instead of answering, I shake my head. "Of course he wouldn't. He was getting laid and getting paid. Show me one fifteen year old horny male that wouldn't jump at that chance."

"I suppose," I reply. "But, I still think it's disgusting."

"Depends how old the landlady is. If she's like eighty in the shade then that's nasty." We both laugh at her comment.

"She was in her thirties, he said," I tell her in a disgusted tone as I roll my eyes.

"Pfff," she says flicking her wrist. "I know plenty of people in their thirties that are still hot. This all happened before you even met him, so it shouldn't really bother you."

"Well that's the thing. He promised me he wouldn't go there again," I confess.

"And he did? Is that where he was yesterday?" she asks, her eyes widening as she waits for my answer.

"I think so. He had some parts on hold at Mr. Gregory's shop because he couldn't afford them. Today, he had the money."

"That's doesn't mean he got it from her. Maybe his mum gave it to him." If it hadn't been so much money, then that could've been a possibility.

"The parts were over a thousand dollars, Meg. His mum doesn't work and I can't see Mr. Shepard forking over that kind of cash. When I asked him where the money came from, he said that he'd come into some money yesterday, but didn't elaborate. How is a seventeen year old going to earn over a thousand dollars in one day without, you know ...?"

"Shit, if she paid him that much money just for sex, he must be fucking amazing in bed. Like, mind-blowing." She's probably right, but I have no plans of finding out. I need to stay as far away from Carter-friggin'-Reynolds as I can get. It's going to be hard when I live next door to him, but if I want to protect my heart I don't have a choice.

CARTER

I sat up half the night waiting for her to come home, but she never did. By morning I'm fucking pissed off. Pissed I let my guard down with her. Pissed that she weirded out on me and I have no clue why. Pissed that she never came home.

I don't even bother waiting to give her a lift to school. What's the point? Even if she was home, after her performance yesterday afternoon she probably wouldn't accept one anyway. Fuck her. Maybe it's for the best if we go back to what we were. *Nothing.* This shit is too complicated. It hurts my fucking head.

During the day I see her a few times, but when she notices me she turns and walks in the other direction. It only serves to piss me off even more. At lunch she has Brad at her table again. It makes my blood boil.

When afternoon rolls around, I'm not surprised when she doesn't turn up in the car park. On my drive home, I see her waiting at the bus stop. It tells me everything I need to know. I flip her off when I pass. The anger has worn off. It's now replaced by hurt. I hate this feeling.

It's been a long time since I felt like this. *Rejected.*

I did plan to work on my car this afternoon, but I've even lost interest in that. Instead, I grab my sketchpad from under the passenger seat and go to my room. The first thing I do is close my blinds. I don't need any reminders of Indiana. And I certainly don't want to risk having to see her.

I sit on my bed with my back against the headboard. If I can lose myself in my drawing I won't have time to think about her.

As soon as I open the cover I see the number Candice wrote in there. I'm tempted to call her. Maybe losing myself in some random pussy is exactly what I need. Indi has made it quite clear she's not interested.

Pulling my phone out of my pocket, I decide to call her. "Candice speaking," she says when she picks up.

"Hey Candice, it's Carter. I was in there on Sunday—"

"Oh I know who you are. You have the kind of face a girl would never forget. Have you decided to take me up on my offer?" she purrs after cutting me off.

"Yeah. You still up for it?"

"Of course. Name the time and place and I'll be there, handsome," she says seductively.

"Tonight?"

"Tonight sounds perfect. I get off work around 6:00pm. How about I meet you at 8:00pm?"

"Great. I'll text you my address," I say apprehensively. I'm not even sure if I want to do this.

"Looking forward to it," she replies.

Once I end the call I text her my address and ask her to call me when she's close. I don't explain why. She'll find out when she gets here I suppose. I'm not sure how she's going to feel about me sneaking her through my bedroom window, but I'll worry about that later.

••••

"Fuck. You didn't tell me you still lived at home with your parents. How old are you anyway?" Candice asks as I haul her through the window.

"I'll be turning eighteen soon."

"Shit. You're still a kid," she says in a shocked tone as I set her on the floor.

"I'm not a fucking kid," I snap. Of all the words she picks, it's fucking that.

"You look older." What does age have to do with anything? I may be young, but I know I'll be the best damn fuck she's ever had.

"Are we going to do this or not?" I ask frustrated as I begin to lose my patience with her.

"Calm down," she replies, taking a step towards me and sliding her arms around my waist, pressing her soft body against mine. "I didn't say there was a problem with it, handsome. I'm just surprised, that's all." Her lips find my neck as she kisses a trail across my jawline until her mouth covers mine. I wrap my arms around her waist and pull her closer. She's the first person I've kissed since Indi. Surprisingly I feel nothing. I definitely felt something when my lips were locked with Indiana's. She made me feel things I'd never felt before, which I fucking hate.

Opening my eyes, my gaze moves in the direction of her window. *Great.* She's standing there watching us. Even from here I can clearly see the hurt etched on her beautiful face. Then in an instant she draws her blinds and she's gone. What the fuck am I doing?

Pulling out of the kiss, I look down at Candice. "I'm sorry I can't do this," I admit looking over towards Indi's bedroom window again.

"What? Why?" She follows my line of sight as I continue to stare where Indi stood only a few moments ago. "What's the problem?" I pull away from her and make my way towards my bed. Sitting, I lean my elbows on my knees and bury my face in my hands.

"It's not you," I say without making eye contact.

"Then what?" she asks, coming to sit beside me. What can I tell her? I've got this love/hate relationship going on with the girl next door? I can't say that, but surprisingly that's exactly what I say. I tell her everything. Well kind of. We end up sitting on my bed talking for over an hour before she eventually leaves, unsatisfied. Makes two of us. One simple kiss and the fucking *kid* has ruined me.

I feel like a prick for what I've done. To both her and Indi. Thankfully, Candice was a good sport about it. I have a sinking feeling in my gut that's not going to be the case with Indiana.

And I was right.

••••

Six days have passed and I've barely seen her. She won't even make eye contact with me. Stubborn arse. Her bedroom blinds have been closed ever since. After the incident with Candice, Indi locked herself in the house for two days. Two fucking days. She didn't even go to school.

I asked her father if everything was okay with her when we were working on my car. He told me she was just a little under the weather.

Under the weather my arse.

I can't understand her. She was the one who went all weird on me, ignoring and avoiding me at every turn. It doesn't take a genius to figure out she's upset about Candice though. Which is a total mind fuck. What happened to my fiery girl? The one who refused to take my bullshit? I wish she'd let me have it. Tell me what the fuck is going on. At least I'd know where I stood. The alternative is making my head hurt.

Even Megan is giving me death stares whenever I run into her. I asked her how she was doing the other day and she fucking flipped me off. What pisses me off more than anything is on the few occasions I have seen Indi at school, that prick Brad has been with her. If she's hanging around with him to upset me, then it's working.

I'd like to knock that fucker out.

ELEVEN

INDIANA

"BRAD WANTS TO COME OVER THIS AFTERNOON," I TELL MEG over lunch. "Mr. Jenkins has paired us up to do our English assignment together. He wants to get a start on it. I'm not sure what to do."

"Let him. Make sure you get him to climb through your bedroom window though. Give that arsehole next door a taste of his own medicine."

"I'm not getting him to climb through my window," I laugh. "Two wrongs don't make a right. Plus, if I do, Brad will get the wrong idea."

"No he won't. Tell him your front door is broken," she says seriously. Has she lost her mind? I can't do that.

"You're such a dork," I say. "I'm not even sure I should have him over. My dad has forbidden me from seeing him, remember?"

"This is school related. He'll be at work anyway, won't he?" she states with a flick of her wrist. "He'll never know." She might be used to doing things behind her parents' backs, but I'm not.

"He will if Carter tells him. He's the reason I'm not allowed to see

Brad in the first place."

"It's up to you, but I'd be all over that shit if it was me. Not only is Brad a total babe, it's the perfect revenge for what Carter's done." Good point, but I'm still not sure if I'm comfortable with this. I'm not really into revenge.

"What if he tries to, you know?" I ask. I'm not comfortable about going against my dad's wishes. I've never defied him in the past. Like Meg said, it is school related. Do I really have a choice? I'm certainly not going to go to his house.

"Have sex with you?" she giggles. "You can say the word you know. You're such a prude." My eyes scan the room to make sure nobody is listening.

"I am not," I reply, throwing a chip at her.

"Just make it clear that you'll be doing your assignment. Nothing else. Your father's a cop. It's not like he's going to force himself on you. Unless he has a death wish."

"I guess you're right." My dad would kill him if he laid a finger on me. Changing the subject, we talk about Derek, Meg's latest lover. I've met him a few times. He seems nice enough. He doesn't go to this school.

"Can I join you ladies?" Brad interrupts a few minutes later. I want to roll my eyes, but I refrain.

"Sure, handsome," Meg purrs. She's so forward sometimes. Of course he takes the seat right next to me. I'm really getting tired of him hanging around all the time. He's really sweet to my face, but I don't trust him after what Carter told me.

"Are we still on for that assignment this afternoon?" he asks.

"I guess. We only have a few days to get it done," I reply.

"About that," Meg chimes in. "If you're going to do the assignment at Indi's place, you'll need to climb through her bedroom window. Her front door is broken." Oh. My. God. She did not just say that to him. I kick her under the table.

"What?" he replies, looking at me confused. "Can't I just use the back door?"

"Nope. She has a vicious dog that doesn't like strangers. He'll probably try and eat you," she tells him with a serious face. I can't help it. I burst out laughing. Lick him to death would be more like it. She is such a schemer. Sometimes I wonder how we became friends.

••••

"I can't believe you said that to him," I say to Meg as we make our way to our next class.

"I knew if I didn't, you wouldn't. Let Carter see. It's alright for him to have girls jumping through his bedroom window. See how he likes it when you do the same." *He won't care*, but I don't say that to her.

"Can we not go there again?" I plead. I'm still reeling over what happened. I can't believe I let myself develop feelings for that douche.

••••

My stomach is in knots as I sit here waiting for Brad to arrive. I have Meg's number on speed dial just in case he tries to make a move. She's already promised to come straight over if I need her. So she should, since she's the one that's gotten me into this mess in the first place.

It's just getting dark when I hear the tap on my bedroom window. I was hoping he could've come earlier, but he had football practice. As I make my way towards the window, I see him smiling up at me. He really is good looking, but in my eyes he has nothing on Carter.

"Hey," I say as I slide open the glass.

"Hey, pretty girl." I have to hold back the eye roll. He can put on the charm all he likes, but he still has no chance of getting into my pants.

He places his hands on my windowsill ready to launch himself up, but in an instant he disappears. What the hell? I hear a growl, followed by, "I don't fucking think so." Carter. Shit. He pulls Brad backwards, making him stumble. When I stick my head out, I see them standing face-to-face.

"What the fuck, Reynolds?" Brad snaps. "What's your problem?"

"You are," Carter spits. Oh shit. I've never seen him look so angry. His face is red and there's a vein protruding from his neck. This isn't going to end well. Fucking Meg and her brilliant ideas. *Not.*

"Carter," I screech, my nails digging into the wooden frame.

"You stay the fuck out of this, *kid*. I'll deal with you later." He doesn't even look my way. His eyes are firmly fixed on Brad. He looks like he's ready to rip him apart. I bite my tongue. As much as I'd like to retaliate, common sense tells me to keep my mouth shut.

"You've got five seconds to turn around and go back to where you came from, or ..."

"Or fucking what, Reynolds? What are you going to do?" Brad retaliates, getting up in his face. Shit. Does he have a death wish? That murderous look on Carter's face alone would have me running for the hills.

"After I kick your arse, I'll drag you down to the police station. That's what."

"That's real smart, dumb-arse. You'll assault me and then take me to the cops. It'll only result in you getting charged, so go right ahead," Brad retorts with a chuckle. God he can be so cocky sometimes.

"I don't think so. When I tell her father I caught you trying to sneak in through her bedroom window he'll thank me for what I did." *Carter's right, he will.* Then my dad will rip him apart.

Brad doesn't move. He stands strong. Then he goes and does something incredibly stupid. Instead of taking Carter's advice like he should, the imbecile pushes him. *Dumb move, dipshit.* Carter stumbles back slightly and then smirks. Actually smirks at him. Like he's saying, *'is that the best you got?'.* Shit, he's crazy.

Stepping back into his face, Carter says in a calm, yet intimidating voice, "One." What is it with Carter and his damn counting? My eyes move to Brad. He's no longer looking so sure of himself. I don't blame him. This is like watching a train wreck. As much as you'd like to look away, you can't. "Two." I want to call out, *run Brad*, because that's exactly what I'd be doing. The idiot just stands there.

On the count of three, Brad raises his hand to throw a punch. Carter's quick and catches it mid-air. "Four, five," he says quickly before launching at him. He tackles Brad to the ground with a thud. Raising his fist, he brings it down, connecting it with Brad's face. *Fucking hell.*

Climbing out the window, I run towards them. Probably not a wise thing to do. "Carter," I scream as I grab hold of his shirt. "Carter." With my other hand I reach for his arm and try to pull him off. He doesn't budge.

"Get off me," Brad whines. I'm relieved when Carter finally listens. He's breathing heavy as he stands. Brad snakes his way backwards on his elbows, never once taking his eyes of Carter. He eventually manages to stand, wiping the blood from his mouth with the back of his hand. "You'll pay for this, Reynolds," he spits before turning and walking away.

"I look forward to it, Cartwright," Carter says to his retreating back. *Idiots,* the pair of them. I turn in a huff and make my way back towards my window. I'm so mad right now.

Climbing back through, I reach for the glass to close it. "I'm not finished with you," Carter says as he pushes the window back open and hauls his arse into my room in one bound. Fuck. I take a step back. When I get a glimpse of the look on his face, I take another step. "What the fuck were you thinking?" he growls.

I continue walking backwards as he stalks towards me. Eventually my back comes into contact with the wall. Shit. Closing the distance between us, he places his hands on either side of my head, caging me in. Leaning forward he pushes his body into mine, pinning me against the wall. I'm trapped.

"Get out of my room," I sneer as I try to push him off me. As mad as he is with me right now, I'm surprised I'm not scared of him.

"I don't think so," he says, roughly grabbing hold of my face and tilting it up so my eyes meet his. "I thought you were smarter than that."

"Well you thought wrong," I retort narrowing my eyes at him. Who in the hell does he think he is?

"After everything I told you about him, you still invited him over?"

"Yep," I say smugly, because it's none of his business why Brad was here. He growls angrily in my face. Fuck him. He can think what he likes. You didn't see me ripping that pink-haired bimbo out of his window the other night, even though the thought did cross my mind at the time.

"You wanna act like a slut, then I'll treat you like one," he says, roughly bringing his lips down to mine. I'm shocked. I wasn't expecting him to kiss me. I wasn't expecting him to insinuate I was acting like a slut either. How dare he? What a hypocrite. He's the whore, not me.

I try to push him away for all of a second. His kiss is hard, bruising almost. Nothing like the sweet kiss we shared last time. But it's hot. Smoking hot. I'd be lying if I said I hadn't thought about having his lips on me again. I hate him and lust over him all in the same breath.

Fisting his shirt in my hands, I pull him closer and deepen the kiss. He groans into my mouth. "You want this don't you?" he breathes, thrusting his erection into my stomach.

"No," I lie, but the answer is yes. I want him so bad. I want him to do all the things that he has done to those other girls, to me. How pathetic is that?

His fingers glide down the sides of my body until he's cupping my arse in his hands. He easily lifts me off the ground and my legs wrap around his waist. His hardness is pressing right against my centre giving me the friction I crave. Leaning my head back against the wall, I moan. The feeling is exquisite. Like nothing I've ever felt before. I dig the heels of my feet into his back, bringing him even closer as I grind myself against him.

His mouth moves across my jaw and down my neck. "Your body is telling me you want me. Stop denying it," he says into the crook of my neck.

"You're full of yourself. I don't," I pant. Another lie. He chuckles against my skin. Lifting his head, he looks me in the eye.

"If I was to touch you now, I know you'd be wet." I know I would be too, but I'm not going to admit it.

"Well you'd be wrong." He cocks one of his eyebrows. I know it's a challenge.

"We'll just see about that," he says with a cocky smile as his hand slips into the waistband of my yoga pants. Oh God. He's going to know I'm lying, but surprisingly I don't care. I want him to touch me there. No, I need him to. "Your panties are soaked," he groans pulling back to look at me. "Now tell me you still don't want me." The anger I saw in his eyes when he pinned me against the wall has vanished. It's now replaced with red hot desire. The way he's looking at me right now has my heart beating out of my chest. "So you don't want me to do this then?" he asks, pressing his fingers in a circular motion against my clit.

"No," I lie as my eyes roll back in my head. I've never been this intimate with anyone before, but I want this. I want him. Badly.

"You're so wet," he breathes as his fingers move inside the silk fabric of my underwear and slide through my wetness. "What about this, then?" he asks as his fingers continue their assault on my clit. I feel my face flush. I hate that he knows how wet I am for him.

"No," I whimper. God. It feels amazing. Nobody but me has ever touched down there. I love how his fingers are making me feel. Unexpectedly, I don't feel as nervous as I thought I would being in a situation like this. I'm not entirely sure if it's because it happened so fast, and I had no time to overthink things, or if it's because it's with Carter. Either way, I'm tempted to scream out, *Don't you dare fucking stop.*

"So you definitely wouldn't want me to do this then?" he breathes, slipping a finger inside me. "Christ. So wet. So tight," he growls out as his eyes shut.

"No. Definitely not that," I moan pushing my pelvis further into his hand.

"I'll stop then," he says, stilling his fingers. My eyes shoot open to find him smiling at me. *Bastard.* He slowly slides his fingers out, so I reach down between us and grab a hold of his wrist. Shit. He knows exactly what he's doing. He's trying to get me to admit that I want him. *Never.*

"Don't stop," I breathe and his smile widens. My head is spinning and my heart is pounding. I can't believe a simple touch is capable of igniting such pleasure. The rougher he is, the more intense the feelings become. Why don't I feel like this when I touch myself? Damn him and his magical fingers. He's playing me like a skilled musician would play their instrument.

"Why don't you want me to stop?" he asks smugly. I narrow my eyes at him.

"Because ..."

"Because why?"

"Just because it feels good, doesn't mean I want you," I say, and his smile widens, revealing his perfect, white teeth. The way he looks when he smiles like that is a sight I can tell you. It takes my damn breath away.

"Oh you fucking want me," he says all cocky. "You don't have to admit it, *kid*. Your dripping pussy tells me everything I need to know." He smirks before sliding his fingers back into my panties and through my wetness. His eyes close again. "*Everything I need to know,*" he breathes.

"You're so full of yourself."

"No. I think it's you that's full of me," he says pushing two fingers inside me.

"Oh God," I moan. My hands move up to his shoulders for leverage. Digging my nails into his flesh through his shirt, I push my hips towards his hand.

"My name's Carter, not God." He's such a smartarse. Ignoring him, I continue to ride his delicious hand. It feels wonderful. Amazing. I'm so close.

"Open your eyes, beautiful," he commands. "I want you to see who is making you feel like this ... Who's giving you pleasure." *He called me beautiful.*

Doing as he asks, my eyelids open as I gaze into his hauntingly stunning brown eyes. He's smiling at me again. "Deny it all you want. We both know the truth. If I was to slide my cock into that tight little pussy of yours, you'd be begging me for more." Nobody has ever spoken to me like that before. His filthy mouth only turns me on more. Picking up the pace, I continue moving my hips against his hand. "Yes. Fuck my fingers," he growls.

My fingernails dig further into his shoulders. "I'm ... I'm ..." I'm trying to say I'm coming but the words are lost as the most intense orgasm I've ever had rocks my body. "Ohhh, Carter," I moan as I throw my head back.

"Yes. Yes, that's it. Come for me, beautiful. I love hearing you say my name like that," he breathes as his fingers continue their assault. *I love hearing him call me beautiful.* "Fuck that was hot," he says as his lips trail a path across my jaw until they find mine. "I almost blew in my pants just watching you come undone."

His fingers are still inside me. I slide my hands up his neck and thread my fingers through his hair, deepening the kiss. If he can make me feel like this with only his hand, I can't wait to see how it feels when we go all the way.

Suddenly, he pulls out of the kiss. He removes his fingers and steps back. My legs slide down his until my feet hit the ground. I watch as his hand moves up towards his mouth. He pops his fingers inside and licks off my juices. "Mmm. You taste as sweet as I thought you would," he groans, closing his eyes like he's savouring the taste. I find this incredibly hot. "Is this what you brought Brad over for?" he asks when he opens his eyes again.

"What? No. We had an English assignment to do together," I confess. He smiles. I guess he likes my answer.

"Have you ever let anyone touch you the way I just did?" he asks.

"No," I admit honestly. I've touched myself on occasions, but I'm not telling him that. All these questions are killing the mood. I wish he'd just shut up and take me the way I want him to.

"Good. Make sure it stays that way," he commands as he takes another step away from me. He abruptly turns and walks towards the window. What? That's it? This is as far as it's going to go? Why am I suddenly overcome with disappointment? "If I find a guy at your window again, I'm going to tell your father." *What the hell?*

I'm instantly consumed with rage. How dare he come over here, scare off Brad, give me the most incredible orgasm I've ever had, and then walk away as if nothing happened?

"Fuck you, Carter Reynolds," I spit. I reach down and pick up one of my shoes off the floor, throwing it at him. It hits him square in the back of the head. *Bullseye.* Take that you bastard.

He laughs as he reaches up and rubs his head before jumping down off the windowsill and disappearing into the darkness. The fact that he finds this humorous only makes me angrier. *Arsehole.*

TWELVE

CARTER

WHEN I HEADED OVER TO HER PLACE EARLIER, I WAS FUMING.
Ready to tear that fucker a new arsehole. Now I'm leaving with a huge
motherfucking smile on my face. Well, I might be smiling, but my cock
isn't. Crazy. Everything about her makes me fucking crazy. Christ it
was hard to walk away from her just now. It took every ounce of
strength I had.

I never intended for that to happen. It was the last thing I expected.
When I had her pinned up against the wall, my hand roughly holding
her face, her cheeks slightly squashed making her sexy-as-hell lips
pucker, I had to kiss her.

Those delicious lips of hers will be the death of me. And now I have
the memory of her pussy to contend with. The way she moved when
my fingers were deep inside her. Those little fucking noises she made
when I brought her undone. No woman has ever had me as turned on
as much as she just did. What I wanted to do was sink my cock into
that heavenly pussy of hers. She would've let me, too. I know it.

When she admitted nobody had touched her that way, it not only made me happy, but it also confirmed that I couldn't screw her. As much as I would like to be her first, it should be with someone special. Someone that's going to treasure her like she deserves. That's not me. I'm only out for a good time. Nothing more.

After I jump through my bedroom window, I head straight to the shower. I'm gonna have to do something I haven't done since I was fifteen. *Flog my log*. If I don't get rid of this boner I'll never get to sleep tonight.

····

Going by the shoe she threw at the back of my head last night, I kind of figured she wouldn't be waiting for a lift this morning. I knock on her front door just in case. When she doesn't answer, I jump in the car and head towards the bus stop. She *will* be riding to school with me this morning, whether she likes it or not.

"Get in the car," I demand when I pull up beside her.

"I don't think so," she snaps, narrowing her eyes. Christ, I love her attitude, but this free bus stop entertainment for all the onlookers has got to stop.

"Are you going to make me count again?" I sigh in frustration. This shit is getting old. She's not alone at the bus stop this morning, but if she thinks it's going to stop me from throwing her over my shoulder and hauling her arse in the car again, she's mistaken.

A smile tugs at my lips as I watch her look around at the other commuters. All eyes are trained on her. I know I've won as soon as her shoulders slump and she lets out a deflated breath.

"Fine, arsehole," she says sharply as she storms around the front of the car, making her way to the passenger side. It only makes my smile grow with satisfaction. Having the upper hand when it comes to her is the best feeling ever.

"Sleep well last night, Princess?" I ask once she's settled in beside me. She ignores me. After the orgasm I gave her, I bet she slept like a baby. "I did," I add. "I fell asleep with your delicious scent all around me." I move my fingers up towards my nose when she looks in my direction.

"Ewww," she says pulling my hand down. "You're a pig." I throw my head back and laugh. Why do I get so much pleasure out of riling her?

"You weren't calling me a pig last night when my fingers were buried deep inside that heavenly pussy of yours," I whisper as I lean towards her. I hear her breath hitch and I know she's affected by my words. "If I remember correctly, it was *'Ohhh, Carter'*." I'm not sure if bringing up last night is torturing her more, or me.

"Shut up," she shouts crossing her legs. Her pretty face is flushed. My words are definitely turning her on. Knowing this is making my cock grow even harder. I want to keep going, but decide not to. I don't want to push her too far. I'm just having a little fun.

For the rest of the drive, she keeps her head turned away from me looking out the window, refusing to speak a word. I notice her squirm in her seat a few times and I know she's thinking about last night. "You okay over there, Princess?" I can't help but note her breasts rising high as her breath hitches again. It makes me happy to know I affect her. I bet if I was to reach down between her legs I'd find her wet and ready for me. I clench the steering wheel tight, because now that's exactly what I want to do. *Touch her.*

When we pull up outside the school, she's out of the car in a flash. "Make sure you're here this afternoon," I demand, leaning over in my seat looking up at her standing next to her open door. Ignoring me, she slams it in my face before turning and walking away in a huff. I have a feeling she'll show up. She knows what will happen if she doesn't.

She manages to avoid me most of the day. That is, until lunch. I purposely make sure I sit at her table. At least that fucker Brad has got the message and stays away. I've copped a few death looks from him today. He's real fucking tough when he has his mates around him.

"Can I join you ladies?" I ask when I approach them. Indi and Megan both say, "No," in unison. I ignore them and take a seat anyway. They don't say a word to me the whole time, but I'm not fussed. When the bell sounds, I rise. "It was a pleasure dining with you both," I chuckle. I hear Indi growl as I walk away. It only serves to make my smile grow.

As I leave the lunchroom, Brad shoulder-barges me as he walks past. "Watch out fucker," I say as he walks off. He laughs as he hurries away. Gutless prick. He'll keep.

When the final bell sounds for the day I make my way towards the car park. As I approach my car, I notice a few people crowded around. As I get closer, I see exactly why.

What the fuck!

INDIANA

I debated whether to get a lift home with Carter, but he's such a stubborn arse. I knew he'd hunt me down if I didn't show up. I actually make it to the car park before him. As soon as my eyes land on his car, my heart sinks into the pit of my stomach.

I stand there in shock, until a minute or so later when Carter arrives. I watch on in horror as he drops his backpack to the ground. His hands fist in his hair and complete devastation crosses his face. I don't blame him. I know how much he loves his car. Who would scoop so low? My first thought is Brad. I'm guessing it was him anyway. *Lowlife.*

Someone has slashed all four tyres. The windscreen is smashed in. There are dents all over the exterior and, what looks like paint, splashed across the hood. Someone has definitely taken to it with a baseball bat.

"Carter," I say as I rush towards him. "I'm so sorry."

I reach out and try to grab hold of his arm, but he shrugs me off. "Don't," he says through gritted teeth. He briefly makes eye contact with me before his gaze moves back to his car. His poor smashed up car. My heart hurts for him.

He looks angry. I'm not sure if it's directed at me, or whoever is responsible for this. If it is in fact Brad, Carter may blame me for what's happened. Either way, nobody deserves something like this. Reaching into my bag, I pull out my phone.

"Daddy, it's me," I say as soon as he answers. "Can you come to the school? Someone has trashed Carter's car."

"What? What do you mean trashed his car?" he asks.

"The tyres are slashed and the windscreen and exterior look like they've been taken to with a bat. There's paint thrown all over the hood, too," I reply.

"What?" he screams. "I'm on my way. If there's any witnesses, make sure they hang around." I can tell he's upset. I know he loves this car just as much as Carter does. Who would do something so sick?

My dad arrives within five minutes. Carter is still standing there in shock. He hasn't said a word. His body language screams what hasn't been said. I feel for him. After my dad talks to all the bystanders, he makes his way back to us.

"Nobody saw anything," he says in a disappointed tone. "Don't worry, we'll get to the bottom of this." Carter still doesn't speak. "We'll get it back to the way it was, son," my dad reassures him resting his hand on his shoulder. "I'll help you." Carter doesn't react, but my father's words make me smile. I know he means what he says.

Once the tow truck comes and takes the car away, my father drops us off at home. "Carter, wait," I call out as he jumps out of the car and storms towards his house. He doesn't stop. I feel my shoulders slump. I feel so bad for him.

"Leave him be," my dad says from behind me. "Just give him some time to calm down. I can understand why he's upset. Don't take it personally."

"Thanks for coming out," I say when he leans down and kisses my forehead. He needs to get back to work. "I hope you find who's responsible for this, Daddy."

"Do you have any idea who may have done this?" he asks.

"I know he had a run-in with Brad Cartwright yesterday. That may be a good place to start." I don't go into detail. That'll only serve to get me *and* Carter into trouble as well.

"Okay, Pumpkin. I'll look into it." He kisses me before getting back into the car. I stand there and watch him drive away. As I head towards the house, my eyes are fixed next door. I really want to go to him, but my dad said give him time to calm down. I think that's a good idea. I decide to call Meg instead.

"What the hell happened to Carter's car?" she asks. Thinking about his car makes me instantly agitated.

"Brad Cartwright would be my best guess."

"You think?" she asks in a shocked tone.

"I'm not sure if Carter has any other enemies at school. Although with his attitude, he's probably pissed a lot of people off," I admit.

"Maybe."

"I wish I could do something to help him, Meg," I confess. "I feel so bad for him. You should've seen his face. He loves that car."

"Yeah, it was a pretty shitty thing to do. He may need to sell his body again to get the money for the repairs."

"God. Don't say that." I feel sick in the stomach now. I hope that's not the case.

● ● ● ●

Once my homework's done, I make something to eat before having a shower. As I lay on my bed, I can't stop thinking about Carter. I wonder how he's doing. Standing, I look over towards his bedroom. The light is on, but the blinds are closed. Do I dare go over there? I know I'm not going to be able to sleep until I find out if he's okay.

My mind made up, I climb out of my window. "Carter. You in there?" I call out after knocking on the glass.

"What the hell?" he says opening his blinds a few seconds later. His hair is wet and his chest is bare. He must've just had a shower. God he's delicious.

"Can I come in?" I ask. Do I even dare enter his room after what happened between us yesterday?

"What do you want?" he asks annoyed when he opens the window.

"I just wanted to make sure you were okay."

"I'm fine. Go home," he bites. I hate it when he speaks to me like that. I understand that he's upset, but he's taking it out on the wrong person.

"Okay," I say disappointed and a little annoyed. What an arse. I know he's upset, but he doesn't have to be so damn rude. I turn and head back towards my house.

"Wait," he shouts. I stop but don't turn around. "I'm sorry. I didn't mean to take it out on you."

"So, can I come in?" I ask with a smile when I turn around to face him. He exhales and then rolls his eyes.

"Fine. If you must." I head back towards his window where he leans out ready to haul me inside.

"Wow. Your room looks different from in here," I say as my eyes dart around everywhere. It's so neat and tidy for a boy's room. Tidier than mine. It's quite bare. No pictures or posters hanging on the walls. He has a bed, desk, bedside table and a set of drawers, but that's about it.

When my eyes finally meet his, he's smiling for some reason. I try my best not to look any lower than his face. I don't want him to think I'm checking him out, because I know that's exactly what I'll be doing.

"So does your room," he smirks. Memories of yesterday enter my mind making me blush. "Why are you turning red?" I narrow my eyes at him. Coming here was a bad idea. Turning, I head towards the window. "Wait. I'm just messing with you, *kid*. Don't go."

He reaches out and pulls me back until my body lands against his. My back is flush with his chest. Having him so close sends tingles running through my body. My senses are engulfed by his delicious scent. God he smells so good.

Not moving, I keep my body right where it is—against him. One of his arms snakes around my waist drawing me even closer, while his other hand reaches up, pulling my hair to the side. He runs his nose from the base of my neck up to my ear.

"You smell delicious," he whispers against my skin, making me shiver. He sucks my earlobe into his mouth, swirling his tongue around it. "You taste good, too." I lean my head back against his chest and whimper. "I love those little noises you make. It turns me on," he breathes. His warm breath against my skin makes it pebble with goose bumps.

He thrusts his hips forward to prove his point. I feel his erection pressing into my lower back. Knowing I have that effect on him does funny things to my lady parts. Slowly, he turns me in his arms and slightly tugs on my hair, tilting my head back until I'm looking up at him. The desire I see in his eyes makes me ache between my legs. He gazes down at me for what seems like forever, before his face slowly inches towards mine.

"Can I kiss you?" he whispers when his lips are near mine.

"Yes," I answer without hesitation. He places his mouth gently on mine. He lets go of my hair and slides his fingers through my locks, digging them into my scalp to bring my face closer. My arms curl around his waist as I push my body further into his, causing him to groan into my mouth. This kiss is sweet and incredibly hot, just like our first time. He really is an exceptional kisser.

When I open my mouth slightly, he slips his tongue inside and deepens the kiss. Turning me, he walks me backwards until my legs come in contact with his bed. He gently lays me down, climbing over me, never once breaking the kiss.

Pulling back he gives me one of his rare, breathtakingly beautiful smiles. He brushes my hair back off my face before leaning down and placing his lips on mine again. We make out for what seems like an eternity. I'm so turned on.

Eventually pulling out of the kiss, he looks down at me, smiling. "I can't believe I have you here sprawled out on my bed. Now what am I going to do with you?"

"Whatever you want," I answer shamelessly. I want him to do anything and everything. His eyes close briefly as he groans at the thought. When they open again he gives me a mischievous look. My heart starts to race. Is it wrong that I want him to do bad things to me, because I do?

"As much as I'd like to, kid, I'm not going to fuck you. Your first time should be with someone special. That's not me." He must see the disappointment cross my face, because by Christ that's exactly what I'm feeling. "It doesn't mean we can't do other things," he smirks. I'm upset this isn't going to go all the way. I want him to be my first.

I want that more than anything.

He brings his lips down to mine again. I'm so incredibly turned on by his kisses. I desperately need some friction down below. I shift my legs from underneath him, spreading them before pulling him down on top of me. He settles in between them.

His hand slides underneath my pyjama top. He growls into my mouth when he feels I'm not wearing a bra. He cups my breast in his hand and runs his thumb over my hard nipple, thrusting his pelvis forward at the same time. *Yes.*

"Your skin is so soft," he whispers against my mouth. His erection hits me right where I need it, making me moan. He does it again, and again. My hands slide down his muscular back until they are resting on his arse. He has the most amazing arse. All round, tight and delicious. Using my hands to push him down, my hips lift up meeting him thrust for thrust. There's only two thin pieces of fabric separating us. *God I wish there wasn't.*

We both continue to move in sync. It's like we're having sex, but with clothes on. I really want to be doing it with him. I want to feel him inside me. "I ... I think I'm going to come," I mutter a few minutes later. He groans into my mouth again, pressing his erection hard against my clit, moving his hips in a circular motion. It feels amazing.

"Come for me, beautiful," he urges. Within seconds my orgasm hits me hard.

"Yes," I moan as my head pushes back into the pillow and my body trembles from the intensity. My nails dig into his arse cheeks as wave after wave of pleasure courses through my body. He doesn't stop moving until I'm finished. Pulling back, his hooded eyes meet mine.

"I need to taste you now," he breathes. Sitting back on his haunches, he slides my pyjama bottoms down my legs, taking my panties with them. Nobody has ever seen me naked before, but for some reason, with him, I don't feel self-conscious at all. "Sweet Jesus. You're more beautiful than I imagined," he states.

The thought of him imagining me naked pleases me. A lot. He spreads my legs wide, gazing down at me. Appreciation is written all over his handsome face. He exhales and then smiles. Leaning forward he lifts my back slightly off the bed as he pulls my top over my head. "I need to see all of you." Returning to his haunches, I watch as his eyes caress my body. The look he gives me is so hot I'm surprised it doesn't scorch my skin. "Perfect," he breathes, making me smile. *He thinks I'm perfect.* His fingers lightly caress my skin leaving a trail of goose bumps in its wake.

His impressive hard manhood is straining against his pyjama bottoms. I want to do something for him, but I have no idea what. I just want to please him like he pleases me.

Placing his hands on either side of my hips, he leans forward. He lays a sweet kiss on my stomach before his tongue trails a path up to my breasts. His eyes meet mine as he sucks one of my nipples into his mouth.

"Mmmm," I say as my eyes close and my fingers thread through his hair. I never knew my body was capable of feeling such extraordinary pleasure. I could easily get addicted to these feelings.

"Open your eyes. I want you to see who's making you feel like this," he demands as his tongue makes a trail over to my other breast. "You're perfect," he whispers against my skin as he kisses down my abdomen. I find every word, every movement he makes completely erotic. "I love how your body responds to my touch."

I should be nervous that he's heading south, but I'm not. I want to experience everything with him. *Everything.*

When he settles between my legs, he looks up and smiles as he inches forward. He parts my lips with his fingers before blowing his warm breath over my clit. His eyes never once leave mine. It makes my breath hitch and my body shiver in anticipation. His tongue darts out and he licks a line straight up my centre. His eyelids flutter shut and he groans against my sensitive flesh.

"So sweet," he murmurs. Reaching down I thread my fingers through his hair.

"Oh God," I moan. I have no words for how incredible this feels. *No words.* His eyes spring open and he pulls back slightly.

"That's not my name," he grumbles. *Shit.* We had this discussion last night.

"Carter," I breathe.

"That's better," he says as his tongue finds me again. I thought his hands were magical last night, but his mouth ... Oh. My. Fucking. God. Amazing. He is a man of many talents.

Within minutes I'm on the verge of another orgasm. I'm trying my best to suppress it. I don't want him to ever stop what he's doing. "I could do this to you all day," he says, like he has just read my mind. *Freaky.*

"I wouldn't complain if you did. It feels amazing," I reply, but it comes out more like a whimper. He growls against my sensitive flesh as he inserts two fingers inside me before hooking them. Fuck. I can't hold back any longer. "Carter," I moan as my hands tug on his hair. His tongue and fingers work feverishly as my orgasm hits me hard, followed closely by another one. *Holy crap.* I think I'm going to pass out.

He kisses his way back up my body until his lips meet mine again. I can taste myself on him, but it doesn't turn me off in the slightest. My hand reaches down between us as I grip his shaft. Shit, he's huge. "Let me do something for you," I offer. I'm tempted to beg him to have sex with me, but I know that will just make me sound lame. Ending the kiss he looks down at me.

"You don't have to. Just seeing you come undone is enough for me," he replies as his face softens. I wish he was this sweet all the time.

"I want to. *Please.* I have no idea what to do, but you can show me. I'm a fast learner." God, like that sounded any better. I feel my face flush. I should've just begged for sex. I hate that compared to all the other girls he's been with, I'm so inexperienced. I'm sure they all knew how to please him. I clench my eyes shut. Somebody kill me now.

"Open your eyes," he demands. I'm surprised to see him smiling when I do. "I like that about you. I love your innocence and that nobody has been where I've been." I feel relieved that my naivety isn't turning him off.

"Can you show me what to do? Show me what you like? I want to please you like you please me." Leaning forward he brushes his lips against mine.

"Nobody has ever said that to me before," he whispers as his eyes lock with mine.

"I'm sorry," I say, feeling my face turn even redder. Now I feel like a complete idiot.

"Don't be. Nobody has ever asked me what I like. What I want. They've only cared about what I could give them."

"Well I care," I say, reaching up and running my hand gently down the side of his face. And I do care. More than I'd like to admit.

His lips meet mine again as he rolls over onto his back, taking me with him. He lifts his hips slightly off the bed and pulls his pyjama bottoms down around his thighs. Grabbing hold of my hand, he wraps it around his shaft. My small hand barely reaches around his impressive girth. Placing his fingers on top of mine, he slowly moves my hand up and down his length.

"Yes, that's it," he moans pulling my lips towards his. "Just like that, beautiful." I love that he keeps calling me that. I wonder if he says that to all the girls. I try not to let my mind go there. I want to believe that what we have is unique.

Eventually he lets go and I'm doing it on my own. He's groaning as his hips buck against my hand. I pause the kiss to look down. I want to watch. I love that little old, inexperienced me is making him feel like this, that I'm capable of giving him pleasure.

His penis is the first I've ever seen in real life. Meg always says how ugly they are. She obviously hasn't seen Carter's, because his is beautiful. I continue stroking it as I sit up. I can see the pre-cum beading at the tip. I want to taste it. Leaning forward I run my tongue around the head.

"Fuck," he hisses through a clenched jaw. I open my mouth and slide the tip inside. He starts to gently pump into my mouth as his hand threads through my hair, holding my head still. "I'm gonna blow," he says suddenly trying to pull my head back. I don't move. I want to keep going. I open my mouth wider and take him in deeper. Closing my lips around his shaft, I continue to work him with my hand. He pumps into my mouth a few more times. "Indi," he cries out as his body shudders beneath me. "Sweet Jesus … Indiiii."

This is the first time he's ever called me by my real name.

••••

"Indi. Wake up," I hear someone say. Opening my eyes, I'm surprised to see Carter's handsome face smiling down at me. "We must've fallen asleep," he says in a sleepy voice as he rubs his eyes. What? I'm still half asleep and dazed. Then I remember where I am and what we did. I bolt upright.

"Crap."

"It's okay. It's still the middle of the night. I just thought you might want to get home before your dad finds you missing," he says sweetly. Looking over towards his bedroom window, I see that it's pitch black outside. In his room, however, it's not. His bedside lamp is on. Shit. I'm still naked. My hands fly up to cover my breasts as my eyes frantically search the bed for my pyjamas. I can't see them anywhere. I feel my face turn red. "Are you okay?" he asks, propping himself up on one elbow.

I can't bring myself to make eye contact with him. "Do you know where my clothes are?"

"Hey," he says, placing his hand under my chin to raise my face to meet his. "Are you okay? Are you having regrets?" he asks when our eyes meet. I'm not. How could I? What we shared tonight was amazing.

I just feel a little uncomfortable now. It's one thing to be naked in front of him in the throes of passion, but now not so much. It's the first time I've ever let somebody see me like this.

"No, I'm not," I reply honestly. "I just want to put my clothes back on." He reaches out and removes my hands that are covering my breasts.

"Please don't hide yourself from me," he pleads. He almost sounds like he's hurt by my actions. "Your body is beautiful. Don't ever be ashamed or embarrassed by it. Especially with me." He says it with so much sincerity I can't help but smile. Who knew he was capable of saying something so sweet?

"Thank you." What else can I say? He reaches down and retrieves my clothes off the floor.

"I mean it," is all he says as he passes me my pyjamas. My smile widens.

Once I'm dressed I rise from the bed. I'm still shocked by what's happened tonight. I'm not sure where this is going to take us, if anywhere, but I'll never regret what we did. *Never.*

Standing, Carter follows me towards the window. I'm not sure if I should kiss him goodbye, so I don't. "I'll see you tomorrow," I say as I swing my legs over the windowsill.

"Hey." He reaches out and gently grabs hold of my arm. "I know we were just mucking around here tonight, but don't let it make things weird between us, okay?"

"Okay." I turn my head and give him one last smile. "Goodnight," I say as I jump off the window ledge.

"Night, *kid*." Looking over my shoulder I narrow my eyes at him, making him chuckle. He stands there and watches until I'm safely back in my room. I lift my hand to wave before closing the window, and he flips me off. He's smiling when he does it though. I guess that's his way of keeping things normal between us.

CARTER

AS SOON AS SHE LEAVES, I LAY IN BED WITH A HUGE SHIT-ARSE grin on my face. Christ. My mind is spinning. Did that really just happen? I've never *not* gone all the way with a chick before, but fuck me, if what we just did didn't satisfy me more than any of the others have in the past. I'd give anything to be able to fuck her. *Anything.* But, I can't do that to her. She deserves so much better than a one-night stand. That's all I can offer. I don't do commitments. *Ever.*

I'm not sure what time it is when I eventually fall back to sleep, but I do know I dreamt of her when I did. I even woke up with a smile on my face. Shit. That's not like me. I hope today things aren't weird between us. I want things to stay just the way they are.

I don't even notice that I'm whistling when I walk into the kitchen for breakfast, until my mum mentions it. "Someone got out the right side of bed this morning," she chirps. "It's been a long time since I've seen you looking so happy. It's so good to see, sweetheart."

"Morning, Mum," I say kissing her cheek and ignoring her observation. My mood actually surprises me as well.

"With everything that went on yesterday, this is the last thing I expected to see this morning. I know how much you love that car."

Fuck. *My car.* For a minute I thought she was talking about me and Indi. My head is so clouded with her that this shit with the car completely slipped my mind. The smile instantly drops from my face and that sick feeling I had all yesterday afternoon returns. I'd like to get my hands on whoever is responsible.

"I hope they find out who did this," she says placing my breakfast in front of me. Suddenly I no longer have an appetite. I don't know how I'm going to find the money for the repairs. My insurance only covers the other party if I have an accident. That's all I could afford. "I won't be needing my car today, sweetie. You can use it to get to school if you like."

"Thanks, Mum."

"Eat something," she encourages, gently rubbing my back from behind me. "I'm sure Ross will get to the bottom of it."

I fucking hope so.

••••

Making my way towards the car I'm not sure if Indi is going to turn up, but I'm hoping she will. I'm surprised my stomach is churning about seeing her. I have no regrets about last night. How could I? I just want things to be normal between us again. I need to pull my shit together and play it cool. Last night was a one-time thing. As much as I'd like a repeat, for both our sakes, it can't happen again.

I throw my backpack in the back seat just as Indi comes through the side gate. I hate that I have to take my mum's car today. I hate that someone fucked mine up. God help whoever it was when I find out. Even though I'm pretty sure it's that prick Brad.

"Hey," she says walking towards me. "I thought we'd be catching the bus today."

"Who said I'm giving you a lift?"

"What?" she gasps before narrowing her eyes. "I see you didn't forget to put your arsehole attire on again today." I chuckle at her comment. Thank Christ we're okay.

••••

"I heard what happened to your car," Brad laughs as I pass him in the hall on the way to my locker. "Sucked-fucking-in." I had planned on ignoring that prick until I had some kind of proof it was him, but not now. Not after what he just said. Something inside me snaps. My backpack doesn't even hit the ground before I lunge at him.

I only get a few good hits in before I'm being dragged off him by one of the teachers. "Cartwright, Reynolds, principal's office now!" he screams pointing down the hall. Great. After all the trouble I got in at my last school, I promised my mum I'd try and keep my nose clean here. Guess I just broke that promise.

The teacher leaves us both seated outside in the waiting room once he's had words with the principal. "You'll pay for what you did to my car, cocksucker," I say through gritted teeth as I glare over at Cartwright.

"Good luck proving it, arsehole. You think I was stupid enough to do it in front of witnesses?" I fucking knew it was him. I rise from my chair, ready to give him another serving.

"Sit back down, Mr. Reynolds," the principal says sternly from the doorway of his office before turning his attention to Brad. "Did I just hear you correctly, Mr. Cartwright?" Christ, I fucking hope he heard his confession.

"What?" Brad says as the colour drains from his face.

"If I'm not mistaken, I just heard you admit to vandalising Mr. Reynolds' car."

"Noooo," that lying cocksucker squeals.

"So now you're going to add lying to your list of offences. I had the police here earlier this morning, making a few inquiries about this particular incident. I think I may need to call them back."

"I didn't do it," he screeches, panic lining his voice. Like shit he didn't. I'm so glad that smug bastard couldn't keep his big mouth shut.

••••

I received lunchtime detention for my part in the fight, but Cartwright got his pretty boy arse suspended. Indi's dad came back to the school and took him away for questioning, and he was later charged with vandalism and malicious destruction of property.

After school was out, Indi and I made our way home. I'm glad last night hasn't changed things between us. Although we still act like we annoy the crap out of each other, I think we're actually becoming friends. I haven't had a real friend since I was a boy.

After the day I found out the true meaning of what a bastard was, I started to act out. The older I got, the worse my attitude became. The friends I had back then were soon stopped from hanging around me. I guess their parents thought I was a bad influence. Maybe I was, but it only served to make me feel more worthless than I already did.

Indi's dad comes out to greet us when we pull into the driveway. "Hey, Daddy," she says as he walks towards the car.

"Hi, Pumpkin. Do you mind if I have a few words with Carter?"

"Not at all. I'm going to take Lassie for a walk before I start my homework." We both watch her walk towards the house. Of course my eyes are glued to her arse again. Well I thought we were both watching, until I turn to face Mr. Montgomery and find him staring at me. *Fuck.*

"Can I ask what your intentions are with my daughter?"

"We're friends, nothing more," I lie. Well it's kind of true. Friends with benefits you might say, but I don't have a death wish so I'm not going to tell him that.

"I'm not stupid, son. I see the way you both look at each other." I nervously shove my hands into the pockets of my jeans. It's one thing for me to know how I feel, but it's another for anyone else to know. I don't like where this conversation is heading. I'm waiting for him to tell me I'm not good enough for his daughter. I know that, but it's gonna suck to hear him say it. Up until now I've liked the way he's treated me. "It's the exact same way I used to look at my wife when she first moved to town," he confesses.

"Yeah. I'm sorry about ... you know ... what happened to your wife," I say.

"Thank you." The sadness I see in his eyes makes me feel bad for him. I've never been in love so I can only imagine how he feels, but I can tell that he is far from over her death. "If her passing has taught me anything, it's to live life to the fullest. You never know what's around the corner." He exhales then shakes his head.

"I'm sure it hasn't been easy for you."

"It's been tough, but having Indi has helped. She's so much like her mother." I smile when I see his face light up. I'd never admit it, but she has the same effect on me. "Do I need to warn you not to hurt her? To always treat her with respect? She's all I have and she means the world to me, Carter."

What? That's the last thing I expected him to say. "No, Sir," I answer before clearing my throat. Shit. Is that the right answer, or was that a trick question?

"Good," he says gripping my shoulder. "I like you, son, but if you hurt or disrespect her in any way, I won't hesitate to kick your arse. You understand?" When he smiles at me, I feel the corners of my lips turn up. This is not how I envisioned this conversation going. Indi and I will never be more than what we are, but it's nice to know that her father isn't repulsed by the idea of his daughter being with someone like me.

"Yes, Sir." He nods and taps my shoulder like he's pleased with my response.

"I called past the wreckers this morning and collected your personal belongings from your car," he says passing me the plastic bag he's holding. "I threw out the cancer sticks I found in the glove compartment. Don't let me catch you smoking again, you hear."

"Yes, Sir," I answer dropping my head. I feel like a child being scolded, but on the other hand, I like the fact that he seems to care.

"I also found this." He pulls a crumpled piece of paper out of his pocket. Without even opening it I know what it is. The sketch I did of Indiana. Fuck. Why did I leave that on the floor of my car? I should've thrown it in the trash, but for some reason I couldn't bring myself to do that. "Did you draw this?"

"Yes," I answer reaching for it. He pulls his hand back.

"It's good. Do you mind if I keep it?" Christ. This conversation is getting more awkward by the minute.

"Sure," I tell him. I'm sure I could draw another one if I wanted, which I don't. We're friends. Nothing more. "You're not going to show her are you?"

"The picture?" he asks, a small smile playing on is lips.

"Yes," I answer shyly. I don't want her to think I'm obsessing over her or anything, because I'm not.

"Not if you don't want me to," he says, his lips turning up further. I have no idea why he's smiling. I divert my eyes. The way he's looking at me is the same way Indi does. Like he can see straight through me. He clears his throat. "Why didn't you have full insurance on your car?" he asks changing the subject. I'm grateful for that.

"I couldn't afford it."

"Fair enough. The guy at the wreckers owes me a few favours, so I've asked him to get started on the repairs to the body. You can sue Cartwright for the damages. His parents can afford it. I'm going to talk to his father about it. He'll probably agree to pay for the repairs before it comes to that. He won't want this going public."

"Thank you," I say extending my hand out to him. Even though I'm still pissed about my car and the fact it's going to take weeks, possibly longer before I get her back, I couldn't ask for a better outcome.

••••

The rest of the week goes by without incident. On the days my mum needs her car, she drops Indi and I at school. The other times she lets me take it.

Ross talked with Cartwright's father. He was right. He didn't hesitate to agree to pay for any repairs needed for the car—in exchange for our silence, of course. Fat lot of good that's going to do. This is a small town. Shit's already spreading like wild fire.

Late Friday afternoon, Ross comes knocking on my door. "Got a spare half hour?" he asks. "I need your help with something."

"Sure. Just let me tell my mum I'm going out." I have no idea what this is about, but I go along with it. Once I'm seated in the passenger seat of his car, he informs me why I'm needed.

"It's Indiana's birthday on Sunday, so I've decided to buy her a small car. That's where you come in. I'm working all day tomorrow, so if I'm going to have it here for Sunday, I need to pick it up today. You're going to need to drive it home from the car yard."

"Are you giving it to her today?" I ask.

"No. Frank across the road is letting me hide it in his garage until Sunday morning. I'm taking that day off to spend it with her."

"Okay. Cool. Does she have her driver's licence?" She's lucky her father can afford to buy her a car. I know if my mum had ever been in that position she would've done the same for me. She always let me borrow hers though, until I could afford to buy my own.

"Yes. Only her provisional licence," he answers.

••••

It's getting dark when we arrive back at the house. Ross got me to park down the road for five minutes so he could go in the house and distract Indi. Frank was already waiting out front with his garage door open when I pulled into his driveway.

I had no idea it was her birthday this weekend. It has me thinking, should I get her something? We're kind of friends. Friends do shit like that I guess. Christ. I don't want her getting the wrong idea about us.

••••

Saturday, Indi's dad invites me to come over Sunday night for a birthday dinner. I guess that means I have to get her something now. I'll admit I did lay awake half the night wondering what sort of gift she'd like before he even asked me. I suppose my mind was already made up.

"Mum, can I borrow your car?" I ask walking into the kitchen.

"No," Fuckwit says cutting in on the conversation.

"John. That's not nice," my mum replies. "Why can't he borrow *my* car?" He clears his throat and squirms in his seat. As much as I hate him, I almost want to laugh. He's usually very calculated with his attacks against me. Guess he's slipping.

"If he can't look after his own car, why should we reward him by letting him use ours? How is he ever going to learn his lesson?"

"That's a little unreasonable," my mum says holding her hand against her chest like she's hurt or shocked by his words. If only she knew, '*unreasonable*' is his middle name. "Carter had no control over what happened to his car. Why should he be punished for that?"

"You're right, Elizabeth," he says in his fake-arse full of shit voice. Placing the paper he was reading on the table, he rises from his chair, making his way towards her. "I'm sorry, sweetheart," he adds sliding his arms around her waist. My mum smiles up at him. Fuck, he has her hook, line and sinker. Of course he doesn't apologise to me. *Arsehole.*

"My keys are in my handbag, sweetie," she says smiling at me. I shift my gaze and hold it on Fuckwit.

"Thanks, Mum."

"You can wash your mother's car when you get home to thank her for her generosity," Fuckwit grunts. Christ I'd love to smack that smug look right off his face.

"He doesn't need to do that," my mum says frowning.

"It's okay, Mum. I don't mind washing your car for you." I walk out of the room before either one of them have a chance to say anything else. Or more importantly, before I say something that may upset her.

••••

After two hours of walking around the damn shops, I finally find the perfect gift for Indiana. I'm not used to doing shit like this. I hate shopping. I hate buying fucking gifts, period. It's something I've never done before. With my mum, I always gave her money. I'm sure there were a lot of things she went without, but she needed money more than anything.

I'm grateful the lady at the jewellery store offers to gift-wrap it for me otherwise she'd be just getting it how it is. I have one more thing to get before I get the hell out of here.

When I arrive back home, I stash my purchases in my room and head outside to wash my mum's car. I don't mind doing things for her, but I hate that *he* has asked me to do it. Just another thing that cocksucker can gloat over.

An hour later I'm done. I empty the bucket, wash the sponge and start to roll up the hose when Fuckwit decides to come around the side of the house. "Before you put all that away, you can wash my car as well," he snaps.

"What?"

"You deaf as well as dumb?"

"Neither," I reply through gritted teeth. I'd love to knock this prick out. If it wasn't for my mother, I wouldn't hesitate. "I didn't borrow your car, so why should I wash it?"

"Because you live in *my* house, eat *my* food and use *my* electricity, that's why, smartarse. You're nothing to me and you're not a damn charity case, so if you want to continue to live under my roof, you'll do as you're bloody told." I exhale an exasperated breath while counting to ten in my head. The longer I stay in this house with him, the harder I'm finding it to keep my cool. "Get it done," he adds before walking back towards the house. "You better do a good job as well or I'll make you redo it." *I hate him with a fiery passion.* What I'd really like to do is ram this damn sponge down his fucking throat.

Snatching the bucket off the ground and heading towards the tap, my gaze moves towards Indi's room. Great. She's fucking standing at the window looking at me with a sympathetic smile on her face. I don't want or need her damn sympathy. I hate that she just witnessed that cocksucker handing me my balls.

Once the bucket is full and I add the detergent, I slap the sponge onto the hood of his car. "Hey. You want a hand?" Indi asks from behind me, making me jump.

"What are you trying to do, give me a damn heart attack?" I grumble.

"That's a little dramatic don't you think?" she says sarcastically, placing her hands on her hips. I love her attitude. "I was only trying to be nice."

"Well don't." She narrows her eyes at me and I try hard to suppress my smile. Is it wrong that I like getting under her skin?

"You shouldn't let him treat you like that?" she says as I turn back to the job at hand.

"When I want your opinion, *kid*, I'll ask for it."

"You don't need to be such an arse," she says, pursing her lips.

"And you don't need to be such a busy body," I retort.

"Fuck you, Carter."

"Oh I know you'd like that, but sorry. Like I said before, I can't do that." She growls at me and turns in a huff, making me chuckle. I think I've had enough fun with her for now. "Hey," I call out as she storms off towards her house.

"What?" She stops walking but doesn't turn around.

"Thanks for the offer." When she flips me off over her shoulder I throw my head back and laugh. I'd also like to thank her for lifting my mood, but of course I don't.

••••

Later that night I'm sitting in my room, sketching, when I hear the side gate next door creak open. Jumping up I take a look. Indiana. Where in the hell does she think she's sneaking off to this time of night?

Opening my window, I jump out in a flash. "Hey. Where do you think you're going?" I ask when I move up behind her.

"What the hell, Carter?" she angrily whispers while clutching her chest. "Are you trying to scare me to death?" Smiling, I decide to throw her words from earlier today, back at her.

"That's a little dramatic don't you think?"

"Ha ha. I think this is a little different, Carter. It's dark, it's late and I'm a girl."

"All the more reason you need to tell me what the hell you're doing out here," I snap. She better not try and lie to me either. I'm ready to lose my shit with her. I'll haul her arse over my shoulder and deposit her back inside her room if I have to.

"None of your business," she replies, quickly moving one of her hands behind her back. Yeah I don't think so *kid*. I'm not sure what she's trying to hide, but I intend to find out. Reaching towards her, I grab hold of her arm.

"What do you have behind your back?" I ask.

"Nothing," she says trying to step away from me. Nice try. I'm way too strong for her and easily manage to snatch the bag out of her hand.

"Give me that," I say taking it from her.

"No. Be careful with that!" she cries out trying to reach for it, but I hold my hand high in the air. She's a shrimp so there's no way she can reach it. When she jumps up to try and grab it, it only makes me laugh.

Stepping back, I lower my arm and look inside. Opening the bag instantly has me gagging. The smell alone should've been enough to warn me of the bag's contents. What the hell? I quickly drop the bag to the ground.

"Fucking shit. What are you doing with a bag full of shit?" She throws her head back and laughs.

"It's Lassie's. That'll teach you for snooping." She bends down and picks up the bag off the ground before turning and walking away.

"Where are you going?"

"To right a wrong," is all she says. I have no idea what she's up to, but if she thinks I'm letting her go out on her own in the dark, she's mistaken. I go to follow, but when she stops next to the driver's side door of my stepfather's car, I'm stopped in my tracks.

My mouth turns up into a smile when I see what she's doing. She opens the bag and tips the contents out right next to the driver's side door. It's still dark when he leaves for work in the mornings so I know he's going to step straight in it. Fucking brilliant.

When she's done, she walks straight past me with a cute little smug look on her face. "Night, arsehole."

"Night, *kid*," I chuckle. "And thank you." I can't believe she'd do something like this for me. I'm not used to people having my back. She's taking a big risk as well, especially after the way he carried on when Larry shit on his lawn a few years back.

"You're welcome," is all she says as she climbs through her bedroom window. I stand there and watch in awe. For an annoying little shrimp, she's one kick-arse fucking chick.

••••

I set my alarm for 5:15am. There's no way I was going to miss the show. My stepfather leaves for work at 5:30am. He only has to go and open up the store he owns on the weekends. He's usually back by breakfast time. He works Monday through to Friday. He has staff who manage the weekend shift. Don't ask me what he does. I have no clue. My mum did tell me once, but I wasn't really listening. Anything she has to say about him doesn't interest me.

His performance was well worth getting up at the butt crack of dawn. It was hilarious. After cursing his head off when he stepped in the shit, he marched over and bashed on Indiana's front door. He had no proof it was her, or Larry, but of course I knew he'd blame them.

I couldn't see the front of her house from my bedroom window, but I clearly heard Mr. Montgomery rip him a new arsehole. I kept my bedroom light off, but Indi didn't. My eyes were glued on her while I listened to her father going off his nut.

Her ear was pressed up against her bedroom door as she listened to her father tell my stepfather off. A few times she covered her mouth and threw her pretty little head back, laughing at the things he was saying. I could feel my smile growing wider as I watched on. She's a fucking legend in my eyes for what she did.

••••

I'm not sure what time it was when I finally fell back to sleep, but I know I was beaming when I did. It's kind of surreal how one person can make such a huge difference in your life. As much as I hate living here with Fuckwit, somehow the kid makes it all worthwhile.

Crazy but true.

Suddenly, I'm jolted out of my sleep by a high-pitched squeal. At first I'm in a daze, but then I remember it's Indi's birthday, and going by that scream, she's just seen her car. Jumping out of bed I rush towards my window, just in time to see her launch herself into her father's arms.

Sitting there in the driveway is the car her father bought her. There's a huge red bow tied around it. Seeing her happy like this does something to me. I can't really put it into words, but I know I'm fucking smiling again. Go figure. I've smiled more in the past few months since moving here, than I have in the previous twelve years since my life changed.

I watch on for a few more minutes before I head to the bathroom to take a leak. I want to give her the present I bought her and wish her a happy birthday, but I'll wait until I go over there tonight. I'll let her have this time with her father. I know she doesn't get to see him as much as she'd like to.

For the rest of the day I just hang around the house, mainly in my room. I don't feel comfortable in this place when Fuckwit's home. I use this time to put the finishing touches on the drawing I made for Indi. When I'm finished, I place it in the frame I bought for her.

I'm not sure how I feel about giving her this, but fuck me, I want to see the look on her face when she sees it. I drew a picture of her and Larry. It was just from memory, but I'm happy with the way it's turned out. It was from the first day when I arrived here, when they were playing ball out the front. She's holding the ball high in the air, and Larry is jumping up trying to retrieve it.

Of course I couldn't help myself. I've titled the picture, 'My Man Larry and the Kid'. I know that's going to piss her off. That's exactly why I did it. Should be good for a laugh if nothing else.

FOURTEEN

INDIANA

MY BIRTHDAY HAS BEEN WONDERFUL SO FAR. BEST PART IS, it's not even over yet. Meg and Carter are coming over for dinner and cake tonight. I have no idea why my dad invited him, but I'm glad he did. Not that I'd ever admit that out loud. I shouldn't love being around him, but I do.

Meg comes over every year to help me celebrate. Usually I'd just wear jeans or something casual, but tonight I decide to make a bit of an effort. It's not because Carter's coming over. I just feel like dressing up. Well, that's my story and I'm sticking to it.

I find myself smiling as I look out of my bedroom window at my new car sitting in the driveway. I friggin' love it. I had no idea I was getting one. My dad is wonderful like that. It's the most extravagant thing he's ever bought me. I thought maybe I'd get one for my eighteenth or twenty-first. I'm not complaining though.

After my shower, I blow dry my long brown hair and apply a touch of makeup. I've decided on an emerald green sundress. It matches my eyes perfectly. I've only worn this dress once before, and received a lot of compliments. *I hope Carter likes it.*

"You look pretty, sweetheart," my dad says when I walk out onto the back deck.

"Thanks, Daddy." Making my way towards him, I wrap my arms around his waist. I love him so much. "Do you want me to order the Chinese food?" I ask.

"Nope. Already ordered. I got all your favourites," he says. Looking up at him I smile.

"You're the best." He kisses the top of my head before looking down at his watch.

"That reminds me, I need to go pick up dinner."

"I'll drive you," I offer and he chuckles.

"You need to stay here and wait for your guests." He's right, but I've been finding excuses all day to drive my car. I drove us to our favourite pancake place for breakfast. I then drove to the shops to get some groceries. I even took the long route home because I wasn't ready to get out of my car. It's going to be great not having to get public transport everywhere. I'll even be able to drive myself to school. I'll miss travelling with Carter, but it's probably for the best. He keeps reminding me that there is, and never will be anything between us. I wish that wasn't the case, but I'm grateful he's upfront and doesn't lead me on. I've noticed the more I'm around him though, the more attached I'm becoming. I don't seem to be able to control these feelings I'm developing.

Once my dad leaves to pick up dinner, I go about setting the table out back. I love it out here. The deck is raised high enough that you can see the view of the lake over the back fence. I'm lost in thought when Carter comes through the side gate. It's only that Lassie bolts past me and down the back stairs, heading straight for him, that I even notice his arrival. Why does my heart race and stomach go into a flutter whenever he's near?

He stops when he reaches the base of the steps. His eyes travel the length of my body before making their way to my face. The corners of his lips turn up into a smile. Why does the looks he gives me do funny things to my insides? He exhales before shaking his head.

"Well look at you. The *kid's* all grown up," he says smirking as he makes his way up the back stairs.

"Ha ha," I reply narrowing my eyes at him. "You know, technically we're the same age now, so if I'm a *kid* that means you are, too." He throws back his head and laughs.

"Nice try. At least I look my age, if not older." God he infuriates me. How can he turn me on with just a look, and piss me off the next. "Happy Birthday, Indiana," he says with a teasing, cocky smile. Ugh! I can tell he gets pleasure out of getting under my skin.

"Oh you know my name?" I ask sarcastically, even though hearing him say it did make my heart skip a beat.

"Of course I do. It's not the first time I've used it either," he whispers, leaning forward. "Have you forgotten that already?" I feel my face heat up. How could I forget that? He called out my name when his dick was lodged in my throat as I made him come. As embarrassed as I am right now, memories of that night send desire coursing through my whole body. So much so I have to clench my thighs together to try and relieve the throbbing that's now present.

"No," I whisper as I drop my head.

"It's nothing to be embarrassed about," he says placing his finger under my chin and tilting my face upwards. When my eyes meet his, my heart starts to race again. He looks hurt. I don't want him to think I regret what we did that night, because I don't.

"I'm not embarrassed by what happened," I tell him honestly.

"Good," is all he says as his face inches towards mine. He places his lips softly against my mouth. "Happy birthday, beautiful." Before I get the chance to take the kiss any further, he pulls back. "This is for you."

I hadn't even noticed he was carrying a gift bag in his hand. I can't seem to tear my eyes away from his handsome face when he's near. Unless he's shirtless of course, then I'm all over that.

"You bought me a present?" I ask sceptically.

"I did. I bought you something, and I also made something for you," he says with a smirk. That immediately has my suspicions rising.

"You made me something? It's a bomb isn't it?" He chuckles at my comment.

"No, it's not a bomb."

"Well, what is it?" I ask, holding the strings of the bag by my fingertips at arms-length.

"Open it and find out."

"Okay," I reply, still uncertain if this is a joke. Coming from him it's liable to be anything. There are two things inside the bag. Something large wrapped in tissue paper. It looks like a picture frame or something like that, and a small gift-wrapped box. I pick up the smaller present first.

After I shake it and hold it to my ear, just to make sure it's not ticking, my eyes meet his again. "It's not a bomb," he laughs. "I promise."

Carefully unwrapping it, I open the small velvet box. I gasp when I see what's inside. It's a silver necklace with a dog charm pendant. It looks exactly like Lassie. I feel tears burn my eyes. This is the sweetest gift anyone has ever given me. Coming from someone who acts like he hates me most of the time makes it all the more special. I want him to like me. I want us to be friends. Maybe more, but I'll settle for friends.

"Do you like it?" he asks.

"I love it."

"Good. I've never bought a present for anyone before, so I didn't know what to get you." There's definitely a sweet side to him. As much as he would hate me to say it, I'm seeing more and more of the real Carter. The one he tries so hard to keep hidden.

"Can you help me put it on?"

"You want to wear it now?" he asks surprised.

"Of course. I'm going to wear it every day."

"You are?"

"Uh huh." His face lights up. Taking it out of the box, I pass it to him. Turning around, I lift my hair out of the way. When his fingers lightly graze over my neck, I shiver and he chuckles. Arsehole. I swear he did that on purpose. Once he's finished I'm surprised when he leans forward and places a tiny kiss on my shoulder, making my skin pebble with goose bumps.

I look at him over my shoulder. What is it with this guy that sends my body into overdrive? Nobody has ever made me feel the things he does, by just a look or a simple touch.

I'm surprised when I see a look of pure lust in his eyes. Just like the one he gave me that night when I was in his bedroom. His hands skim lightly down my arms before snaking around my waist. He then pulls my body against his. I can feel his erection pressing into my back. I guess I have the same effect on him.

His lips find my neck as they kiss a path up towards my jaw. I tilt my head to the side and softly moan. He turns me in his arms and my hands slide over his chest and around his neck, just as his lips meet mine. We agreed not to go there again, but when we're together, it's like there's this magnetic pull drawing us to each other. I can't explain it, but the way he looks at me sometimes, I know he feels it too.

A few minutes later when the doorbell chimes, we both pull apart from each other like we've been caught doing something wrong. How can something that feels so right be wrong? Carter clears his throat and I feel my face flush.

"That must be Meg," I say brushing my hands over the front of my dress nervously. He runs his hands through his hair while staring at me, dumbfounded. I get the impression he doesn't understand this thing between us either. "I better go answer the door." I turn and walk away from him before he has a chance to say anything.

"Happy birthday, babe," Meg says when I open the front door. "I saw your new car in the driveway. Eeeek. I'm so friggin' jealous."

"I know. I still can't believe I have a car. Tomorrow, you and I are going for a cruise around town."

"Awesome. Hey, are you okay? Your face is all flushed." Which I'm sure only causes my face to go even redder.

"I'm fine," I lie and she narrows her eyes at me. I hate that she can see straight through my bullshit. "Come in. Dad's gone to pick up the

Chinese food." She hands me a present as she passes. "Thank you," I say plastering a smile on my face.

I follow her out towards the back deck. She stops in her tracks when she sees Carter standing there, patting Lassie. Looking over her shoulder she smirks at me. Bitch. I guess she's making her own assumptions as to why I was flushed when I answered the door.

"Carter," she says turning her head back in his direction.

"Megan," he replies with a nod. She smiles, looking between the both of us before she makes her way towards the table and takes a seat. I follow. I can just imagine what's going through her head right now.

"Open your present," she says when I'm seated.

"I still have one more present to open from Carter first." Leaning forward I reach for the gift bag that's sitting on the table.

"Oh. Did Carter give a you present before I arrived?" she giggles.

"Yes," I answer. She's such a smartarse. I know exactly what she is insinuating. "He gave me this necklace." I hold it up for her to see.

"Jewellery? Hmm. Oh, that's so pretty," she says grinning when she leans over to get a closer look. "What else did he get you?" Her eyes move over to him and he squirms in his seat. Poor thing. Meg can be such a stirrer sometimes.

"You can open it later if you like," Carter replies looking over at me.

"No she can't. I wanna see what else is in the bag."

"Meg," I snap.

"What? I think it's sweet that he got you a present." Ugh! I wish I hadn't said anything now. Opening the bag I pull out the other gift. I gasp when I unwrap the tissue paper. It's a framed picture of Lassie and I playing fetch.

"Did you draw this?" I ask meeting his gaze.

"Yeah," he shrugs nervously fiddling with the collar of his T-Shirt. I've never seen him look so unsure of himself. This picture is amazing. There's so much detail in it. It looks exactly like us. Who knew he was so talented?

My eyes scan over the drawing and then I see the title written down the bottom. 'My Man Larry and the Kid'. My gaze moves back towards him. I fight the grin on my face while trying my best to give him a dirty look. I know I've failed miserably when he laughs.

"Let me see," Meg says snatching it out of my hand.

"Wow. You drew this? You should do this for a living."

"I'm considering it," he tells her. "I sold some of my drawings to a tattoo place a few weeks ago. I'm still surprised by how much money they made me."

"No shit," Meg says. Then she gives me a look. I know exactly what she's trying to convey. I guess he didn't go to see that whore-bag after all. I feel terrible now. It was wrong of me to make assumptions about where he got his money from. Meg even said there was probably a reasonable explanation, but being the stubborn person I am, I refused to listen to her.

••••

Meg ended up sleeping over so I didn't get any more alone time with Carter. I'll admit I was disappointed, but it's probably for the best. He's definitely not a one-woman man, so I guess if this thing between us continues, I'm only going to wind up getting hurt.

Monday is a public holiday, so we have no school today. Meg and I spend the day cruising around in my car. "You wanna grab some lunch at the little café mum took us to a few weeks ago? I want to try that dish she ordered," Meg asks.

"Sure. I might have the same. It looked yummy." I park in the car park just off the main road. It's near impossible to get parking on the street this time of day. It's only a half a block walk to the café from here anyway.

Meg links her arm through mine as we walk down the street. "Is that Carter over there?" she asks pointing across the road. Of course my head immediately snaps in that direction. *It's him.* My heart starts to race for some reason. I hate that he makes me feel like this.

"What's he doing going into a bar?" I ask more to myself than her.

He's not even eighteen yet.

"I don't know. Maybe he wants a drink."

"It's the middle of the day. He's underage," I say.

"So, we're not all goody-goodies like you, Indi. I've been in plenty of bars before." Reaching up, I pinch her on the arm. "Ouch. What was that for?" she laughs.

"I'm not a goody-goody," I snap. Sure I haven't done half the things she's done, but since Carter has been my neighbour, I have crossed the line a few times.

"Name one thing," she challenges. I can name a few, but I haven't told her about the things Carter and I have gotten up to. Only because I know she'll never shut up about it if I do. She stops and waits for me to answer. "Exactly," she says when I don't.

"I put dog poop next to Mr. Shepard's car the other night." Lame I know, but it's the best she's getting.

She starts laughing. "You did not."

"I did too. He trod in it the next morning. He came bashing on our door screaming like a raving lunatic. My dad went off his head when he blamed Lassie."

"No fucking way. You really did that? Why?" she asks.

"Because he was being mean to Carter. I hate the way he treats him." She stops walking and turns to face me.

"You really like him, don't you?" I shrug. The answer is yes, but I'm trying my best to fight what I'm feeling. No point wishing for something that's never going to happen. "Why don't you tell him how you feel? I can tell by the way he looks at you that he feels the same. This just proves it," she adds, flicking the necklace around my neck. "When a guy buys a girl jewellery, it says a lot."

"It's a necklace with a dog charm on it, Meg. It's not a damn engagement ring."

"Why don't you make a move on him? Maybe that's what he's waiting for."

"He doesn't want a girlfriend," I tell her.

"He told you that?"

"Kind of. He said things could never go any further …" Shit. I clench my mouth shut before I say anything else. I didn't mean to say that part.

"Any further? Any further than what?" she asks yanking on my arm when I try to walk away.

"Nothing," I reply looking down at the ground. She's gonna know I'm lying if I look her in the eye.

"You lying bitch. Spill. I know you're keeping something from me."

"I'm not," I lie, raising my head and meeting her steely gaze. When a smile creeps onto my face she reaches out and pinches me. "Ouch." I start to laugh as I rub my arm to try and relieve the pain.

"I'm waiting," she says impatiently, raising her hand like she's going to pinch me again.

"Okay," I reply pushing her hand away. "We may have snuck into each other's room and did some things. Not sex. Other stuff."

"What? When? Why am I only hearing about it now?" she screeches in a high-pitched voice. I drag her towards the café, promising to tell her everything once we're seated. She's never going to shut up about this, I know it, but I don't really have a choice. I can't lie to her.

••••

I tell her the whole sordid mess as we wait for our food to arrive. We're sitting outside the café. I told her I wanted to sit out here for privacy so we could talk, but my real reason was so I could keep an eye on the pub where Carter is. I'm still wondering why he's in there. I hope he hasn't gone in to meet, or even worse, pick up a girl.

That thought makes me feel sick in the stomach.

"I can't believe all this has been going on behind my back and I'm only hearing about it now. I tell you everything about my hook-ups," she complains.

"Yes I know," I reply rolling my eyes. "All the sordid details as well. Sometimes after talking to you I feel the need to bleach my brain."

"Fuck off," she says and we both laugh. We both stop talking when our food arrives so we can eat, although the whole time my eyes keep drifting over towards the building that houses Carter. Half an hour has passed since he entered.

When we've finished eating we ask for the bill. We split it and make our way back towards the car park. We don't make it far when Meg turns and starts dragging me across the street. "Where are we going?" I ask.

"To see what lover boy is up to."

"What? We can't go in there, we're underage," I say horrified.

"So is he. We can both pass for eighteen. Well I can. Not sure about you," she laughs.

"Ha ha, bitch. Just because I'm short ..."

"Undo those buttons," she says reaching for my top. I slap her hand away.

"No!"

"Do you want to see what Carter's up to?" she asks. Do I? I'm not sure. If he's in there with another female, I don't know how that's going to make me feel. Not good that's for sure. "Your only chance of getting in is those perky little tits of yours," she says reaching for my buttons again.

"Fine." I slap her hand away again and undo the top two buttons of my blouse. I'm not sure it's going to help, but it's worth a shot. I'm glad I wore my black lace, push-up bra today.

"Ladies," the bouncer at the door says when we approach. I shouldn't have even bothered with my buttons—he didn't even look my way. Of course he couldn't take his eyes of Meg's girls. They're huge and put mine to shame. What is it with men and boobs?

He opens the door and gestures for us to enter without even asking for any ID. He winks at Meg as she passes. I roll my eyes. My stomach is churning as we enter. This place is a dive. It smells of stale beer and cigarette smoke. If my dad knew I was here, he'd kick my arse and probably close this place down.

"I can't see him," I say as my eyes dart around. "Let's go."

"Oh, stop being a big baby." She grabs my arm and drags me further into the establishment. This is the first time I've been in a place like this. I hope none of my dad's friends are here. I grab hold of her hand and clutch it tight.

As she pulls me further towards the back, I scan the room. I feel like everyone's eyes are on us. We walk past one table and this guy with a shaved spiky head and tattoos all up his arms looks me up and down before licking his lips. Ewww.

"Can we just go, Meg," I beg. "This place is creeping me out."

"Not until we find your lover boy."

"He's not my lover boy. Stop saying that," I angrily whisper. "He's probably already left."

"The way you were scoping out this place from across the street, I think you would've noticed if he had."

"Ha ha. Please, can we just go?" Pulling me over towards the wall, she places her hands on my shoulders.

"Stay here and don't move."

"Where are you going? Don't leave me here alone," I plead. I can hear the horror in my own voice as I speak. Meg just laughs.

"You crack me up. Stop being such a goody-goody. Live a little, babe." She releases my shoulders and turns and walks away before I even get a chance to protest. Great. My eyes nervously scan the room. When they land on that tattooed, scary guy again, I find him staring at me. Shit. He gets up from the table and starts making his way towards me. Double shit. My heart is beating out of my chest.

I'm kind of relieved when I notice *he* has boobs. It's really a she. Or a shim. Whatever you want to call it. They're way too big to be man boobs. I still don't like the way she's looking at me though. God, I hope she doesn't want to fight me or something.

"Hi," shim says when she stops in front of me.

"Hi," I manage to squeak out.

"What's a pretty little thing like you doing in a place like this?"

"Ummm ... ummm." I want to say something, but can't seem to find the words. She takes a step closer. She's now mere inches from me. I can smell the alcohol on her breath. What the hell does she want? My question is answered almost immediately when she reaches out and grabs me right between the legs. I'm frozen with fear, or shock. Shim has hold of my vagina and there's not a damn thing I can do or say to stop it.

She's not even touching me up, just holding it, like I said, *"Excuse me could you hold my vagina for a second?"* which of course I didn't. I stand there for what seems like forever while this stranger has hold of my crotch. I want to ask her to let go, or at the very least push her away, but I'm terrified. She's twice the size of me. I briefly make eye contact with her. She's smiling at me. Can you believe it? She's standing in the middle of a public bar, holding my fucking snatch, smiling. *Crazy bitch.*

"Hey. What the fuck do you think you're doing?" someone says from behind her. Relief floods through me when I recognise Carter's voice. "Keep your hands off my fucking girl," he warns as he pulls her off me. As horrified as I am right now, I'm happy. *He called me his girl.*

"Sorry bro," Shim says holding up her hands in defence before backing away. My eyes meet Carter's. Oh crap, he's pissed.

"What the fuck?" he says. "Why are you here?"

"Ummm ... Meg needed to use the bathroom," I fib. There's no way I'm going to tell him we were here spying on him.

"Are you okay?" he asks, gently placing his hand on my shoulder. "You're awfully pale." Well yeah. How would he feel if a stranger manhandled his private parts? Scratch that. It's Carter. He'd more than likely enjoy it.

"That girl just had hold of my ..." I'm not sure why I can't say the word out loud, but I point in the direction of my vagina instead. God I'm so lame. "How do you think I am?" I'm mortified by what she did, but even more so that he witnessed it. Even though his eyes look angry, I see a small smile play on his lips. *Bastard.*

"I know. I saw. She's lucky she has tits or I would've knocked her the fuck out."

"Carter," Meg says from behind him. "What are you doing here?" Thank god she said that. I love how she always has my back.

"Did you find the bathroom?" I ask with a wink when Carter turns his head in her direction.

"Yes. Yes I did. Are you okay? Your face is all white," she observes frowning.

"Some girl just grabbed me on the ... you know what," I tell her. I still can't believe that just happened. Who does that kind of thing? Of course the bitch starts laughing.

"What's a 'you know what'?" she asks. *Fucker.* She knows exactly what I mean.

"My lady parts," I admit as I feel my face burn up.

"Your vagina? Your hoo-ha? Your snatch? You can say the word you know," she says giggling. I'm glad she finds this amusing. *Not.*

"Shut up," I snap narrowing my eyes at her. She's just adding to my humiliation.

"You're shitting me right?" she asks like she doesn't believe me. Why would I lie about something like that?

"No, she isn't," Carter chuckles. *Somebody kill me now.*

"I'm glad you two think it's amusing," I retort as my eyes move between them. Of course they're both snickering.

"It's not amusing, it's fucking hilarious," Meg laughs. "Who was it? Point her out." I just glare at her. I need to get the hell out of here.

"Serves you right for being in a place like this when you're under-age," Carter chimes in. Who asked for his damn opinion anyway?

"Excuse me? I believe you're underage too," I respond. What a hypocrite.

"Only by a few months. I came in to play pool. Besides, I'm a guy. I can handle myself. You, on the other hand, are a kid. Your little run-in with the she-man just proved that this is no place for you." I hear Meg snigger again from beside me and I want to kick her. Carter just stares me down. I can tell by the look on his face that he's trying to rile me up.

"Whatever." I want to say more, but I don't. He'll only have another smartarse remark to come back with. *So much for Meg having my back.* To hell with them both. I turn on my heels and stomp towards the exit.

I'm sure one day I'll find the humour in this situation, but right now I don't.

••••

Carter begrudgingly agreed to hang with us for the rest of the afternoon. "I suppose being around you two is better than being around my stepfather," he said sarcastically. Although initially it pissed me off, he was smiling when he said it. I swear he does shit like that just to get under my skin. Although he'd never admit it, I think he was grateful.

He confessed to not wanting to go home because his stepfather had the public holiday off work. It made me feel sad for him. Things must be pretty shitty living with that arsehole. Especially since he makes it quite clear he's not welcome. I know he's lost without his car, as well. It's still going to be another week before the repairs are complete.

Thankfully, the little incident back at the pub isn't mentioned again. I'm sure I haven't heard the last of it though, especially from Carter. On our walk back to the car, Meg remembers she has to pick up some photos her mum is having printed. Carter waits for us outside the shop while I go in with her.

I see that they have some T-shirts on display behind the counter, where you can print your own image on them. It gives me an idea. After speaking to the lady who served Meg, she says she can definitely make what I want. Thankfully, I've got the perfect image on my phone. After she downloads it onto her computer, she tells me I can pick it up tomorrow. I smile. I can't wait to see Carter's reaction when I give it to him.

We drove around for a while before heading back home to swim in the lake. He even came with Lassie and I later that afternoon when we walked Meg home. I still find it hard to be around him after everything we've done, but I'm hoping in time it will get easier. I'm glad that we're somewhat friends at least.

••••

Tuesday morning, I head for my car—my first day of driving myself to school. I didn't ask Carter yesterday if he'd like a lift. He's forward enough to ask if he wants one. He has his mum's car if he doesn't.

"Morning, *kid,*" he says when I round the corner, almost scaring the life out of me. I wish he'd stop surprising me like that. He's leaning up against my car looking all smug and sexy. Obviously he's travelling with me.

"Can I help you with something?" I ask raising an eyebrow at him. He never makes things easy on me, so I intend to do the same.

"I'm just here for my lift," he replies as one side of his mouth turns up into a cocky smile. It really should be illegal to be that damn good looking.

"What lift? I didn't offer to take you," I retort, trying to keep a straight face.

"You don't need to," he says all smug. "You owe me."

"I don't think so," I chuckle.

"What about all the lifts I've given you?"

"If I remember correctly they were under duress."

"Duress or not, a lift is a lift, *kid,*" he says as he walks around the passenger side and opens the door.

"Stop calling me kid."

"As long as I know it annoys you," he chuckles, "I'm never going to stop." Remind me again why I put up with him? Grrrr.

As much as I hate to admit it, I like having him around.

••••

After school, I told Carter I needed to swing by town so I could pick up the shirt I ordered. He was cool with that. He waited in the car while I ran inside. I burst out laughing when the lady showed me the finished product.

I'd gotten a large image of Lassie's face printed on the front of the

T-shirt, with 'My Man Lassie', in big bold letters. Dumb I know, but I was over him calling Lassie, Larry. He thought the picture he drew me was funny, well ditto to this shirt. My little bit of revenge you could say.

"What did you have to pick up?" he asked when I got back into the car. I tossed the plastic bag on his lap.

"A present for you."

"You bought me a gift?"

"Yes. Open the bag." He looked sceptical as he reached in and pulled out the T-shirt. When he held it up and read what it said, he threw his head back and laughed.

"I fucking love it, but she spelt Larry's name wrong."

"No she didn't." I couldn't hide the smile on my face. Finally, one for Indi.

Well that's what I thought until the next morning. He actually met me at the car before school wearing the shirt. I couldn't believe it. I should've known he was up to something by the big-arse grin on his face. My gaze immediately moved to the bottom of the shirt where Lassie's name was printed. Ugh! He'd crossed it out with a thick black sharpie, and written 'Larry' next to it in big capital letters. *Touché, arsehole.*

CARTER

OVER THE NEXT FEW WEEKS, LIFE SEEMS TO GET HARDER. EVEN though I finally have my car back, *which is a fucking relief,* Indi and I are spending a lot of time together. I'm finding the more I'm with her, the more I don't want to be without her. It's so fucked up. It sucks to want someone when you know you can't have them.

I try my hardest not to show it and continue to give her a hard time whenever I can, but with every passing day I'm finding it harder to resist her. I should've just taken her when she offered it up to me, but for once in my life I tried to be the good guy. I put her wellbeing before my own needs.

Not a day goes by that I don't think about what we did that night, or that sweet pussy of hers. I want to be buried balls deep inside her. *More. Than. Anything.* Don't even get me started on that mouth of hers.

Things at home are getting worse as well. I'm not sure how much longer I can continue to bite my tongue around Fuckwit. I think he's figured out that I won't fight back because I don't want to upset my mum. He's using it to his advantage. He now taunts me every chance he gets. *Fucker.* I need to get the hell out of here before I *ruin* everything.

If I lose my shit with that motherfucker, it will *ruin* things for my mum. As much as I hate *him*, I love seeing her happy. I'll never understand why, but *he* does that for her.

And then there's Indi. If I let this thing between us go any further, I'll *ruin* her as well. I don't want to cloud her sunshine with my darkness. She's pure and I'm not. How can something that feels so right be so wrong? *Life can be a real bitch sometimes.*

I feel like the walls are closing in on me. Some days it gets so bad, it's a struggle to even breathe. It's still a few months before I turn eighteen. In my heart I know I'm not going to last that long.

••••

On Saturday night I'm sitting at my desk in my bedroom, doing homework, when I see Indi climb out of her bedroom window. Where in the hell does she think she's going? *Fuck.* Today I've avoided her like the plague. I just needed some space to sort through all these unwanted feelings I have for her. Looks like that was a waste of fucking time. I can't sit here and watch her sneak off to God only knows where. Anything could happen to her.

I watch to see which direction she's heading before throwing on a shirt. For some reason she's walking down towards the lake. Although it's a warm night, she's got rocks in her fucking head if she intends on going for a swim.

By the time I put my shoes on and jump out of my window, a few minutes have passed. I hope she hasn't gone too far. I should've grabbed a torch. It's so fucking dark out here. I have a good mind to throw her over my knee and spank her for leaving the house at this time of night on her own. Christ, she makes me fucking crazy sometimes.

I'm mumbling profanities under my breath when she comes into view. She's sitting on the dock all alone, her feet dangling over the edge. I can only see her silhouette by the aid of the moonlight. It's casting a silvery glow over the water, illuminating her.

My heart rate picks up as I get closer. I have this love/hate thing going on with the feelings she ignites within me. Although I kind of like it, it's also foreign and scares the crap out of me, When I'm around her I feel alive. I thought that part of me died a long time ago. I can't explain how this tiny little spitfire, who annoys me to no end, can make me feel that way, but fuck me she does.

"What are you doing out here all alone?" I ask annoyed when I'm standing a few feet behind her. She doesn't answer, but I clearly see her hand come up and wipe her eyes. Fucking great, she's crying. I don't know how to deal with this shit. I haven't cried since I was a kid. Why do women have to be so damn emotional?

What I want to do is turn around and walk the fuck away. But I can't do that to her. Jesus Christ. I know I'm gonna regret asking this. "Are you okay?"

"I'm fine," she sniffles. She's not fucking fine. "Can you just leave me alone?" Even though she just gave me the out I was hoping for, I can't walk away from her. One: because she wants me to, and the stubborn part of me won't allow her to tell me what to do. Two: because for some reason, seeing her upset tugs at my heartstrings. *Shit.*

I take the few steps that are separating us and sit down beside her. "If you're fine, why are you crying?" Did I just ask her that? Now I want to punch myself in the mouth for being so stupid. For some reason though, I want to know why she's upset.

"I told you I'm fine."

"Okay. If you say so." I know she's lying but I'm not going to push it. I'm not leaving her though. We sit in silence for a few minutes staring out over the lake. When I see her raise her hand to her face out of the corner of my eye, I know her silent tears are still falling. It hurts me to see her like this.

I move my hand slightly to the left and lace my fingers through hers. She may not want to talk but I find myself hoping that me being here is comforting. "Today is the anniversary of my mum's death," she whispers. Fuck. That explains the tears.

"I'm sorry," is all I say. Lame I know, but I'm not good with shit like this.

"My dad locks himself in his room every year on this day. He drinks a bottle of scotch and cries. I can't stand it. It tears me up inside. That's why I'm sitting out here. So I don't have to hear him." Christ. I have no words for what she just told me, so instead I squeeze her hand.

Holding her hand and being so close has all my senses on high alert, but I have a feeling tonight she needs a friend more than anything. "I'm sure you both miss her. I'd be lost without my mum," I confess.

"We do. The only memory I have of her is being sick. My dad tried his best to shelter me from her illness. She was in bed a lot. I remember on her good days my dad would let me lie with her. She'd sing to me sometimes and stroke my hair." A small smile graces her face when she says that. "It makes me sad that her life was cut so short. She was only twenty-eight when she passed. Mostly I'm sad for my dad. He's so lost without her. It's like when she died, his light went out. I know he loves me, but it's a different love to the one he had for my mum. He does a good job of hiding it most days, but days like today shows just how much her death has affected him. I also hate that she missed seeing me grow up, and before you say anything smart, I've grown a lot since I was six."

"Really? You must've been fucking miniscule when you were six then."

"Ha ha," she says bumping my shoulder. She walked right into that one.

"Jokes aside," I chuckle, "it would've been tough for him. Losing his wife and having to bring a child up on his own."

"It was. I'm sure it still is at times. Is your dad still alive?" she asks. Usually that question would get my back up, but tonight it doesn't. I've never talked about this with anyone before, but surprisingly for the first time in my life I want to talk about it. I want to open up to her.

"I have no idea. The day he found out my mum was pregnant with me, he took off."

"So you've never met him?" she asks turning her face to look at me.

"No. It's only ever been my mum and I. Well it used to be until she married that cocksucker."

"I'm sorry," she whispers squeezing my hand. "Do you have any other family? Like grandparents?"

"No. My mum's parents kicked her out when she got pregnant. Apparently she brought shame on the family. She lost everything because of me. She took me back there when I was five. It didn't go down too well. My grandfather called me a bastard and slammed the door in our face."

"What? Oh. My. God. That's awful. I'm sorry that happened to you. Is that why you always refer to yourself as a bastard?" she asks. I can hear the sorrow in her voice as she speaks. I probably shouldn't have opened up, but I actually feel a kind of relief talking about it. Like a weight has been lifted off my chest.

"It's the truth. I am a bastard. Nothing can change that." After all these years I still feel shame when I think about that day and what that word means. She lets go of my hand and reaches up to turn my face towards her. When I see tears welling in her eyes it brings a lump to my throat.

"You're not a bastard, Carter. Please don't ever think that way about yourself."

"I still remember the day I looked up the meaning of bastard in the dictionary." I exhale when I think back to that day. The motherfucking day I learnt what I really was. *A person born to parents not married to each other. A person considered to be mean or contemptible. A person, especially one considered to be unfortunate. Irregular, inferior, or of dubious origin.* "I was crushed, but I was just a kid. I guess I've learnt to live with it over the years."

"You're not a bastard, Carter. Just because you choose to act like one sometimes, it doesn't mean you are one," she enforces as another tear falls from her pretty green eyes. Seeing her shed a tear for me makes the lump in my throat grow. She almost sounds like she believes what she's saying. I want to believe her, just like I wanted to believe my mum all those years ago, but it's a fact.

"It's okay," I tell her as I reach up and wipe her tear away with the pad of my thumb. "As you can see I've embraced the fact that I'm a bastard," I chuckle, but she doesn't. My words actually make her look sadder. It tears at my fucking heart.

"Lots of people have children before they marry these days. It's no big deal. It's stereotyping at its worst. The older generations may have believed that bullshit, but in my opinion they should be ashamed of themselves. Those poor kids never asked to be born, yet they had to suffer that narrow-minded injustice for the rest of their lives. Hypocrites like your grandfather are fucked in the head if you ask me." Her words make me laugh. "It's not funny, Carter. Look at what it has done to you. It makes me so mad," she adds frowning. She looks so fucking adorable when she does that.

She goes to say something else, but I lean forward and cover her mouth with mine. I love that she feels so passionate about this subject, and I love that she doesn't think I'm a bastard. Everything she said is true, but sadly it still doesn't make me feel any better about myself.

I'm still a bastard.

Maybe in time her words will help, but right now all the blood has left my brain and rushed straight to my cock, so I can't think of anything else but *her*. I know we said we wouldn't go there again, but I need this. *I fucking need her.*

When I tilt her head back and deepen the kiss, she moans into my mouth. Sliding my hands under her arms, I lift her up and onto my lap so she's straddling me. Wrapping her legs around my waist, her hands snake around my neck. Mine slide around her tiny waist and I draw her body flush with mine. I love the way she kisses. The way her lips feel against mine. The way her soft body moulds against my hardness. I don't think I'll ever tire of it. Actually I know I won't. I'm hooked—*on her.*

SIXTEEN

INDIANA

MY HEART IS STILL HURTING FOR HIM. THINKING OF HOW HE must've felt as a small boy, and the fact that he's been carrying that stigma around for all these years. It breaks my heart. Although unfounded, his attitude since the day we met suddenly makes sense. I hate that he feels so lowly of himself, especially since they were circumstances beyond his control. How could his grandfather, his own flesh and blood, label him like that? He was just a fucking kid. He didn't ask to be born.

As I kiss him, I try my hardest to show him without words, how special he is, how much I care for him. How he's nothing like the perception he has of himself. We've both tried so hard to keep our friendship completely platonic the past few weeks, but tonight I need him. I think he needs this, too.

I need to lose myself in him so I don't have to think about my dad falling to pieces back at the house. So much for my damn 'Distraction' playlist. In between songs I could still hear his muffled cries. That's why I came down here. Every year I dread this date. I've always hoped as the years passed, things will get easier for my dad, but not this year. Hopefully next.

Carter's hands slide from my waist down to my arse. He draws me in, my centre pressing hard against his erection. I moan into his mouth. I don't even recognise myself when I am with him like this. He makes me so wild. One of his hands move under my top as his fingers lightly skim up and over my stomach, making me shiver, until he's palming my breast and pinching my nipple through the lace fabric of my bra. My hands tangle in his hair as I rock my hips forward.

I've only been kissing him for a few minutes and I'm already on the verge of coming undone. I could get addicted to the way he makes my body feel. Our kiss soon turns primal. It's like we can't get enough of each other.

His hand moves down between us as he rubs my clit through the thin material of my shorts.

"Come for me, beautiful," he whispers as his lips make a trail across my jaw and down my neck. I lean my head back and moan. It only takes me a few seconds before I call out his name when my orgasm hits. When I open my eyes I find him looking at me, smiling. "I love watching you come." I feel my face heat. "Don't go all shy on me now," he adds as he leans forward and plants a soft kiss on my nose.

I can still feel his erection pressing into my inner thigh. Sliding my hand down his body, I stoke him through his jeans. "Don't," he says pulling my hand away.

"What? Why? I want to give you relief."

"No. I've been trying my hardest to behave around you for weeks. I let this go as far as it did tonight because you needed it. If we don't stop this now, I may not be able to control myself. You make me crazy," he admits.

"Well don't stop."

"I told you, we can't go there, Indi. Your first time should be with someone special. That's not me." I move my hand up to cup his face.

"You are special, Carter. I want you to be my first." I mean every word, too. I may regret it, but I doubt it. Even if we can't be together after tonight, I'll still treasure the fact that he was my first.

"You don't mean that," he says placing his hand on the back of my head, pulling my face into his chest. I can hear his heart beating wildly. I love being held like this, by him. When I'm with Carter, he makes me feel like nobody else but us exists in the world. He obviously has no idea how much I want this.

"I do. Please, Carter. Don't make me beg."

"I don't do commitments, Indi. I'm not boyfriend material."

"I'm not asking you to be my boyfriend," I say pulling my head back so I can see his face.

"Well what then?" Even in this light, I can see his vulnerability. I wish he didn't have such a low opinion of himself. I wish he could see himself through my eyes then he'd know just how special he is.

"I'm asking you to be my first. Nothing more. Just one night. I want you to do all the things you've done to the others." Did I just say that? Yep, I did. It's true though. Since the moment I saw Jennifer climb in his window, I wished it was me. Then there was the pink-haired bimbo.

"What others?" he asks.

"The girls that climbed through your window. Jennifer and the girl with the pink hair."

"I didn't do anything with the girl with the pink hair," he chuckles.

"You didn't? But I ..."

"When I saw you watching us, I couldn't go through with it," he confesses.

"You couldn't? Why?"

"Because you cock-blocked me."

"I did not," I say playfully slapping his arm. "Tell me the real reason."

"Fuck. Enough with all the questions. I just couldn't okay. I felt bad." My lips turn up into a smile.

"Why did you feel bad?" I ask, my smile widening. I probably shouldn't be probing him like this, but I want to know the reason.

"Just drop it," he snaps.

"No. I want to know why." He lifts me off his lap and places me back beside him in annoyance.

"I'm not going to answer that," he says as his handsome face scrunches up into a frown. When he turns his head away from me, I get the impression he's feeling uncomfortable, so I let it lie. Although, secretly I'm dying to know why.

"So are we going to do it?" I ask changing the subject.

"Do what?" he replies turning his head to look at me.

"You know ... sex." I can't believe I'm even having this conversation with him. He chuckles at my comment making me blush. He probably thinks I'm so lame.

"Trust me, kid. As much as I'd like to deflower you, you'll regret giving me your virginity." Even though his words are telling me 'no', I can tell by the look in his eyes he wants this as much as I do.

"I won't," I say reaching for his hand. "I want this, Carter. I really do. Please don't make me beg, because I will. No strings. I promise. Just one night, that's all I'm asking." *God I'm so pathetic.* He holds my stare, but doesn't speak. *Please say yes* I silently chant in my head.

"You really want this?" he eventually asks.

"Yes. I want you." He breaks into a full smile, showing his perfect white teeth.

"You're not going to expect me to marry you or anything, are you?"

"What? No way. I don't even want you as a boyfriend," I screech.

"That's just lovely, that is. Way to dirty talk it up," he replies placing his hand on his chest, mocking fake hurt.

"I'm serious," I say trying to hold a straight face. "I'm just using you for your body." Seeing him like this makes my insides all warm and gooey. Even when he's scowling he's breathtaking, but when he smiles ... *no words.*

"So I was right all along then?" he says when he stops laughing.

"About what?"

"You do want me." He is so fucking smug sometimes, but he's right. I do. I'm not even going to justify that with an answer. There's no way

I'm going to give him the satisfaction of being right.

"You're so full of yourself," I say nudging him with my shoulder.

"You'll be full of me in a minute," he chuckles, reaching for my hand as he goes to stand. I pull him back down.

"Can we stay down here? I'm not ready to go back up there yet."

"You want me to fuck you down here? In the open?" he asks with surprise in his voice.

"It's dark. No one will see us."

"If you're sure," he says with a smile. "I never would've picked you to be so adventurous."

"Well there's a lot you don't know about me." That's such a crock of shit. He's right. I'm not the adventurous type at all, but he brings something out in me: A desire to let loose. To live a little.

"I'm gonna have to run back to the house and get a condom." Leaning forward he brushes his lips against mine. "I'll be back in a minute."

"Okay," I reply as he stands. You'd think I'd be nervous that I'm about to have sex for the first time, and in the open of all places, but I'm not. Not with Carter. I'm actually looking forward to it.

He returns a few minutes later with a huge grin on his face and a blanket and pillow in his hand. "Can't have you getting splinters in your back, ruining that beautiful skin of yours," he says as he spreads it out on the dock. When he's not being an arse and giving me a hard time, he says the sweetest things. "You sure you want to do this?"

"Positive," I answer as I reach for his outstretched hand. He pulls me to my feet and straight into his hard chest. He wraps his big strong arms around my waist, looking down at me.

"No regrets?" he asks.

I shake my head gently. "No regrets." His lips meet mine. His kiss is soft and sweet, making my toes curl. I slide my arms around his neck when he scoops me up. Falling down to his knees, he gently lays me on the blanket, placing my head on the pillow. He lays down beside me, pulling me into his arms.

"You sure you don't want to go back to my room?" he asks. God.

Enough with all the questions.

"Just fuck me already," I blurt out. I'm not even shocked by my words. I want this to happen. *Like yesterday.* I appreciate that he's trying to do the right thing, but I'm not changing my mind no matter how hard he tries to talk me out of it.

"Jesus, those words coming out of your sweet mouth are hot," he says. He sits me up and removes my top. I reach for the hem of his T-shirt, lifting it to reveal his heavenly abs and mouth-watering chest. He grabs hold of his shirt behind the neck and pulls it over his head. His hands then reach behind me, unclasping my bra. After I slide it down my arms and discard it, he gently lays me back down.

Moving his face forward, he draws one of my nipples into his mouth while his hands work feverishly on the button of my shorts. Leaning back on his haunches, he slides my shorts and panties down my legs. I watch his smile grow in the moonlight as he looks down at me.

I hear a growl come from deep in his throat as his lips trail a path down my abdomen. I push my head back into the pillow and moan when his face settles between my thighs. He grips the back of my legs and pushes my knees towards my chest, spreading my legs wide.

"I need to taste you again," he whispers against my sensitive flesh. "I haven't been able to get your pussy out of my mind." I find myself smiling knowing he's been thinking about that night, about me. I've thought about it as well—a lot.

He groans as his tongue swirls around my aching clit. I thread my fingers into his hair holding his head in place. His mouth is magnificent. I don't want him to ever stop.

Within minutes he has me coming undone. He slides two fingers inside me as my orgasm pulses through my body. He doesn't stop until my trembling body stills. "You're so wet for me," he says as he withdraws his fingers and pops them in his mouth, licking them clean. God, I love when he does that.

He stands and pulls the condom out of his pocket and removes his jeans. As much as I love being outside under the stars with him, I wish we had some light so I could see more of him in his naked glory. His body is breathtaking.

He rips open the condom wrapper with his teeth and slides it onto his impressive length. All I can think as I watch on is, *I hope that monstrosity fits inside me.* I'm definitely not having second thoughts, but I'll admit the nerves are starting to settle in.

He crouches down, placing his hands on either side of my body before hovering over me. Leaning his face forward, his lips briefly meet mine again. I can taste myself on him. "This is going to hurt," he says as he settles between my legs, lining himself up with my opening. "Are you sure you want to go through with this? It's not too late to pull out."

"I'm sure. I want this, Carter," I tell him honestly as my hands come up to cup his face. He smiles before brushing his lips against mine.

"I'll be as gentle as I can, okay. Try to relax."

"Okay," I reply. He glides the tip of his dick through my wetness before slowly pushing the head inside me.

"Sweet Jesus," he groans before stilling, giving me time to adjust. Pulling back slightly, he pushes in a little further. His head falls back as a primal growl escapes him. I can already feel the sting as he stretches me. I'm not gonna lie though, knowing it's me making him feel like this is an incredible turn on. "You feel amazing," he breathes looking down at me. "Are you ready?"

I nod as his lips meet mine. He kisses me for a minute or so without moving. I'm sure he's trying to distract me. It's working. Without warning he withdraws before pushing all the way in. It stings like a bitch, but doesn't hurt nearly as much as I thought it would. He stills again, giving me time to adjust.

"Are you okay?" he asks, gently brushing back the hair off my face.

"Perfect," I answer. I can't believe I'm actually having sex. And with Carter Reynolds of all people. The guy I love and hate all in the same breath. I'm no longer a virgin and I have no regrets. None whatsoever. I'm glad my first time is with him.

"I've gotta start moving," he says a few seconds later. He groans again when he slowly withdraws before pushing all the way back into me. After a few more thrusts the burning sensation dissipates and I'm now moving with him. It feels amazing. *He feels amazing.* "I think I'm in love with your pussy," he moans as he picks up the pace. I think I'm falling in love with him, but I'd never say that out loud. I shouldn't even be feeling like this, but I have no control over my heart. "I'm not sure how much longer I'm gonna last. You feel too good. I need you to come again."

"I'm close," I say as I wrap my legs around his waist and dig the heels of my feet into his backside, pushing him further inside me. He lifts his body up slightly and moves his hand down between us to rub my clit as he continues to push into me, in short, fast thrusts. It's all I need to send me over the edge. "Ohhh ... I'm ... I'm." That's all I manage to get out as the sensations take over, and I have the most intense orgasm I've ever experienced.

"Fuuuck," he grunts as his body starts to jerk above me. I know he's coming too. His body did the same thing when I gave him a blow job in his bedroom a few weeks ago. After a few more thrusts he stills inside me. "I think you've ruined me," he says breathlessly as his lips find mine again. I fist my hands in his hair as I hold his face against mine. I don't want this night to ever end.

Our kiss goes from soft to wild within minutes. He's still inside me and I feel him harden again. We're now on round two. This time he rolls over, pulling me with him so I'm on top.

His hands glide up my body before cupping my boobs and rolling my hard nipples between his finger and thumb. I tilt my head back and moan as pleasure floods my body. My palms smooth over his chest, gripping his shoulders to give me some leverage so I can ride him. I love the friction that this position provides. Carter lifts his head and sucks one of my nipples in his mouth. I love his mouth on me. I wrap one of my hands around his neck while my other one runs through his hair, holding him against my breast.

Now I know why Meg fucks like a rabbit. I could easily get addicted to this feeling—only with Carter of course. I'm not the type of person that would just sleep around with anyone.

Carter's hands move back down to my waist. Gripping my hips, he lifts my body slightly before guiding it back down. He does this over and over. I have no words for the sensations I'm experiencing right now.

"You have a magnificent pussy," he groans. "I could fuck you all day." All day sounds wonderful. I don't want this feeling to ever stop.

"Don't stop what you're doing ... *please*," I beg as my hips start to swirl in a circular motion, making my clit grind against him.

"I have no intentions of stopping," he says breathlessly. "I need to kiss you." He pulls my face down to his. Sliding my hands up his neck, I thread my fingers through his hair. He's now pounding into me as our kiss heats up. The noises coming from both of us are feral. I think he's just as lost in me as I am in him.

I'm right on the edge. I've been trying to hold off because I don't want this feeling, or my time with him to end, but I can no longer stop the orgasm that's looming. "Carter," I moan into his mouth as my body convulses with the intensity of it.

"Fuck," he grates out as my inner muscles clench around his dick. His hands grip my hips so hard I swear they are going to leave marks. He pumps into me as his own release comes, setting off another orgasm for me.

"Oh. Shit ... I'm coming again," I moan tugging on his hair as I throw back my head, crying out his name. When our bodies finally still, I collapse onto his chest. My skin prickles with the cool breeze.

"Christ, you're so beautiful when you're coming. You have no idea what seeing you like that does to me," he sighs, kissing my forehead and wrapping his arms tightly around my torso. If I wasn't so worn out I'd offer to show him again.

I get the strongest vibes from him, whenever we've been intimate. I can't quite put my finger on it. Even though I have no experience, nothing to compare it to, I'm pretty sure what we have is special. It's like he's feeling everything I am. It's so intense. But then he'll say or do something that tells me he wants distance. It's confusing. Maybe it's just part of his charm. Maybe I'm reading too much into this. Or maybe he does feel everything I do. I doubt it. *He's probably like this with all the girls.*

We stay motionless, wrapped in each other's arms for what seems like ages, before he eventually slides out of me and places me beside him. I'm surprised by the loss I feel from no longer being connected to him.

Standing, he passes me my clothes before removing his condom and getting dressed. Tears sting my eyes when I realise my time with him is over. I don't want this night to end. I don't want this to be our last time together. When I told him one night, I honestly thought I'd be okay with that. Now I know that's not the case.

Once I slip back into my clothes, I go to stand. "Don't get up," he says squatting down beside me and stroking his hand gently down the side of my face. "I don't want you to go yet." I feel my lips curl into a smile when he leans forward and kisses me. He lays down beside me and pulls me into his arms. Reaching behind him, he pulls the other half of the blanket over us. "Just let me hold you for a while."

CARTER

'No regrets' we said, but that's exactly what I'm having. Not because of what we did. *No way.* I'll never forget what she gave me last night. I'm not just talking about her virginity either.

My regret is now I've taken it this far with her, crossed the line I swore I'd never cross, I have to leave. It's for her own good. I don't have a choice.

It was sometime in the early hours of this morning that I made my final decision. I only hope I have the strength to go through with it. I haven't slept a wink all night. It was around 3:00am when we finally left the lake and made our way home.

In my heart I knew it would be our last time together, so I didn't want it to end. I even offered to let her spend the night at my house, in my bed, but she declined. I've never invited anyone to spend the night with me before. It's funny; when it comes to her, my previous rules, the ones I've never broken cease to exist.

I'm in the midst of both heaven and hell. Last night she took me to a place I never thought possible. Bliss. That's what I experienced with her. *Fucking bliss.* Never in my life did I think sex could be like that. Sure, it's always good, but with her ...

Sweet Jesus.

The things she made me feel blew my fucking mind. What we shared was fleeting in the grand scheme of things, but I know it's something I'm not going to forget in a hurry—if ever. I only wish things could be different between us, but they can't.

Rising from the bed, I head to the bathroom to shower. If I'm going to go through with my plan I need to get my shit together. Standing under the spray of hot water, I contemplate what my actions today are going to do to the two people I care about the most in this world.

My mum has given up the last eighteen years of her life for me. It's time I gave it back. She has her *fuckwit* of a husband to help pick up the pieces. Then there's Indi. She has so much promise for a bright and happy future. She has her whole life ahead of her. A life I'm pretty sure will be a lot richer without me in it.

I have no idea where I'm heading, or what I'm gonna do. I was hoping for a few more weeks to get a plan in place, but after what happened last night, this needs to be done today. The sooner, the better. Things are only going to get complicated if I stay. The consequences are just too high. My feelings for her are far too strong. I've tried to fight them, but I've lost the battle. This thing between us can't last. It will eventually lead to heartbreak. I know it. That's a chance I'm not willing to take, for her, or for me.

I've had enough of that shit to last me a lifetime.

Sadness washes over me as I pick up the body wash and remove her scent from my skin. Never again will I be able to smell her sweetness, feel her silky soft skin beneath my fingertips, or taste her lips. It brings a motherfucking lump the size of a goddamn basketball to my throat.

Once I'm dressed I throw my things into my suitcase, stowing it under the bed before going in search of my mum. I find her in the kitchen cooking. As devastated as I'm feeling right now, just seeing her brings a smile to my face. I'm going to miss her cooking, but more than anything I'm going to miss her.

"Hey, sweetie," she says smiling at me. "Breakfast won't be long. As soon as John gets home we'll eat."

Walking to her, I wrap her in my arms. "I love you, Mum."

"I love you too, Carter."

"Thank you for always loving me. For keeping and wanting me when nobody else did." I hear my voice crack when I speak.

"Baby? What's brought this on?" she asks looking up at me. "Is everything okay?"

"Everything's fine. I just needed you to know how much I appreciate you and everything you've done for me over the years. It's meant everything to me. You mean everything to me." I see her eyes well with tears from my words.

"Are you sure you're okay?" I see concern etched on her beautiful face. I nod, tightening my embrace. "You're part of me, sweetheart. You'll always be a part of me. Not having you in my life was never an option. Not a day goes by that I'm not thankful that you're my son," she says, gently running her hand down the side of my face. I can't speak. The lump in my throat is growing bigger by the second.

I'm surprised I'm not choking on that fucker.

This is my goodbye. I don't know when or if I'll ever get to see her again. That thought makes my heart ache. If it wasn't for her, my life growing up would've been nothing. Meaningless. She gave up her future, her family, everything for me. Words will never be able to express what that means to me.

She loved the bastard that nobody else could.

Leaning down I place a gentle kiss on her cheek. "I'll be in my room," I say as I turn and walk away. I don't bother looking back. I can't. If I do, she'll see the tears that now glisten my eyes.

"Okay, sweetie. I love you, Carter," she calls out behind me.

"I love you too, Mum," I whisper.

Reaching under the bed, I grab the bag I just packed. Emptying out the contents of my school backpack onto the bed, I head back into my bathroom. I throw my deodorant, toothbrush, toothpaste and brush into the bag. Walking back into my room I grab my sketchpad and a photo I have of my mum and I from when I was a boy, and stuff them inside. Looking around my room, I check to see if there's anything else I need.

Heading towards the window, my gaze moves towards Indi's house. I'm shocked to find her standing in her bedroom watching me. She's smiling. *Fuck.* I was hoping I didn't have to see her before I left. I can't say goodbye to her, I just can't. It will gut me.

Tearing my eyes away from her I drop my suitcase out of the window. It lands with a thud. When my eyes meet hers again, I watch as her gaze moves down to the bag on the ground, and then back up to meet mine. The smile drops from her beautiful face. *A face I know I'm never going to forget.*

She steps forward and presses her palms flat against the glass. Fuck, she knows. The devastation I see cross her features rips my fucking heart in two. I watch as a lone tear cascades down her cheek. What I wouldn't give to hold her right now. Kiss her. Tell her I don't know how I'm going to survive without her in my life.

Jumping out the window, I pick up my bag and start walking towards my car. I take one last look over my shoulder at the only other person on this earth, apart from my mum that I love. Yes, I love her. I love her so much it fucking hurts. Last night just confirmed it.

She's the only person that has made me feel like I'm somebody. The only person that has accepted me for who I am—the real Carter Reynolds. The person I am on the inside. Not the illegitimate child. *The bastard.* The real me. She knows my story and still cares. Still wants me around.

I'm not used to people wanting me, so the fact that she does is something I'll never forget. I'll treasure the time I've spent with her. She'll always have my heart. I know that for a fact.

As much as it kills me, I need to let her go. Although she may not think so, she deserves so much more than I can ever give. *So much more*. I was born a bastard and I'll die a bastard. That's never going to change. In time I know my doom and gloom will dull her sunshine. I couldn't do that to her. She's perfect just the way she is.

I open the trunk of my car and place my suitcase and backpack inside. My heart is so heavy as I move around to the driver's door.

"Carter, please don't go. Don't leave me," I hear her cry from behind me. *Christ*. She's come outside. I don't turn around. I can't. I wish I could stay. Better still, I wish I could take her with me, but that's not an option.

Ignoring her, I open the door and climb in. Tears cloud my eyes. I didn't think this would be so hard. I turn the key in the ignition and back out of the driveway. My eyes betray me as I take one last look at the *kid*. The *kid* that stole my heart. The *kid* that managed to penetrate my darkness, and for the briefest of moments showed me what it was like to have light in my heart again. Fuck I'm going to miss her and her smart mouth.

She needs to forget me. I swear I literally feel my heart shatter into a million pieces as I watch her standing there. Her arms wrapped around her tiny body. Tears are streaming down her beautiful face. It takes every bit of strength I have not to go to her.

There's so much I want to say to her. *So much*. So much I want to thank her for. But, instead I do what I need to do to help her forget me. To help her move on. I flip her off as I put my foot down and drive away. Drive away from the only two people who'll ever hold a place in my heart ...

PART
TWO

CARTER

five years later ...

I'M JOLTED OUT OF MY SLEEP BY *OUR* **SONG; LET HER GO, BY** Passenger. Well technically it's not our song, but it's the one that reminds me of her. Of us. I heard it a few days after I left. For the first time in years I cried. *Cried like a fucking baby.* It's been the ringtone on my phone ever since. I don't know why I torture myself by keeping it. All it does is remind me of what I've lost. Of the one and only girl I've ever loved.

I reach for my phone on the bedside table just as the brunette beside me stirs. Fuck, is she still here? "What time is it?" she asks.

"Time you got dressed and left," I answer looking at the clock. Shit. 4:30am. Who'd be calling me at this hour? It better be a life or fucking death situation or someone's gonna get their arse kicked. When I see my mum's number on the screen my heart drops. Jumping out of bed, I turn to the chick that shouldn't be here.

I can't even remember her name. Is it Sarah ... Samantha ... Shona?

Fuck me. I'm sure it starts with an 'S'. Either way, *I don't do sleepovers.* I'm always upfront with every girl I bring home. They know exactly what they're getting into. I'm pretty sure I told her to leave last night after we fucked. I guess I fell asleep and she didn't listen. I fucking hate it when they do that.

"Get your shit and go," I snap.

"I want to go back to sleep," she whines, pissing me off even more. Scooping her clothes off the floor, I toss them on the bed. It's not like I didn't make it perfectly clear last night. This was a hook-up and nothing more. The majority of them are pretty good, but occasionally you get one of those needy ones that think they can change me. Like they have some kind of magical pussy that's gonna keep me coming back for more. *Sorry, not happening.* There's only one girl on this earth that can do that for me—*my Indi.* Nobody will ever live up to her. *Nobody.*

"Go," I say in a warning tone as I turn and walk out of the room so I can take this call. "Mum?"

"Carter," she cries.

"Shit, Mum. What's wrong?" I ask in a panic.

"It's ... It's John." Just hearing that fucker's name has my blood pressure rising. If he's hurt her in any way I'll rip him apart. "He's dead." Well I wasn't expecting her to say that.

"What? What do you mean he's dead? What happened?" To be honest I don't give a shit that he has died, my only concern is my mum. I've always hated him, but I need to remember my mother loved him. *God only knows why.*

"Carter," she sobs. "I don't know what happened. I rolled over in bed and put my arm around him. He was so cold. He ..." She starts to cry uncontrollably. It breaks my fucking heart to hear her cry. "I need you to come home, please." Can I go back there? I suppose I don't really have a choice. This isn't about me. She needs me. It only takes me a split second to make my decision.

"I'm coming, Mum. I'll be home in a few hours. Will you be okay until I get there?"

"Yes," she whispers.

"I'll be there as soon as I can," I assure her.

"Thank you, sweetie," she sniffles. It kills me to hear her so upset. "I feel so alone." Christ, I hate that she feels that way. I know all too well what *alone* feels like.

Going back there is the last thing I want to do. I've spent the last five years trying to forget. My mum needs me, though.

••••

After showering and packing a few things into a bag, I'm on the road by 5:00am. As soon as I hit the freeway I pull out my phone to call my mum. I'm living in Newcastle these days. It's a two-hour drive, north of Sydney. There's nothing I don't love about this place. It's my home now and I'll never leave. The people are great, I love the pace of life, it's not as hectic as Sydney, and the beaches are spectacular. Originally I moved up north to try to put some distance between Indi and I. I thought it would help, but even if I moved to the ends of the earth I know she'd still be on my mind and in my heart.

When I was working with Jax, I was only a half hour drive away. Sometimes the temptation to drive past her house was hard to ignore. Being up here hasn't stopped that desire to see her, but over time I've managed to deal with it.

I hate that I'm so far away from my mum right now. She's all alone and sounded so distressed when she called. Understandably, I suppose. I'm itching to get to her as soon as I can.

"Hello," a male voice says. I recognise it straight away. I feel my lips curve into a smile. Thank fuck he's with her. Relief washes over me.

"Ross. Hi, it's Carter. Christ I'm glad you're there with her."

"Carter, my boy," he says affectionately. I can tell by the tone in his voice he's happy to hear from me. It's the same reaction I've gotten whenever we've talked over the past five years. "As soon as I heard the call come into the station I came straight here."

"I appreciate that. Thank you. How's she holding up?" I ask.

"Not good I'm afraid."

"Can you tell her I'm on my way?"

"Will do. I'm sorry it's under these circumstances, but I'm happy you're finally coming home, son. I'm looking forward to seeing you." I've never considered that place my home. Fuckwit ruined that for me. As long as my mum and Indi reside there though, my heart will too.

"I'm looking forward to seeing you, too," I tell him. If I'm honest with myself, he's not the only one I'm longing to see.

When I first ran away it took Ross less than a week to track me down. I guess in his line of business I should've expected that. I'd headed to Jax's tattoo parlour the day I left with some drawings I'd done. I was hoping to make some quick cash. Something to help get me by until I could find some work. I guess running away without a lot of money to my name wasn't my smartest move.

That's where Ross Montgomery found me, the tattoo parlour. Thankfully, Jax not only bought my sketches that day, he offered me a job. He took me under his wing, and over the coming months taught me everything he knew.

Ross was pissed off when he confronted me. Pissed that I'd walked away without saying anything to anybody. He said my mum and Indi were devastated that I left the way I did, not to mention going out of their minds with worry.

"Why didn't you come to me?" he'd asked. "I could've helped. Running away like you did wasn't the answer, son." He tried his best to talk me into coming back home with him. He even went as far as offering me a room at his house. I guess he knew my stepfather was part of the reason for me fleeing. He wasn't the only reason. I never told him that though.

He was disappointed when I refused to go with him. But, being the easy-going man he is, he accepted that I had my reasons, even if he didn't agree with them. At the time, I was sleeping on Jax's couch. Ross didn't like that idea, so the next day he helped me secure a place of my own. A little one-bedroom apartment. He also promised he wouldn't tell anyone where I was when I asked him not to. However, he demanded I call my mother and let her know I was okay, which I did.

Ross called me every few days for the months that followed. The calls dwindled to weekly and then a couple of times a month, but he always ended the conversation by saying, "I'm here if you ever need anything, son. Don't ever forget that." I really appreciated that. The fact that he cared meant a lot, and still means more to me than he'll ever know. Over the years he's became the father figure I've never had. The kind of father I've been pining for my entire life.

I've accomplished so much in the last five years. I learnt at a young age that, with hard work, anything was possible. I owe so much to Jax. With my steady hand and artistic skills, I soon surpassed all his expectations and became his number one artist.

Not only was I working full time at his parlour, I was also doing private jobs after hours at my apartment. I was sensible with my money, just like I had been when I was a kid. Within a year I'd saved enough cash to open my own parlour. 'Indi Ink'. Yes, I named my place after her. Don't ask me why. I guess I still wanted her to be a part of my new life. Even if it wasn't the way I'd like it to be.

I'm the sole owner of 'Indi Ink', but I have a second parlour that Jax and I own together. It's called 'Wicked Ink'. We're hoping one day to own a whole chain of them. The way business is booming, I can definitely see that in our future.

Jax and I have stayed close friends over the years. Although he was upset to lose me at his parlour, he didn't hesitate to help me get set up at 'Indi Ink'.

Initially, being a tattoo artist was not a path I would've chosen if I hadn't met him. I'm thankful my journey led me to him. I love what I do. One night over a few beers, he told me about a guy he knew that was selling up and getting out of the business. That's when he asked me if I was interested in a partnership. I jumped at the chance.

Candice run's 'Wicked Ink' for us. Yes, she's still in the picture, and her hair is still hot pink. I don't think she'll ever change it. We never ended up getting together after the night I knocked her back when she snuck into my room, but we've become close friends. She helped me to deal with the loss of Indi after I left.

Ross has supported me all the way as well. He even came to the official opening of 'Indi Ink'. I had no idea he was coming. He never said a word about what I'd named the shop. To this day I still wonder if he knows I named it after his daughter. I guess it's pretty fucking obvious that I did.

I can't describe what I felt when he walked through the door that night. It blew my fucking mind. I'm so thankful that he gives a shit. He's the only male in my life that ever has. He's told me numerous times how proud he is of me. I fucking love him for that. As far as I know, Indi and my mum have no idea that we've stayed in contact all these years.

My mum and I talk on the phone regularly, but I haven't seen her in the flesh since the day I left. She always invites me home for the holidays, but I use my work commitments as an excuse. Don't get me wrong I wanted to see her. I fucking miss her like you wouldn't believe. Her husband though, not so much. If I never had the displeasure of seeing him again, it would've been too soon. I would've invited her up here to my place. I thought about it a lot, but I didn't want that Fuckwit tainting my space. My serenity. Thankfully, that's something I no longer have to worry about. *I can't wait to see her again*.

I've never asked my mum, or Ross, how Indi's doing. As much as I wanted to, I just couldn't. I guess I was scared. What you don't know won't hurt you, right? I have no idea what she's been up to all these years. She could be married with kids for all I know. That thought makes me feel sick to the stomach. I suppose it's because after all this time she still holds my heart.

Sure there's been other women since I've been gone. I'm not a fucking saint. I never claimed to be. No one serious though. How can you commit to someone when your heart belongs to another? There's not a day gone by that I haven't thought of her, missed her.

I hope she's happy, I really do. If I am honest with myself, I hope she is single and happy, but that's my selfish side talking. Although the thought of actually seeing her again excites me more than I care to admit, it also scares the crap out of me. I know nothing of her last five years. Not a damn thing. I have no idea what to expect. Ross and I never talked about anything to do with my old life. It was the way I wanted it.

The alternative was just too hard. I couldn't move on if I was still stuck in the past. He understood that, but the day he helped me move into my apartment, he said, "I hope you know what you're giving up. I hope you don't live to regret your decision." I knew he was referring to Indiana. I think I'll always regret walking away from her, but I did what I thought was best. *For her.*

••••

By the time I pull into my old street, I'm feeling nauseous at the thought of being back here again. I'm not even sure if she still lives with her dad. It's been five long years, but in a way it only seems like yesterday that I held her in my arms. Kissed those delicious fucking lips of hers. I'm sure some lucky bastard has snapped her up. Who wouldn't? Anyone would be fortunate to have her. She's the perfect girl. The one I let get away.

Stupid fucker.

My heart skips a beat as I drive up to the house. Wouldn't you know it, the first thing I see is her. *Just my fucking luck.* It looks like she's washing her car. She's bent over the hood wearing these tiny little denim shorts. That fucking arse. Jesus I can't tell you how many times I've thought about that arse.

I find it ironic, because the first day I arrived here, her arse was the first thing I saw. Now here I am five years later, and the same fucking thing happens. Déjà vu at its fucking worst. Is the universe trying to fuck with me, or what?

My hands are slightly trembling as I pull into the driveway. My gut is churning. My eyes are trained on her. *Please be happy to see me*, is my first thought. She straightens up. Her back still to me. When her body stiffens, I know she knows it's me. The sound of my car probably gave it away.

I still have my Monaro. I'll never get rid of her. I finally got to finish it. It looks so bad-arse. I fucking love this car. It still has the original Flamenco Red paintwork. I just had it redone. I also kept the black GT stripes on the hood. I replaced the tired old motor with a Blown 350 Chev and a manualised automatic transmission. The interior has been refreshed using a soft black leather. The seats have been recovered in black leather as well, with a red leather stripe through the centre. It has chrome-spoked mags on the fat eighteen-inch tyres. It looks fucking sick. Nothing gets the adrenaline pumping more than being in control of 750HP of pure muscle. I've had so many offers to buy this beauty, but I'd never part with her. I've spent a small fortune getting her to where she is now, but it was worth every cent. She's my baby.

Everything seems to slow down as I stay seated in my car staring in her direction. It's like the world's suddenly moving in slow motion. She turns. When her eyes meet mine she takes my breath away, literally. Fuck she's even more beautiful than I remember. Her eyes widen in shock and the sponge in her hand drops to the ground.

I can't seem to move as I drink her in. My heart is thumping furiously against my ribcage. Fuck I've missed those eyes, those lips— her. She hasn't changed much, just grown. A sixteen year old Indi was beautiful. A twenty-two year old Indi—fucking stunning. My *kid* is no longer a kid. She's a sexy-as-hell woman. *Drop dead fucking gorgeous.*

Only when I manage to pull myself together do I get out of the car. Her eyes are still trained on me. I feel my lips turn up at the corners. Words can't express how good it feels to see her again in the flesh. I take a step towards her. Her eyes narrow and my smile grows. I've missed her spunk, and the attitude that not only pissed me off all those years ago, but turned me the hell on.

"Hey," I say as I walk towards her. She doesn't reply. Instead her hands move to her hips and her scowl deepens. I guess after all this time she's still pissed off with me. I can't really blame her. "Well look at you," I add as I bend down and retrieve the sponge she dropped by her feet. As I stand, I can't hold back the whistle that escapes my mouth as my eyes travel up those sexy, lean legs of hers. It makes my cock twitch. The effect she has on me hasn't dwindled one bit. What I wouldn't give to run my fingers, better yet, my tongue, up the length of her legs, burying my face in her sweetness. "The kid's all grown up," I smirk when my eyes meet hers again.

Fuck me she's fine.

"I'm not a fucking kid anymore," she snaps.

Leaning forward so my face is only inches from hers, I whisper, "I can see that." Her pupils dilate and I hear her breath hitch. I immediately know my effect on her hasn't diminished either. It takes everything in me not to pull her into my arms and squeeze the fucking life out of her. Why did I leave it so long to see her? Just being near her again makes me feel alive. "It's good to see you again, Indi."

"Well, the feeling's not mutual," she says frowning. She's lying, I can tell. Her body language is saying the complete opposite to her words. She's still a stubborn arse I see. My eyes leave hers and gaze down at her lips. I can't tell you how many times I've dreamt of those lips over the past five years. Too many to count. I want to kiss her so bad my fucking chest aches. I let my eyes drop a little lower. That's when I see the necklace I bought her for her seventeenth birthday. I can't believe she's still wearing it. It has me smiling like a damn fool. You have no idea what seeing that means to me.

I watch her chest rise and fall as her breathing quickens. She can deny it all she wants, but she's effected by me. "My eyes are up here, buddy," she spits. I want to laugh at her comment. I love her smart mouth. I'm glad this part of our relationship hasn't changed.

Underneath the material of her white top, I can see a hint of her white lace bra covering the swell of her breasts. It gives me an idea. I can't help myself. I lift the sponge in my hand until it's hovering over her tits. I hear her gasp when she realises what I'm about to do. I clench my fist tight and the water drips out. It soaks into the fabric of her top, making it transparent. Her nipples harden and so does my cock. Christ. I haven't even touched her yet and I swear I could break diamonds with this fucker.

Peeling my gaze from her spectacular rack, I make eye contact with her again. I'm feeling quite pleased with myself, but that feeling doesn't last long. The anger I see in her eyes is not what I'm expecting. When did she lose her sense of humour? I guess I should've known from past experience, when it comes to her, I'm playing with fire. Especially since she has five years of pent up anger towards me inside her.

This is one time I'm not anticipating her next move. So when it comes, I'm totally taken by surprise. She raises her right leg slightly and then, *BOOM*. She knees me fair smack in the nuts. Hard. *Jesus fucking Christ.*

All the air gushes from my lungs as pain radiates through my whole body. My dick goes instantly limp. Fuck, I think she just killed it. I'm pretty sure my boys are now lodged somewhere in my throat.

A feral, high-pitched sound escapes me as I fall to my knees in agony. "Stay the fuck away from me, arsehole," she screams as she turns and runs inside.

Somebody call an ambulance. I think I'm gonna die.

INDIANA

TEARS THREATEN TO FALL AS I STORM DOWN THE HALL TO-
wards my room, but I will them back down. I shed a lot of tears after
he left, too many to count. I *refuse* to shed another. Fuck him.

Ripping my wet shirt over my head, I throw it across the room in
anger before flopping face first onto my bed. *He's back.* After all this
time he's come home. I don't know how I feel about that. Actually, yes I
do. I'm elated, devastated, and pissed off like you wouldn't believe. Is it
possible to feel so many emotions at the same time? I guess it is,
because I'm feeling all of them right now.

I knew in my heart what I felt for him all those years ago was still
lurking somewhere in the background. Hidden deep within the depths
of my soul. Seeing him now has brought everything flooding back to
the surface. It took me years to move on after he left. Fucking years.

I can't go there again, I just can't.

There was a time I would've done anything to see him again.
Absolutely anything. But, he's come back five years too late. I have

Mark now. Next week we'll be celebrating one year together. I care for him deeply. Maybe even love him. To be honest, I'm not sure. He's already told me he loves me, but I can't say it back. Not until I'm one hundred percent certain. Maybe because what I feel for him doesn't hold a candle to what I once felt for Carter. I think that's what's throwing me.

Mark's handsome, successful and hardworking, but he's never been able to ignite the burning desire within like Carter could. Mark and I met at college. He chased me for months before I eventually gave in and agreed to go on a date with him. We've been together ever since. He's the first guy I've been intimate with since Carter. I stayed clear of any kind of relationship after he left.

For years my shattered heart still belonged to him.

Finally, I gave in to the notion that he wasn't coming back, so I decided I needed to at least try and love again. Mark's a good guy. The total opposite to Carter. He's definitely not what you'd call the bad boy type. He's safe. Stable. Most importantly, *he loves me*. He'd never walk away from me. Never crush me the way Carter did all those years ago.

••••

I locked myself in my room for most of the morning. I wasn't aware of what was going on next door until I finally surfaced. I had no idea Mr. Shepard had passed away during the night. That's obviously the reason why Carter has returned. To be honest, I'm glad he's dead. The way he treated his stepson and what he did to me after Carter left, I can't say I'm upset about his passing.

"Elizabeth's a mess," my father says over lunch.

"I bet she is," is my only reply.

"Carter came home this morning," he adds giving me a strange look. I know he's waiting to see my reaction. Well he's not getting one.

"Yeah I know. I've already had the misfortune of running into him." I take a bite of my sandwich so I don't have to say anymore.

"You're still angry after all these years?" he asks reaching across the table and placing his hand over mine. I sigh.

"No," I lie. My dad cocks an eyebrow. I try to act like I'm unaffected, but I get the impression he can see straight through my facade. I divert my eyes and take another bite of my sandwich.

"Five years have passed, Pumpkin," he says tightening his grip on my hand. "Maybe it's time to let all that hurt and anger go. He may have been a little misguided in his thinking, but he did what he thought was best." Does he think I haven't tried to let this go? Tried to forget him? I know he had his reasons for leaving. I get that. In my eyes though, the way he went about it was wrong. The fact that I haven't heard a word from him in five years cuts me to the core. I'm not sure if I can get past that.

"Can we change the subject, Daddy? I don't want to talk about Carter Reynolds."

"Fair enough. Let's talk about the funeral then." He gives me a weak smile before continuing. "I know how you feel about John, Indi," he says. "I feel the same way. In saying that though, I think we should attend the funeral. For Elizabeth and Carter's sake. As a sign of respect to them." I roll my eyes. Going to that cocksucker's funeral is the last thing I want to do.

"Fine," I sigh. I don't like that idea one bit, but I'll go for Elizabeth's sake. Nothing else. She's a sweet lady. I'll never understand what she saw in that jackass, but he was her husband, so I guess she'll need all the support she can get.

••••

I've managed to evade Carter for the past two days. My emotions are still all over the place since seeing him again. I've spent the last two nights at Mark's house which is something I rarely do, but it was the only way I could avoid running into him.

Thankfully, work's been flat out, so during the day I haven't had time to think about anything else. To think about him. *The guy that crushed my heart.*

Today is Mr. Shepard's funeral, so avoiding him isn't going to be an option. That's if Carter even attends. I know how he felt about his stepfather. We share a loathing for him. I'm pretty sure he'll be there for his mother though. It's the only reason my dad and I are going.

"You look lovely, Pumpkin," my father says smiling when I walk into the kitchen. For funeral attire, I suppose I look okay. I'm wearing a knee-length, black fitted pencil skirt, a short sleeve black silk blouse and black heels. My long, dark hair is pulled into a tight bun on the top of my head.

"Thanks, Dad. You look nice, too," I reply as I walk towards him and plant a soft kiss on his cheek. He looks handsome in his black suit. I'm sure he has a lot of lady admirers. I understand how much he loved my mum, but I wish he could let go of the past. It's been sixteen years since her death. It's time he started to live again.

I'm concerned about him going today. I hope it doesn't bring up memories of my mum's funeral. Things are still hard for him. Well, the fact that he continues to lock himself away those two days every year, tells me they are.

There's a black car parked in next door's driveway when we leave. I feel sick in the stomach on the drive to the crematorium. Not about the funeral, but about seeing Carter. I feel like a fraud going to the funeral of someone I hate. I'll never be able to find it in my heart to forgive him for what he did. *Never.*

Once we park the car, dad and I head over to the chapel. We mill around outside with the others. All of ten people I might add. I guess being the world's biggest prick meant he didn't have many friends.

My dad makes small talk with the two men standing beside us, while I try and calm the inner turmoil raging within me about seeing Carter. I overhear one of the men tell my father he's Mr. Shepard's brother. I'm not usually judgemental, but I'm immediately sceptical of him. After all, they're related. The other man says he's one of Mr. Shepard's employees. It makes me wonder if any of the people here were actually his friends. People like him don't have friends I guess. Just enemies.

My stomach's doing flip-flops when the funeral car arrives. I presume Carter and his mother are in the black car that pulls up behind it. It was the one that I saw parked in their driveway before we left. My hands are trembling so I wrap them around my middle. The driver gets out of the car and makes his way towards the back door. I try not to look when he opens it, but my damn eyes aren't doing what they're told.

Carter gets out of the car first. I swear I stop breathing as soon as I see him. He's dressed in a black suit. He looks so different. So grown up. So damn hot. For some reason it makes my heart ache. I've never seen him in anything other than casual attire. He is absolutely breathtaking. No other words could describe how good he looks. Seventeen year old Carter was a sight, but an adult Carter ... *no words.*

He reaches for his mother's hand and helps her from the vehicle. My heart hurts for her when I see how broken she looks. Poor thing. I feel bad that I haven't given her my condolences yet, but there was no way I was going over to her house knowing Carter was there.

Carter leads her over towards the chapel. When she gets a glimpse of the coffin in the back of the hearse, a fresh load of tears fall from her red, puffy eyes. I feel my own eyes well just watching her. She looks so broken. Carter wraps her in his arms and holds her tight. Memories of what it felt like when he held me like that flood my mind. I try to push those thoughts away. That's the past and exactly where it needs to stay. I have Mark now.

When he first left all those years ago, I was heartbroken. I cried for weeks. Part of me understood why he felt he had to go. I didn't like it, but I understood. As the months and years passed though, and I got no word from him, none whatsoever, that hurt turned to anger. I know the night I gave him my virginity we'd agreed it would only be one night, but that night, I not only gave him my virtue, I gave him my heart. When he left the very next day without so much as a goodbye, it crushed me. I'm not sure if I can forgive him for that.

We may not have been in a relationship, but first and foremost, he was my friend. Friends don't treat each other like that. He made me and what we shared in our short time together seem inconsequential. Did I mean so little to him? I guess so.

After shaking Carter's hand, my dad wraps Mrs. Shepard in his arms. She cries into his chest. He's lost his spouse as well, so if anyone knows what she's going through right now it's him. As I watch them together, I can feel Carter's eyes boring into me. I don't dare look. Thankfully, I'm wearing my large, dark sunglasses so he can't see my eyes.

When my father lets go of Mrs. Shepard, I wrap my arms around her. "I'm sorry for your loss, Elizabeth," I say.

"Thank you, sweetie," she sniffles as she returns the hug. Letting go, I step back so she can move on to the next guest. A shadow falls over me. Looking up, I find Carter standing in front of me. The cheeky fucking bastard has his arms outstretched, waiting for his hug. *I don't think so buddy.* I see a smirk cross his face when my brow furrows. Before I get a chance to say anything he pulls me into his arms. *Fucker.* He knows I'm not going to make a scene at a funeral.

God he smells amazing.

I know I should push him away, but for some reason I can't. My arms seem to have a mind of their own when they slide around his waist. He exhales, pulling me in tight. "Christ I've missed you," he whispers so only I can hear. Tears sting my eyes. I've missed him too, but it's too late for that. I waited for years for him to return, and when he didn't I moved on.

When reality hits, I have no choice but to pull away. All these feelings that I'm having towards him are consuming me with guilt. Making me feel like I'm doing wrong by Mark. As much as I hate to say this, once the funeral is over, I hope Carter goes back to wherever he came from. Having him around again is too hard. I have a new life now. A life that doesn't include him.

••••

For the rest of the service I don't leave my father's side. The whole time I feel Carter's eyes on me. Only once do I give in to the temptation to look his way. Of course I find him staring straight at me. The sad look on his face as his eyes bore into mine makes my chest ache for some reason. I quickly divert my eyes back to the front of the room.

After we left the Chapel, Mrs. Shepard invited us to her house for the wake. I had no intentions of going back, but the pleading look in her eyes when she asked had me saying yes. *Damn it.* Carter better stay the hell away.

"I'm not going to stay long," I tell my father when we pull into our driveway. I can't handle these feelings Carter evokes in me when he's around. Staying away from him is the only way.

"Sure, Pumpkin. I'm sure Elizabeth and Carter will appreciate you making an appearance."

Of course when we enter the house the first person I see is him. His eyes immediately find mine. The corners of his lips turn up slightly, making his gorgeous face even more handsome. He's standing in the corner of the main room looking completely out of place. Why I feel bad for him, I can't say. I suppose it would suck to feel uncomfortable in your own home, I guess. I find myself wanting to go over and talk to him, but I don't. Instead I head towards the kitchen to see if there's anything I can do to help. At least in here I'll be away from his watchful gaze.

Just my luck they have caterers hosting the wake, so when I'm told there's nothing I can do to help I head back into the main room, deflated. My heart sinks when I find my dad standing with Carter. There's no way I'm going over there to join them. Thankfully, they're lost in conversation and don't notice I've re-entered the room. I don't know anyone else here, so I slip outside and take a seat on the front step. I need the fresh air. I need the space. I need to be as far away from Carter as I can get.

Ten minutes later, I hear the front door open behind me. Turning my head, I find him standing there looking all smug and delicious. Great. Everything in me wants to get up and walk away, but that's not the adult thing to do. As angry as I am at him, we're not teenagers anymore.

"I was wondering where you got to," he says coming to sit beside me. "Here, I brought you something to drink." He holds up a glass of wine. I have a good mind to tell him to jam it up his smug arse, but the truth is, I need it.

"Thank you," I reply reaching for it, but he pulls back his hand. I narrow my eyes at him. Ugh! "I see some things haven't changed. You're still an arsehole." He laughs at my comment like it's funny. It wasn't meant to be funny.

"I'm just messing with you," he says passing it to me for real this time. He's already removed his tie and suit jacket. The sleeves of his shirt are rolled up to his elbows, revealing a full sleeve tattoo on his arm. *He didn't have that last time I saw him.* It only serves to make him look even more like a bad boy. Three words come to mind—Sexy. As. Hell. I hate that his presence still has a huge effect on me.

I find myself wondering what his life's been like since he left. A long time has passed since we were last together. Going by his past, he's probably still a man whore. I hate it that that thought upsets me. "So how have you been?" he asks taking a pull of the beer in his hand.

He must've been wondering the same thing as me. I shrug. Is it wrong that my eyes are focused on his lips wrapped around the head of the bottle? I remember all too well what those lips felt like. Being near him again seems so surreal.

"It's had its ups and downs," I answer with a shrug. His eyes lock with mine. The look I see on his face is so intense I have to turn away, taking a huge gulp of my wine. I'm not sure if I can have this conversation with him. It's funny; for years I longed for him to return, and now he's here, I wish he wasn't.

"How's my man, Larry?" he asks, breaking the awkward silence. My heart sinks. He hasn't been around, so I guess he doesn't know. "Would you mind if I went to see him? I've thought about him a lot over the years." Just hearing him ask that has tears rising to my eyes. I quickly lower my face so he can't see them.

What I wouldn't give to see Lassie again. Reaching up, I grab hold of the necklace Carter bought me, clutching it in my hand. I took it off after he left, but when Lassie passed I put it back on. The necklace and the picture Carter drew are all I have left.

"He died," I choke out. Even after all these years it still breaks my heart whenever I think about him. When I think about what happened.

"What?" he says in a tone that makes me think he doesn't believe what I said. I wish I was lying. My eyes move back to Carter's. Even through my tears I can clearly see the colour drain from his face. "Fuck," is all he says as he puts down his beer and engulfs me in his arms. I go willingly, burying my face in his chest. "What happened? He was still young ... so healthy." A sob escapes me as the memories of that morning flash through my mind. I don't think I'll ever get over that day.

"It was all my fault," I admit for the first time ever. I've always known I was the reason behind Lassie's death, but I've kept that to myself all these years. The truth was just too hard to live with. I'm ashamed that my childish actions were the result of his death.

"What? How?" he asks in disbelief as his hand strokes my back to comfort me. I can feel his body trembling as he holds me. I know he loved Lassie as much as I did, so I'm sure he'll be upset by my news. For some reason I don't hesitate to tell him the truth, it's time I confessed.

I keep my face buried in his chest. I can't bring myself to look at him. I don't want to see the judgement in his eyes when he hears what I have to say. "After you left, I was so angry with your stepfather. I knew in my heart he was part of the reason you went away. Every day, for weeks, I threw Lassie's droppings over the back fence into his yard. It was my revenge. My way of saying 'fuck you' for the way he treated you when you were here. At the time it felt so good. I knew it would piss him off, I just didn't know how much." I feel his body stiffen.

"Did he do something to him?" he asks, grasping my shoulders and pulling me back so he could see my face. Yes he did. Fucking arsehole. I hope he rots in hell.

"Yes," I choke out as memories of that morning flood my mind. I can clearly see the anger cross his handsome features when I admit that. He stares at me for a moment before pulling me back into his chest.

"What did he fucking do?" he seethes through gritted teeth.

"One morning, I went out back to feed Lassie before school, as I always did. That's ... that's when I found him," I say as fresh tears begin to fall. God I wish I could erase that image from my mind. "He was fitting in his bed. There was green foam coming from his mouth. He was struggling to breathe. Oh, Carter. It was horrible," I cry as his hold on me tightens. "I don't think I'll ever get that image out of my head."

"Fuck. Did he poison him?" His body is clearly shaking with anger now.

"Yes. He poisoned him with snail bait. It's something we never used in our gardens because we knew how toxic it was for dogs. The amount of poison the vet found in his system suggested he'd ingested a large amount. An autopsy showed traces of minced meat that must've contained the pellets to entice Lassie to eat it."

"Jesus Christ."

"By the time we got him to the vet it was too late. He was too far gone," I continue.

"Did he get charged for what he did? My mum never mentioned it in our phone calls."

"My dad tried. We couldn't prove it was him, but we both knew it was. We took a sample from his garden. It was the same type that was used to poison Lassie. Unfortunately, it's a commonly used brand, so without any concrete evidence there wasn't much we could do." Tears are streaming down my face as I feel my heart break all over again. I miss him so much. He didn't deserve to die like that. He was a good dog.

"I'm fucking sorry," Carter says squeezing me to him. "So fucking sorry. That must've been a hard thing to see. I know how much you loved that dog. Fuck. If that *motherfucker* wasn't already dead, I'd make him suffer for what he did." His tone tells me he means every word. That's exactly how I felt when it happened.

When Mr. Shepard pulled into the driveway that afternoon after work, my dad marched straight over there and punched him square in the mouth. It would never make up for what he did, but it gave us some satisfaction.

THREE

CARTER

***SHATTERED*. THERE'S NO OTHER WORD TO DESCRIBE HOW I'M** feeling right now. I'm lost for words. I loved that dog. If I'd known what Fuckwit had done before today, I would've spat on that fucker's coffin. How did I not know? Why didn't Ross tell me? I guess it was his way of looking out for me. That's the only thing that makes sense. I'm sure he knows that I wouldn't have let this slide so telling me would've only landed me in trouble.

My heart is hurting for her. I want to comfort her any way I can. Having her in my arms again is amazing. Best feeling ever, but I hate the reasons behind it. I wish I could've done something to stop this from happening. She blames herself, but ultimately the blame lies on me. I'm the one who left. I'm the one he hated. I'm the one who caused her to lash out like she did.

Poor fucking Larry.

I continue to hold her long after the tears have stopped. If she's content to be in my arms, then that's exactly where she's going to stay.

I've fucking missed holding her. She's where she's supposed to be. I don't know why she makes me feel things the others can't, but fuck me she does. *A kaleidoscope of fucking emotions* would be the best way to describe it.

I have an overwhelming compulsion to kiss her. Kiss all her sadness away. But, I can't do that. I'm leaving in a few days. I can't start something that's going to end the minute I drive away and return to my new life. That wouldn't be fair on either of us. Our past has already messed me up enough. I'm worried what would happen if I went there again. Nothing good could come from it, that's for fucking sure. Only more heartache.

"Hey. I was wondering where you two got to," her father says from behind us. Indi pulls away from me with a start, like she's been busted doing something she shouldn't. *What the hell!* I'm sure the look I give her is one of utter confusion. Tearing my eyes from her, I look over my shoulder at Ross. "Is everything alright out here?" He has a huge smile on his face. I guess he's happy seeing us together.

"Yes, Daddy," she replies, standing and tugging at her skirt at the same time. "I'm going to go home if that's okay. I have a headache." She doesn't look at either of us when she speaks.

"Okay. I'll be home shortly, Pumpkin."

Before walking away she meets my eyes briefly. "Bye," is all she says as she turns heading towards her place. I'm left sitting here stunned.

••••

Later, after all the guests have left, and my mum's lying down, I head to my bedroom. I hate being back in this house. I never intended to come back here, but in saying that, I also never thought I'd feel as uncomfortable as I do. Even with him gone, it's still his house so I fucking hate it.

Indi and Larry are both on my mind as I sit on the side of my bed, burying my face in my hands. I wish there was a way I could make this right, but there isn't. I hate to think what she would've gone through finding Larry the way she did. And how much she would've suffered after that. *How he fucking suffered.*

I'm pulled from my thoughts a few minutes later when I hear a horn sound in the driveway next door. Standing, I make my way to the window to see who it is. Instantly I feel my blood pressure rise. There's a fucking guy in Indi's driveway.

I know I have no right to be mad, but I am. I'm the one who walked away from us. It would be selfish of me to expect her not to move on. To be honest, as much as I've missed and thought about her over the years, I had no intentions of ever coming back for her. Sure I thought about it, *constantly*, but I believed it was for the best if I didn't. Seeing this rude prick just now though has me doubting my decision.

He sounds his horn again and I see red. *I don't fucking think so buddy.* If this is her boyfriend, and I hope it isn't, someone needs to teach him some manners. I slide open my window and jump out, just like old times.

"Hey," I say when I approach the driver's side window.

"Hey." The first thing I notice is he's a fucking pretty boy. I should've known.

"Why are you sounding the horn?" I ask annoyed.

"What?" he says squaring his shoulders. If he thinks that's going to intimidate me, he's mistaken. I don't scare easy.

"Are you deaf as well as fucking rude?" I ask, placing my hands on the open window of the door, causing him to pull his head back. *Gutless prick.*

"Who are you?" he asks with trepidation.

"Who the hell are you?" I'm in no mood for this back and forth bullshit.

"I'm Indiana's boyfriend." My heart sinks. She couldn't possibly be going out with this dick. I have to take a few seconds to recover from this devastating revelation.

Fuck, she has a boyfriend.

"Well if you are in fact her boyfriend, why the hell are you honking your horn? If you were a gentleman, which it's quite obvious you're not, why aren't you getting out of the car to get her like she deserves?" I snap.

"It's none of your business." Like hell it isn't.

"I beg to differ," I sneer, folding my arms over my chest. I give him a look that surprisingly has him opening up to me.

"Her father can be very intimidating," he admits with a sigh. "I'm not sure if he's keen on me dating his daughter. I get the impression he doesn't like me much."

"I can see why," I reply, giving him a look that says I don't particularly like you either. Because I don't. Not another word is spoken while we have a kind of standoff staring competition. My eyes are fucking burning, but there's no way in hell I'm blinking. I'm not backing down. Immature I know, but there's no way I'm letting this prick win.

"Carter," Indi snaps from behind me. "What in the hell do you think you're doing?"

"Trying to teach this moron some manners," I answer turning to face her. Thank fuck she showed up. I don't know how much longer I could've lasted. I blink a few times to try and moisten my dried up eyeballs.

Sweet Jesus. I inhale a sharp breath as my eyes take her in. She looks gorgeous in that sexy-as-hell red dress.

She still takes my breath away after all this time. I hear her dick *boyfriend* open his car door from behind me. "Get back in the car," I say through gritted teeth without even looking his way. I can't, because my eyes are glued to her. When I hear his door close, I smirk to myself. Just what I thought—coward. She deserves so much better. *So much fucking better.* My smile widens when I hear her growl at me with disdain. She's so fucking adorable when she's pissed off.

"Look, Indi," the *wanker* says from within the car. "How about we give tonight a miss?"

"What? No." She frowns, pursing her lips at me before turning her attention back to him. "I've just spent the last hour getting ready,

Mark." I can tell. *She looks stunning.* I have to stop myself from licking my lips as I drink her in. What I wouldn't give for a taste of grown up Indi.

Before he gets a chance to reply, I turn my head and glare at him. Silently warning him not to change his mind. His eyes dart from me to her as he swallows nervously.

"Carter," she snaps. "How could you?" She places her palms on my chest and pushes me. I have to hold back my smile. She's so damn cute. "You're only back a day and you're already trying to make my life miserable," she sneers, pushing me again. Christ I've missed her smart mouth.

"You're glad to have me back," I say smugly. She falters for a second before answering, making me think whatever she's going to say is the opposite of how she really feels.

"No, I'm not." Bingo. She's fucking glad. I knew it.

"Don't tell me you haven't missed me," I say so only she can hear as I take a step closer. I'm so close now her perky little tits are almost brushing against my chest. Her scent envelopes me, making my dick come to life. I could drown in her smell, in her. I'm tempted to move in even closer, but I don't. Even after all this time I remember exactly what her soft, warm body feels like pressed against mine. When her eyes widen and I hear her breath hitch, I know damn well I'm right. She's missed me just as much as I've missed her.

I saw how content she was in my arms earlier today. If this *wanker* holds her heart, there's no way she would've been so comfortable letting me hold her. For some reason it gives me hope. Maybe all is not lost.

Her hands come up giving me another shove. She's pretty strong for a squirt. "Didn't you learn your lesson the other day?" she scoffs, cocking one of her eyebrows. Shit. I take a step back as my hands instinctively cover my crotch. My fucking boys are still paying for my little prank with the sponge. I'm pretty sure they couldn't survive another blow like that.

The determined look on her face has me retreating another step. I hold up one of my hands in defeat, while my other hand protects my nuts. If I had a white flag I'd be waving that fucker with a vengeance right now. What is it with her? When did she become a ball-busting warrior? I wonder if pretty boy has ever been introduced to her knee. Scratch that. I just witnessed him in action. He doesn't have any balls.

"Okay. I get the message loud and clear. Please don't go all ninja on my nuts again," I plead. Her face relaxes slightly and I see a small smile play on those luscious lips of hers.

"Good. Now stay the hell away from me," she says as she walks around me and gets into the car. My heart sinks as the car reverses out of the driveway. That prick gives me a smug look and I have to hold myself back. Indiana's eyes lock with mine briefly before she turns her head and looks out the passenger side window. Fuck. My damn heart hurts.

Stupid fucker.

Once the car is out of sight, I head back into the house. I need a fucking drink. Opening the fridge I grab a beer before shoving it back on the shelf. I'm not drinking anything that belonged to Fuckwit. Besides, the mood I'm in calls for something stronger. Heading back into my room, I grab my car keys. *Time to get shitfaced.*

••••

A few hours later, I'm halfway through my bottle of Jack when I hear a car pull up next door. I'm not sure if it's Indi and her *boyfriend*, or Ross. I drag my drunken arse off the bed and head to the window to look. It's Indiana.

I'll admit I'm pleased that she isn't spending the night with him, but I feel a pang in my heart when I see her lean over the centre console and lock lips with him. I remember all too well what a spectacular kisser she is. When his hand comes up and threads into her hair, pulling her in closer, I have to look away.

I'm not sure if it's the alcohol running through my veins or not, but I want to jump out of this window and drag that cocksucker out of the car and away from her. I'm blaming the alcohol. Coming back here was a mistake. I think I was better off not knowing what she's been up to.

Flopping back down on my bed, I reach for my bottle of Jack and take a swig. It burns like a motherfucker on its way down, but I welcome it. I need to be numb, so I take another gulp. I've only ever drunk straight from the bottle once before, and that was a few days after I left here all those years ago.

I see her bedroom light come on from where I sit. Everything in me wants to go over there, but what good would that do? She's moved on. I suppose I can't really blame her. In all honesty, I had no intentions of coming back. Even though I did entertain the thought a million times over the years.

I watch as she heads towards her drawers and retrieves what I presume is a pair of pyjamas. Her gaze moves towards my window as she stares into the darkness of my bedroom. I'm tempted to switch on my bedside lamp so she can see me, but I don't.

She turns suddenly and heads back out of her room. A few seconds later I see the bathroom light come on. She's probably going to have a shower. That thought makes my dick twitch. It pisses me off. I push the thoughts of her naked and rubbing soap all over her delicious body out of my mind. I'm only torturing myself if I don't.

INDIANA

MY THOUGHTS STRAY TO CARTER AGAIN AS I LET THE HOT water wash over my body. I was supposed to be spending the night at Mark's, but after dinner I asked him to bring me home instead. I feel bad that I let Carter get in the way of our plans tonight, but my head is pounding.

Fuck him and his bullying tactics. Who in the hell does he think he is? Poor Mark was so intimidated by him. They're worlds apart when it comes to personalities. Mark is so timid, Carter not so much.

After drying myself and dressing in my PJ's, I grab a few headache pills out of the medicine cabinet and pop them in my mouth. I need to lie down.

Walking back into my bedroom, my traitorous eyes land on Carter's bedroom window again. His lights are out so he must be asleep. I feel bad for the way I left things between us earlier, but he can't butt into my life like that. He's the one who walked away, not me.

"I'm not in my room," I hear a male voice slur, almost making me jump out of my skin.

"What the fuck, Carter?" I screech when I see him sprawled out on my bed. "Get the fuck out of my room."

"Can't do that, sweetheart," he says clumsily sitting up. Is he drunk? I take the few steps towards my bed and reach for his arm, tugging on it.

"You can't be in here," I growl. He looks up at me, and smiles. One of those panty-melting smiles that he used to give me all those years ago. I hate that he still makes me feel things after all this time. "You need to go."

"Nope. I need to talk to you first," he says, reaching out and pulling me forward with so much force I land on top of him. Being pressed against his hard body, on my bed, is not a good idea. "I've missed you," he slurs wrapping me tightly in his arms. I can smell the alcohol on him. *It's so strong, if I stay near him like this, I'm sure the fumes will make me tipsy.* I try and push myself up off his chest as he tightens his grip. I've missed him too, but that's irrelevant. I decide not to voice that out loud.

Being this close to him is too much. I shouldn't be feeling what I'm feeling. It's wrong. My mind is flooded with memories of our time together. I can't go there again. "Carter. Let me up."

"Nope. Not until you talk to me." He buries his face in my hair and inhales. "Fuck you smell good. Just like I remember."

"Stop," I say annoyed as I pull my face back, looking down at him. The sweet look on his face almost makes me smile. Almost. He shouldn't be here. I've moved on. Being so close to him again only confuses me. He can't just expect things are going to pick up from where they left off.

"I'm not letting you go until you agree to talk to me."

"Fine," I say sighing. "I'll talk to you, but you need to let me go first."

"Okay," he says, releasing me. I immediately stand. If we're going to talk, I need distance. A lot of distance. I take a few steps back from the bed. "Why are you here?"

"I told you, I miss you," he replies, sitting up again.

"I have a boyfriend, Carter. Remember? You can't just waltz back into my life five years later, after no goodbye, no contact, and expect to carry on as if nothing happened. You broke my heart when you left." I feel tears sting my eyes, but thankfully I manage to keep them down. I refuse to let him see my weakness.

"I'm sorry," he apologises, exhaling. "I thought leaving you behind was for the best ..." His eyes meet mine and the sadness I see tears at my heart. "I fucked up. I know that."

"Yes, you did. I understand why you felt you had to go, but you could've contacted me. Anything would've been better than nothing." I wrap my arms around myself, trying hard to hold my emotions at bay.

"Do you love him, Indi?" I turn my face away from his. I can't look at him and say this.

"Yes." Although he doesn't evoke the kind of feelings Carter did in the past, I care for Mark. A lot. He's sweet. He treats me like a princess. He'd never leave me the way Carter did. With him I have a future. With Carter, all I have are memories. That's all I'll ever have. He doesn't speak for the longest time. When my gaze moves back to him, I find his head bowed and his shoulders slumped. I feel like a bitch. "I'm sorry, Carter."

"Don't be," he says, his sad eyes meeting mine. "I let you go, and now I have to live with it."

"Carter," I whisper, walking towards the bed and sitting beside him. "I'll always treasure the time we spent together as kids. Always. But, that was in the past. We're not kids anymore."

"I guess," he replies. "Although, you were the kid back then, remember? Not me."

"Whatever," I say bumping my shoulder with his. I see the corners of his lips turn up. I knew that would have to come up eventually. Some things will never change. "Surely you have someone special back home?" He's gorgeous. I don't doubt that the girls fall all over him, just like they used to when he lived here. I'm not sure I want to hear his answer, but I'm in a relationship. It would be selfish of me not to want the same for him.

"No. You know me, I was never one for commitment." Don't I know it? It saddens me that he still hasn't changed after all this time. He's a good guy deep down. He deserves someone special in his life.

"That's sad, Carter."

"That's my life, I guess," he says with a shrug. My hand comes up and rubs his back. I'm not sure how much of this is the alcohol talking.

"Tell me about your life. What have you been up to? Where are you living?" It's something I've always wondered, but I also want to change the subject. This conversation is too depressing.

"I live up north, in Newcastle."

"Really? It's beautiful up there," I say. Meg and I went up there for a weekend away a few years back. I can't believe I was so close to him.

"It is. I have my own business. I'm a tattoo artist."

"Wow. I'm glad you put your talent to use. You were always so good with your hands."

"You better believe it, sweetheart," he says wiggling his eyebrows, making me laugh.

"You're still full of yourself I see."

"Don't tell me you don't miss my hands on you? I bet lover boy doesn't make you feel the way I used to."

"I'm not going there with you, just drop it," I snap, standing. His words sting because they're true.

"Because I'm right," he replies in a cocky tone. He is, but I'd never admit it. *Never*. My sex life with Mark is pretty bland. It's rarely spontaneous, and always in a bed. He's not as adventurous as Carter, but he still satisfies me, so that's the main thing. Sometimes I wish for more, but great sex isn't everything, I suppose.

"Can we change the subject, please?" I'm happy to talk about our current lives, but not sex. Mark wouldn't approve of that, and I'd have to agree. It's totally inappropriate. Especially given our past.

"Sure," he says with a sigh. "Tell me about you. What have you been up to since I left?"

"Not much. College, work, that sort of thing."

"I had a feeling you'd go to college. What did you study?" he asks.

"Veterinary Science. I'm a Veterinarian."

"Really? Wow. I never knew you wanted to be a Vet."

"I didn't, but after Lassie ..." I hear my voice crack as I speak.

"Fuck," he says rubbing his hands over his face. "I'm sorry. Poor fucking Larry." When I look at him, I see tears glisten his eyes. I can't go over this again. Earlier today was hard enough.

"You hungry?" I ask trying to change the subject. I need to get him out of my room. I can't seem to function properly with him sitting on my bed.

"I guess. But, not just for food." His hands reach out for me, but I slap them away.

"Well food is all I've got," I tell him as I turn to leave. When he doesn't get up, I look at him over my shoulder. "Are you coming or what?"

"Sure," he says half-heartedly. His disappointment is evident. That's too bad. It pisses me off that he thinks it's okay to make advances at me. No matter how much he's had to drink, he should know better. He needs some food to sober up, and I need distance. Thankfully, he follows me into the kitchen.

"Do you want a toasted cheese sandwich?" I ask.

"Okay, thanks." When he starts to walk towards me, I point at the table. *Distance.* I need distance. Having him close is just too much.

"Sit," I command. A boyish smile appears on his face before he turns and does what I asked. He's a little unsteady on his feet. It makes me wonder just how much he's had to drink. "Do you get drunk like this often?"

"Nope."

"Then why tonight?" I ask, placing a glass of water in front of him. His glassy eyes meet mine. I see sadness and maybe a touch of anger.

"Cos I felt like it. I see you haven't changed. You're still fucking nosey," he retorts. I suppose being back here isn't easy for him, so I ignore his snide remark.

I make four toasted sandwiches. Two each. I didn't eat much when Mark and I went out for dinner. My stomach was in knots after our little altercation with Carter. "Here you go," I say, placing the plate in front of him.

"Ta," is all he says as he picks up one of the sandwiches and takes a bite. I find myself sneaking glances at him when he's not looking. His face is so rugged, so handsome. Is it possible he's grown even more beautiful over the years, because I'm certain he has? I shouldn't even be thinking that, but I am.

Mark is pretty to look at, but in my eyes he has nothing on Carter in the looks department. Carter's sinfully hot, all man, and those tattoos make him look so bad-arse. He's every girl's fantasy. It's a shame he's a non-committal man whore.

It's a surreal feeling that we're actually having a meal together, after all this time. Well, if you class a toasted sandwich as a meal. So much has changed since he left, but in a way, nothing has.

He looks up and catches me staring. "You don't like your food?" he asks with a mouth full.

"Of course. Why would you ask that?"

"Because you look like you'd rather be eating me instead," he says with a cheeky smile.

"What?" I screech. He throws back his head and laughs. "Nooooo. You're delusional if you think that."

"Just calling it how I see it, sweetheart." When he winks at me I feel my face flush. Shit. I probably was looking at him like that. I need to get him out of this house, and away from me, ASAP.

••••

For the next few hours, we eat, we chat, and we laugh—just like old times. I think it's exactly what we both needed to heal, to completely move on. There was so much unfinished business between us, but now I feel like it's all water under the bridge. I'm hoping after tonight, I can finally let all the hurt go.

Let him go.

My heart hurts to think this is more than likely the last time we'll be alone again. He mentioned earlier he was leaving tomorrow. I'm sure I'll see him around when he visits his mum, but not like tonight. I shouldn't want him to stay, but for some reason I do. Well, part of me does. The part of me that now belongs to Mark, knows him leaving is for the best.

"I should get going," he says.

"Okay." I try not to let my disappointment show. I've missed being around him. I've missed the banter we shared. When he reluctantly turns, I follow him towards the front door. "Thanks for the food ... for the catch up," he says when we walk out onto the front porch.

"It was nice," I reply, getting up on the tip of my toes and planting a soft kiss on his cheek. Taking a step back, my eyes meet his. My heart is sad knowing this is our final goodbye. At least I'm getting one this time around. "Take care of yourself, okay?"

"You too, kid," he says, reaching up and gently running his hand down the side of my face. His touch is so gentle, so sweet. I feel tears burn my eyes. We stand there for the longest time staring at each other. His hand is still resting on my cheek. I find myself leaning my head into his palm. I briefly close my eyes and savour the last time I'm going to feel his skin against mine. I'd give anything for him to wrap me in his arms again. *Anything.*

When I open my eyes, I find him watching me. He gives me a sad smile. "Goodbye, Carter," I finally say, taking another step back. I'm thankful I got to say it this time. It doesn't seem to lessen the ache in my heart though.

"Goodbye, Indi." He continues to stand there, not moving. That electric pull between us, the one we shared in the past, is still as strong as ever. As much as I'd like to stay out here all night with him, I can't. Someone needs to be the strong one here. I turn and take the few steps towards the door. Out of the corner of my eye, I see his hand reach towards me, but then he drops it back by his side. I'm grateful for that. We need to make a clean break.

••••

I manage to hold in my tears when I walk into the house, but they're already falling by the time I reach my bedroom. My heart feels like it felt all those years ago when he left—broken.

I'm grateful that he came back, that I got to see him again. In saying that though, seeing him has conjured up all those old feelings. The ones that took me years to suppress. Guilt consumes me. I shouldn't be feeling like this when I have a boyfriend.

Wiping my eyes, I dig my phone out of my bag. Turning it on, I find a message from Mark.

Night, babe. Hope your head is feeling better. x

Again the guilt hits hard. Technically I've done nothing wrong, but if Mark completely holds my heart, I shouldn't be feeling what I'm feeling.

I'm feeling better, thanks. Sorry I had to cut the night short.
See you at work in the morning. xxx

That's a total lie. My headache is worse than ever, but I don't want him to worry about me because I know he will. He replies straight away.

That's good. Night, gorgeous. Sweet dreams. Wish you
were here. x

I don't reply to his last message. I'm not sure what to say. I do and don't wish I was there with him. My head is so clouded right now it's probably best that I'm not.

Finally, I climb under the covers. My thoughts are still well and truly on Carter. I know he's next door. Only a few metres away. I wish I could spend more time with him before he leaves, but it's probably safer for my heart if I don't.

FIVE

CARTER

AS MUCH AS I HATE BEING BACK IN THIS HOUSE, I THINK WALK-ing away tomorrow, leaving my mum and Indi behind again, is going to be just as hard as it was the last time. For Indi's sake it's probably for the best, or is it? I'm not sure about that anymore. Especially after meeting that *wanker* she's dating.

Once I would've said she was way too good for me, but in the past few years I've grown up, a lot. Sure, technically I'm still a bastard, but Indi's words that night, all those years ago, have stuck with me. I'm not the same person I was. I no longer try to let that word define me. I still have my moments, but as a whole, I've come a long way. I'm a good, hardworking, and honest guy. That's what I try my best to remember. Not all the other bullshit.

Going over there tonight, drunk, may not have been my smartest move, but I'm glad I did. I think she needed it just as much as I did. Being with her again was nice, but it only reinforced how good we are together, and how much I've missed having her close. She's the only girl I've ever felt comfortable with. The only one who I can completely be myself with.

••••

When I wake the next morning, she's still on my mind. My head hurts like a bitch from all the alcohol I consumed. I finished off the bottle when I got back home. My heart was hurting after saying goodbye to her. Because it was more than words, it truly was a goodbye. That doesn't sit well with me for some reason. I have this feeling in my gut that if I walk away again I'm going to regret it for the rest of my life. I'm going to lose her forever. If I haven't already.

After showering and eating breakfast, I decide to head next door. I don't know what I'm going to say when I get there, but I feel compelled to see her one more time before I leave. Jax called me this morning to see when I'd be heading back. I told him today. I have a great team, so I'm not really worried about the shop. I know I also have Jax and Candice if anything goes wrong, but either way, I still need to get home. I need to sort out what I'm going to do. To figure out a way I can come back here more often. Well, if Indi wants that of course. I got mixed messages from her last night. She said she loves that *wanker*, which was hard to hear, but I also get that feeling in the pit of my stomach there's still something between us. Maybe it's just wishful thinking on my part. Who fucking knows?

"Carter, my boy," Ross says with a smile when he answers the door. "Come in."

"I was hoping to speak to Indi before I leave," I divulge as I follow him down the hall towards the kitchen.

"She's already left for work. Sit." Disappointment consumes me. I take a seat at the kitchen table as he sets about making us a cuppa. Is missing her a sign, or just rotten luck?

"Oh." I hear my own displeasure in my voice.

"Tell me something?" he asks as he stops what he's doing, turning to face me. "Do you still have feelings for Indi?" Whoa. Where did that question come from?

"What?"

"Come on, Carter. Don't pussyfoot around with me. Do you still have feelings for my daughter, or what?" I try my best to remain calm and not give anything away.

"Why do you ask?" He exhales in frustration. I know he knows I'm avoiding answering.

"I'll tell you why," he says in a stern voice, walking towards the table and taking the seat opposite me. "That dick, Mark. Indiana's boyfriend." I can't help but smile when he refers to him as a dick. My sentiments exactly.

"What about him?"

"He called me last night ..."

"He did? Why?" My first thought is, *fuck*, he's dobbed me in for accosting him in the driveway, and Ross is going to chew me out about it.

"He asked for my permission to marry Indiana." *Hell no.* By the way his shoulders just slumped, I'd say he's not too happy about it. That makes two of us. "To be honest I'm not sure how I feel about it. I'm a pretty good judge of character, and I've never been able to completely warm to that guy, if you know what I mean." I sure do. I only met him for a few minutes and I didn't like him. Under other circumstances I might, but as long as he's associated with Indiana, I know that's not going to happen.

"Did you give him permission?" My heart starts to race as I wait for his reply.

"Not in so many words, but I told him if it's what my daughter wants, and if it makes her happy, than I'm fine with it. What else could I say? I'd never stand in the way of her happiness. I just don't think she'll get that with him." He rubs his hands over his face as he contemplates everything. "I still can't believe the coward rung me instead of asking me face to face. Christ, I hope she doesn't say yes."

"Can I ask you something else?"

"Sure," he replies.

"Why are you telling me this?"

"Because I don't think Mark is the right man for her. Indi seems happy enough with him, but there's something missing. That spark. I just don't see it when they're together. Maybe I'm just being an overprotective father. She's all I have left, but I want her to be truly happy. I want her to experience the kind of love I shared with her mother. Is that too much to ask?" I feel my lips turn up. I couldn't agree with him more. It still doesn't explain why he's telling me this.

"Do you want me to rough him up?" I ask. Maybe that's why he's sharing this with me.

"No. I want you to get your shit together and decide what you want." Hold on a minute.

"You want me to be with Indi?" I look at him in disbelief. Surely he couldn't want that.

"Yes. If that's what you both want, of course." My lips turn up into a smile. I like the fact he thinks I'm good enough for his daughter because I know how much she means to him. He exhales before looking me in the eye. His expression is serious. "If you still have feelings for her, which I get the impression you do, this may be your last chance. You can both deny it all you want, but I'm not stupid, Carter. I saw the way you two looked at each other all those years ago. It's the same look I saw yesterday if I'm not mistaken. You only get one chance at true love, son. Believe me, I know. I also know my daughter. She's as loyal as they come. If she marries him, it will be for life."

Uneasiness settles over me with every word spoken. I swear my heart's beating so hard I can hear it thumping in my ears. The thought of losing her to him, forever … It doesn't sit well with me—at all.

"I don't know what to say," I confess, making eye contact with him as I shift around in my seat. This whole conversation is agitating me. Of course I have feelings for her. I don't know what he expects of me though. Does he want me to marry her? He's got rocks in his head if he thinks that's what I want. I'm not the marrying kind. Even for her. Fuck no. Girls like her don't marry guys like me.

"You don't have to say anything. Just think about what I've said. I thought it only fair to tell you. I just wanted to make it an even playing field," he says smiling. Cunning old fool. I fucking love this man.

"Thanks. I'll give it some thought." What else can I say? As much as I hate the thought of them together, is it fair to come between them when I'm not even sure I can give her what she wants? What she needs? Fuck it. *Yes I can.* Even if it's just to get her away from him. She deserves better. Standing, I reach for Ross' hand. "I'll catch you next time I'm in town," I say. "Can you do me a favour and keep an eye on my mum until I get back?"

"Sure thing. Are you leaving already? We didn't even have a coffee." He clasps his hand in mine.

"I don't have time. What's the address of Indi's work?" His face lights up at my question.

"It's just off Tuckers Road, the second street on the left. A big horse-shit coloured building. You can't miss it." His description of the building makes me chuckle.

"Let us know you got home safely. And don't worry about your mum, I'll keep a close eye on her." He reaches out and grips my shoulder. "Remember, I'm always here if you need anything, son."

"I know," I reply smiling. I love that he always says that. I love that he gives a shit.

••••

As I drive towards Indi's work my head is all over the place. This place hasn't changed much in the five years I've been gone. Well, the buildings haven't. *I wish I could say the same for Indi and I.* I contemplate turning around and heading back home at least ten times. I know how I feel about her, but can I really come between her and that *wanker?* Chasing after another guy's girl is not my style, but this isn't just any girl, it's Indiana. *My* Indiana. She was mine first.

A song comes on over the radio. It's one of those mushy love songs. I hate that shit. Reaching out, I go to flick the station when the chorus cuts in. The guy sings about having a hole in his heart. Why does this resonate with me? Because that's exactly how I feel. There's been a piece of my heart missing since the day I drove away five years ago.

Instead of changing the station, I turn it up. I listen as he sings about starting again. Is this a sign? Can we start again? Are we too far gone to get back what we once shared? Once I've parked, I sit in the car until the song ends. "That was Start Again, by Conrad Sewell," the DJ announces. I rest my head on the steering wheel as I inhale a deep breath. I know in this moment, this hole will never mend until I have her again. I have to try. I'm going to regret it for the rest of my life if I don't.

Doubt settles in. "What am I doing here?" I mumble under my breath when I exit the car. What am I going to say to her? I have no fucking clue. All I know is from the minute Ross told me that *wanker* was going to propose, I knew I had to see her before I left. She can't marry him. She just can't.

I shake my head as I walk towards the building. One thing's for sure, Ross was right. The colour of the building does resemble horse shit. I'd say this guy has taste in his arse, but he has Indi, so that couldn't possibly be true.

My hand rises, pushing open the glass door. "Here goes nothing," I mutter to myself as I step inside.

Time to work on getting my girl back. Well, at least try to.

INDIANA

I STILL FEEL GUILTY ABOUT LAST NIGHT. EVEN THOUGH NOTH-ing happened, I feel compelled to tell Mark about it. I don't want to keep secrets from him. He knows nothing about my past with Carter. Maybe if I come clean, I won't feel so bad. I don't want him to think I'm doing things behind his back, because I'm not.

When I finish up giving Mrs. Smith's poodle, Poppy, her vaccination, I decide to go and talk with Mark. I knock before walking into his examination room, even though Stephanie, the receptionist, told me he was alone. Of course his room is three times the size of mine. I swear the broom closet is larger than the pissy little room he's shoved me in.

It's his practice I guess, so it's only fitting he get the best room. But, it annoys the hell out of me sometimes. His parents bought the clinic for him when we graduated. At first I wasn't too keen about working together, but he practically begged me to, so I agreed. So far it's worked out pretty good. We get on well. Being in each other's pockets all day isn't as bad as I thought it would be. We don't live together, so we still get time away from one another.

"Hey," I say when I enter the room.

"Hey, sweetheart." He walks towards me and wraps me in his arms. "Everything okay?"

"Yes," I reply, encircling his waist and resting the side of my face on his chest. "Carter came over last night after you dropped me off."

"Who?"

"Carter. My neighbour. The guy from yesterday afternoon."

"Oh. The thug." You can clearly hear the disdain in his voice.

"He's not a thug," I say in his defence. He does act like one sometimes, but he's definitely not a thug. Just a little misguided on occasions. Mark doesn't know him like I do, so I resent him for calling Carter that.

"I beg to differ, but you're telling me this why?" I can tell by his voice he's annoyed. I can't really blame him. I wouldn't like it if the shoe was on the other foot.

"Because I don't want to have any secrets from you." I feel his body stiffen. He pulls back and puts his finger under my chin, lifting my face towards his.

"What kind of secrets? Did something happen between you two?" The uncertainty on his face makes me feel bad.

"What? No. He just wanted to talk, that's all."

"What's the story between you two? I've never seen him around before, and you've never mentioned him. He seemed awfully protective of you yesterday." I was hoping I didn't have to go into this, but I guess I should tell him.

"We got together when we were younger. Ummm ... he was my first ... you know, sexual encounter. Then he left. I haven't seen him again, until now."

"I see," he says, letting me go and taking a step back. "I don't like this situation, Indi. I saw the way he looked at you yesterday. Do you still have feelings for him?"

"No. We're friends. That's all. As I said before, I just didn't want to keep any secrets from you." I see his face soften as he steps towards me reaching for my hand.

"I'm glad, but I'd prefer it if you stayed away from him from now on. I don't trust him."

"That's a little unreasonable don't you think? He's my friend, my neighbour, nothing more." Even as the words leave my mouth I doubt them. But Mark seems to believe me.

"Okay. I don't like it, but I trust you. If he gives you a hard time though, please tell me. I'll have a talk to him."

"Sure." I seriously doubt that though. He seemed pretty intimidated by Carter yesterday. I know what Mark's like. He's definitely not the confrontational type. You only have to see the way he lets his parents order him around to know that. He leans forward and brushes his lips against mine.

"I love you, Indiana, and I *will* protect what's mine."

"Thank you, but there's no need. I can handle myself around Carter." He pulls back from me when there's a knock on the door. It's Stephanie.

"There's a Mr. Reynolds here to see you, Ms. Montgomery." Fuck. The only Mr. Reynolds I know is Carter. My eyes dart to Mark. He smiles at me. Of course he has no idea who Mr. Reynolds is. I don't think he's going to be impressed when he finds out.

"Okay. I'll be out in a minute."

"Are you okay?" Mark asks when she closes the door. "You've gone a little pale."

"I'm fine," I lie giving him a tight smile. I'm far from fine. What does Carter want? Why has he come to my work?

I turn from Mark and head towards the door. Just my luck, he follows. Shit. When he sees Carter standing there, he falters. "Him," I hear Mark growl from beside me. Carter's hands are buried in his pockets. He looks nervous, which for some reason on him I find endearing. I love his vulnerable side. It's a side of him he doesn't show often. My heart starts to race as I take him in. Why am I still so affected by him after all this time?

"What can we do for you?" Mark asks, draping his arm over my shoulder like a possessive caveman. Carter's eyes move between Mark and I.

"I need to have a word with Indiana. In private," Carter says locking eyes with Mark.

"There's nothing you can't say to her in front of me," he snaps. *Far out.* You could cut the air with a knife. Carter ignores Mark, turning his attention to me.

"Please, Indi. It will only take a minute."

"I said no," Mark reaffirms. I reach for his hand, giving it a squeeze. Now is not the time to turn all alpha. Carter will tear him apart.

"I think Indi can make up her own mind," he sneers with contempt before turning his attention back to me. "I just need to talk to you before I leave. A few minutes, that's all I ask." The pleading look on his face tugs at my heart. I can't believe he's leaving again, already. He's only just got here. I thought he'd stick around for a few more days.

"You're leaving right now?" I try not to sound disappointed, but I fail miserably.

"I've got work commitments," he replies giving me an unsure smile. Mark's not going to like it, but I have to talk to him. I need to know what he wants.

"Oh." I turn to Mark. "It'll only take a few minutes." He doesn't say a word, but the anger in his eyes is clearly visible.

"Fine," he exhales in defeat before turning and storming back into his room. I flinch when he slams the door. He's seriously overreacting here, but I guess I can't blame him for being upset. After all, I just finished telling him that Carter and I have a history.

"Outside?" Carter asks flicking his head towards the door. The insistent look on his face has me nodding. My gaze moves to Stephanie. Her eyes are firmly fixed on Carter as she eyes him up and down. Why that annoys me, I can't say. Actually, yes I can. I hate that women just fall all over him. Don't they realise how pathetic they look? I've seen her giving Mark that same look on occasions, but surprisingly that didn't seem to bother me as much as it does right now, with Carter.

I follow him out into the street. He's quiet for the longest time. I watch on as he paces the sidewalk. His hands are threaded through his hair. I presume he's trying to calm himself down first. When he finally stops, he turns to face me.

"Remind me again, what do you see in that guy?"

"Excuse me? Is that why you came here?" I give him a look of disbelief. He better not have come all this way just to tell me that.

"No," he says exhaling. His big brown eyes search out mine.

"Then why? What do you want, Carter?"

"You can do so much better."

"Really?" Again with this bullshit.

"Yes. Can't you see how wrong he is for you, Indi?" He steps forward and reaches for my hand. He met him for all of a minute. How would he know if he's right for me or not?

"That's not for you to decide, Carter," I snap, pulling my hand from his. He doesn't even know Mark. He has no right to judge.

"Indi, please." His hands fist in his hair again. He's definitely struggling with something. I have no idea what. Surely he didn't come all the way here to tell me Mark was the wrong guy for me. He already made that quite clear last night. "If you stay with this guy, you'll regret it. Trust me. There's someone better out there ... waiting." What the hell is he talking about?

"Like who? You? Mr. I-don't-do-commitment. You're asking me to throw away a future with Mark, for what? Friends with benefits? Been there done that, remember? The day I gave you my heart was the same day you ripped it out and stomped on it. I'm not stupid enough to go through that again." His shoulders slump slightly at my verbal assault, but every word I spoke is the truth.

"I'm sorry. Hurting you was the last thing I wanted," he says. The sincerity in his voice is clear. I'd like to believe he would never purposely hurt me, but the fact is he did.

"Well you did. That's irrelevant now because it's in the past. I'm over it." Which is a lie. I'm not sure I'll ever completely be over it. "Why did you come here?"

"I don't know. Fuck," he says with a sigh.

"You don't know what?" I'm really starting to lose my patience with his indecisiveness. "Spit it out, Carter. If there's something you want to say, then just damn well say it."

"I don't know if I'm that guy, but I do know it's definitely not him." He's not even making sense. He doesn't want me to be with Mark and he doesn't want me either. *What the hell*? His words cut me right to the core.

"Thanks for the advice. If that's all, I need to get back to work. You've already pissed my boss off. I don't want to lose my job." I turn to walk away. Even more confused than I was the moment I saw him standing in the reception area. If he only came to cause trouble, then he's achieved that. Disappointment consumes me. Funny thing is, I can't even tell you why.

"Wait." I stop when he reaches for my elbow. "Maybe I should've thought about what I was going to say before I got here, but I didn't. I came on an impulse. I came ..."

"For what, Carter?" I ask in a frustrated tone as I turn to face him again.

"I came to tell you ..." I raise an eyebrow when he pauses. I'm waiting. "Look, I'm not sure if I can give you what you need, Indi, but I do know I don't want to lose you to *him*." He flicks his head towards the clinic when he says that. "I don't want to lose you to anyone for that matter. I know you told me you loved him last night, but does he make you feel what I did when we were together? We had something special. I know you felt it too."

No he doesn't, but I'd never admit that out loud. My heart rate picks up. Is he asking me to break it off with Mark, so we can have a relationship? Has he lost his mind? "Had being the operative word here, Carter. I still have no idea what you are trying to say."

"To be honest, I don't even know what I'm trying to say," he chuckles, rubbing his hands over his face in frustration. I feel my lips curve into a smile as I watch him. I've never seen him looking so unsure of himself. "It's just ... I'm lost without you. I've spent the last five years trying to deny it, but it's true. I miss you. I've felt like I've had a hole in my heart since the day I drove away and left you crying in the driveway. I want you in my life again."

"What are you asking me to do, Carter?" He reaches out, grasping both my hands in his. I hate how even the simplest touch from him sends my heart into a flutter.

"I've gotta go back home today. I have some things I need to sort out with work. I'm hoping to be back here by the end of the week. Can you just think about what I've said while I'm gone? I miss you. The last few days have made me see just how much. I need you in my life, Indiana."

"You do?"

"I do. I can't promise you anything. I don't know what the future holds for us, but I want things to be the way they used to be between us. I want to see where it takes us. I'll admit I'm not the commitment type, but if anyone could make me one, it's you. It'll only ever be you."

My head says I should tell him to go to hell, but my heart speaks a totally different language. My smile grows. If it gets any bigger, I'm sure my face will split in two. What he's said is a lot to take in, such a huge risk to even consider. And then there's Mark. I know he doesn't make me feel the kind of things Carter does, but I'm not sure if I can just walk away from him either. Can I even trust Carter with my heart anymore? He broke it once, who says he won't do it again? I think my head is going to explode. This is too much to process all at once.

"Okay," I finally say. I hope I don't regret this. I can't believe I'm even entertaining the idea. But there's a part deep inside that knows exactly why I am.

"Okay, what?" he asks, a look of hopefulness on his face.

"Okay, I'll think about what you've said." He lets out the breath he was holding while waiting for my answer. "I said think, Carter, that's all. Don't go getting your hopes up. I'm not sure if I can walk away from what I have with Mark." And that's the truth.

"That's all I'm asking." He pulls me into him, wrapping me in his arms. Mark never makes me feel like this when he holds me. *Never.*

Why am I even thinking that? Can I take a chance on a guy that I know has the potential to destroy me? Because that's exactly what will happen if he breaks my heart again. "I'll see you at the end of the week," he says pulling back and cupping my face in his hands.

"I'm not making any promises, okay. I'm not sure—"

"I'll respect any decision you make," he says cutting me off. "I might not like it, but I'll respect it. If you decide Mark is the guy for you, then I'll walk away. I promise."

"Okay."

"Okay," he responds, smiling. God I love his smile. There's something about it that turns my insides all mushy.

"I've got to get back to work." I go to step back, but he pulls my face to his, planting a warm, soft kiss on my mouth. It leaves my lips tingling, and it was only a peck. I have a feeling my headache isn't going to go away anytime soon. It's going to be a really long, agonising week.

•••••

Three days have passed and thanks to my current predicament, I still have this damn headache. Mark was upset with me after my little talk with Carter, but by the afternoon he came around. He asked me what Carter wanted, and I lied. I told him he wanted to say goodbye, which made me feel awful. It still does, but what can I say? I need to make up my own mind without any influence from either one of them.

To be honest, I'm totally confused. I'm not sure if I want to give up either of them. My screwed up heart screams Carter, but unfortunately my head doesn't. This is one time I wish I wasn't so sensible. I believe Carter when he says he wants more, but is he capable of more? Does he think he wants me because I have Mark, or does he really miss me? It's a total mind fuck. Can I walk away from Mark and take a chance on an uncertainty?

"Hey, babe," Mark says coming up behind me, sliding his arms around my waist. I was so lost in thought that I jump. "Are you nearly ready to leave? I'm taking you out for dinner."

"Can I have a raincheck? I have a really bad headache. I was actually looking forward to going home and lying down." That's the truth. I'd even considered not coming in today, but I knew Mark needed me to assist him in surgery.

"Nope. I have big plans for us tonight. We're going out. That's final," he demands as his lips trace a trail down my neck.

"Mmmm," I moan, tilting my head to one side. "Can we go out tomorrow night instead?"

"Come on, Indi," he begs, turning me in his arms. "Please. I've put a lot of effort into tonight. Don't spoil it over a lousy headache." The pleading look in his eyes has me giving in.

"Fine," I say with a sigh.

"Good girl." He leans forward and places a kiss on the tip of my nose. "We'll swing by your place after work so you can change and pick up some clothes for tomorrow. I want you to stay over tonight."

"I agreed to dinner. I'm not in the mood to stay over." It's not just my headache that's stopping me from spending the night. It's all this stuff with Carter as well. Until I sort through that, I can't be intimate with Mark. It wouldn't be fair on him. Plus it would only confuse matters.

As much as I've missed Carter over the years, I can't believe I'm even contemplating the idea. Mark's safe. Mark would never break my heart.

••••

It's around a fifty-minute drive to the restaurant. We end up at an upmarket waterfront restaurant on the North Shore. Usually we eat locally, so I'm surprised that he would bring me here.

My eyes immediately scan the surroundings when we enter. It's beautiful. The waiters are all dressed in tuxedos. The restaurant is all white, with splashes of black, silver, and a deep cherry red throughout. It screams class and money. I've never been to a place so swanky before, I'd hate to see what it costs to eat at a place like this.

"Reservation for two under Thompson," Marks says to the maître d.

"Right this way," he replies with a pleasant smile. My eyes are darting around the room as we walk across the restaurant floor, heading towards the outside terrace overlooking the harbour. Mark pulls out my chair when we reach the table. "Thank you," I say as I take a seat. He places a soft kiss on the top of my head when he pushes my chair in. The maître d spreads a white linen napkin on my lap before making his way around to Mark. I'm not complaining about being here, but again I wonder what the special occasion is.

When we're alone, he reaches for my hand across the table and I smile at him. He really is easy on the eye. It brings all of my worries to the forefront. Can I really let him go? Can I allow Carter to waltz into my life after being absent for five years and disrupt everything?

"You okay?" he asks. I love how caring he is towards me.

"I am. It's lovely here. Thank you for bringing me."

"Only the best for you, sweetheart," he replies pulling my hand towards his mouth and placing a soft kiss on my knuckles. It makes my stomach churn as guilt consumes me. Again I'm plagued with doubts. Doubts on whether I can give up what I have with Mark for an uncertainty. Doubts if I can let Carter go. Carter shouldn't even be on my mind when I'm here with Mark, but he is.

When the waiter comes over to take our drinks order, Mark orders a bottle of their finest wine. His mother usually frowns upon me when I drink. *"Drinking alcohol isn't very ladylike,"* she has said to me on numerous occasions. A wine here and there never hurt anyone. She can be such a pretentious cow sometimes.

Usually when we're out with them, which thankfully isn't very often, I don't order wine anymore. His mother has a way of making me feel inferior. Like I'm not good enough for her son. Tonight though, I actually welcome the alcohol. It may help me relax a little.

The waiter pours a tiny amount into each glass. I hate how they do that. Mark picks up his glass and swirls the liquid inside before bringing it to his nose. I almost want to laugh. He wouldn't know the first thing about fine wine since his family are non-drinkers. God, some rich people can be so fake. It's all a show. It's a two hundred dollar bottle of wine. How bad could it taste? Finally he takes a sip and nods, so the waiter proceeds to fill both our glasses.

As soon as he walks away, I lift my glass to my mouth and take a huge gulp. "Easy there," Mark chastises. "It's expensive wine. You're supposed to savour the taste, not guzzle it down." I roll my eyes at him before taking another gulp. I'm not interested in the taste. The faster I drink this baby, the quicker the alcohol will be pulsing through my veins.

"So what's the special occasion?" I ask. I'm curious. He never usually goes to this much trouble on a date.

"All in good time," he says with a wink. Great. Now he's going to make me hang out. I'm not a fan of surprises. He smiles at me before looking over at the maître d' and nodding his head. What's he up to? I find out soon enough when a violinist appears at our table. Of course he stands right next to me when he starts to play. It's not like I hate the sound of the violin or anything, but with this headache it's like nails on a chalkboard. He may as well be bashing me over the head with the damn thing. It would have the same effect.

Mark reaches for my hand, giving it a light squeeze. I plaster a smile on my face. I don't want him to think I don't appreciate the effort he's making, I do. It's very sweet. Thankfully, he only plays one song before walking away. "Are you having a nice time?" he asks.

"I am."

"Good."

"Are you ready to order now, Sir?" the waiter asks reappearing at our table.

"Yes, thanks," Mark replies. As the waiter rattles off the chef's suggestions, I tune him out. I already know Mark's going to order for me. He always does. His father orders for his mother as well. I guess he thinks that's the way it's done.

Maybe in the sixteenth century.

While we wait for the food to arrive, we talk about work. Our conversations seem to always divert in that direction. I guess when you and your partner do the same thing for a living that happens. I must admit though, I think it's the only thing we really have in common. That thought saddens me for some reason.

My mind drifts to Meg. God I miss her. It's times like this I could use her shoulder. Her advice is what I crave. She's the only one I could talk to about this situation. She knows me better than anyone.

She's living on the other side of the world with her husband, Drew. He's in IT. That's how they met. She hated school, so instead of going to college like me, she headed straight into the workforce when she finished her senior year in high school.

She instantly fell head-over-heels in love, which was surprising for her. I guess he was the one. It was a whirlwind romance. They were married within a year. Then he was offered a position looking after the company's overseas branches. It was a huge opportunity for him. Naturally Meg followed her husband.

There's a huge gap in my life without her in it. We talk on the phone when we can, but it's not the same as having her living nearby when I need her. Like now. She adores her husband, but hates being shuffled around from one place to the next. As soon as she gets settled, they up and move again. I can hear the sadness in her voice every time we talk on the phone. She has so many of her own dramas going on at the moment, I suppose it wouldn't be fair to burden her down with mine.

Once we've eaten, Mark asks me if I'd like to dance. I almost say no, but when I see the look of expectation in his eyes, I don't. He's gone to a lot of effort tonight. The least I can do is go along with it.

He holds me in his arms as we move to a slow song. "Do you know how much I love you?" he whispers in my ear when the song comes to an end. Guilt consumes me again. I'm not sure how much longer I can do this. I tighten my grip around his waist, holding him against me, savouring the feeling of being held by the man who loves me.

When the music stops, Mark releases me. Turning to walk back towards our table, I'm stopped when he reaches for my arm, holding me in place. Facing him again, my heart drops into the pit of my stomach when I realise what he's about to do. He takes a step backwards, and to my horror, gets down on one knee.

Holy fucking crap! I'm not ready for this.

"No, no, no," I blurt out in a panic as I try and pull him back to his feet. Noooo. *Please don't ask me to marry you in front of all these people*, I want to scream, but before I get a chance, he pulls the ring out of his pocket and holds it out towards me.

"Indiana Montgomery, I love you. Please say you'll spend the rest of your life with me." At first I stand there in stunned silence. I feel dreadful. My eyes dart around the restaurant. Everybody has stopped what they're doing and are now watching this horrible scene unfold. I find myself wishing a big black hole would open up beneath me and swallow me whole.

Even before Carter came back on the scene, I knew I wasn't ready for this kind of commitment. I'm only twenty-two. There's so much I want to experience before I even think of settling down. Like traveling the world for one. How can I say no to him in front of all these people? I can't lie and say yes either. That would be so much worse.

My eyes meet his again as he waits for my answer. I see hope, then desperation cross his face. I feel tears burn my eyes. The pleading look in his eyes makes my heart hurt, but I still can't bring myself to answer him. Then his expression turns to anger. I continue to stand there in stunned silence.

A few seconds later he rises to his feet. "I can't believe you'd embarrass me in front of all these people," he snarls through gritted teeth. How is this my fault? We've never even discussed marriage.

"I'm sorry," is all I manage to get out, in a voice that doesn't even sound like mine. He doesn't reply. Instead he turns and storms away, heading towards the exit. I run after him. Words cannot express how terrible I feel.

"Mark. Mark, wait," I call out as I chase after him.

"Go to hell," is all he says as he abruptly pushes the restaurant door open and walks out into the night. I continue after him.

"Mark, please. Let's talk about this."

"There's nothing to talk about. We're through," he says as he opens the driver's side door and climbs into the car. I'm stopped in my tracks. Did he really just say we're through?

"Mark," I cry as tears rise to my eyes. Ignoring me, he starts the car. What? Is he just going to leave me here all alone? The car inches forward, and I have to step out of the way so he doesn't run me down. Surely he's not going to just drive away. He's just upset. I can understand that. "Please," I call out as he passes me. "Talk to me." He slows, inching down his window.

"There's nothing you can say that's going to fix this," he snaps angrily.

"Can we at least talk about it?" I plead. "You're not even giving me a chance." Anger sweeps through me. He's acting like a complete dickhead. "We've never even discussed marriage. Hell, I haven't even told you I love you yet. What possessed you to think I was even ready for this?" He continues to look straight ahead. The gutless prick won't even make eye contact with me. He exhales a large breath before meeting my steely gaze.

"Because I panicked," he admits. "I didn't want to lose you." Tears rise to my eyes again when the anger on his face is replaced with sadness. I hate that I've hurt him, but he's acting like a tool. This is not the Mark I thought I knew. "You've changed since that thug has returned. I'm not stupid, Indiana. I see the way he looks at you ... the way you look at him. Deny it all you want, but any fool could see the connection you two have." I can't reply because in my heart I know everything he's saying is true. "That's what I thought," he says in a defeated tone when I don't deny it. "I think it's for the best if you find another job." *What the hell!*

When he winds up his window and drives forward, anger broils inside me. I'm so pissed with him, I'm tempted to kick his stupid, ridiculously expensive car as it passes, but that would only bring me down to his level. He's carrying on like a spoilt brat.

Wrapping my arms around my torso, I watch him drive towards the exit of the parking lot before pulling into the traffic. *He'll be back.*

Regardless of what he said, I know deep down he's a good guy. He's just hurt. He'd never leave me stranded like this. He'd never walk away from me like Carter did. *Never.* I wait, and I wait, but he doesn't return.

Wow. I guess he would.

CARTER

FIVE LONG DAYS PASS BEFORE I RETURN. I'VE WORKED MY ARSE off to get back to Indiana as quick as I could. I can only stay for a few days, but it's better than nothing. I'm still not sure how this back and forth thing is going to work, but I'm not giving up yet. Truth is, I'd travel to the ends of the earth for her if I had to.

Jax and I changed our usual Friday night card game to last night. We've been doing this for years now. I love catching up with him and having a few drinks. It's our way of unwinding after a busy week. We used to alternate between my place and his, but lately he seems to be coming up my way. He likes it up here. We have the best pubs and nightlife.

He cheats his arse off at cards, but I don't care. I'm just grateful for the company. After I left mum and Indi behind, he was all I really had. I'm not sure where I would've ended up if it weren't for him.

He knows all about my predicament with Indiana. Only because one night I had too much to drink and blurted it all out. Confessing my love for the girl I left behind. He'd only seen the other side of me before then. The fuck 'em and chuck 'em side. He thought I was a legend until he found out I was secretly hung up on a chick from my past.

He gave me shit about it for weeks. One night he went too far and we nearly came to blows over it. It wasn't mentioned again until last night. I was the one who brought it up. I needed his advice. We discussed opening up another parlour close to where Indi lives, but there's already five existing tattoo shops within a twenty-kilometre radius. It just isn't viable at the moment. I'll work something out, or die trying.

My stomach is in knots as I drive into my old street. I have no idea what to expect. I've had no contact with her since I visited her at work five days ago. I pray she's given what I said some serious thought. I pray that fucker hasn't proposed to her yet. *Fuck.* What if he has? What if she said yes? I suddenly feel like I'm going to be sick.

Pulling into my mum's driveway, I look over towards Indi's house. Her car and Ross' are both parked under the carport. It makes me wonder why she's not at work today. Unless she got a lift with that *wanker.*

As I turn off the ignition and go to exit the car, Ross comes out of my mum's house. I smile as he walks towards me. I'm grateful to know he's been here comforting her. My mum told me when we spoke on the phone that Ross had been calling in every day to check on her. He'd been bringing over food and running errands. He's such a great guy.

I've called her every day since I left, sometimes more than once. She cried every time we spoke. I still find it hard to comprehend her devastation. Especially for Fuckwit. But, I guess I didn't love him like she did. If only she knew what a cocksucker he really was, but who am I to burst her bubble? I'm pretty sure she wouldn't think he was so wonderful if she knew how he treated me when she wasn't around, or what he did to Larry.

"Hey, son," Ross says smiling. I love how he always seems happy to see me. "I wasn't expecting to see you back so soon."

"I tried to get back here as soon as I could," I reply, reaching for his outstretched hand. "How's my mum doing today?" He shrugs.

"As well as can be expected." From our phone calls I was kind of expecting him to say that.

"I appreciate you keeping an eye out for her. Is Indi home from work today?" I ask, flicking my head in the direction of her car.

"She's been home all week."

"What? Why? Is she sick?" I feel panicky when I ask that.

"Heartbroken more like it," Ross replies, making my mind race. What does he mean by heartbroken? What the fuck has happened?

"Why?" Ross shakes his head in disgust. The anger rolling off him is as clear as day. What the fuck is going on?

"Thinking about it still makes my blood boil," he confesses.

"Don't leave me hanging. Tell me what the hell you're talking about." I can already tell I'm not going to like what he has to say.

"That lowlife, Mark," he sneers. I don't even know what he's done, but I already want to kill him. "He took Indi to a fucking restaurant on the North Shore. He got upset because she didn't accept his proposal, so the mongrel abandoned her. Left her all alone in a strange place late at night. She was an absolute mess when she called me to go and get her. He's lucky I didn't damn well kill him for treating her like that."

"He fucking what?" I scoff. I can clearly hear the venom in my voice. Utter rage consumes me. My hands are trembling as I turn and walk back towards my car.

"Where are you going?" Ross asks reaching for my arm.

"To pay that prick a visit."

"There's no need. I've already done that." I thrust my arm out of his grip.

"I don't care. He's getting one from me, too."

"Hold on there, son. Don't go off all half-cocked," he pleads, coming around to block me from getting into the car. My brow furrows. "If you really want to help, go see Indi. She's been locked in her room for days."

I have to give him credit. He has a way about him. A way of calming me with a look or a few words. I guess he's trained in this type of thing. I let out a frustrated sigh. I'd love to go see her, but if she's broken-hearted over that putz, would she really want to see me? *Fuck it.* Seeing her is all I've thought about all week.

"Okay. I have something for her anyway." Opening the back door, I pull out the envelope that contains the old drawings of Larry. I went searching for them before I returned. It's not much, but it's something. Shoving the envelope under my arm, I reach for the box that's also sitting on my back seat.

"What's in the box?" he asks smirking. I open one of the flaps and show him what's inside. He chuckles and slaps me on the back. "She'll love it. You're a good guy, Carter. Don't ever doubt that." I felt compelled to get it for her. Fuck I hope she likes it.

••••

"Indi. It's Carter," I call out knocking on her bedroom door. "Can I come in?" I'm really apprehensive about seeing her. I have no idea what kind of welcome I'm going to get. The nerves kick in as I stand and wait for a reply. I'm relieved a few seconds later when she opens the door.

Her eyes are all red and swollen. She looks so broken. The sight makes my heart hurt. I've never seen her like this before. I don't like it. Where's my fiery girl gone? It makes me hate that fucker even more. I place the box and the drawings on the ground and pull her into my arms. "I'm sorry," is all I say. I'm not sorry that they broke up, but I am sorry about the way he treated her. I'm sorry that she's so hurt by it.

She cries softly into my chest as I hold her. I'm still going to pay that prick a visit, whether Ross likes it or not. "I'm glad you came back," she whispers. Relief floods through me when she says that. I was kind of expecting her to go all ninja on me again. I feel partly responsible for the predicament she's in.

Was it my plea that stopped her from saying yes?

"I told you I'd be back," I reply looking down at her. "Your dad told me what happened." She bows her head, taking a step back and wiping her eyes.

"It was for the best, I suppose. Can we not talk about it? I'd rather forget it ever happened."

"Sure." My eyes drink her in. Her hair is piled up on the top of her head in a messy bun. She's wearing a cute pink onesie that, believe it or not, looks incredibly sexy on her. She looks just like the kid I fell in love with. There's something so sweet about her. She's like nothing I've ever known. Perfect is the word that springs to mind. "Can I come in?" I ask.

"Of course." She moves to the side so I can pass. I hear a whimpering sound coming from behind me. I stop, remembering the gift. "What was that noise?"

"I bought you something." Christ I hope I did the right thing.

"You did?" A brief smile crosses her face. Bending down, I pick up the envelope that contains the drawings.

"I found these. Don't look at them now. They're some drawings I did years ago of Larry. I thought you might like to have them." Tears pool in her eyes and now I feel like a dick. It probably wasn't a good time to give them to her. She takes the envelope out of my hand, hugging it to her chest. I resist the urge to console her.

"Thank you. I'll treasure them."

"I got you something else," I say hesitantly. I'm now rethinking my decision. Bending down again, I retrieve the box. Jesus. I hope this doesn't backfire in my face. Seeing how down she is right now, this could go either way. Extending my arms, I hold it out to her. "Open the flaps." Another brief smile appears on her face as she places the envelope on her bedside table before her hands move towards the box. I lower my arms. After all she is a shrimp. She can reach the top, but won't be able to see what's inside if I don't.

I hold my breath when she looks inside. "Oh. My. God. Carter. You didn't ..." When she looks up from the box, her beautiful green eyes are brimming with tears. *Fuck.* I'm not sure if that's a good sign or not.

"Oh. My. God," she repeats.

"I hope you don't mind. I know he'll never replace ..." I can't bring myself to finish that sentence. "It was my way of trying to ... you know ... right the wrong." I'm fumbling with my words like a damn fool. I'm not good at shit like this. I don't know what to say to her. The way I see it, she tried to right the wrong that was committed against me all those years ago, and now I'm trying to return the favour. I also feel partly responsible for what happened to Larry.

Tears are streaming down her cheeks as she reaches into the box and lifts the little puppy out. I find I'm holding my breath again as I watch her. She clutches him to her chest and sobs. It warms and breaks my heart all at once. The puppy extends his neck and starts to lick her chin. Even through her tears, she giggles. "I love him," she sniffles as her eyes meet mine. "I don't know what to say, Carter. Thank you." I place the box on the ground and pull her into my arms.

"You don't have to say anything," I tell her. "I'm just happy you like him. I have all his things in the car. Food, bed, toys, leash, stuff like that. He's only six weeks old, so this is the first time he's been away from his mum."

I searched online for days until I found him. He's a cute little guy. I bought the same breed as Larry, a long-haired German Shepherd.

"Thank you. You have no idea how much I needed this. How much I needed you back here." I'm pretty sure I'm fucking beaming when she says that. She gets up on the tips of her toes and plants a small kiss on my cheek. My heart is singing. "I need to give him a name," she says making me chuckle nervously.

"No need. Going on past experience, I took the liberty of already naming him." She looks up at me again, slightly narrowing her eyes. It makes me laugh. "No offence, but you kind of suck at that."

"I do not," she replies, playfully nudging me with her shoulder.

"His name is engraved on his tag." Looking down, she grasps for the heart-shaped medal attached to the pup's collar. She starts to laugh. I feel my smile grow when she reads it out loud. *I couldn't help myself.* The name I chose is brilliant.

"Larry Junior," she laughs. "I love it, Carter. It's perfect."

••••

It took a bit of convincing, but I manage to talk Indi into having a shower and getting dressed. She needs to get out of the house. While she's getting ready, I head over to see Mum. I take Larry Junior with me. He's an awesome little guy. If she didn't want him, I definitely would've kept him for myself.

Indi and I end up going out for lunch. Nothing fancy. We go to our usual burger joint, but get the food to takeaway. Indi couldn't bear to leave the puppy at home so we brought him with us. We take Larry Junior, or LJ as he's now affectionately known, to the park for a picnic. First picnic I've ever been on, but fuck me if I didn't enjoy it. I'm realising that it doesn't matter where I am. As long as I have Indiana by my side, I'm happy.

As the day goes by, Indi becomes more like her old self. We both laugh as LJ bounces around and barks at everyone and everything. It's nice to see her happy again. She's even opened up a bit about what happened with that dick, Mark. I struggled to keep my temper at bay as she explained everything.

Not only did he leave her stranded so far from home, but he left her with the four hundred dollar restaurant bill, and basically fired her from her job. One thing is for sure, I need to get my hands on that fucker and teach him some damn manners.

She confessed he'd left a few messages on her phone the next day, but she ignored them. I'm happy about that because he showed his true colours in the end. No amount of grovelling can make up for that.

I get the impression she's upset about the breakup, but more so by the way it came about. I don't blame her. What he did was a low act. He never should've left her like that. I'm pretty confident she'll get over him quick. I'll make sure of it. If I have my way, she'll forget he even exists. For the first time in my life, I truly want this. I want her for myself. I want to own her, possess her, and be able to call her mine.

There's no talk of *us* over the course of the day, but I'm cool with that. We need to rebuild our friendship first, and she needs to get over that *wanker*. I don't want to be her rebound. If we do end up getting together, I want the timing to be right. I certainly don't want it to be when she's still hung up on someone else. It's going to be all or nothing.

After dropping her and LJ off at home later that afternoon, I head back out. I want to spend some time with my mum tonight, but there's one stop I need to make first. I'll never be able to sleep if I don't get this off my chest.

Pulling up outside the building, I take a deep breath to try and calm myself down before going inside. To be honest I'm anything but calm when I push through the door. I've been stewing on this all day.

The reception area is empty, so I make my way towards the room where I presume he'll be. I don't even bother knocking. "Oh God," he mumbles when he looks up and sees me standing in the doorway.

"Sorry, but not even God can help you now," I say stepping into the room and locking the door behind me. He swallows nervously, taking a step backwards. As much as I'd like to kick his arse right now, that's not why I came. Messing with him is much more fun.

"You ... you can't just barge in here," he stammers.

"I can do whatever the hell I like," I retort taking another step forward. He raises his hands in front of him as he retreats another step. I follow suit and take two more steps. He's cornered. The first thing I notice when I get closer is his black eye. It brings a smile to my face. The swelling's gone down, but it's a beauty. Compliments of Ross I presume. Maybe I should give him a matching one. *Fucker.* He deserves it after what he did. Anything could've happened to Indiana after he left her stranded like that.

When he realises I'm not going away, he squares his shoulders and stands tall. It doesn't intimidate me in the slightest. He can act like he's not affected by my presence, but he is. His trembling hands and the uncertainty on his face says it all. It wouldn't surprise me if he pisses his pants. *Fucking coward.*

"You owe Indiana four hundred dollars," I state in the calmest voice I can muster.

"Excuse me? I don't owe her a damn thing." I beg to differ, arsehole.

"Are you going to hand it over, or am I going to have to come and get it myself?" I take another step towards him, letting him know I mean business. He owes her a hell of a lot more than money, but it's a start. Knowing Indi like I do, she probably doesn't even want the money back, but I'm going to get it for her. After everything he's done, she should at least get reimbursed for that.

"Fine," he says as he reaches for his wallet in his back pocket. "I'll give you the money and then you can leave. If you don't, I'll call the police." I chuckle at his reply.

"You really think they're going to show up after the way you treated Indiana?" He inhales a sharp breath as the colour drains from his face. He knows I'm right. There's no way they'll be rushing over here after the way he treated Ross' little girl.

He pulls the money from his wallet and throws it on the examination table in front of him. "There, now go." I extend my hand, staring him down; I don't need to speak the words, my look says it all. His shoulders slump and his hands shake as he reaches out and picks up the money off the table. The uncertainty in his eyes as he slowly approaches me has me smirking. *Pussy.*

When he's close enough to put the money in my hand, he slaps it in my palm before taking a step backwards. I'm too quick for him though. Using my free arm, I reach out and fist my hand in his white coat, dragging him towards me.

"What were you thinking leaving her stranded at night on her own?" I seethe. "Anything could've happened to her."

"I was hurt ... angry. I didn't really think." Is that all he's got? His piss poor excuse makes my fucking blood boil. Reefing him closer, I growl in his face. "Please don't hurt me," he begs like the mother-fucking sissy he is. Shoving the money in the pocket of my jeans, I hold him in place with my other hand.

"Give me one reason why I shouldn't?"

"Because I'm sorry I left her there. I've sent her a few messages, but she didn't reply."

"You think a message is enough after what you did?"

"I'd go around and tell her to her face, but her dad said he wouldn't hesitate to put a bullet in me if I went anywhere near her." That statement has me smiling. "If I could make it up to her, I would." Like fucking hell.

"Wrong fucking answer, arsehole." Without hesitation, I raise my fist and pound it into his face. "Now you have a matching pair," I say. Fuck that felt good. He deserves a hell of a lot more after what he did to her, but I decide to give him a break. He's just lost the best thing that's ever happened to him. I've been exactly where he is right now, so I know firsthand that he's gonna regret it for the rest of his life. Letting him go, he stumbles backwards.

"My eye," he cries.

"You're lucky that's all you got. Stay the fuck away from Indiana. If you don't, next time I *won't* be so forgiving." My tone is full of warning as I turn and unlock the door and head back to my car.

EIGHT

INDIANA

I LET LJ SLEEP IN HIS DOGGY BED IN MY BEDROOM LAST NIGHT.
He's too little to sleep outside. Plus it's coming into winter, so the nights can get pretty cold. I love this little guy already. He brings back so many memories of Lassie when he was a pup, all the good ones that have been clouded by his death. I want to embrace all those wonderful memories and try and forget the horrible ones I have of that day.

For years I've wanted another dog, but I couldn't bring myself to do it. I didn't want to feel like I was replacing Lassie. I could never do that. I'm grateful that Carter took that choice away from me. He has no idea how much his beautiful, thoughtful gesture means. He can be the sweetest, gentlest, most caring man when he's not being an overbearing, infuriating arse. I can't bring myself to look at his sketches of Lassie yet, but I will in time.

I didn't see Carter again after he dropped me off yesterday afternoon, but when I was going to bed last night, he was in his bedroom. When I waved to him, he blew me a kiss. It sent my heart into a flutter. It beats the finger he used to give me.

I laid in bed for hours thinking about him being only a few metres away—just two walls and a small distance separating us. It's too soon after Mark to go there with him. I want to take it slow. I need to know he's going to stick around this time. I can't give him my heart again until I'm sure. If I did and he left me again, I know it would break me.

I'm awoken early Sunday morning by LJ's little cries. A smile graces my face as soon as I look over the side of the bed and find him sitting there looking up at me. He has the sweetest face. After taking him out back to do his business, I feed him before carrying him back into my room and climbing into bed. My headaches are still playing havoc. Some days the pain is bearable, other days not so much. I know it's all the stress I'm under. The sooner I can get my life back to normal, the better.

Surprisingly, I'm not missing Mark as much as I thought I would. I think I miss my job and the animals I cared for more. I loved working there. The hardest part for me is the way things ended between us. I gave him a year of my life and I hate that it ended so abruptly. I guess he wasn't the good guy I thought he was. That's the part I'm still trying to wrap my head around. As it turns out, the only two men I've cared about did the same thing; walked away from me, and everything we shared, without a backwards glance. I can tell you that's a huge knock to the ego. You think you know someone, then *boom*, you realise you don't know them at all.

A little later, I'm pulled from my sleep by the sound of a lawn-mower. Looking over at the clock on my bedside table, I notice it's 10:30am. It's not like me to sleep in this late. Rising, I rub my eyes as I make my way towards the window. That's when I see him. Holy hell. *Swoon.* I say a silent prayer to the sun gods for blessing us with a reasonably warm day for this time of year. Carter is in the back yard mowing his mum's lawn, shirtless. I swear I lick my lips as my eyes take him in. What a sight to behold.

His body is even more muscular and defined then I remember. He's wearing a pair of faded denim jeans that are ripped at the knees. *So sexy.* They hang low on his waist, revealing his delicious V and the band of his boxer briefs. Don't even get me started on those tattoos of his. What I wouldn't give to run my hands over every inch of his body again. I remember all too well what his hard, toned muscles felt like against my fingertips.

I stand there staring for the longest time. I can't seem to drag my eyes away from him. I'm pulled from my thoughts when LJ whimpers at my feet. Picking him up, I run my hand over his fur. "I'm just checking out your daddy," I whisper. "Shhh. Don't tell him." He cocks his head to the side, staring up at me with his big brown eyes. It brings a smile to my face. "He looks mighty fine without a shirt. *Mighty fine,*" I murmur. I turn LJ's face in the direction of Carter, and he lets out a cute little bark when he sees him.

After peeling myself away from the window, I take LJ out back again before jumping in the shower. Having Carter home makes me feel invigorated. I no longer want to be locked away in my room. I want to be outside, or wherever he is.

••••

I may have made a little effort in my appearance this morning, but after the hot mess Carter found me in yesterday, I find myself wanting to look nice for him. I'm only wearing a white top with a pair of black tight jeans and my black long boots. But I took extra time with my hair and even added a touch of makeup to my face.

When I'm done, I head into the kitchen to get a cold drink for Carter out of the fridge. I can still hear the mower, so I know he's still out there. "You look pretty today, Pumpkin," my dad says looking up from the paper he's reading at the kitchen table.

"Thanks, Daddy. I thought I'd take a cold drink over to Carter."

"That's nice," he says smiling at me. "Oh here. This is for you." He picks up an envelope off the table and passes it to me.

"What is it?" I ask.

"I believe it's the money that dick owes you from the restaurant."

"What? How did you get it?" I ask, annoyance lining my voice.

"Does it really matter how? Just be thankful you got it back," he says angrily. I can tell by his tone he's far from over what happened. I thought he was going to burst an artery when he picked me up from the restaurant after Mark left me behind. I've never seen him so mad. He wanted to head straight over to his place, but I begged him not to. Beating him up wasn't going to solve anything.

"Did you go and see him?" I ask frowning. I specifically asked him not to. He ignores my question. "Daddy, what did you do?"

"I didn't do anything," he says looking back down at his paper. Did nothing my arse. I know Mark. He wouldn't just hand it over. His family is very well off, but as tight as you can get. They don't part with money easily. I open my mouth to say something, but my father raises his hand to stop me. "Just drop it, Indiana. Why don't you go and give Carter that drink. I'm sure he'd be grateful for it." I know, when my father says that, the conversation is over. Ugh! *Men.*

After putting LJ on his leash, I walk down the side of the house and out the front. That's where Carter's moved to. LJ pulls back on his leash as we approach. I guess the loud noise of the mower is frightening for him. Bending down I pick him up, cuddling him into my side so he feels safe.

When Carter looks up and notices me approaching, he smiles. Reaching for the lever, he shuts down the mower. "Hey," he says as I walk toward him.

"Hey. I heard the mower. I thought you might like a cold drink." I hold up the can of Coke in my hand.

"Thanks," he says, taking it with one hand and wiping the sweat off his brow with the other. The shimmer of perspiration covering his delicious body only seems to enhance his muscle tone. My eyes travel down to his chest. That's when I notice one of his nipples is pierced. *Holy cow.* I find myself wanting to lean forward and swirl my tongue around it. "Hey, my eyes are up here," he says with a chuckle. I feel my face flush when I make eye contact with him again. They're the same words I used on him when he was checking out my tits that day.

"Sorry," I say as embarrassment consumes me.

"Don't be. I like that you find me irresistible."

"I do not," I scoff, screwing up my face.

"Deny it all you want, beautiful, but you and I both know the truth." I don't bother responding because he'll only have another smart comeback. Besides, he's right. *Plus he called me beautiful.* It's been a long time since I've heard him say that to me. "You're looking rather fine today. Did you go to all that effort just for me?" He smirks and then winks. "I'm touched." God he's a cocky arse.

"No," I screech. Even though the answer is yes. LJ barks in my arms, and it's only then that Carter realises that I'm holding him.

"How's our little boy today?" he asks, reaching out and ruffling the fur on the top of his head. The fact he referred to him as ours makes me smile. "Did he sleep okay?"

"He did. I put him in my room last night." His eyes look up from the dog and lock with mine.

"He got to sleep in your room? Lucky bugger. Maybe I should've climbed in the box yesterday, then I could've slept in your room, too."

"Ha ha. Nice try," I laugh.

"Well you've got to give me ten points for trying," he chuckles. "So, what are your plans today? Do you have any?" I shrug.

"Not really."

"Wanna do something with me? I'm nearly done here."

"Like what?" I ask sceptically. I can never tell with Carter.

"We could go for a drive, or to the movies."

"The movies? Have you ever been to the movies?" I ask surprised. It doesn't seem like his thing.

"No, but there's always a first." I smile. I love that he wants to spend time with me and is willing to suggest anything so he can.

"Can I pick what we watch?"

"As long as it's not some sissy-arse movie, then yes," he replies.

"Okay." He smiles at my response. It makes my heart race. I have no idea where this thing with us is going, but God I hope it goes somewhere.

"Give me an hour. I need to finish up here and then have a shower."

"Alright. I'm gonna take LJ for a walk. Come get me when you're ready." After placing LJ down, I walk across the lawn towards the sidewalk. Turning my head, I take one last glance at Carter over my shoulder. He's standing there watching me. I give him a smile and he winks at me. It sends my stomach into a flutter. God, he's sex on legs.

••••

"How's your mum going?" I ask him on the drive into town. He shrugs. I need the distraction because all I can think of is all the bad things I'd like to do to him. Like run my tongue over every inch of him. For some reason he's always brought out my wild side. He's freshly showered and smells divine which doesn't help matters. I could seriously drown in his scent.

"Okay, I guess. Your dad's been great. I'm thankful for everything he's been doing."

"I like that they're becoming friends," I tell him as I turn my head in his direction. He has such a beautiful profile. While his eyes are firmly planted on the road ahead, I use this time to look over his handsome face. "They both have the loss of a spouse in common. Hopefully having each other will do them some good," I add. Well that's my hope. His eyes briefly leave the road and look my way. Why does a simple look from him turn me on?

Elizabeth will be good for him. It's been sixteen years since my mum died. My dad still locks himself away on her anniversary and birthday. He's never dated anyone since her death. I know he loved her, but he needs to move on. Live again. I'm sure my mum would've wanted that for him.

Carter opens my door and helps me out of the car when we arrive at the movies. We originally planned to have lunch beforehand, but as it turns out we don't have time. "We can go eat afterwards," Carter says as we line up for tickets.

"Okay." I smile up at him when he places his hand on the small of my back as the line moves forward. I still can't believe we're here together. "Are you gonna get some popcorn?" I ask.

"Do you want popcorn?"

"Hell yeah. You can't watch a movie without popcorn. It's unethical." He throws back his head and laughs.

"If you say so. You'll need to get me up to speed on the ethics of movie watching then. This is my first time remember." After we grab the tickets, popcorn, and a large Coke, we head towards the cinemas.

"I can't believe I'm popping your movie cherry," I tell him as we walk along. He looks down at me and grins.

"Well I popped your cherry, so I guess it's only fair you get to pop one of mine." I swear my eyes must be bugging out of my head when what he says registers. He did not just say that! I feel my face flush. Leaning towards me, he whispers in a husky voice, "I love it when you blush like that. It turns me on like you wouldn't believe." Oh God. I'm positive my face is as red as the cup he's holding in his hand. He flicks out his elbow and nudges me. "Don't go all shy on me now, beautiful. I'm just messing with you." Some things never change. I see exactly how much enjoyment he gets out of messing with me.

Bastard.

Following him up the stairs towards the seats, I ask, "How far up are we going?"

"Back row."

"I don't think so," I say as I tug on his arm to stop. "Just here is fine."

"Why don't you want to sit in the back row?" He's kidding right? "Don't you trust me to behave myself?" He gives me a look like butter wouldn't melt in his mouth. Nice try. I know for a fact it would sizzle.

"I don't think you know how to behave," I laugh.

"I resent that remark," he says mocking fake hurt. He knows damn well I'm right. His next comment just confirms it. "Do you really think sitting here is going to stop me from misbehaving? Because you know as well as I do, it won't." Although his words make me want to clench my thighs together, I swallow nervously.

The predatory look in his eyes as I pass him to take my seat has my insides doing flip-flops. I know I'm not ready for anything like that yet, but in saying that, I know I wouldn't be able to stop if he tried. I remember all too well just how good he made me feel all those years ago.

I can't tell you how many times I'd wished Mark could make me feel even a fraction of what Carter used to, but sadly he never did. I shouldn't even compare them, but after being with Carter it's pretty hard not to.

Carter sits beside me, placing the popcorn on my lap. "Thank you," I say looking straight ahead. The intense look on his face just now has made me nervous for some reason. I can't bring myself to make eye contact with him. It has me feeling apprehensive about agreeing to come. For my heart's sake, I need time. I need to be sure this is going to work before it goes any further.

"Relax," he says nudging me with his elbow. "You're lucky I'm in a behaving mood." My eyes dart to him and I find him smiling. It's sweet and reassuring, but I still have my doubts. I can't help but roll my eyes. This is Carter Reynolds we're talking about. I pick up a piece of popcorn and pop it into my mouth, relaxing back into my seat. We'll just see about that.

The movie I chose to watch is Fast and Furious. It's the seventh movie in the franchise. He gets to drool over the cars, and I get to check out the hot guys. Although I already know they won't compare with the one sitting next to me. I haven't seen the first six movies, but he was kind enough to bring me here, so the least I could do is pick something he might enjoy.

We sit in silence waiting for the movie to start. Sure enough, a few minutes in and his antics start. *Behaving mood my arse.* He's trying to act inconspicuous, but I see straight through him. Every time I reach into grab some popcorn, he does as well. His fingers always brushing against mine. It sends tingles up my arm each and every time. When I look at him, his head is forward focussing on the movie, but the smirk on his face tells me it's intentional.

I watch as he takes a sip of the soda before offering it to me. My eyes move from the cup back up to him. This salty popcorn is making me thirsty, but I'm not a fan of sharing drinks. Never have been.

"What? I don't have cooties," he says pushing the cup my way.

"That's debatable," I retort, raising an eyebrow.

"I don't." The tone of his voice makes me believe he's offended. Of course I know better. Carter doesn't offend easy. He leans forward into my space. "If I recall, you've had your tongue down my throat. Actually, now that I think about it, you've had my cock in your mouth. You didn't keel over and die, so take a fucking sip," he says shoving the drink towards my hand. My eyes widen. I can't believe he just said that. My head turns towards the people sitting behind us. I hope they didn't overhear.

"Fine," I snap, snatching it out of his hand. He smiles when I wrap my mouth around the straw.

"See, no cooties," he says when I pass it back to him. It makes me giggle.

"It's early days," I whisper, leaning towards him. "I'm sure cooties isn't an instant death." He playfully bumps me with his elbow.

"Again, I resent that remark." His comment makes me laugh.

A few minutes later, his antics continue. Picking up a piece of popcorn, my hand moves towards my mouth when Carter's fingers suddenly wrap around my wrist, stopping me midair. My eyes immediately move to his as he gives me a mischievous smile. Tugging on my arm, I watch on in horror as he pulls my hand towards his mouth. His eyes are locked with mine as his lips slowly close over my fingers and he sucks the popcorn out of my grip. When his tongue darts out and he seductively licks the salt off my skin, I inhale a sharp breath and clench my thighs together as desire sweeps through me. I recall with ease how magical that mouth of his feels. Releasing his grip on my wrist, he licks his lips.

"Delicious," he breathes. *Far out.* He has me so turned on right now. Ugh! I'm sure that's his plan.

I find myself stealing glances at him as we watch the movie. He's so gorgeous. He seems to be enjoying it. I've caught him laughing a few times. It brought a smile to my face. Seeing him happy does something to me. I can't explain it. He's come so far in the last five years. He's nothing like the troubled teen I knew all those years ago. He seems to show more of the real Carter these days. You have no idea how that makes me feel.

I'm surprised that apart from the popcorn incident, he now actually seems to be behaving. About halfway through the movie, that changes. I see him watching me out of the corner of my eye. Pretending I don't notice, I keep my focus trained on the screen ahead. Then he goes and does one of those fake-arse yawns. You know, those lame ones you see in the movies. The ones that have the guy yawning with their arms stretched wide, before slyly wrapping it around the girl's shoulder.

"You did not just try that lame move on me," I laugh.

"What? I yawned," he says giving me a sheepish grin. He doesn't fool me for a minute. "Ain't a guy allowed to yawn these days without the girl getting the wrong idea?"

"You're such a nerd sometimes," I say throwing a piece of popcorn at him. He picks it up off his shirt and pops it in his mouth.

"That may be true, but the nerd always gets the girl in the end." He winks at me before looking back at the screen. Of course he doesn't remove his arm. Giving up, I rest my head on his shoulder and he pulls me in closer. When my eyes look up at his face, he's smiling. It has me doing the same. I love being in his arms. I've really missed it.

NINE

CARTER

TODAY'S GONE BETTER THAN I EXPECTED. GOING TO THE movies is not something I thought I'd ever do, well not as an adult anyway. When I was a kid, that's a different story. Unfortunately, back then my mum could never afford to take me.

I offered to take Indi because I thought she'd like it. Girls like that shit don't they? I've never dated before so this is all new to me. I just wanted us to be together. To spend time with her any way I could.

Surprisingly, I actually enjoyed the movie we watched. I was sure she was going to pick some sappy chick flick, but she did good. Real good. My highlight though, was *her*.

After we left the cinema, I casually slipped my hand into hers, lacing our fingers together. She didn't seem to mind, which pleased me more than I care to admit. Whenever I'm near her, I have an overwhelming desire to have my hands on her. I know we're taking it slow, but a touch here or there isn't too much. I can tell by the way she reacts to my slightest touch that she can feel this thing, whatever the fuck it is. It's still as strong as ever. Given half the chance, we could be explosive together. I know it.

We walked a few blocks until we found a nice restaurant, laughing and talking about the movie as we did. This is the closest I've ever come to being on a real date. But fuck me if I don't want to experience all that with Indiana. I get a buzz whenever I'm with her. It's electric. She makes me feel alive. When we were kids, the feelings she evoked within me freaked me the hell out, but now I embrace them. I need them. I crave them. Crave her. I've denied myself for too long.

Later that afternoon, Ross invited my mum and me over for a barbeque. Having the three most important people in my life together is a great feeling. Is it wrong that I wish we were a family, because I do? I wish Ross was my father, but more than anything, I wish Indiana was my girl. I guess if I eventually get her, I'll get him by default.

I'm gonna try my damned hardest to make that happen.

••••

It was late by the time mum and I arrived back home last night. I'd planned to drive back to Newcastle, but decided to leave early this morning instead. I was enjoying my time with them too much. I didn't want it to end. It's been a long time since I've felt like part of a family. My mum even seemed happier than she has since Fuckwit died. There were no tears, and even a few smiles.

Ross and Indi both walked us out, so I never got to say the proper goodbye I would've liked. She knows I'm going back home again, but I promised her I'd return at the end of the week.

It's 5:00am when I throw my bag in the car. I need to get on the road before the traffic gets too bad. Peak hour is a real bitch. I'll never get back in time to open the shop by 8:30am if I don't leave soon.

I've looked over in the direction of Indiana's bedroom a dozen times since waking, hoping to see her light on. I'm silently willing her to wake up. I need to see her one more time before I go. It's going to be five long days before I'm back. I exhale when I open the driver's side door. Her room is still bathed in darkness. I continue to stand there staring. *Fuck it.* I gotta see her.

Jogging over to her window, I tap lightly. "Indi. Indi. Are you awake?" I hear LJ bark from inside her room. I know that will wake her. *Good boy.* I need to bring him back a huge motherfucking steak when I return. Her light comes on so I tap again. "Indi. It's me, Carter."

"Carter. What are you doing? It's 5:00am," she says in a sexy-as-fuck sleepy voice that has my cock stirring. It takes every ounce of control I have not to jump through that window and have my way with her. She rubs her eyes and squints as she tries to adjust to the light. She looks so fucking sweet when she just wakes up. Her hair is all over the place, but fuck me if she isn't the most beautiful thing I've ever seen.

"I know. Sorry. I just wanted to see you again before I left." She smiles when I say that. "Can I get your number, if that's okay? I'd like to call you during the week."

"You would?" Her face lights up like she's surprised that I'd want to. Doesn't she realise how hard these five days away from her are going to be for me?

"I'm going to miss you," I tell her. Because I am.

"I'm going to miss you, too." Now I'm the one smiling like a fool. When she starts rattling off her number, I pull my phone out so I can program it in.

"I'll call you, alright," I say sliding the phone back into my pocket.

"Okay. Drive carefully."

"I will." I stand there looking up at her. Why is it so hard for me to walk away? "I'm sorry I woke you."

"I'm glad you did." My eyes drift from hers down to her lips. I want to kiss her so fucking bad, but I'm not sure if she'd want that. *Fuck it.* I'll never know if I don't try. Reaching up, I cup her face in my hands. *I'm going in.*

Gently, I pull her face forward until her lips meet mine. I give her a soft, sweet kiss. Not the kind I'd like to give, but anything more than this and I'll never leave. When I pull away, I rest my forehead against hers.

"I'll be back Friday night."

"I look forward to it," she whispers.

"Go back to sleep."

"Okay," she breathes as she straightens, reaching for the window.

"Bye, beautiful."

"Bye, Carter."

I'm smiling as I walk back towards my car. I swear there's even a spring in my step that wasn't there previously. Taking out my phone, I send her a quick text.

Dream of me ...

Her reply makes me laugh.

You wish. x

•••••

For the next few days she's on my mind night and day. Even though I'd like to, I refrain from calling her every fucking hour. I manage to limit it to one text in the morning and a call each night. Monday night we talked for nearly an hour. It's amazing how much you can learn about someone when you sit down and have a full-on conversation with them.

I still give her a hard time whenever I can. I'm not sure I'll ever tire of riling her up. It's too much fun. She gives as good as she gets. I love that about her. She's really opened up to me over the past few nights, and I have with her. It's all the silly insignificant things I'm learning about her that I love most.

Like how she prefers savoury food over sweets. *That's because she's already plenty sweet enough.* She has a vast taste in music. Her favourite colour is pink. When she was little she wanted to grow up to be a fireman or a princess. She's wanted a horse since she was four years old. All the little things that make her, her. That make her special.

Last night we talked for nearly three hours until Indi eventually fell asleep with the phone next to her ear. I stayed on the line for ages afterwards, just listening to her breathe like some crazy-arse stalker. I don't know why I torture myself like that. It only made me want to climb through the phone and hold her in my arms.

What's she fucking doing to me?

I shook my head with disgust when I finally ended the call and headed into the bathroom for a cold shower. I haven't even looked at another girl since I first went back home for the funeral. My eyes are only for her. She's under my skin again, but this time I'm afraid it's for good. *Fuck me.* I may as well cut my damn balls off and mail them to her.

••••

One more sleep. I sound like a fucking kid. It's Thursday and all I can think about is tomorrow we'll be together again. I've been wishing the days away all week. Not only for the weekend to roll around, but for the nights to come so I can call her.

After finishing off a job, I look at the time on my phone. 1:00pm. I was running late this morning so I didn't get time for breakfast. My receptionist, Justine, got me a coffee on her way to work. She always does that. She's a good kid.

There's a twenty-minute break before my next job so I decide to head out to get some lunch. I need some fucking food. "I'm getting something to eat," I tell Justine as I walk past the front desk. I'm not even out the door and my phone rings. Ross' name lights up my screen. *Fuck.* Why would he be calling me in the middle of the day? My heart is beating out of my chest when I answer the call. My first thought is something is wrong with Indi or my mum.

"Hey, Ross. Is everything okay?" I ask before he has the chance to speak.

"That's why I'm calling you. I'm not sure, son. Has Indi mentioned anything to you about the headaches she's been getting?"

"What? No. Why?" This is the first time I'm hearing about it.

"She's been getting a lot lately. She didn't tell me, but I've noticed she's been lying down a lot during the day. That's not like her. This morning I confronted her. Apparently she's been getting them for the past two weeks."

"She hasn't said a word." Sure I'm not happy about it, but she's been going through a lot lately, so I don't think much of it. "I'm sure it's nothing, Ross. It's probably just stress."

"That's what she said. I'm worried, Carter. She won't go to the doctor. She's so damn stubborn sometimes." You can clearly hear the frustration in his voice. "I was hoping you could talk to her."

"If it was anything serious, I'm sure she'd go and see about it," I say trying to reassure him, or maybe myself.

"I don't think you understand, Carter. This is exactly how things started with Isabella."

"Hold on," I say. He's lost me. "Who's Isabella?"

"My wife. Indiana's mother." My heart drops into the pit of my stomach. Now it all makes sense. She died of a brain tumour. *Oh fuck, does he think Indi has a tumour?* When my knees buckle beneath me, I place my hand against the wall in front of me to hold myself up. "Carter. Are you still there?"

"Yes. She needs to go and see about it straight away," I blurt out in a panic.

"I've tried to make her. She won't listen. I even lost my temper with her this morning. I've never screamed at her before. *Never.* Carter, I can't lose her too," he pleads. When his voice cracks it feels like a knife is being plunged into my heart. The thought of losing her is unfathomable.

"Leave it with me," is all I say as I end the call. I feel like the wind has been knocked out of me. My shoulders slump and my hands fist in my hair as I exhale a huge breath. This can't be fucking happening. When I'm steady on my feet again, I turn to face Justine. "Cancel all my appointments for the rest of the week."

"Are you okay? You don't look so good."

"I've gotta go," I say as I turn and push through the door.

Fuck. I think I'm gonna be sick.

TEN

INDIANA

I'M HIDING OUT IN MY ROOM AWAY FROM MY DAD WHEN Carter comes barrelling through my door. Have I got my days mixed up? I thought he wasn't coming back until tomorrow night. The look on his face tells me he's not happy. He stalks towards me without uttering a word. Suddenly, I'm lifted from my bed and slung over his shoulder in one swift motion.

"Carter! What the hell?" Has he lost his damn mind?

"If I was you, I'd keep that trap of yours shut. I'm in no need for your bullshit," he snaps as his hand comes down hard on my arse. Ouch.

"What the fuck is your problem? Put me the hell down, arsehole." All the blood is rushing to my head making it throb.

"Zip it," he says as he storms through the kitchen heading towards the front door. I'm upside down, but I can clearly see the smile on my father's face as I pass.

"Daddy, help me. He's lost his mind," I scream.

"Sorry, Pumpkin. Can't do that. It's for the best." *What*? Next thing I know, I'm being seated in the passenger side of Carter's car. Immediately I try to get back out. I'm not going anywhere with this crazy-arse bastard.

"Don't even think about it," he growls, giving me a look that instantly has me recoiling in the seat. He reaches for the seatbelt and leans over me, clicking it into place. "If you try and escape you'll be sorry." He locks the passenger side door before stalking around to the driver's side. All the while my dad stands on the front porch with a grin on his face. I pinch myself. This has to be a nightmare. *Ouch.* Nope I'm awake.

"Where are you taking me?" I ask when he's seated in the car. His angry eyes meet mine.

"Where do you think? To the fucking doctors." Oh hell fucking no. Christ, my dad must've called him. *Traitor.* How could he?

"You can't make me go," I say reaching for the buckle of my seatbelt.

"I can and I will," he replies grabbing my hand to stop me. Tears burn my eyes. I'm not sure if it's from anger because he's forcing me to do this, or from fear. I have no interest in hearing what the doctor has to say. None whatsoever.

"You can't force me to do this," I sneer through gritted teeth.

"I've got news for you, sweetheart. I can, and I fucking will."

"This is kidnapping." If this fucker didn't just snatch me from my bed without giving me the chance to grab my purse or my phone, I'd be calling triple zero right now.

"Kidnapping," he chuckles like some evil psychopath. "Your father's a police officer and he doesn't see it that way." His head snaps in my direction when I reach for the door handle. He looks at my hand before making eye contact with me. One of his evil eyebrows raise as he gives me a warning look that say's, *don't try me.*

"I can't believe you two," I snap letting go of the door and crossing my arms over my chest like a spoilt child. Talk about overreacting. It's a damn headache. I exhale an exasperated breath as he starts the car and backs out of the driveway. "I hate you right now." His brow furrows and his grip on the steering wheel tightens making his knuckles turn white, but he chooses to ignore my comment.

No words are spoken on the drive to the doctor's surgery. I'm pissed that they're making me go. When he parks the car, he gets out. Crossing my arms over my chest in protest, I don't move. He walks around to my side of the car and opens the door. "Get out," he demands.

"Make me." He sighs before bending over and undoing my seatbelt.

"Have it your way," he growls before lifting me out of the car and slinging me over his shoulder again.

"Put me down, arsehole. I'll walk." I'm mortified that he's going to carry me inside.

"Nope. You had your chance."

"You suck," I tell him as I slap his back like a brat. I don't want to be here. I don't want to hear what the doctor has to say. I suddenly understand how my mum felt when she was faced with this. Tears of frustration rise to my eyes. Sometimes it's better off not knowing the truth. In my heart I know what he's going to say. I've had my headache for over two weeks. At first I thought it was stress, but when things settled down and they still didn't go away, I started to have my doubts. Although it worried me, I pushed all my concerns to the back of my mind. I refused to believe it was anything but a simple headache. Even though logic told me it was more.

This morning when I confessed to my dad the reason why I've been lying down so much, not only did the colour completely drain from his face, but he had to reach out and grab hold of the table because his legs threatened to give out from underneath him. I knew in my heart my concerns were founded. I'm only twenty-two years old. I haven't even experienced all that life has to offer.

I don't want to die.

••••

An hour later we leave the doctor's surgery. It's safe to say my stomach is in knots. I have to fast from midnight tonight and be at the hospital by 8:00am tomorrow for a blood test and a CT scan. The doctor seemed quite concerned by the duration of my headaches and, of course, my family history. He called the hospital before we left to arrange my appointments for the morning. Dread fills me when I think about everything I'm going to have to face tomorrow.

We're both silent on the drive home. Carter held my hand from the minute we entered the doctor's room and didn't let go until we left. He has no idea what having him by my side means. I'm still angry that he brought me here against my will, but I understand why he did. I'm grateful that he cares enough to make me come.

"How you feeling?" he asks when we pull into the driveway. I shrug. Numb would be the best word I guess. "It's going to be okay," he says reaching over the centre console and squeezing my leg. I appreciate the sentiment behind his words, but is it going to be okay? Am I going to end up another statistic, just like my mum? Tears burn my eyes when I think of what this is going to do to my dad.

"I need to go and talk to my dad," I say, my voice cracking. I remove my seatbelt and reach for the handle on the door. "Thanks for forcing me to go against my will, I guess." What else can I say to him? This is exactly why I didn't want to go in the first place.

I don't want to know.

Carter removes his seatbelt and quickly exits the car. Before I know it, he's opening the passenger side door and pulling me into his arms. He squeezes me so damn tight I think I'm going to bust. When he eventually lets go, he cups my face in his hands. The look I see in his eyes is almost my undoing. I can't break down in front of him. He'll think I'm weak.

"Whatever happens tomorrow, I promise you we'll get through it together." That's all it takes for the dam to burst. Shit. I've been trying to keep my emotions at bay since we left the doctors. I inhale a large breath to force the tears back down, but as I do, an ugly sob escapes me. "Fuck," he says as he engulfs me in his arms again, pinning the side of my face against his chest with his hand. I hear the erratic beat of his heart as his body trembles against mine.

••••

Carter is on my doorstep at 7:00am. I never asked him to come with me this morning, but I guess he's invited himself. My dad didn't take the news too well last night. Carter insisted that he come with me to break it to him, but I felt it was something I needed to do alone. I hate that my dad has to go through this all over again.

When his shoulders slumped and he buried his face in his hands and cried, it broke my heart. That was when I realised I need to fight this with everything I have. I need to be strong for him. No matter how I'm feeling on the inside, no matter what the outcome of the tests, I have to put my big girl panties on and deal with it the best way I can.

"You don't have to come with us this morning," I tell Carter when I answer the door. "My dad has taken the next few days off work to be with me."

"Well tough, I'm coming as well. For both of you," he says as he pushes his way past me and enters the house. His pigheadedness should piss me off, but it doesn't. I find myself smiling at his retreating back as he walks down the hall towards the kitchen. I may or may not be in for the fight of my life, but it's good to know if I am, I'm not alone.

ELEVEN

CARTER

ONCE ALL THE TESTS ARE COMPLETED, WE HAVE TO WAIT TWO
agonising hours for the results. After Indi's mini breakdown when we
arrived home from the doctors yesterday, I was worried how she'd
cope today, but she's been a real champ. I'm proud of her. Surprisingly,
I'd say she's faring the best out of the three of us.

Her dad has been quiet since I arrived at their house this morning.
He's barely said a word. When she was taken in for her tests, he paced
the corridor until she came back out. It tore at my fucking heart. I can
only imagine what this must be like for him. Indi's all he has left.

As we sit here waiting to hear her fate, my stomach is churning.
Ross' leg is bouncing up and down nervously, and Indiana is sitting
there as cool as a fucking cucumber. That both astounds and worries
me. Fuck I pray we get good results.

"The doctor will see you now, Ms. Montgomery," the nurse says
appearing in front of us.

"Good luck, Pumpkin," Ross says grasping her hand and giving it a squeeze.

"Everything is going to be okay, Daddy," she replies smiling. Now I understand why she's been acting so calm today. She's doing it for her dad.

"This way," the nurse says gesturing with her hand for Indiana to follow. We both stand at the same time.

"I've got this, Carter," Indi says, turning her head in my direction. "I've already discussed this with my dad. I'm going in to get the results alone."

"You discussed it with him, not me. I'm coming whether you like it or not," I snap. She's not fucking doing this alone.

"Or not," she says narrowing her eyes at me. It brings a smile to my face. I reach for her hand and lace my fingers through hers.

"We're doing it together. End. Of. Story." She tries to pull her hand from mine, but I tighten my grip. *I don't think so.* When she realises I have no intentions of letting go, she sighs.

"Fine, you stubborn arse," she mumbles, making me chuckle.

"Takes one to know one," I whisper in her ear as I follow her into the doctor's room. She pinches my hand spitefully and I smile. I love her spunk.

"Take a seat," the doctor says when we enter. "I'm Doctor Emmerson, the oncologist here at the hospital." After the introductions, we're seated. My eyes drift to Indiana. From the outside she looks so calm. Reaching over, I grasp her tiny hand in mine again. When I feel it trembling, I know she's anything but. It tugs at my heart. *Please let her be okay.* "I have your results back," he says, the passive look on his face giving nothing away. Fuck doctors and their poker faces. At least if his expression gave a hint of what was to come, I could prepare myself. Then he goes and says the exact words I've been dreading. "Indiana, I'm sorry …" That's all I hear as the rest of the words are drowned out by the thumping of my heart. I feel Indiana's grip on my hand tighten.

Noooooo! This can't be fucking happening.

••••

Our sombre faces say it all. *Devastation*. I offered to drive Ross' car home from the hospital. He was in no state to get behind the wheel. I listen intently as Indiana recounts everything the doctor told her. Everything I missed as my world around me crumbled.

She has a tumour. On a positive note it's small. The doctor's pretty confident *if* they find no other cancers, six weeks of radiation therapy may be all she needs. He assured her it's the best solution for her particular diagnosis. It cuts out all the unnecessary risks associated with brain surgery.

Ross doesn't respond to anything Indi says. I glance at him in the rear view mirror, and the pain, shock, and disbelief that this is happening again, is plain to see. He's usually so tough, so put together. It brings a lump to my throat. To find out your only child has the same disease that killed your wife would be a pretty hard pill to swallow.

"Everything is going to be okay, Dad," she says turning and reaching for his hand in the back seat. I'm in fucking awe of her. She's just been told she has a tumour on her brain, and she's the one comforting and reassuring him. She's the one who's being positive and optimistic when it's plain to see he's consumed with doubt. "The doctor even said that medicine has come so far since Mum's diagnosis all those years ago. Plus, we found it early. Hers came years after the symptoms started."

Every word she speaks has a calming effect on my aching heart. I'm devastated that this is happening. I'd give anything to change her situation. I don't want to lose her before I've even got her back, because over the past few weeks I've realised that my life without her in it, is unimaginable. She completes me.

She sounds so confident, so sure of herself. If she thinks she's got this, then fuck me she has. Who am I to rain on her parade? Her positivity is inspiring and may be just what she needs to beat this motherfucking tumour.

She has to go back to the hospital on Monday for an MRI. The doctor wants to make certain that the cancer is confined to her brain, that there's no secondary cancer present in her body. If there isn't, he gives her as high as an eighty percent chance of survival. I'm fucking stoked about that. I'd rather a hundred percent, but if eighty is the best he can give then so be it. They're pretty good fucking odds. I'd be lying if I said that twenty percent didn't scare the living shit out of me though.

Now we just have to pray the tumour is confined.

When we arrive back at the house, the three of us go inside. Ross heads straight for the fridge and grabs a beer. "Want one?" he asks me.

"Sure." Alcohol is not the answer I guess, but I think in this situation it's needed.

"Would you guys mind if I had a lie down? I didn't get much sleep last night. I'm tired," Indi asks.

"Of course not, Pumpkin," her father says as he walks towards her and wraps her in his arms. "I'm sorry I haven't been very supportive today, it's just ..."

"Shhhh, Daddy. You have nothing to be sorry about," she replies sliding her arms around his waist. "I love you. I know this is hard for you, but it's going to be okay."

"I love you too, baby girl," he says leaning down to kiss the top of her head before letting her go. She takes a step back and looks over at me.

"Thanks for coming today, Carter. It meant a lot to me."

"Don't sweat it," I reply, the corners of my mouth turning up briefly. My heart feels so heavy. "I'll be with you every step of the way." And I will be, whether she wants that or not. She smiles, but it doesn't quite reach her eyes. For a split second she almost looks like she's going to cry, but she recovers quickly. It makes me wonder. Maybe she's not faring as well as she's making out. I can't blame her. I'm not sure I would be, if I was in her predicament.

I continue to sit at the kitchen table with Ross while he drinks himself into oblivion. To be honest I feel like doing the same, but I don't. What good is that going to do? It's not going to fix anything. Instead, I choose to be his rock. The one he's been for me for the past five years.

The hours pass and Indiana doesn't re-emerge from her room. Everything in me wants to go to her. To make sure she's alright. "I can't go through this again," Ross says suddenly, his voice cracking. He buries his face in his hands, and I can tell he's on the verge of a breakdown. I feel for him, I do, but he needs to pull himself together. His daughter needs all the support she can get right now.

"Look at me, Ross." He raises his head and his glassy eyes meet mine. "You can, and you will. She's your daughter. It sucks, I know, but you've gotta get your shit together, mate. She needs you."

"I know ... I know," he says shaking his head. I've never seen him like this before. "She's my baby girl. She's all I've got." He looks up at me, his eyes brimming with tears. "I don't think I could go on if I lost her too."

I get up from my chair and make my way around to his side of the table. He's had enough to drink. "Come on," I say placing my hands under his arms and helping him up. He stumbles, but finds his feet. "I think you need to lie down."

"Maybe you're right," he slurs. "I'm glad you're back, son. You're just what my girl needs." His words make me smile. I love that he thinks I'm good enough for her, even though I still have my doubts if I am. I guide him towards his bedroom before laying him down on the bed. As I remove his shoes and pull the blanket over him, he closes his eyes.

"I'll see you tomorrow," I tell him as I turn to leave.

"Carter."

"Yeah." I stop, looking at him over my shoulder. His eyes remain closed.

"I love you like you were one of my own," he mumbles. I feel the corners of my mouth turn up. I can't tell you what it means to hear him say that. I stand there briefly watching him. He's the closest thing to a father I've got. Before I get a chance to reply, he lets out a loud snore. I shake my head and chuckle. Fuck me if I don't love him too.

I gently close his bedroom door as I leave. As I head down the hall towards the front door, I stop. I feel compelled to check on Indi before

I go. Turning, I head back down the hall towards her room. I raise my hand to knock, but I pull back. If she's asleep, I don't want to wake her. She needs her rest.

Reaching for the handle I quietly open the door, trying not to make a noise. I'll look in on her then leave. I smile when I see her lying on her bed, her back to me. What I wouldn't give to be beside her right now. As I turn to leave, I hear a sniffle. Is she crying? I see her hand come up to wipe her face. Fuck, she is.

"Indi," I say as I take a step towards her bed. She turns her head and looks at me over her shoulder. Her eyes are red and puffy. She looks so sad. It breaks my fucking heart. I don't hesitate. Kicking off my shoes, I climb into the bed beside her. No words are spoken as I pull her towards me and wrap her in my arms. She slides her arm around my waist, crying softly into my chest. Tears rise to my eyes as I tighten my hold. The enormity of today and what lies ahead, finally hits home.

It makes me hate myself even more. Why couldn't I have had my shit together all those years ago? We've waisted so much time. One thing is for sure. I'll be beside her every step of the way from now on. I'll cherish every second of our time together. However long that may be.

Losing her to this isn't an option I ever want to face.

••••

I open my eyes to find sunshine flooding the room. At first I'm disorientated. I'm wrapped in warmth. My gaze moves down to find Indi sound asleep on my chest. It brings an instant smile to my face. Christ she's beautiful. Her long dark lashes are splayed against her cheeks. Her sexy-as-fuck plump lips just itching to be kissed. Her leg is thrown over mine, pinning me to the bed. Her arm is still draped around my waist.

My morning wood is straining against my jeans. Having her wrapped around me isn't helping matters. Fuck. What I wouldn't give to be able to flip her over and have my way with her.

Lifting my head off the pillow slightly, I place a soft kiss on her forehead. A smile graces her face as she lets out a sexy little sigh and snuggles in closer. The leg that's draped over me rises slightly. It's now inches away from my cock, making it grow even harder. Shit. I need to adjust that fucker because it's become painful, but I don't want to wake her.

I've never spent the night with someone like this before. If I could stay here like this, wrapped up in her forever, I would. I lay here watching her until she finally stirs. "Morning, beautiful," I say when I see her eyes open. She lifts her head off my chest as her eyes dart around the room before landing on mine.

"Carter." The shock on her face makes me smile for some reason. "What time is it?" I turn my head to look at her bedside clock.

"8:00am."

"Shit. Did you stay here all night?"

"It appears so. We must've fallen asleep." She tries to sit up, but I tighten my grip. I'm not ready to let her go yet.

"Let me up," she pleads.

"Nope. I'm not done holding you." She sighs as her eyes meet mine again.

"That's nice, but I've gotta pee."

"Oh." I chuckle as I let her go. "How are you feeling today?" I ask as she climbs over the top of me.

"Fine," she says smiling. It doesn't reach her eyes, so I know she's lying.

Whilst she's in the bathroom I adjust my cock, but don't move from her bed. I'm gonna need to keep her busy today. I don't want her moping around worrying about the MRI on Monday.

When she re-enters the room, I sit up. "I better get going before your dad finds me in your room. He does own a shotgun." She giggles at my comment.

"He likes you, Carter. I think you're safe. Besides, I'm not a kid anymore."

"Finally, you admit it," I say as I reach down and grab my shoes off the floor.

"Ha ha. Very funny." Sliding my feet into my shoes, I stand. I take the few steps that separate us, snaking my arms around her waist. Thankfully she doesn't seem to mind.

"Get ready. I'll be back to get you in about an hour."

"Where are we going?" she asks, the corners of her lips turning up.

"Out for the day. Do you mind if we take our parents with us? I think it will do them both good to get out of the house."

"Of course not," she answers, her smile widening.

"Wear something comfortable and warm." She's gonna need it where we're going.

"Okay," she says. Inching my face forward, I place my lips gently on hers. It's just a simple peck, but I feel compelled to kiss her. I'm a patient man. I'm willing to wait as long as it takes. In the meantime though, I'm going to sneak in whatever I can. Anything that could possibly hurry her along.

I need her. Her diagnosis yesterday only intensifies my desire to have her, sooner rather than later. Situations like this make you realise life is short. You need to live everyday like it's your last.

"Your dad had a lot to drink yesterday," I tell her. "I had to put him to bed. He's probably going to be feeling pretty shitty today, but try and talk him into coming with us. I don't like the idea of him being alone."

"You're very sweet, Carter Reynolds," she says reaching up and running her hand down the side of my face. "Who knew?" She's smiling when she says the last bit, so I don't take offence.

"What can I say? You bring out the best in me. You always have." This time she cups my face in her hands and pulls my head down towards hers. When her mouth covers mine, I pull her body closer, groaning. *Hot damn.* Now this is the kind of kiss I've been pining for.

Fuck I've missed her lips. Missed these crazy-arse feelings she makes me feel. It's electric. Her touches and kisses make me feel electrified. That's the best way to describe it. It's like a current that shoots through every inch of me. Sweet Jesus.

She makes me feel alive.

TWELVE

INDIANA

MY LIPS ARE STILL TINGLING EVEN AFTER CARTER LEAVES. I'M grateful for everything he's done for both me and my dad. He's been so supportive. I'm not sure how I would've got through yesterday without him. As pissed as I was that he forced me to go to the doctor in the first place, I'm thankful for it now. It was the push I needed. He only had my best interests at heart. I can't be mad at him for that.

It may just be the difference between living and dying. My mum waited years before getting her diagnosis. Thanks to Carter, I only waited weeks. I at least have a fighting chance of kicking this tumour's arse. Sadly, my mum didn't have that luxury.

It's made me think a lot about everything she went through. I'd be lying if I said it doesn't upset me. I hate that she waited so long to see someone, despite my father's pleas. If she hadn't, there's a good chance I may not have had to grow up without a mother. My dad may not have had to live without his soulmate.

My poor dad. I'm gonna fight this motherfucking tumour with

everything I have. I refuse to let this be the end for me. I refuse to bring more heartache to him. This would destroy him, I know it. After mum passed, having me to care for was the only thing that gave him the will to carry on. To keep existing.

After I shower, I make my way into the kitchen to find him sitting at the table drinking coffee. Carter was right: he does look like death warmed up. "Morning, Daddy," I say in a chirpy voice. Today I'm feeling optimistic. The tears I shed last night will be my final ones. I refuse to shed anymore. Positive thinking from this day forward. No matter what the MRI shows, I'm going to live every day to the fullest. I refuse to live like I'm dead while I'm still alive.

"Morning, Pumpkin. How are you feeling this morning?"

"A lot better than you by the looks of it," I reply as I walk towards him, wrapping my arms around his neck from behind and kissing his cheek. He clears his throat, a slight red tinge appearing on his handsome face.

"I'm happy to hear that," he says. "I'm sorry about the way I acted yesterday ..." Removing my arms, I take a seat next to him.

"You have nothing to be sorry about. I understand how hard this is for you. I'm sorry that you have to go through this again. We're going to beat this, Daddy. I promise." I reach for his hand and grasp it in mine. "Okay?" Meeting my gaze, he smiles.

"Okay." Squeezing his hand, I rise. No more talk of tumours today.

"Now, what would you like for breakfast? Carter and Elizabeth will be here soon. The four of us are going out for the day."

"Some toast will be fine, Pumpkin," he says smiling. It doesn't quite reach his eyes, but at least he's trying.

••••

We end up driving to the Blue Mountains. It's just over an hour's drive from where we live. Apparently, this is the area where Carter grew up. It's a beautiful place. I understand why he said wear something warm. It gets pretty cold up here. In winter it's not uncommon to see snow.

Parking the car when we arrive at Katoomba, we all get out. Dad offered to drive today. Carter's car is only a two-door, so getting in and out of the back seat can be a pain in the arse. Dad and Elizabeth sat in the front. Carter and I were in the back. He reached for my hand before we even got out of our street, and he held it all the way here. I love the feel of my hand wrapped in his.

My dad walks around the front of the car and helps Elizabeth out, while Carter gets out on his side and offers me his hand. I grab my woollen beanie and scarf off the seat beside me before sliding over. Carter takes the scarf out of my hand and wraps it around my neck, while I place the beanie on my head.

"You look so cute," he says tugging on my scarf and pulling me forward, placing a tiny kiss on my nose. Have I mentioned how much I love this side of him? He can say and do the sweetest things sometimes. Lacing his fingers through mine, we walk towards the lookout to see the large rock formation known as the Three Sisters, and the breathtaking Jamison Valley below.

Carter explained the large sandstone rock eroded away over time creating the three tall rock formations that sit side by side, towering over the beautiful valley. Aboriginal legend says, that three sisters who fell in love with three men from a neighbouring tribe, causing a war to break out, were turned into stone becoming trapped forever. Hence the name.

Even though he grew up in the area, I'm surprised by his knowledge. When I asked him about it, he confessed he came here a few times on school excursions when he was a boy.

I can't believe how vast and beautiful this place is. I've always known of its existence, but sadly have never visited until now. After zipping up my coat, I wrap my arms around myself. The icy wind has a real bite to it.

"Are you cold?" Carter asks draping his arm around my shoulder, pulling me into him. I smile to myself.

Once we've looked around up top, Carter suggests we ride the

Scenic Railway down the cliffside to the valley below. Apparently, it's a really steep drop, so Elizabeth ops out. My dad offers to take her for a coffee in the café, so Carter and I can still go.

Holy crap, steep is not the word. It's a fifty-two percent incline, earning the title of the steepest passenger railway in the world. You also have the option to recline your seat back another twenty percent, which of course we did. Carter holds me tight against him on the journey down, which to me is the best part. Again, he links his fingers through mine as we walk the tracks of the valley below.

We fall into easy conversation as we walk along. When we come to a stop by a beautiful waterfall, Carter pulls out his phone to take a selfie of us. He drapes his arm around my shoulder and pulls me in against his side. "Smile, beautiful," he says. After snapping a few shots, he releases me and places the phone back in his pocket. Presuming we're going to continue on down the trail, I take a step forward. "I'm not finished with you yet," he says reaching for me and pulling me back to him. Turning me in his arms, he cups my face in his hands. The look he gives me has my heart melting. He looks like I feel—*happy*. "I'm going to kiss you now," he warns before covering my mouth with his.

It's another one of those sweet, hot kisses that has me weak at the knees. My arms slide around his waist and my hands fist the back of his jacket to hold myself up. Opening my mouth slightly, I deepen the kiss when his tongue meets mine. This is not the kind of kiss that you would call acceptable for a public place, but I don't care. I'm too lost in him to give a shit.

I can't even put it into words what being here with him in this magical place feels like. I can't remember the last time I felt this happy, this alive. Not once have I thought about my illness and what lies ahead. *Not once.* Instead, I'm lost in every look, every word, and every touch from Carter. I'm consumed by him.

••••

It's late in the afternoon by the time we arrive back home. When we finally made our way back up the mountain to our parents, Carter suggested we head to Leura for lunch. It's a quaint little town, with the cutest little shops, galleries, cafés and restaurants.

We ate in a nice place complete with a fireplace, which was a welcome escape from the cold. All the food was made with local produce. It had wall to ceiling glass windows that overlooked the valley below. The food and the company were amazing. Today was something that we all needed: a nice escape from the dramas awaiting us back home.

The only downfall was it had to come to an end. I enjoyed every second of my time with Carter. When my dad and I came inside, and Carter and his mum went to their house, I can't even explain the emptiness I felt. After Dad and I had dinner, I went to my bedroom, hoping Carter would be in his room so I could catch a glimpse. Sadly he wasn't.

Eventually, I gave up and headed in for a shower. It had been a big day, and to be honest I was tired. The quicker I got to sleep, the faster tomorrow would come. That meant I'd get to see Carter again. It's funny how quickly I've become attached to him. I guess, even after he left all those years ago, he still held my heart. In a way we've just picked up where we left off.

Later as I lay in bed, all I can think about is him. He's proven over the past week how much he cares. Maybe it's time I take down the walls I've erected around my heart and let him back in.

THIRTEEN

CARTER

I'M AWOKEN BY A SOFT VOICE CALLING MY NAME. "CARTER ... Carter, are you awake?" *I fucking am now.* Reaching out blindly, I flick the switch on my bedside lamp. The light hurts my eyes. Squinting, I try and adjust my sight to the sudden fucking brightness that has now filled my room. This better be a damn emergency.

"Indi." She's standing just inside my window, wearing a silky black dressing gown. I have no idea why she's sneaking in my room. Or am I dreaming? My heart starts to race when I realise something must be wrong. I sit up rubbing my eyes. "Are you alright? Is everything okay?"

"Everything is fine," she says taking a step towards me. "I couldn't sleep. I was thinking about you, about us."

"You were?" I'm confused.

"I was." Why that has me smiling like a fool, I can't say. I guess I like the fact she was thinking about me. Hopefully in a good way. She takes another step towards me. I watch as she takes in a long breath before releasing it slowly. She looks nervous. Shit, that can't be a good sign.

Have I misunderstood her reasons for coming here?

She doesn't speak another word. Instead her hands move up to the tie of her dressing gown. I gulp in some air as she slowly undoes the bow. Nope. I haven't misunderstood. I feel my dick twitch with anticipation.

Her hand slowly moves up to her shoulder as she pushes the silk fabric down one arm. It's like a torturous, erotic striptease. It immediately has my dick growing. If this is a fucking dream I'm going to be pissed. I almost want to pinch myself just to make sure. I hold my breath as I wait for her next move.

She moves to the other side, sliding the dressing gown over her other shoulder. When she lets go, my eyes follow the fabric as it falls to the floor, pooling at her feet. As my gaze moves back up her legs, I almost swallow my tongue when I realise she's totally naked underneath.

I rub my eyes again. I can't fucking believe it. Here is the woman of my dreams. The one I've been pining for, for the past five years, standing in my bedroom wearing nothing but a smile. *Fuck me.* Have I died and gone to heaven?

I'm off the bed in a flash. "I want you," is all she says, shyly, as I stalk towards her, closing the distance between us. If she wants me, she's got me. Hook, line and fucking sinker. I don't give her a chance to say another word. Pulling her into my arms, I cover her lips with mine. I've been fantasizing about having her again. *For ... five ... damn ... years.*

My mouth and hands are everywhere. "I can't tell you how many times I've dreamt about having you again," I whisper as my lips trail a path across her jawline and down her neck. "Please tell me this is really happening."

"Oh God, it's happening," she moans, tilting her head back and pushing her tits further into my bare chest. "We've wasted enough time apart." *She's got that right.* My hands run down her lean back, cupping that delicious arse of hers. Lifting her off the ground, she wraps her legs around my waist as I carry her over towards my bed.

Once I've laid her down I reach behind me, untangling her limbs from my waist. I need to see her. All of her. Standing, I feel my lips turn up into a smile as my eyes rake over her naked body. *Fucking perfection.* "You're even more beautiful than I remember," I breathe, leaning forward to place my hands on either side of her waist. When my eyes meet hers again, she's smiling too.

Reaching up, she runs her hand down the side of my face. "I missed you when you left," she admits.

"I missed you too," I reply, lifting my hand and brushing her hair off her face. "So much." Straightening up again, I untie the string on my pyjama bottoms, letting them fall around my ankles. Stepping out of them, I kneel on the bed before climbing on top of her. My cock is so hard for her it hurts. "Are you sure you're ready for this?"

Please say yes.

"Yes. I've never been more certain of anything in my life." I smile at her words. She is too, but there's also a twinge of uncertainty on her face. "You're not going to run away again are you, like last time?"

"I couldn't leave you again if I tried," I admit. And that's the truth. She's it for me. I want her. I fucking need her. I've denied my heart long enough. My life without her in it is something I don't want to experience again. "If the past five years have taught me anything, it's that I'm nothing without you." My confession brings tears to her eyes. Fuck me if I don't mean every word.

Raising her arms, she slides her hands around the back of my head and pulls my lips down to hers. I groan into her mouth. I agree, enough talking. *My* girl is lying beneath me, ripe, ready and naked. I've waited years for the chance to devour her again. There'll be plenty of time for words later.

My hand is trembling as it caresses over her heavenly body. I never get nervous before sex, but for some reason I am now. This moment seems too good to be true. My heart is beating out of my chest. *Pull your shit together, Reynolds.* This isn't just some random hook-up. Tonight I need to bring my fucking A game.

I need to show her that I'm the one she wants. I need to erase any memories she has of that *wanker* and their time together. She's mine now, and that's the way it's gonna stay. I'll do everything in my power to make sure that happens.

My hands skim over her toned stomach heading towards her little piece of heaven. The place I've been dying to touch, to taste. Using my knee to open her legs wider, I run my fingers over her mound until I reach her clit. Fuck, she's so wet for me. "Christ, I've missed your pussy," I say as my mouth kisses a trail down her neck.

She moans, pushing her hips forward as I slide through her wetness before slipping a finger inside. I've missed those sexy as fuck little whimpers she makes when she's turned on.

I already feel like I'm on the edge and I'm not even inside her yet. My fingers continue to work their magic until she's coming undone. This is going to be her first of many orgasms tonight. I'm not going to stop until she's passed out from exhaustion. I need to get my fill of her, and I have five years' worth to make up for.

"I forgot how skilled you were with your hands," she breathes coming down from her bliss.

"I'll remind you again later," I tell her, sucking one of her perfect tits into my mouth while kneading the other one with my hand. I'm not going to stop until I've tasted every fucking inch of her. "First I need to get you reacquainted with my mouth and my cock."

"I look forward to it," she replies, threading her fingers through my hair and lifting my face to make eye contact with her. "But your mouth can come later." The flush from her arousal spread over her flawless skin turns me on like you wouldn't believe. Especially since I was the one responsible for putting it there. "I need you inside me. I've missed that connection with you more than anything," she pleads. I've missed it too. Nobody has ever been able to make me feel the things she does.

"You don't need to ask me twice," I say placing a soft kiss on her lips as I reach for the drawer next to my bed. "The sooner I'm buried balls deep in your heaven, the better."

Once I've retrieved the condom, I kneel back on my haunches and roll it on. Her spectacular green eyes watch my every move. I smile down at her. I still can't believe I'm lucky enough to be given a second chance. I can assure you I won't fuck it up this time.

When she opens her legs for me I settle in between them, leaning on both elbows to take the weight. My heart is beating out of my chest with anticipation of what's to come. I know once I take her this time, there's no going back for either of us. I want this so bad.

"I'm not sure how long this is gonna last," I confess as I look deep into her eyes. She's mesmerising. "I'm gonna fuck you hard and fast this time round. Then I'll take my sweet time with you, okay?"

"God, yes," she whimpers as her hands skim down my back before resting on my arse. Her electrifying touch sends shock waves coursing through me. It's so powerful. She brings every inch of me to life. Her fingers dig into my arse cheeks, pulling me forward towards her opening.

As soon as the head of my cock is inside her, I'm already throwing back my head and groaning. She's so tight, just like I remember. By the time I'm all the way in, I feel like I'm on the edge. Fuck I've missed this. She pushes her head back into the pillow and lets out a sound of pure ecstasy. I know exactly how she feels. Together we're magic. We were fucking made for each other. There's no denying it.

My hand runs down her side to her hip, holding her in place. I pull out to the tip and thrust back in. *Fuck.* I'll be lucky if I last a minute. Indi's hands find their way into my hair again, pulling my face towards hers. "Fuck me, Carter," she whispers against my mouth before deepening the kiss. I plan to. Christ I love the way she kisses me.

"Sweet Jesus," I groan. If she keeps talking like that it will be over before it even starts. My fingers dig deeper into her hip as I pick up the pace. She feels like home. Fucking home. Her pussy was made just for me. Only me. No one will ever touch what's mine again.

By some miracle, I manage to hold out until she comes again. As soon as her pussy constricts, contracting around my cock like a vice, I lose it. "Indi," I practically scream as my body starts to shudder before stilling. My orgasm is so intense I swear I'm seeing fucking stars by the time it's over. If I could climb inside her pussy, I'd never leave. We're both trying to catch our breath when I collapse down on her chest. "Are you okay?" I ask.

"I'm wonderful," she says, turning her head to the side and placing her lips on my cheek. "Never been better."

Lifting my head, I smile down at her. Christ she's beautiful. My hand comes up to brush back a few strands of hair that are stuck to her forehead from perspiration. "I've missed you so much."

"Me too," she says cupping my cheek with her hand. "Please don't hurt me again, Carter." Her words cut. I hate that I hurt her, but doesn't she realise I was hurting too?

"Never," I reply. "You're mine now, you know that right? Nobody else is allowed to touch you. Only me." She smiles, cocking one of her eyebrows.

"Is that so?" she asks narrowing her eyes slightly. I suppress my smile. I don't want her to think I'm joking about this, because I'm not.

"Damn straight," I say with all seriousness.

"Well, that works both ways, just so you know."

"You're all I want. All I've ever wanted," I confess as my lips find hers again. I'm still inside her and my cock is already hardening again. "Ready for round two?"

"God yes," she whimpers, making my lips curve up.

"That's my girl," I breathe placing a soft kiss on her lips. This time I'm gonna take my sweet time with her. I have all night to get reacquainted with this luscious body of hers. Reaching for her hands, I pin them above her head before lacing our fingers together. My lips trail a path across her jaw and down her neck as I push my hips forward, rocking into her tight little pussy with slow, short, agonising strokes. I want to stay like this forever. Closing my eyes, I find myself wishing for a lifetime of moments with her. My heart burns for her.

It always has, and it always will. She's my addiction, my air.

FOURTEEN

INDIANA

CARTER AND I STAYED AWAKE UNTIL THE EARLY HOURS OF THE
morning. If we weren't being intimate with each other, we were lying
in each other's arms talking. I'm so glad I worked up the courage to
come over here, because this whole experience has been magical. Even
better than our first time together. Nothing's changed, but
everything's changed if that makes sense. We're not kids anymore.
We're adults, making adult decisions and having adult feelings.
Although there's a tiny part of me that's terrified he's going to leave
again, my heart believes he won't. I hope my heart's right.

The alternative is incomprehensible. Last night I let down all my
barriers. I think he did too. He was nothing like the old smartarse
Carter. He was loving, attentive, and extremely sweet. I gave him
everything. Every piece of me. Even my heart. Last night just
confirmed that I'm still in love with him. He's it for me. What Mark and
I shared doesn't even compare to what Carter and I have when we're
together. It's mind-blowing.

We stayed in bed until late Sunday afternoon. I woke midmorning to find him lying beside me watching me sleep. It was a little daunting. I hope I wasn't dribbling or anything. I woke again a few hours later to his smiling face between my legs. Let me just say it's an amazing way to be woken up. We've had so much sex, I'm not sure if I'm going to be able to walk when we finally get up.

We need to get out of bed soon. Elizabeth is cooking dinner for us. She found out I was in here with Carter when he snuck out to the kitchen to get us some food. Apparently my dad is coming over as well.

I'll have to go home to shower and change. I only have the dressing gown I wore here last night. That's definitely not appropriate for dinner attire. Especially since it's with our parents.

"I suppose I better go home and shower," I tell him, rolling on to my side to face him.

"I'm not ready to let you go yet," he replies, pulling me into him. "Shower here, with me."

"I have to go home. I have no clothes." When he smiles sheepishly, I know he's concocting a plan.

"If I get you some clothes, will you stay and shower with me?" He raises his eyebrows, hopefully. I love his sweet side. It's adorable.

"What? You're going to go to my room and pick me out something to wear?" I ask, intrigued and a tad horrified.

"Hell yeah. Don't you trust me?" With a smile like that, I don't think so.

"Definitely not," I screech. He flips me onto my back and pins me to the mattress. "I can just imagine what you'd choose. We're eating with our parents remember?" The look on his face has me smiling. He's trying to act offended, but I know he's not. He knows I'm right. He'll probably dress me like a damn hooker. The skimpier the better. I know his type.

"I'll prove you wrong," he says leaning forward and planting a soft kiss on my nose before pushing himself up and off the bed.

"Carter. I'll go and get something and come back and shower with you," I offer, sitting up.

"No need. I've got this." He winks at me as he pulls on a pair of jeans. Got this my arse. I'm not sure how I feel about him going through my drawers. I have nothing incriminating in there. Well I hope I don't.

When he jumps out the window, I get up and grab one of his T-Shirts, pulling it over my head. By the time I rush towards the glass he's already inside my room. Ugh! This should be interesting.

He's back a few minutes later looking all pleased with himself. When he passes me his selection through the window, I burst out laughing. A tiny pair of shorts and a skimpy little top. I knew it. I know him better than he thinks.

"You do realise it's winter, don't you?"

"You don't need warm clothes, you've got me," he smirks. I shake my head. I can't help but laugh at his serious face.

"Can you go and grab something more suitable? Better still, let me do it," I say rolling my eyes.

"So you're not going to wear these?" he asks, taking them out of my hand and holding them up, disappointed. "I wanna see you in these, you'll look hot." I start to laugh.

"I'm not wearing that to dinner, Carter."

"Will you dress in them later when we're alone?" The pleading look on his face has me nodding my head.

"But not for dinner." I lean forward and plant a kiss on his lips.

"Fine," he says, his shoulders slightly slumping. "I'll go get something a little less revealing." Before I get a chance to protest, he's heading towards my house again.

"I need underwear too, by the way."

"I'm on it," he calls out, looking over his shoulder before hauling himself into my room. My eyes are glued to his arse. God it really is one fine arse. Round, tight, and delicious.

A few minutes later he reappears at my window smiling like a fool. My gaze moves to the black lace teddy in his hand. *Far out.* He's going through my underwear drawer. I shake my head vigorously, but he nods before screwing it up and stuffing it in his pocket. I bury my face in my hands. I knew this was a bad idea.

I can't help but admire the strain of his muscles when he uses his arms to push himself through the window of his room a few minutes later. He really is a sight. This time he has a red hoody and a pair of black yoga pants in his hand. *That's more like it.* His smile grows when he passes me my black lace bra and matching panties.

"Fuck you have some sexy underwear," he says with a whistle. "I'm expecting a fashion parade in the near future."

"I don't think so," I laugh as I snatch my clothes out of his other hand. "And the teddy you stashed in your pocket," I demand holding my hand out to him.

"Fuck no. That's for later," he replies as he pulls it out, placing it into the top drawer of his bedside table. "So is this," he adds, pulling my pink vibrator out of his back pocket. *Fucking hell.* I'd forgotten that was in there.

"Give me that," I snap as I lunge towards him, but he's too quick. He raises his arm, holding it high in the air so I can't reach. When I jump to try and grab it, he starts laughing. "Carter," I whine. "Give it to me."

"Sorry, beautiful. I can't do that. From this day forward, I forbid you to use it without my permission. If you want to get off by a toy," he says waving it in my face, "then I'm gonna watch." Forbid me my arse. Who the hell does he think he is?

"You can't forbid me to do shit," I retort, folding my arms across my chest.

"I hate to break it to you, sweetheart, but you're mine now. So, I can, I will, and I just did." He places his finger gently on the tip of my nose, so I swat it away.

"You're an arse," I retort, but the *mine* comment he made is not lost on me. I'm smiling on the inside.

"I know, but I'm your arse," he says pulling me into his arms, covering my mouth with his. He slides his hands up my outer thighs, moving them under his T-shirt and cupping my arse. "Fuck you look sexy wearing my clothes."

••••

D-day. My stomach is in knots as we travel to the hospital for my MRI. *Positive thoughts.* That's what I keep telling myself. Carter, my dad, and Elizabeth are with me for moral support. I'm grateful, but if I had my way I would've gone it alone. Hearing that I had a tumour the other day was the worst, but seeing the look of devastation on Carter and my dad's faces was even harder.

When we arrive, I have to see the doctor first. He just wants to touch base and explain what will be happening today. Of course Carter follows me into the room without a formal invite. Presumptuous arse. I do love how supportive he's been, but I still narrow my eyes at him when he sits beside me in the doctor's office looking all smug. Naturally, he smiles and reaches for my hand when I do that. It's obvious he enjoys getting under my skin.

The procedure seems pretty straightforward. The doctor explains that an MRI (Magnetic Resonance Imaging) uses a powerful magnetic field, radio frequency pulses and a computer to produce detailed pictures of organs, soft tissue, bone and virtually all other internal body structures.

There are no side effects associated with the scan, but he informs me that I may feel claustrophobic being confined in such a small space for around an hour. If that's the case, I'll have a buzzer in my hand that I can press, and I can be given a light sedative to relax me if needed. Personally, I think staying still for that long is going to be the hardest part.

"When will we have the results back, doc?" Carter asks.

"I'll schedule an appointment for tomorrow. We can discuss the results and figure out a plan from there," he replies, smiling briefly as he stands and walks towards the door. "I'll get the nurse to escort you to the imaging room. They're waiting for you."

"Thank you," I say rising from my seat.

"Yes, thank you," Carter adds, reaching for the doctor's hand when we reach the doorway.

"I'll see you both in the morning."

The nurse informs Carter that he won't be able to come in, but he still insists on walking with me all the way. He pulls me into his arms and kisses the top of my head before I enter.

"I'll be right out here waiting for you," he says. And that's exactly where I find him when I'm done.

The whole experience was very daunting, so I'm relieved when it's over. The four of us decide to stop off and have some lunch on the way home. Not much is said about the MRI and my appointment tomorrow. It's like a dark cloud hanging over our heads. I'm not going to worry until I have to. I've already been diagnosed with a tumour, so it can't get much worse than that.

When we arrive back home later that afternoon, Dad invites Elizabeth inside for a coffee. When we're alone, Carter pulls me into his arms. "I've gotta run a few errands," he says planting a soft kiss on my lips. "We'll do something together later, okay?" His fingers travel down my sides, cupping my arse in his hands. He pulls me against him and covers his mouth with mine. I'm looking forward to spending time with him later. I wish it could be now, but he has a life outside of me. I can't be selfish. He's been putting his needs aside to be here for me since my diagnosis.

••••

After taking LJ for a walk, I watch a movie while Dad and Elizabeth sit in the kitchen. When it's finished and Carter still hasn't returned, I head to my room. I'm surprised to find a large white box wrapped in a red bow, sitting on my bed. I have no idea how it got there. It wasn't here when I left this morning. My first thought is Carter. My head snaps in the direction of his place, but he's nowhere to be seen.

I'm smiling as I approach the bed. I lean forward towards the box and listen, for what I'm not sure. A tick? Which is dumb I know, we're not kids anymore. That's when I notice a card has been slipped underneath the ribbon. Sliding it out I read, *Indiana,* that's been handwritten on the front of the envelope. Well it's definitely for me.

Hesitantly I open it to read what's written on the card.

> *I want you to be ready at 7:00pm, sharp. I won't take no for an answer. You know I won't hesitate to throw you over my shoulder if I have to. Make sure you're wearing ONLY what's in the box. Nothing else. I know how stubborn you are, so I've taken the proper precautions to make sure this happens.*
>
> *Carter. x*

My first thought is, how dare he boss me around like that? Who in the hell does he think he is? Needless to say, I'm smiling like a damn fool when I think it. I secretly love his demanding side. It turns me on. I've been missing him since he dropped me off earlier. I love that he wants to spend time with me.

I start to wonder what he means by saying he's taken the proper precautions. I know him, that can't be good. I can only imagine what's inside the box.

Reaching for the bow, I untie it. If it's something he wants me to wear, I'm apprehensive to see what's inside. If it's skimpy lingerie, I'm gonna kick his arse.

Removing the lid, I gasp when I see what's inside. It's a dress. A beautiful, and by the looks of it, ridiculously expensive dress. It's a pretty jade green colour, and the fabric is soft and shimmery. Lifting it out of the box, I hold it up. It's exquisite. It sits just above my knees and has shoestring straps. My gaze moves to the tag. It's my size. How did he know that?

I guess when he was in my room getting my clothes yesterday he could've snooped. Ugh! I wouldn't put it past him. I place the dress against me and twirl around in a circle. My smile grows. I love it. Never in my life have I owned something so pretty.

When I carefully lay it on my bed, I notice a pair of matching green heels in the bottom of the box. They are the right size as well. Although sceptical, I'm extremely touched that he would do this for me. This is something the real Carter would do. The sweet one. Not the bastard he pretends to be most of the time.

To be honest, this is the last thing I expected. My thoughts drift back to the note. What does he mean I can't wear anything else? Is he trying to say I'm not allowed to wear any panties? That's definitely something Carter would suggest. I rush straight to my underwear drawer. I gasp when I look inside. It's empty. All my underwear is gone. *Everything.* The only thing left is a lone box of tampons.

My eyes immediately move towards Carter's bedroom. He's standing at his window with my white lace thong hanging from the tip of his finger and a smug look on his handsome face. *What an infuriating arse.* A big, fat, beautiful, infuriating arse. As annoyed as I am with him, the gorgeous, playful smile on his face has me smiling too. I'm tempted to go out and buy the most unflattering pair of granny undies I can find, just to spite him, but the thought of being panty-less around him actually excites me.

I can't wait to see what tonight holds for us.

FIFTEEN

CARTER

WE HAVE NO IDEA WHAT TOMORROW'S GOING TO BRING, SO tonight I want to do something special. I want to take her out before she gets her results. Before the treatment starts. Give her a night to remember. Something to hold on to if the times ahead get tough, which I'm sure they will.

As I walk up the steps towards Indi's front door, the nerves settle in. I'm not cut out for this shit. My stomach is in knots and this damn tie feels like it's choking me. I hate wearing these fuckers. I wipe my sweaty palms on the front of my pants before knocking. A few seconds later the door swings open. *Fuck me.*

I inhale a huge breath and hold it as my eyes take in what's in front of me. "Wow," is all I manage to get out. I knew that colour would look perfect on her, but the image I had in my head doesn't even come close to what she looks like in the flesh. I chose the green because the moment I saw it, it reminded me of her eyes.

Stunning.

"Hey," she says smiling.

"Hey. You look nice." Seriously, nice doesn't even cut it. Gorgeous, sexy as hell, edible, would've been a better way to describe her. My eyes move to her perky little tits beneath the dress. Even without a bra they sit perfectly. The sight of her hardened nipples underneath has my cock stirring. I thought this no underwear thing was a brilliant idea, now I'm not so sure. How in the hell am I going to be able to keep my hands off her all night?

Impossible.

"You look nice too," she replies, breaking my train of thought. When my eyes meet hers, the corners of her lips turn up. "Very handsome." Christ, she has me smiling like a damn fool. What is it with her? I clear my throat and tug at the air-constricting tie around my neck. "Do you want to come in?" she asks. I look down at my watch. We really need to get going if we're going to make it on time.

"We're pressed for time. Are you nearly ready to leave?"

"Yes, I just need to grab my coat. I'm allowed to wear a coat aren't I?" she asks sarcastically, rolling her pretty green eyes.

"Of course. You're going to need one," I chuckle. It is winter after all. She'll freeze in that dress without one. I don't want her getting sick.

"Where are we going?" she questions. If she thinks I'm going to tell her, she's mistaken.

"It's a surprise," I tell her. I organised something simple, but sweet. Just like her. I know my girl well enough. She's not into all the pretentious crap.

"I should've known that's what you'd say," she replies rolling her eyes again. Her attitude turns me on. I want to back her up against the wall and have my way with her, but that will come before the night's out.

I follow her down the hall towards her bedroom. My eyes are glued to that incredible arse the whole way. That little sway in her hips makes my dick twitch. I'm tempted to reach out and run my hand up her legs and under that dress, to make sure she hasn't disobeyed me, but I know if I do we'll never get out of here. Although the anticipation is killing me, there'll be plenty of time for that later. Tonight is about her and making memories. My cock can wait.

"I have pretty good taste," I admit as we walk towards my car.

"How so? Or do I really want to hear the answer?"

"The dress," I reply opening the door for her. My hand brushes over her arse as she lifts her leg to get into the car. I grin to myself when I hear her breath hitch. I don't feel a panty line and my dick stirs. *Good girl.* For once she did as she was told. Knowing she's naked under that dress is going to make keeping my hands off her impossible.

"You did well, but some underwear to accompany it would've been nice." The sarcastic tone in her voice makes me chuckle. I don't think so, beautiful.

"Nope. You're perfect just the way you are. Plus, it will give me better access to that magnificent pussy of yours," I whisper leaning towards her ear. I hear her take in a sharp breath, and it brings a smile to my face. This is going to be fun. Or torture. I'm guessing for both of us.

••••

The drive into the city isn't as bad as I thought it would be. We're pretty much on time. I sent a quick text while we were stopped at a red light, letting Jax know we weren't far away. He's been giving me shit about tonight all afternoon. He thinks I've turned into a pussy. This night was so last minute, so I had no choice but to ask for his help. Maybe he's right. Who knew giving your heart to a woman meant handing over your manhood as well? Fuck me if she's not worth it though. I'd be anything, even a pussy, if it made her happy.

My hand has been sitting just above her knee for most of the drive. I'm impressed that I had the willpower not to slide it between her legs. At one stage, as my fingers drew lazy circles on her skin, her legs slightly parted. I knew it was an invitation to venture up further, but even then I stood strong. By the time I'm finished with her tonight, she's going to be so hot and ready, she'll be begging me to fuck her. It will be the perfect way to end our evening.

When I pull into the parking bay by the curb I reach for her hand, bringing it towards my lips to place a soft kiss on her knuckles. Her eyes are planted firmly on my mouth against her skin. I watch as her tongue darts out and moistens her bottom lip. Everything in me wants to kiss her. So that's exactly what I do.

Reaching across the console I slide my hand around the back of her neck, bringing her lips towards mine. When she opens her mouth and slips her tongue past my lips, I groan. My cock strains against my pants. I should've held my resolve, because now that I've had a taste, I don't want to stop.

My fingers inch up her inner thigh as her legs willingly open. She wants my hands on her just as much as I want them there. As I slide under her dress, Let Her Go starts to play. *Fuck.* My phone. It's probably Jax. Reluctantly I pull out of the kiss and retrieve it from my pocket. Damn him. "How far away are you, fucker? I'm freezing my nuts off here," he complains.

"I'm just parking the car," I reply as my eyes meet Indiana's. Christ she's beautiful. Her big green eyes are locked with mine. Her flawless skin is flushed from her arousal. Her full lips are red and swollen from my kiss. I'd like nothing more than to skip the first part of the evening and take her straight to the hotel, but I can't do that. I remind myself, *tonight is about creating memories—tonight is about her.*

"Good. Hurry up, pussy, so I can get the fuck out of here." I chuckle at his comment.

"We'll be there in a minute."

"Who was that?" Indi asks when I end the call.

"My mate Jax. You'll meet him in a minute." I lean forward and brush my lips with hers. "This," I say when I pull back and point between the two of us, "will have to wait till later." She gives me a disappointed smile. I feel the same. She's all I've thought about all day. In all honesty, it's just going to make the ultimate prize at the end of the night all the more sweeter. I only hope my aching cock and blue fucking balls can wait until then. I'd like nothing more than to bend her over the hood of my car right now and plough into her sweetness.

After I help her out of the car, she wraps her black woollen coat around herself. "It's freezing tonight," she says slightly shivering.

"I'll keep you warm," I tell her as I snake my arm around her shoulder and kiss the top of her head.

"I like the ringtone on your phone," she says as we cross the road. "It's a great song."

"Thanks," is my only reply. There's no way I'm going to tell her I've had it for the last five years because it reminded me of us. I've already lost enough of my manhood for one night.

As we walk underneath the Harbour Bridge and onto the grassed area overlooking the spectacular Sydney Harbour, my eyes seek out Jax. When I see the small table I asked him to set up, along with candles in the centre, my nerves kick in again. I want this night to be special, but I'm kind of feeling like a dick now. Jax is right. I'm a fucking pussy.

"This way," I say as I guide her to the right. I see the smug smirk on his face as we approach. *Fucker.* He's never going to let me live this down. When we reach the table I extend my hand to him. "Hey."

"Hey," he says with a smile before his eyes stray towards Indiana. I watch as he looks her over. His smile grows. Why that gets my back up, I can't say.

"Indiana, this is my friend Jax." Although I'm not sure for how long, if he keeps looking at her like that. "Jax, Indiana."

"So, I finally get to meet the elusive Indiana," he says taking her hand and bringing it towards his mouth. I wanna snatch her hand out of his, but I manage to rein myself in. I'd look like some pathetic, jealous jerk if I did that. *Like hell I'm jealous.* "Carter never shuts up about you." *Motherfucker.*

"He talks about me?" Indi asks, looking over at me with a huge smile on her face.

"All the damn time." The teasing grin he's wearing when his gaze shifts to me tells me he's trying to get me to bite. I'm not falling for his bullshit. He's the biggest shit stirrer I know. I usually find his antics amusing, but not tonight. Not in front of my girl.

"I do not, arsehole," I say trying to come to my own defence. Jax throws back his head and laughs. *Prick.*

"I'm just messing with you, mate," he replies, slapping me on the back. I give him a look that says both, I know, and shut the fuck up. Payback's a bitch. Indiana giggles from beside me. I guess she finds it amusing.

"Is this all for us?" Indi asks looking over the table setting in front of us. I'm grateful for the distraction. He's making me look like a dick in front of her. He's set up the table just as I asked. It's just a small table covered with a white linen cloth. Two white ceramic plates, two wine glasses and silver cutlery. There's a small vase with a red rose inside and two candles either side, in the middle of the table. He's done a good job, for a cocksucker.

"It is," I tell her, draping my arm over her shoulder. "Do you like it?"

"I love it," she says as her arms encircle my waist and she smiles up at me. The smile is exactly what I was hoping for. It makes the ribbing I've been getting all day from Jax, worth it. "Thank you, Jax."

"Don't thank me. Just doing what the big fella asked," he replies, flicking his head in my direction. The look Indi gives me when Jax says that has my heart thumping against my ribcage. I know in that moment, that everything Jax has said today is true. I'm well and truly fucked. "I'm going to duck off and pick up the food," Jax adds looking at his watch. "Then I'm out of here." I pull out Indi's chair for her. Once she's seated I lean down and place a soft kiss on her hair.

"I just need to speak with Jax for a second," I tell her before Jax and I take a few steps away from the table. "Thanks for all your help," I say extending my hand to him. He's really gone above and beyond. I owe him big time. "I appreciate it. You did well for an arsehole." He laughs at my comment.

"No problem. I aim to please," he says pulling out a cigarette and lighting it. I haven't smoked since I was seventeen, the day Ross found my cigarettes in the car. I don't miss it at all, but I could do with one right now. Anything to calm my fucking nerves. "For the record, I'd probably turn pussy for her too," he replies, soft enough so only I can hear.

"Keep your eyes off her, she's mine," I grit out, and he laughs. Christ, he gets me every time.

"Fuck, you really have done your nuts over this one."

"Fuck you," is all I say. No point denying it, because it's true. He's just trying to rile me up because he's a stirring prick. Even though he's given me a hard time about tonight, I know he's happy that Indi and I are finally working things out. He's had to listen to me grumbling about the one I let get away a number of times when we've gotten drunk over the past five years.

He's shaking his head and chuckling as he walks away. I make my way back towards the table. He's set it up so I'm opposite her, but I move my chair around to the side before I sit. I want to be as close to her as I can get.

Yep, I'm a pussy.

"You okay?" I ask reaching for her hand.

"I'm great. I can't believe you went to all this trouble for me."

"There's nothing I wouldn't do for you," I say, tucking a strand of her hair behind her ear. Fuck me if I don't mean every word too. She smiles and my stomach does a flip-flop. *Jesus, I'm a goner.* Leaning forward, I brush my lips with hers.

"Who knew you were such a romantic?" she replies when I pull back and lock eyes with her. Her words make me squirm in my seat as I tug at my tie, trying to loosen it. Great, she thinks I'm a pussy too. I'm far from a romantic. "Hey," she says, reaching out and running her hand down the side of my face when she sees my reaction to her words. "I love this side of you. It's very sweet. It beats the douchebag I usually get." The playfulness I see on her face makes me chuckle. I guess my behaviour towards her has been pretty deplorable at times.

"Like I said the other day, you bring out the best in me."

"I'm glad," she says bringing her face towards mine. "You bring out the best, and sometimes the worst in me." She giggles as her lips meet mine. That's true.

SIXTEEN

INDIANA

WORDS CANNOT EXPRESS WHAT TONIGHT HAS MEANT TO ME.
It's the perfect distraction. I didn't think it was possible to love him more than I do, but the more he lets his guard down, showing me his vulnerable, sweet side, the harder I fall.

"Okay, you two lovebirds," Jax says when he gets back. "You do realise you're in a public place." Carter and I pull away from each other. We made out the whole time he was gone. I'm so frustrated and turned on like you wouldn't believe. Carter's hands have not moved passed my face. I need his hands all over me, desperately. *Why can't he see that?*

I clench my thighs together when he looks at me with hooded eyes. I can tell he wants me as bad as I want him. When Jax clears his throat from beside us, I tear my eyes from Carter, looking up at him. I feel my face flush when I see he's smiling. "Get a room you two."

"You're just jealous, arsehole," Carter says with a chuckle, making my blush deepen.

"Nope. I'm happy with my balls being exactly where they are, thank you." Jax's comment makes me laugh. I love the banter between these two. I'm glad Carter has a good friend like him. He was such a loner when he was young.

Jax places the box in his hands on the side of the table, opening the flaps. I have to hold in my giggle when I see what's inside. With the elegant setup of the table and the location, I was kind of expecting something a little more than burgers and fries, but that appears to be what we're having. It's very Carter, and very us, I guess. Since that's what we always seem to eat when we're out together.

"Thank you," I say when he places it on my plate.

"My mate owns a restaurant not far from here, so they're not just any burgers, they're his speciality. You won't find better," Jax explains as he places Carter's food in front of him. They smell delicious. Next, he pulls out a metal thermos and passes it to Carter. "Since this is an alcohol free zone, Carter insisted on chocolate milkshakes as the beverage of choice." I let out a small laugh. I think it's very sweet.

"It's perfect," I say as my eyes meet Carter. He's smiling as he watches me.

"Yes, it's a perfect choice for a five year old," Jax replies sarcastically. I burst out laughing when Carter growls at him. Ignoring his torments, Carter pours the chocolate milk into the wine glasses that are sitting on the table.

"I'm out of here," Jax says as he picks up the empty box. "I'll be back later to pack everything up. About ten?" he asks, looking at Carter.

"Sure. Thanks, mate," he replies, fist pumping him.

"It was nice meeting you, Indiana," Jax says shaking my hand.

"You too. Thank you for everything you've done tonight," I reply.

"It was no trouble. I'm glad you two finally got your shit together." My gaze moves back to Carter when he says that. I'm glad we did too. "Don't do anything I wouldn't do," Jax adds with a wink as he turns to leave.

"Well that means we can do pretty much anything," Carter retorts to his retreating back. Jax laughs, flipping him off over his shoulder.

Once he's gone and we're alone again, Carter picks up his wine glass filled with chocolate milkshake and raises it in the air. "Cheers to good times ahead," he says with a sweet smile.

"Cheers," I reply clinking my glass against his. I have to fight the tears that threaten to come. I hope we have many more years ahead. I take a sip before placing the glass back on the table. "So how long have you known Jax?" I ask, trying to block all the uncertainty out.

"Five years. He helped me a lot when you know ... I left. He gave me a job and a place to stay until I got on my feet. I owe him a lot."

"He seems like a good guy. I'm glad you had him. I used to worry about you being alone," I confess reaching for his hand.

"Well I'm back now, and I'm no longer alone. Now, let's eat before it gets cold. As you can see I've gone to a lot of effort organising this gourmet meal."

"Yes you did," I reply, popping a fry in my mouth. "It's perfect. Just like you."

••••

After we eat, we talk and laugh. I'm having a great time. If only he'd touch me, it would be perfect. He caresses my hand, my arm, my face, but his hands go nowhere near where I want them to. I'm not sure if he's purposely trying to drive me insane with anticipation, but knowing him, I'm sure that's his plan.

Leaning towards me, he places his lips on mine. I'm not sure how much more I can take. I'm hot and ready for him. I'm so ready that I'm even tempted to touch myself if he doesn't damn well hurry up and do it. I fist my hands in his jacket, pulling him even closer. "How much longer until we can get out of here? I need you." I feel his lips curl up against my mouth. He's driving me crazy on purpose. *Arsehole.* I slide my hand up his inner thigh, cupping his manhood. I'm pleased to find him as hard as a rock. I guess he's driving himself crazy as well. I clench my thighs together as my fingers stroke over his thick length. I need him inside me. I wish we weren't in a public place right now so I could straddle him. "Touch me, Carter."

He hesitates at first, but then his hand moves to the back of my head, pulling me into him. He growls into my mouth as he deepens the kiss. *Touch me with your hands*, I want to scream. Finally, his other hand finds its way to my knee. I part my legs slightly, and the cool night air gushes in, hitting my centre. He forced me into wearing no panties, so why isn't he taking advantage of it?

He slides his hands up the inside of my leg, but stops before it reaches where I need it. I continue to work him over, but still his hand doesn't move up any further. I can't take much more of this. The anticipation already has me on the edge. Using my other hand, I grasp his wrist and move it the rest of the way. He chuckles into my mouth. God he infuriates me sometimes. "Don't make me beg."

"Fuck. You're so wet," he groans as his fingers slide between my folds.

"What do you expect? You've been driving me crazy all night. Since when do you keep your hands to yourself?"

"Keeping my hands off you hasn't been easy," he breathes as his skilled fingers circle my clit.

"Oh God," I moan. "I think I'm going to come already." He pulls his hand away as soon as I say that. *What the hell?*

"I don't want you to come yet," he says. "Wait. It will be all the sweeter." He's fucking kidding me, right? By the look on his face, I can tell he isn't. Me and my big mouth.

"I don't want to wait," I whine as I pull his mouth back to mine. "I need you, Carter. I need you now."

"I need you too, but not here." He pulls back and looks down at his watch. "Jax should be here in ten minutes. I'll shoot him a text and make sure he's on his way." I sit back in my chair, folding my arms over my chest like a spoilt child while he types a message into his phone. I've never been one for public sex, but right now, I'd do just about anything. I'd sit on his lap and ride him with everything I had, even calling out giddy-up on the top of my lungs. I wouldn't care who was watching. That's how desperate I am.

He's done this on purpose. The no underwear thing. Every look, every word, every touch. It's all been part of his big stupid plan. I've heard of blue balls, but is there such a thing as blue flaps? Because seriously, if there is then I have them. I've never wanted something so bad in my life. I clench my thighs together again. Just thinking about it is driving me insane.

Mark never got me this worked up. Not even close. I never craved him the way I crave Carter. "Maybe I should pleasure myself then," I say moving my hand under the table. He stops typing and grabs hold of my wrist.

"Like hell you will." He lifts my hand back on top of the table, pinning it down with his. He uses his thumb on his other hand to finish his text. Once it's sent he places his phone down and locks his eyes with mine. "Surely you can hold out for ten minutes," he says with a cocky smirk on his face. I narrow my eyes at him.

"No, I can't. I'm dying here," I snap. His face drops and his free hand skims through his perfectly dishevelled hair. It was meant as a joke, but then what I said dawns on me. *I'm dying.* Fuck. Am I? I could be. I didn't mean it like that. My stomach churns as he pulls me into his arms and practically squeezes the life out of me.

"Don't say that," he whispers against my hair. I can feel his body trembling against mine. He's done a good job of distracting us both, until now. Uncertainty looms in the air. I refuse to die. Tomorrow we'll find out exactly what we're dealing with. I can do this, I tell myself. I'm tough. I'm gonna fight this illness with everything I have. I just hope I'm tough enough.

••••

Carter walks me to the car when Jax arrives. Once he gets me seated in the passenger seat, he moves around to the driver's side and places the key in the ignition. The heater blasts to life. The warmth is heaven, just what I need. My jacket kept me reasonably warm, but my legs and my feet are frozen. He turns it up to high before smiling at me.

"I'll just help Jax pack everything into his car. It won't take long," he says, kneeling on his seat and leaning across the centre console, brushing his lips against mine. "You stay here and warm up." I smile when he pulls away from me. I'm so lucky to have him. I'm glad he came back. I'm also glad things didn't work out with Mark. I need Carter in my life.

I need him more than he'll ever know.

SEVENTEEN

CARTER

"YOU OKAY?" JAX ASKS AS WE CARRY THE TABLE AND CHAIRS
back to his car.

"I'm good," I answer, which is a total fucking lie.

"Bullshit man. I know you better than you think. Is there trouble in
paradise already?"

"No. Just something Indi said earlier spooked me, that's all." He
gives me a look.

"Fucking women," he says shaking his head. "I knew she was too
good to be true. Is she talking about marriage and kids already?"

"What? Fuck no." I sigh as her words play over in my head. *I'm
dying here.* Fuck I hope she doesn't believe that. I don't even want to
go there. She's been so positive, and I've been drawing from that. In
reality, I know she didn't mean it that way, but under the circumstances, hearing those words leave her mouth really fucked with my
head. "She has a brain tumour," I confess, meeting his gaze. I haven't
told him about her illness.

"She fucking what?"

"Yeah. It's pretty fucked up. I've only just got her back and now I might lose her again. She gets the final results tomorrow. That's why I organised tonight. I wanted to give her something to hold on to. Something to help get her through the treatment."

"Jesus," he says as he stops walking. "I had no idea. I'm sorry for calling you a pussy man. You should've told me."

"Don't be. You didn't know."

"Is she going to be okay? She's not going to die is she?" *I fucking hope not.*

"We won't know the extent until tomorrow. She had an MRI this morning. We already know she has a small tumour on her brain, but tomorrow we find out if there's any secondary cancer. If not, her prognosis looks pretty good."

"Shit. That's fucked up." I nod, passing him the chairs to stow in his trunk. It is. Fucked up is an understatement.

"Thanks for helping me tonight," I say grasping his shoulder. "It meant a lot to both of us."

"Shit, it's the least I could do. I'm sorry I gave you grief about it. I wouldn't have been such a cocksucker if I'd known the reason behind it," he admits.

"I won't hold it against you. I've known you long enough to know being a cocksucker comes naturally. You can't help it. It's just who you are." I chuckle when he punches me in the arm.

"Let me know how tomorrow goes, okay?" The sincerity on his face makes me smile. He's a good bloke. I'm lucky to have him as a friend. He's been like a big brother to me for the past five years.

"I will. Thanks," I say heading back towards my car. I try to push tomorrow out of my head so I can concentrate on tonight. I need to get Indi's hot, willing, and sexy-as-fuck body back to the hotel ASAP, so I can lose myself in her. I can't wait another minute.

Indi smiles at me once I'm seated in the car. She really is a stunner. *Fucking gorgeous.* I don't even think she realises how beautiful she is. She still takes my breath away after all this time. I don't think that will ever change. "You alright?" I ask reaching for her hand.

"I'm perfect. Tonight was perfect," she replies squeezing my hand. "I don't want it to end."

"Who said anything about it ending? It's only just beginning." I reach across the centre console and thread my hand through her hair, bringing her face towards me. She comes willingly. Her soft warm mouth presses against mine, and I'm lost again. I've never been much into kissing, but with her, I don't ever want to stop.

When she opens her mouth and deepens the kiss, I reluctantly pull away. The longer we stay here, the longer it's going to be before I can have her. As I move to start the ignition, she stops me.

"Wait. Don't go yet," she says, unbuckling her seatbelt and climbing onto my lap. "I can't wait another second." Straddling me, she places her hands between us as she fumbles with my belt buckle. I go to protest, but she places her finger over my mouth and cocks one of her eyebrows. I know she's daring me to try her. She's so fucking cute. "I'm taking control now. You've made me wait long enough." I feel my smile grow. The hotel I've booked for tonight is only a one-minute drive away, but she doesn't know that so who am I to argue? I'm not one for giving up control in the bedroom, but I'm interested to see where this goes.

Sure we're parked under the bridge at night, but we're in the middle of the city, so there's plenty of people walking around. To be honest, I never picked her to be this game. I sit there and watch as she gets my belt undone before going to work on my button and zipper. Her brow is furrowed with frustration at the amount of time it's taking to get my cock free. When she bites her bottom lip between her teeth, I almost give in to the temptation to help her. I want to bite those fucking lips of hers too. I'm surprised at the self-control I've shown tonight.

I've wanted to be buried balls deep inside her since the moment she opened the door to greet me. Knowing she's been panty-less all night hasn't helped matters. But, if she wants to take control I'll give it up, just this once. After all, tonight is all about her and what she wants.

Being the cocky bastard I am, I place my hands behind my head, letting her do all the work. My dick is straining painfully against my pants, but I really don't think she has it in her to go all the way. Not here.

I'm wrong. No sooner does she get my cock free, she breathes, "Condom."

"There's some in the centre console," I tell her. I'm glad she thought of it, because I'm so lost in this moment, it didn't even cross my mind, which is not like me at all. I always wrap it. I'd never take the risk of bringing another bastard into the world. I'd never want my child to go through what I have.

Seeing her ripping the foil wrapper open with her teeth is the sexiest thing ever. She places it over the head of my cock, pinching the top before rolling it down. She's never done this with me before, so I can only presume she did it with that *wanker*. That gets my back up for some reason. I have no right to be angry with her. I've had plenty of other girls since I left.

It makes me wonder how many others she's had. It makes me hate myself even more for leaving. When I left I was the only one. I was the one who forced her to have others. I need to push those thoughts out of my head. It's not going to do me any good longing for something I can't change. What I can be certain about is there will *never* be anyone else.

When the condom is in place she hoists up her dress, lining me up with her entrance. In one swift movement, she impales herself on my cock. "Fuck," I groan as my eyes roll back in my head. I unlace my fingers from behind my head and pull her mouth down on mine. *She's so hot.*

"Yes," she moans as she lifts her hips and slides down my length again, and again. I love this wild side of her. My little vixen. I think I need to get her worked up more often. Her pussy grips me like a vice. Our kiss is wild, all lips and tongue. *Smoking hot.* I love that we can't seem to get enough of each other.

I tear at her jacket, tugging it down her arms and discarding it on the seat beside us. I dig my fingers into her hips, lifting her up before pulling her back down. There's nothing gentle about this. It's wild and it's dirty, just the way I like it.

She pulls out of the kiss, pushing the strap of her dress over one shoulder, before pulling my face down towards her now perfect, exposed tit. If she keeps this up, I'm not going to last longer than a minute.

"God, don't stop," she moans as she rides my cock with a fiery passion. "I'm ... I'm ..." I'm sure she's about to tell me she's coming when a loud knock on the window stills us.

"Fuck off, Jax," I growl, because my first thought is it's him.

"Open the window, please," a very stern voice says. *What the fuck?* I don't move her off my lap. Instead I pull her dress back up to cover her, before reaching for her coat on the passenger seat and wrapping it around her. I'm not finished with her yet. I'm gonna wind down my window and tell whoever is there to fuck the hell off.

Again that impatient prick knocks, making my temper spike. When a torch is shone through the window, I almost lose it.

"Look," I snarl, winding down the window a fraction. I quickly bite my tongue when I see a police officer standing there, looking very unimpressed. *Jesus Christ.*

"Oh my God," Indi whispers, her voice lined with shame when the officer shines his torch in her face. She quickly buries her head in my chest as I wrap my arms around her protectively.

"I'd expect this from a couple of kids, but you're adults, you should know better. I'll give you two minutes to clear off, or I'll arrest you both." His words have Indiana burying her face further into me.

"Somebody kill me now," she whispers. I almost want to laugh at her obvious humiliation. She may think twice before attacking me again. Although, I'm certainly not complaining about that part. All I can think is thank god it wasn't Ross. That wouldn't have gone down too well.

"I'm sorry, officer. We're staying at the Park Hyatt tonight, so we'll be on our way."

"That's just over there," he says in disgust, pointing his torch in that direction. "You couldn't wait one minute?"

"She attacked me," I reply raising my hands in my defence. Indi pinches my side, hard. "Ouch," I laugh. The officer shakes his head.

"Don't let me catch you here again."

"Sorry, officer. You won't," I say in a serious voice, trying hard not to smile. I wind up my window and chuckle when he leaves.

"How could you?" Indi cries, beating down on my chest. It only makes me laugh harder.

"If I remember correctly, you were the one who attacked me." She narrows her eyes when they meet mine.

"Yes, but you didn't tell me we were staying here in the city. I only attacked you because I thought I was going to have to wait until we got home." Cupping her red face in my hands, I bring her sweet mouth to mine. She's so adorable when she's angry.

"Did you give me a chance? You were like some sex craved wild animal," I retort, meeting her gaze once again.

"I was not," she snaps, pinching my side once more. This time I laugh, even though her pinches hurt like a bitch.

"It's not funny you arsehole." *I beg to differ. It's fucking hilarious.*

••••

"How about a bit of elevator sex?" I ask, pinning her against the wall as we travel up to our room. She's still upset about our little run-in with the law. She's barely said a word since we've gotten out of the car.

"Ha ha. Not likely. Nearly getting arrested once is enough for tonight. Imagine if it had been my father."

"He doesn't even work in this area," I reply flatly, sliding my hands around her waist and pulling her against me. When she doesn't bite back, I place a chaste kiss on her head. One day she'll find this story amusing.

I know we're only here for the night, but I've booked one of their finest suites. Hopefully once she sees it, she'll cheer up. All I want is for tonight to be memorable. I guess with what just happened it will be. I have to hold back my chuckle as I think about how close we came to getting arrested for having sex in a public place.

"Wow, this place is spectacular," she says as soon as we enter our suite. I smile as I watch her eyes dart everywhere. I place the bag I'm holding on the floor and pull her into my arms.

"Only the best for you, beautiful." I plant a soft kiss on her lips and she relaxes as her body melts into mine. "Why don't you have a shower and warm up?"

"Okay. Will you have one with me?" she asks sweetly, snaking her arms around my waist. Does she even need to ask? I had every intention of accompanying her, with or without an invite. I grab the toiletry bag out of the small suitcase I packed. "I don't have any pyjamas," she says when I follow her into the bathroom. My hand reaches out to touch her perfect arse. My need for her is overwhelming.

"That was my plan," I reply, slinking my other arm around her waist and pulling her back against my front. I run my nose up her sleek neck. Fuck she smells amazing. "You won't need any." My mouth moves along her jaw as my hands slide up her toned stomach before palming her perfect tits in my hand. Her head tilts to the side as a small moan escapes her. Those little noises she makes, make me fucking crazy.

I'd planned to take her in the shower against the tiles, but I can't wait that long. I need to finish what we started back in the car, right now. I take a step back and peel her jacket off her shoulders, tossing it to the side. My hands skim down her sides as I bunch up her dress, lifting it over her head.

I retreat another step as I drink in her perfect naked body. The only think she's wearing, is those sexy as fuck shoes. "Place your hands on the vanity and spread those incredible legs of yours," I command. Like the good girl she is, she does exactly as she's told. I slide out of my jacket and toss it on top of her clothes. As I loosen my tie and remove it, my eyes don't leave her once. She's watching me through the mirror in front of her.

The anticipation is almost too much as I unbutton my shirt. I need to have her now. I pull my wallet out of my back pocket and remove a condom before flinging it to the side. I place the foil packet between my teeth as I work feverishly at my belt. Sliding it out of the loops in one swift movement, I drop it to the floor. I make quick work of my button and zipper on my pants before shoving them down, taking my boxer briefs with them.

Ripping open the packet, I slide it over my rock hard cock as I slip out of my shoes, remove my socks, and step out of my pants. Her eyes rake over my body through the reflection in the mirror. Her beautiful face is flushed and her stance widens as I take the few steps that divide us.

A loud growl rivets from deep within my chest as my arm snakes around her waist and I pull her incredible arse back towards me. "I'm going to fuck you hard and fast," I breathe as my lips find her neck.

"Yes please," she moans as she lifts her arm and slides it around the back of my neck. "Fuck me now, Carter. I can't wait another second." *Sweet Jesus.* Hearing her say that is almost my undoing.

"Place both hands on the vanity," I order. As much as I like her hands on me, she needs to hold on. She's been dying for my dick to be inside her all night, so I'm going to give her exactly what she wants. I'm not going to go easy on her this time.

My fingers slide between her legs. I already know she's going to be hot and ready for me, but I need to make sure before I pound into her. The last thing I want is to hurt her. I groan when I feel her dripping. Lining up my head with her entrance, I push all the way in. I'm balls-deep in her heaven. Christ she feels amazing.

Giving her body a few seconds to adjust, I pull her hair to the side and run my tongue across her shoulder and up her neck before sucking her earlobe into my mouth. Slowly pulling back out to the tip, I thrust back in.

"Oh God yes," she whimpers. "Don't stop." I have no plans of stopping. My fingers dig into her hip, holding her still, while my other hand slides around the front of her and between her legs so my fingers can circle her clit. She lets out a small cry as her pussy clenches around my cock. I know she's already on the verge of coming undone. She's not the only one.

Picking up the pace, I continue to pound into her, over and over. I watch her eyes roll back in her head through the mirror, and she screams out my name. I love it when she does that. I love that even when she's so consumed with bliss, she knows it's me that is making her feel that way.

Her body goes limp, but I hold her tight against me without relenting my assault. My fingers still rub her clit as my cock thrusts into her sweet pussy again and again. Not even a minute later, she cries out again as another orgasm engulfs her. It's enough to send me over the edge.

When her legs give way from complete exhaustion, I lift her into my arms and carry her towards the shower recess. Hopefully the hot water will revitalise her, because I'm not even close to having my fill yet.

EIGHTEEN

INDIANA

I WAKE IN THE MORNING TO CARTER'S BEAUTIFUL FACE BE-
tween my legs. It's a wonderful sight I can tell you. This is the second
time since we've reconnected that I've awoken to him doing this. It's
something I could easily get used to. Mark wasn't a big fan of oral sex.
I, on the other hand, love it. There's something so erotic about it.

"Good morning," he says against my sensitive flesh when I moan
and thread my fingers through his hair.

"Morning," I whimper breathlessly.

After the incredible sex we had when we arrived at the hotel last
night, Carter carried me into the shower when my legs threatened to
give out. After he washed every inch of me, he took me up against the
tiles. I know it's only been a few days, but it's like we can't get enough
of each other.

He seemed concerned about me when we got out of the shower. He
said I looked tired and pale. He had no reason to worry. Although my
headaches are still playing havoc, they don't seem to bother me so

much when I'm lost in him. He's all the medicine I need.

Even though I told him I was fine, he wrapped me in a towel and sat me on the edge of the bath and dried my hair. It was very sweet. When he was done, he ordered me to bed. I'll admit I was a tad disappointed when he wrapped me in his arms and demanded I get some sleep. I was hoping for round three.

I'm surprised I'm not feeling apprehensive about my doctor's appointment later this morning. Maybe that will come after. Right now, I'd be lucky if I could remember my own name. Thanks to Carter and his magical tongue, I'm overwhelmed by the magnitude of feelings pulsing through me. If eating pussy was an Olympic sport he would win the gold medal, hands down.

He pushes two fingers inside me, hooking them to reach my G-spot, at the same time sucking my clit into his mouth. "Oh God yes," I moan, pushing my hips up towards his face while my head sinks further back into the pillow. When he groans loudly, the vibrations sends me over the edge. My body convulses as my orgasm hits hard.

He's smiling as he kisses his way back up my body, his eyes locked on mine. His bed hair is sticking up all over the place, but he still looks as gorgeous as ever. My heart starts to race as his lips meet mine. I'm overcome with love for this man. I wish I could tell him how I feel. I want him to know just how much he means to me, but I don't want to scare him off.

I can't lose him again.

"Can you be my alarm clock every morning?" I ask as my fingers smooth back his hair.

"If I could be between your legs every morning, I'd be a happy man," he chuckles as his lips move along my jawline and down my neck.

"That could be arranged," I say jokingly. Removing his mouth from me, he raises his head. His expression is serious as his eyes meet mine.

"Well arrange it," he deadpans. I start to laugh. "What's so funny?"

"You," I say. "You know if you were to be between my legs every morning, we'd have to spend every night together." Well I suppose he could always sneak in my window before dawn, but that's going to be near impossible since he lives two hours away. I dread him going back home, but I don't even want to think about that right now.

"And your point?" he replies, raising one of his eyebrows. Surely he can't be serious. As much as I'd like to spend every night with him, I'm pretty sure he wouldn't want that. I thought he was joking, but the serious look on his face tells me he's not.

I turn my head to the side. For some reason I'm suddenly finding it hard to meet his gaze. I don't want to get my hopes up. This is Carter Reynolds we're talking about. Mr. I-don't-do-commitment.

"Hey," he says, placing his finger under my chin and turning my face back towards his. "Wouldn't you like to wake up with me every morning?" I can clearly hear the hurt in his voice. The uncertainty on his face tugs at my heart.

"Of course I would," I reply, trying to reassure him. "I thought you were joking."

"Well I'm not. I'm in love with you Indiana. I want this. I want us." I feel the corners of my lips turn up. Did he just say he loved me?

"You love me?"

"I don't just love you, sweetheart. You own me, *completely*. It's crazy how much. I never thought anyone could make me feel like this, but fuck me, you do. You make me feel it all. I loved you when I walked away five years ago, and I've never stopped. It'll only ever be you." His hand comes up to brush the hair back off my face. Tears sting my eyes from his sweet words.

"I love you too, Carter," I admit. My heart is singing right now knowing he feels the same way about me as I do him. I've never said that to a guy before. Well except my dad, but that doesn't count. Carter's face breaks out into a huge smile. Before I get to say another word, his mouth crashes into mine.

He nudges my legs open with his knee as he settles between my thighs. I can feel his erection pushing against my leg. His hand reaches out to the side while his lips remain on me. I know he's feeling for the condoms he left on the bedside table last night.

When he retrieves it he pulls back, leaning on his haunches as he rolls it on. His eyes never once leave mine. "I can't believe you love me," he whispers. *Well believe it.* When he settles between my legs again, the smile I see on his face melts my heart. Despite what he thinks of himself, he's an easy person to love. He laces his fingers through mine, pinning them above my head.

No words are spoken as he ever so slowly slides inside me. His lips meet mine as he gently rocks his hips forward. This time he doesn't fuck me, he makes sweet and passionate love to me. He gives me every piece of him, and I do the same as our hearts merge as one.

I love him right down to the depths of my soul.

••••

We crawl out of bed an hour later. I feel like I'm floating. I've never felt this happy, this whole. Carter runs me a bath to soak in while he orders breakfast. He hasn't stopped smiling since we've told each other how we feel. Being with him just feels so right. It always has. I know that's why I never completely moved on. Why I couldn't give myself fully to Mark. My heart has always belonged to Carter. It always will.

When I get out of the bath I wrap myself in a towel and pick up my crumpled dress off the floor. I guess I'm going to have to wear this home. *We'll have to call to the house on the way to my appointment.* My stomach churns when I think about that. I pray that we're going to get some good news today. Surely life couldn't be that cruel. We've only just found each other again.

"Hey," Carter says coming into the bathroom and snapping me out of my thoughts. "You okay?" His hands slide around my waist from behind as he places a soft kiss on my cheek.

"I'm fine," I reply turning my head to meet his gaze. "We're going to have to call to my place so I can get some clothes."

"I packed some. They're laying on the bed."

"They are?" You can clearly hear the surprise in my voice.

"Uh huh," he replies like he's proud of himself.

"They better not be skimpy." He chuckles at my comment.

"I did consider it, but I knew you had your appointment, so I packed jeans and a sweater thingy, or whatever you call them."

"And underwear?"

"That too," he says, turning me in his arms and planting a kiss on my nose. "Get dressed, breakfast has just arrived. I bought you a new toothbrush as well. It's in the toiletry bag on the vanity. Oh, and some girly deodorant. Can't have my girl stinky." I release a small laugh, playfully punching him in the arm. I'll give him stinky.

"Thank you," I say wrapping my arms around his waist, squeezing him tight. "For everything." I feel tears sting my eyes again. I'm feeling so overwhelmed right now.

It's like this thing between us is too good to be true. I pray that's not the case.

••••

My leg won't stop bouncing as we sit in the doctor's room waiting to be called. I'm trying my best to act cool, but I'm failing miserably. I cross my legs at the same time Carter reaches for my hand. It's just the two of us today. My dad called before we left the hotel, but Carter talked him out of coming with us. Knowing my dad, he wouldn't have been impressed, but Carter did promise to call him the minute we had the results.

Carter brings my hand up to his mouth, placing a kiss on my knuckles. I smile at him trying to let him know I'm okay, even though my stomach is churning inside.

"The doctor will see you now, Ms. Montgomery," the nurse says from behind her desk. Carter stands first pulling me up with him. He laces his fingers through mine as we walk down the small corridor towards the doctor's room. I've given up on trying to stop him from coming with me. Secretly I'm glad. I need him. He's quickly becoming my rock.

"Whatever the doctor says, we face it together," Carter whispers in my ear as his hold on my hand tightens. I'm not sure if I could get through this without him. He's been wonderful. I give him a tight, nervous smile when his eyes meet mine. I'm afraid if I talk right now, I'll cry.

The doctor greets us at the door. He shakes both our hands before offering us a seat. As soon as we're seated, Carter reaches for my hand again. My eyes dart towards him. His eyes are planted firmly on the doctor. His brow is furrowed, worry clearly visible on his face. This time, I squeeze his hand as calmness settles over me. I suddenly realise that whatever the doctor is about to say is irrelevant. We have each other. For how long, who knows, but in this moment that's all that seems to matter.

My eyes leave Carter when the doctor speaks. "I have your results from the MRI, Indiana." I hold my breath as I wait for him to continue. "I'm pleased to say there's no secondary cancer present." My cheeks puff out as I release my breath slowly. My eyes move to Carter, and the relief on his face is evident. His gaze meets mine and his lips turn up into a beautiful smile.

"That's great news," Carter says turning his attention back to the doctor. "What happens from here?"

"Well, I'd like to put Indiana on a course of steroids for the next two weeks to relieve any swelling around the tumour, then we can get started on the radiation therapy. I have some information I'd like you to read through in the meantime. It will answer any questions you may have. It also outlines the benefits, risks, and side effects that may arise, things of that nature."

"What are the risks and side effects?" Carter asks. I'm glad he's got it together enough to ask questions. My mind is on overload at the moment.

"The risks are minimal. That's why I've chosen this avenue instead of surgery. The tumour is small so you'll be receiving small doses of radiation over a six-week period. Longer if required, but I'm pretty confident it won't be needed. The radiation will kill off any cancer cells and hopefully prevent it from growing or spreading. As for the side effects, you may not experience any. People react quite differently to the treatment. You may feel nauseous, or have a loss of appetite. It's important you eat correctly whilst undergoing the radiation therapy. There's a list of foods and things you should avoid in the package. You may experience fatigue and some hair loss, but again, every case is different. Your skin on your head may become dry and itchy, but there are creams that can help with that. All in all, nothing too serious. The benefits far outweigh all of that."

There's so much to take in it's making my head spin. If this radiation therapy is going to cure me, then I'll take any side effect they want to throw at me. In the grand scheme of things, if it's going to save my life I don't really care.

"Everything you should and shouldn't do is clearly outlined in the pamphlets inside the envelope. Please read up on them. It's best if you know everything going into this."

"We will," Carter assures him. I'm feeling very overwhelmed by it all.

The doctor must see the indecision on my face because he adds, "You're young and healthy. You have everything on your side, Indiana." He gives me a reassuring smile as he passes me the envelope. "I'll get you that script for the steroids." I watch as his fingers move over the keyboard in front of him before he reaches for the printed script in the tray. "If you have any concerns after reading through the information, don't hesitate to call me. It's pretty straightforward and should answer any questions you may have."

"Thank you," I say as he leans over the desk handing me the script.

"I'll get you to make an appointment with me for one week's time, and we can discuss any of your concerns and get you prepared to start the treatment the following week. What type of work do you do?"

"I'm between jobs," I admit. I still can't believe Mark fired me, the arsehole. It's not like I could've kept working there under the circumstances, I suppose, but I'm eager to find something else. I love what I do. I miss my animals.

"Well maybe that's a good thing. You're going to need plenty of rest during the course of the treatment, so maybe you should put that off for a few months. Or at the very least, find casual work." Thankfully I live at home with my dad, so I can survive without money for a little longer. I do have savings I can dip into if needed.

When he stands, Carter and I follow. Carter reaches for his hand first before I do the same. "Thanks, doc," Carter says as we're leaving.

As soon as we exit the building, Carter pulls me into his arms before swinging me around. "I'm so fucking happy," he says before placing me back on my feet. "Well I'm happy things aren't worse than we thought. I still hate that you have to go through this." He cups my face, giving me a sad smile. "You've got this in the bag. You know that right?" he adds confidently as he pulls me into a crushing hug. "I've gotta call your dad. He's waiting to hear back from me."

I smile as he releases me and pulls out his phone. Although what lies ahead is daunting to say the least, his happiness is infectious.

NINETEEN

CARTER

WE STOP OFF AT THE PHARMACY ON THE WAY HOME AND PICK
up the steroids. I can't wipe the smile off my face. I know we still have
a long road ahead, but after today's results I'm hopeful. She's tough.
My fiery little kick-arse. I have every confidence she'll come out of this
cancer free. I'm not even going to entertain the alternative. I refuse to
go there. I've just got her back. *I won't lose her again.*

"You okay?" I ask when we pull into her driveway. She's been
pretty quiet all the way home. Well, ever since I told her I'd be heading
back to Newcastle later today. I wish I could stay longer, but my shop
needs me. She'll always be my first priority, but I have a backlist of
clients since I've cancelled so many appointments. I'm going to be
taking a lot of time off when the treatment starts, so I'll need to stay on
top of it until then.

*Doesn't she realise how hard it's going to be for me being away from
her?*

"I'm fine," she replies reaching for my hand and forcing out a smile.

She's not fucking fine. Why do chicks say that shit?

"You sure? You know you could always come home with me. I'll have you back in time for your appointment next week." Her smile widens when I say that, and I can tell she's giving it some serious thought. I'd love to take her back with me. I'm not sure why I didn't think to ask her before now. I guess I was scared she'd say no.

"I don't know," she answers with a shrug. "You've got work every day. I'm only going to get in your way."

"Bullshit. I live above my shop. I converted it into an apartment when I bought the building. I'll be right downstairs. You can come and go as you please. Or I can come upstairs in between clients. The beach is across the road, and I have a small grassed area out the back for LJ." I sound so fucking pathetic the way I'm rattling everything off in the hope she'll say yes. Taking her home with me is a brilliant idea. I want her by my side, in my space. I need it. I'm not going to be able to concentrate all week having her so far away from me. "Please say you'll come," I beg, clutching her hands in mine. "If you hate it up there, I'll bring you straight back."

"If I'm with you, I won't hate it," she admits.

"Then you'll come?"

"I'll come." Before she has a chance to say another word, my mouth is on hers. I can't believe she's agreed to come back with me. I can't wait to show her my place, my work, the area where I live. I'm fucking beaming like a fool when I pull out of the kiss. I'm deliriously friggin' happy.

This just proves she's the one. Once upon a time, the thought of sharing my life and my home with someone would've freaked me the hell out. It's something I wouldn't have even considered. Now I can't wait to get up there. I can't wait to go to bed with her every night, wake up with her every morning, and to share my days with her.

"Why don't you go inside and pack? I'm gonna see if there's anything my mum needs doing before I leave, then I'll come over and get you." I cup her face in my hands, placing one more kiss on her lips.

"Okay. Can I have my underwear back?" Her comment makes me

chuckle.

"I'll think about it."

"You better pack me some, mister," she demands, reaching out and pinching my arm. "I mean it."

"Ouch," I say with a chuckle. "Your fingers are almost as lethal as your knee."

••••

After I run a few small errands for my mum and take her garbage out to the trash bin, I head towards my room. The quicker I get packed up, the quicker I can take Indi home with me. I'm really looking forward to having her up there. Hopefully she'll want to stay the whole week, and I can bring her back for her next appointment with the oncologist.

After throwing my stuff into my bag, I open the bedside drawer next to my bed to retrieve my sketchpad. Inside I find a small piece of paper sitting on top.

You can't tell me where and how I choose to get pleasure!

As soon as I read it, I start laughing. *Like hell I can't.* I can, and I damn well will. Of course, when I rifle around in the drawer I find the vibrator missing. I'll get it back. You just wait and see.

After the rest of my things are packed, I head towards the kitchen to say goodbye to my mum. I've seen a vast improvement in her this visit. She still has her moments, but I'm confident in time she'll get past this. He was not the man she thought he was. When I see her shedding tears for him, I want to tell her the truth about what type of person he really was, but that's only going to upset her more.

••••

"Did you pack the information from the doctor?" I ask Indiana as I place her suitcase in the trunk of my car.

"No I didn't. I better go grab it." I smile as she turns and runs back into the house.

"Look after my girl," Ross says as I reach for his hand.

"You don't need to ask me that. Of course I will."

"I know," he replies placing his hand on my shoulder. "You're good for her, son." His words make me smile. She's good for me is what I want to say, but I don't.

While Indi hugs her father goodbye, I pull my seat forward so LJ can climb in the back. "There's some containers in the freezer with that pasta dish we had a few nights ago, and the chicken casserole from the weekend, if you don't feel like cooking while I'm gone. Oh and—"

"I'll be fine, Pumpkin," he says cutting her off and wrapping her in his arms. "I survived when you were away at college didn't I?"

"I guess," she admits with a giggle. "You should invite Elizabeth over for dinner one night if you get lonely."

"I'll keep that in mind," he chuckles, kissing the top of her head. I open Indi's door for her when she walks around to the passenger side. I can't even put into words how excited I am that she's coming home with me. I feel like a little kid on Christmas morning.

Once I'm seated in the driver's side, Ross leans in my window. "I'm only a phone call away if you need me," he says, soft enough for only me to hear. I know there's an underlying meaning to his words. He has no reason to worry. I intend to keep a very close eye on Indiana while she's staying with me. I'd never let anything happen to her. I think Ross knows that.

••••

For most of the drive we travel in a comfortable silence. Except for when Indi is singing along to the radio. It's sweet. I love how relaxed she is around me. There's nothing pretentious about her at all. What you see is what you get.

"I can't wait to see your place," she says placing her hand on top of mine. "Meg and I went to Newcastle a few years ago for a girl's weekend, when I was at Uni." I look over at her and smile. I would've been living up here then. If only I'd known. It would've blown my mind if I had ran into them.

"How is Meg? Do you still see her?" When we were kids those two were always together.

"She lives overseas with her husband, Drew. We still talk on the phone when we can, but it's not the same." You can clearly hear the sadness in her voice as she talks. "They move around a lot, and with the time differences between countries, it's hard. I miss her so much." I bet she does. *Meg married?* For some reason I can't picture that.

"Does she know about the tumour?"

"No. She has her own worries. She doesn't need to be burdened down with mine," she replies giving me a half-hearted smile.

"Regardless, Indi. She's your friend, she'd want to know." She shrugs at my reply.

"If the opportunity arises next time we talk, I'll tell her." I can see this subject is getting her down, so I quickly change it to something else.

"I can't wait for you to see my shop. There's something special about it that I haven't told you," I say squeezing her hand.

"Really?" Her face lights up when she looks at me. "What?"

"You'll see when we get there."

••••

"Indi Ink," she whispers when I pull up outside. "Oh my God. You named your shop after me," she squeals, her head snapping in my direction.

"I did," I reply smiling when I see the look on her face.

"When?" she asks excitedly as we exit the car.

"When I opened it."

"But that was four years ago." Her beautiful eyes widen when she walks towards the shop, her head tilted back so she can see the sign.

"I know. It's silly I guess, but I wanted you to be a part of it somehow."

"It's not silly," she whispers before launching herself into my arms. "It's amazing. I'm so touched that you would do that." Her lips are on mine before I get a chance to reply. "I love it. I love you," she says against my mouth. My hands slide around her waist, drawing her closer. I love that she loves me, because I love her so fucking much.

TWENTY

INDIANA

"THANK YOU FOR MAKING ME PART OF YOUR SHOP," I SAY WHEN I pull back from the kiss. I got all choked up when I first saw it. I thought maybe he'd changed the name recently, but the fact he named it after me, even when I wasn't in his life anymore, means so much more. It confirms everything I hoped all those years ago—that he *hadn't* forgotten about me after he left, and that I *did* mean something to him.

"You still held my heart the whole time I was gone," he admits, making me melt. The sincerity in his words brings a lump to my throat as my hold on him tightens. I can't believe we wasted five long years of our lives apart. In saying that though, I know it will only make us more appreciative of what we have now.

"Can we go in and take a look around?" I ask with excitement. I want to see what it looks like inside. I want to see him in all his glory. I'm so proud of everything he's achieved. Even though my heart was broken after he left, the hardest part for me was not knowing what had become of him. He was all alone. A teenager with a huge chip on his shoulder and a mountain of anger inside him. That's what worried me the most.

My main concern was that he'd get himself into trouble. Or worse, turn to alcohol or drugs to cope. I'm so grateful that wasn't the case. Even back then, as much as he tried to hide it, I knew his heart was good. He was just tainted by a stupid word.

"Really? You want to go inside now?" The disappointment in his voice doesn't go unnoticed. When he pulls me back against him and I feel his hard on pressing into my back, I know why. "I was hoping to take you upstairs first." The hopeful look on his face almost has me agreeing. But I want to get this out of the way so we can lock ourselves away for the rest of the night. I've been busting to see it.

"Just a quick one. Then you can take me upstairs and ravish me."

"Deal," he says grabbing hold of my hand and dragging me towards the shop. He unlocks the door and flicks on the main switch lighting the place up. My eyes dart everywhere as he disables the alarm system. I love it already. It's nothing like I imagined.

"Okay. You've seen it, let's go." He reaches for my hand to drag me back out the door, but I pull away from him. *Nice try buddy.*

"Let me look around first," I say with a small laugh as I pull out of his grip and step further into the reception area. I hear him sigh behind me, but I ignore it. It's huge. It doesn't look so big from the street. The floors are tiled in a dark charcoal grey. There are two long, black leather sofas right in the middle of the room, sitting on a turquoise blue shag pile rug. A black coffee table sits in the middle of the sofas. There are four large black albums stacked on top.

Walking towards them, I open the first one to see it's full of his drawings. I want to sit down and go through them all, but I know that's going to piss him off, so I'll leave that for later.

Off to the right is a large, black L shaped counter, with three pendant lights positioned strategically above it. This place has so much class. It's nothing like what I imagined a tattoo parlour would look like. I'm fascinated by every detail. My fingers run over everything as I pass. The walls are painted in the same turquoise colour as the rug, and the large black and white framed drawings around the walls stand out against the green. I take it all in as I manoeuvre through the room. There are recessed lights built into the ceiling above each drawing, illuminating them.

My eyes move to Carter, still standing just inside the doorway. His hands are buried in the pockets of his jeans as he stands back observing me. "I love seeing you in my space," he says as he stalks towards me. I love that he brought me here.

"This place is beautiful," I tell him. "I'm so proud of you." My arms snake around his neck as I tilt my head back to make eye contact with him. "Really proud, Carter."

"Thank you," he replies bringing his mouth down on mine. "Can I take you upstairs now?" His comment makes me laugh.

"I haven't finished my tour yet. Show me around the rest of the place." He exhales in frustration.

"Fine, but it's gonna be quick." He reaches for my hand, pulling me through the room towards a long corridor. There is a stack of doors all the way down. At least ten each side, maybe more. "These are the rooms of my artists. Where all the magic takes place," he explains.

"You have that many people working for you?" I ask surprised.

"Yes. I have twenty-three people on the books, not including me: twenty artists, plus Vicki, who does all the piercings. Justine works on the front desk and then there's Jacquie. She does all the stocking and ordering of supplies."

"Wow." I don't know what else to say. For some reason I thought it was just him and maybe one or two other people working here. I'm blown away. "Which room is yours?" He leads me down to the end of the corridor.

"The biggest one," he chuckles. "I'm the boss, I've gotta have some perks." Of course he'd have to have the biggest. That doesn't surprise me in the least. He grabs his keys out of his pocket and unlocks the door.

"Why is the door locked?"

"All the doors have locks on them. My guys each have their own keys, and I have a master key that unlocks them all. The equipment we use is expensive. It just made sense to fit locks on the doors when I had the shop fitted out."

"Makes sense," I say in agreement. When he switches on the light he steps to the side so I can enter. Again it's nothing like I imagined. It's bright and sterile looking. I suppose it has to be given the nature of the business. The walls are painted white. Along the back wall sits a black leather flat bed. Over in the corner is a matching soft black leather reclining chair with an adjustable stool beside it. There's a stainless steel bench off to one side, with two long lamps that have retractable extending arms attached. Another stainless steel cabinet sits off to the side of that. It has small drawers down both sides.

I walk towards the frames hanging along the left wall. They're all certificates. "Did you win all these awards?"

"Yeah. Jax made me enter them when I worked for him. I don't have time for that shit anymore."

"That's amazing," I say looking over my shoulder at him. He has a shy boyish smile on his face that I find very endearing. My eyes are drawn to the large picture behind him. "Oh my God, Carter. That's me." It's a huge framed sketch of my face. It takes up half of the wall. *Far out.*

"Yeah," he replies, scratching his head and bowing his face like he's embarrassed that I've seen it. I step around him to get a closer look. *It's beautiful.* My mouth is curved up into a natural smile. He has drawn my eyes with such detail they actually look like they're sparkling. Is this how he sees me? I stand there for the longest time just staring at it. I'm mesmerised.

Carter comes up behind me as I take it all in. His arms snake around my waist and his lips trail a path up my neck. "Let's get out of here before I bend you over the bed and fuck you senseless. Having you in this room makes me want to do all kinds of crazy shit." I tilt my head to the side and smile as he sucks my earlobe into his mouth. When he bites down softly, I moan.

"I'm game," I breathe, turning in his arms.

"Don't tempt me, because I'm already on edge." The desire I see in his eyes sends tingles down my spine. Sliding my arms around the back of his neck, I pull his lips down to mine. That's all the encouragement he needs. Before I know it, I'm backed up against the wall and my top is being pulled over my head.

His mouth, tongue, and hands are everywhere. Grabbing hold of the hem of his T-shirt, I slide it upwards as my fingers move over his delicious abs. He reaches behind himself, tugging at the neckline before ripping it over his head. My mouth goes straight to his nipple ring, as I swirl my tongue around it before sucking it into my mouth.

Tilting his head back he groans loudly. "I need to be inside you now," he breathes. His hands move around my back as his fingers work at unclasping my bra. Sliding it down my arms, he lets it drop to the floor. My body melts into him as his hands run up my sides until he reaches my breasts, palming them.

My fingers work frivolously at his pants, undoing the button and fly. Once they're undone, I pull them down over his hips taking his boxers with them. Wrapping my hand around his hard length, I stroke it. "I can't wait another second," he groans as he spins me around before lifting and laying me face down on the bed. His hands move around to my front and he makes quick work of undoing my jeans and reefing them and my underwear down my legs. "Get on your knees," he commands. I do exactly as he says.

My arse is high in the air and I'm completely exposed to him, but I'm so turned on I don't even care. I want, no, I need his hands, his mouth or his cock in me now. Like he just read my mind, his finger runs from my clit, sliding through my wetness before sinking deep inside me. My back arches as I push my body into his hand. "Oh God," I moan.

"That's not my name," he says in a stern voice as he pulls his finger out before adding another and gliding them back in.

"Carter. Please fuck me," I beg. When his fingers leave me and I hear the foil wrapper tear, I know I'm about to get exactly what I asked for. I moan loudly when I feel him rub his length around my entrance. His fingers slide up my back until he reaches my hair. Wrapping my ponytail around his wrist, he gently tugs my head back.

"I remember the first day I met you," he whimpers, sliding all the way inside me. "My first thought that day was exactly this. I wanted to bend you over, grab hold of your hair and fuck you hard." He pulls almost all the way out before slamming back into me. He repeats the process over and over until I'm screaming. What we're doing is hot and feels so damn good.

"Don't stop," I moan. The rougher the better. It just turns me on more. Every time he slams back into me, the head of the bed hits the wall with a loud thud. "Harder," I implore as my fingers clutch tightly onto each side, digging into the leather to hold me in place. He's never been this rough with me before, but I love it. It's so primal, so raw. It's fucking at its best.

"Fuck, Indi," he cries as his fingers dig into my hips, stilling me. He continues to pound into me in hard, short strokes. "I love you so much, Indiana." That's all I need to send me over the edge.

"Carter," I moan as my head tilts towards the roof and my eyes roll back in my head. "I'm coming ..."

"I know, baby. I love the way your pussy grips my cock when you come," he groans out as he pumps into me a few more times before his body shudders then stills.

His lips find my neck when he collapses down on top of me. "That was amazing," I pant.

"It was," he replies as his lips curve into a smile against my skin. "I'm never gonna look at this bed the same way again."

"I think we marked the wall," I giggle.

"I don't give a fuck about the wall. I didn't hurt you did I?"

"Not at all," I say turning my head to meet his lips. He smiles as his hand comes up to brush the hair off my face. The love I see in his eyes melts my heart. Nobody will ever make me feel the way he does. *Nobody.*

He plants another kiss on my lips before he pushes off me and stands. "Get dressed. I want to take you upstairs. You can soak in the bath while I fix us something to eat, then I'm taking you to bed." The look of promise I see on his face sends my heart into a flutter. I'm so glad I came up here with him. I already know this week is going to be amazing.

TWENTY-ONE

CARTER

NEITHER OF US REALISED THAT POOR LJ WAS STILL IN THE back of the car until we heard him barking when we exited the shop. Indi rushed straight to him while I retrieved the bags from the trunk. After carrying him over to the grassed area next to my building so he could relieve himself, we head upstairs.

I've always loved living here, but having her with me now makes coming home all the better. I've redone the whole upstairs area, the kitchen, bathroom, everything. At this stage it only has one bedroom, but the old man that owns the adjoining building is only months off retiring and I'm already in negotiations for buying him out.

When I do, I have plans of knocking down the wall between my apartment and the one above his shop and extending my living space, as well as adding two more bedrooms. I'll probably rent out the shop below with plans of expanding my parlour when I have more cash flow.

"Wow, look at the view from up here," Indi says when I usher her inside. When I moved in, I had the pissy little windows on the far wall replaced with floor to ceiling ones. The view of the ocean from up here is spectacular. I only wish I could've added a balcony out here, but council regulations forbid it. *Fuckers.*

You can see all the way to the horizon, and the sunset is really something. I can't wait to share that with Indi while she's here. "The view looks mighty fine from in here, too," I tell her as I wrap my arms around her from behind, resting my chin on her shoulder. I can see her smile reflecting in the glass in front of us. Fuck I'm so stoked to have her here.

Turning, she snakes her arms around my neck. "Thank you for inviting me to come stay with you. It's so surreal to be here in your place. I'm so happy, Carter." For some reason, her words bring a lump to my throat. I can't even reply, so instead I tighten my embrace and savour the feeling of having her in my arms.

••••

"I love your apartment," she says when we sit down to eat. I ran her a bath after showing her around, which took all of three minutes. There really isn't much to see. My living area is open-plan. My kitchen and dining table is off to the left when you walk in the front door. I have an L-shaped black leather sofa over on the far side of the room, facing my large flat screen TV that's mounted on the feature wall. To the left of the sofa, I have a full-size pool table and bar area. Behind that is the door that leads to my bedroom and the bathroom. "It's the perfect bachelor pad," she says with humour in her voice. "And so tidy. Do you have a cleaner or something?"

"Or something," I reply flatly, suppressing my eye roll. I've always been pretty anal when it comes to things like that. Men are capable of keeping a clean house, despite what most people think. "Eat before it gets cold."

I called Justine, my receptionist, before I left Sydney and asked her to pick up the ingredients I needed to make Fettucine Boscaiola. I knew it would be late by the time we arrived here, so I wouldn't have time to shop.

"I can't believe you cooked this," she says twirling her pasta around her fork and popping it in her mouth. "It's delicious." I smile at her.

"Well I've lived alone for the past five years. It was learn how to cook or starve, I guess," I reply chuckling.

"You're a man of many talents." I don't miss the underlying meaning to her words. *You better believe I am, sweetheart.*

My dick stirs as I watch her lips slide over the metal utensil. If I wasn't so worried about her keeping up her strength, I'd say to hell with dinner and throw her over my shoulder and take her straight to bed.

After we've eaten and the dishes are done, I wrap her in my arms. "I'm gonna take a quick shower. Why don't you give your dad a call and let him know we arrived safely?" I say kissing the top of her head, inhaling her sweet vanilla scent at the same time. She smells delicious—good enough to eat, and that's exactly what I plan to do as soon as I get her into my bed. She looks cute in the pyjamas she's put on after her bath, but they need to go. She won't be needing those while she's staying here.

••••

I wake feeling the happiest I've been since moving here. I know it's because I have Indi beside me. Now that I have her up here, I don't want her to ever leave. It may be too soon to want her to move in, but I already know that's what I want. Hopefully in time, she'll feel that way as well. Now that I have her back, I have no intentions of letting her go. She's a keeper. *Mine.*

Rolling onto my side, I feel my lips curve into a smile as I watch her sleep. I do this often. Crazy I know, but I love having her next to me. Her long lashes are splayed out, resting on her cheeks. Her perfect lips are parted slightly. Her dark hair is fanned out over the pillow. Reaching up, I lightly brush back the few strands that have fallen over her face. I never knew it was possible to love someone so completely as I do her.

It brings all my worries to the forefront. A slight panic rises within me. What if her treatment isn't successful? What if she decides she no longer wants to be with me? What if she doesn't want me forever, like I do her? I'm not sure how I'd cope without her now.

The last five years have been hell. I lived in denial for too long, fighting my feelings every step of the way. I can't do that anymore. She owns my heart and my soul. She's my air. I'm nothing without her. I suddenly have this overwhelming compulsion to crush her against me, begging her to never leave me.

Fuck. I'm pathetic.

Maybe I should just wake her up and ask for my balls back. I'm pulled from my thoughts when LJ whimpers beside the bed. "Hey, buddy," I whisper, carefully rolling over and looking over the side of the bed. He's been locked inside all night. I guess he needs to take a piss. "Hold on," I say getting out of bed and throwing on a pair of sweats.

"Hey, come back," I hear Indi call out as I tiptoe across the room. My head swings in her direction as she sits up rubbing her eyes. She's so damn sweet when she first wakes. The sheet covering her drops down around her waist, revealing her spectacular tits. It makes my dick twitch. I love that she makes no effort to cover them back up.

Turning, I quickly head back towards her. "Don't move. I'll be back in a minute," I order, placing my lips on hers and groping one of her tits with my hand. "I'm just gonna let LJ out."

"Okay," she smiles slinking her arms around my neck. "Morning."

"Morning, beautiful," I reply brushing the hair off her face. "How's your head this morning?" She shrugs. I hate that she's in constant pain from this damn tumour. I'd give anything to be able to take it away. The sooner this treatment is over, the better. "I'll grab you some headache tablets on my way back."

"Thanks." I kiss her forehead before gently laying her back down. Pushing myself off the bed, I stand and whistle for LJ to follow. It's gonna be a bitch having to go to work today knowing she's up here all alone.

••••

Indi was asleep by the time I made it back upstairs. Not long after slipping in beside her and wrapping her in my arms, she wakes again. "Your tablets are on the bedside table," I say pulling her into me and kissing her forehead.

We stayed wrapped in each other for another hour or so, before I finally had to drag my arse out of bed. I could easily get used to waking up to her every morning. When I headed for the shower so I could get ready for work, she insisted on having one with me. Of course I had to take her up against the tiles. I can't seem to keep my damn hands off her. I think we're both going to be exhausted by the time the end of the week rolls around. *I'm not complaining.*

After dressing, we had breakfast and went down to the shop together. She wanted to meet my guys, and to be honest I was looking forward to showing her off.

"Oh my God," Justine says as soon as she walks through the door and sees Indi standing beside me. "You're the girl from the picture." I'd forgotten about that damn thing. It's been a talking point around here for years. My eyes drift to Indiana, and I'm surprised to find her blushing.

"Justine, this is the love of my life, Indiana—my Indi," I admit proudly, slinking my arm around her shoulder and tucking her into my side. Indiana's beaming when she looks up at me. *I'm only speaking the truth.*

"Wow," is all Justine says with a stunned look on her face as she walks towards us and extends her hand. "Hi ... Holy crap, you actually exist." I chuckle at her comment. For years they've been bugging me wanting to know who the woman in the drawing is. I usually say that's what the woman of my dreams looks like. I wasn't going to tell those fuckers anything. So I guess I can understand her shock. None of them realised she was actually a real person. They thought she was a figment of my imagination.

"It's nice to meet you," Indi replies with a sweet smile on her face. When the front door of the shop opens, all our heads turn in that direction.

"Look Jacquie," Justine squeals, pointing at Indi. "She's real."

TWENTY-TWO

INDIANA

I'VE HAD THE MOST AMAZING WEEK. IT SADDENS ME TO THINK it's coming to an end. I hope Carter asks me to come back up here again, because I've loved every minute of my time with him. This place is absolutely beautiful.

When he's not working, and we're not having sex on every surface of his apartment, he's been taking me everywhere, showing me the sights of Newcastle and the surrounding areas. It's surprising how much better it is when you see things through the eyes of a local. He knows all the best places. I can tell how proud he is of his hometown. I've only been here a week and I'm in love with it too.

We've been for long strolls along the beach every afternoon, and last night he took me to the most amazing waterfront restaurant at the Newcastle Marina, called Rocksalt. He ordered us a grilled seafood plate for two. It was mouth-watering. I could easily get used to living here.

Even though Carter's been working a lot, he's been trying his hardest to come and see me in-between clients, but he's been pretty flat out. He can usually only stay a few minutes when he pops upstairs, but I appreciate him making the effort. He makes sure to spend the whole of his lunch breaks with me though.

I've offered to cook for him, but he insists on taking me to some of the local cafés for lunch. Today though, it was something different. We had a picnic on the beach. He bought some fresh prawns from the fish market, and we ate them straight out of the white paper wrapping. They were divine, just like my company. I didn't think it was possible to love him anymore than I already do, but with each passing day I seem to fall even harder.

To be honest, I'm kind of glad I haven't had to do much because I'm exhausted. My headaches seem to be getting worse and I'm feeling tired all the time. I've been hiding it from him. I don't want him to worry more than he already is. He's trying to play it down, but I see the unease in his eyes when he looks at me. He's always checking on me or asking how I'm feeling, so I know he's concerned.

After our picnic, he walked me back upstairs to his apartment before heading back to work. The first thing I did was collapse onto the sofa. I've been using our time apart to take naps.

His appointments can take anywhere from one to three hours, so he's none the wiser that I'm usually sleeping while he's not here. It gives me the pick-me-up I need for when he's around, but it's also a welcome relief from the throbbing pain in my head. I'm over it. I'm sick of feeling so *blah* all the time.

I'm woken by tiny kisses being rained all over my face. "Hey, beautiful," Carter says when I open my eyes. "Are you feeling okay?" I can see the anxiety on his face so I smile hoping to ease his mind.

"I'm fine," I reply when he moves back so I can sit up. "I must've fallen asleep. What time is it?"

"4:00pm." Shit it was just after one when we arrived back from lunch. I've been asleep for almost three hours. "I was gonna take you for a spin on my jet-ski, but if you're not up to it ..."

"You have a jet-ski?" I ask excitedly. He sits down beside me on the sofa, pulling me onto his lap.

"I do." He smiles before placing his lips against my cheek. "I usually take it out on the weekends. Jax has one as well, so we go out together when he's up here. Since we're going back to Sydney tomorrow, I thought we could go out now, if you're game." The thought of leaving here tomorrow makes my heart feel heavy. Carter's been wonderful and made me feel so welcome. I want to get as much in as I can before I leave. I've never been out on a jet-ski before.

"I'm game," I tell him as I snake my arms around his neck.

"You sure you're up to it?" he asks, unease masking his voice. I wish he'd stop worrying about me.

"Of course. Let's do this," I reply, standing and reaching for his hand.

"I love how easy-going you are," he says with a sweet smile as he picks a bag up off the ground and passes it to me. "I bought you a wetsuit and life jacket. The water's pretty cold this time of year."

"You did? Thank you," I reply beaming, taking the bag from him and looking inside. He spoils me. The wetsuit is black with large patches of pink throughout, matching the life jacket perfectly. I love that he chose my favourite colour. I'm touched by his thoughtfulness. Getting up on the tips of my toes, I brush my lips against his.

"Go get changed while I hook the trailer up to the car," he says leaning down and kissing my forehead. "I'll meet you downstairs when you're ready."

••••

I had the most amazing time on the jet-ski and being wrapped around his sinful body as he sped across the water. The smell of the salty sea, the sun on my face and the wind in my hair, made me feel invigorated. We stayed out there for close to two hours. Carter took it easy as we navigated through the waves. I'm pretty sure that was for my benefit. I was grateful.

He didn't let loose until we reached the calmer water. Thankfully, it was a nice day, so it wasn't choppy. We did hit one bump that made my face screw up from the sudden jolt to my aching head. Surprisingly though, there's something about being with him that seems to lessen the constant pain in my brain. Maybe I'm just so lost in him I don't focus on it so much. Maybe it's something else.

Before coming back into shore, Carter stopped about a kilometre out to sea. He moved me to the front of the jet-ski and wrapped me in his arms while we sat and watched the beginning of the sun setting on the horizon. It was majestic. We would've stayed out longer but it was starting to get dark. He's promised to take me out again next time I come up. Hopefully that will be soon.

When we headed back to the apartment, Carter sent me upstairs to run a hot bath, while he washed down the jet-ski before stowing it in the small garage at the rear of the shop.

The warmth of the bath water is welcomed after being out on the ocean in the cold wind for the past few hours. I'm lying back relaxing and reflecting on the wonderful time I've had whilst I've been here, when Carter enters the bathroom. Opening my eyes, I find him stripping out of his wetsuit. "Hope you don't mind some company," he says smirking as he stalks towards me.

"Not at all," I reply as my eyes rake over his magnificent body. He really is beautiful, and all mine. I'm one lucky girl. I lean forward so he can hop in behind me, and sigh contently when he wraps me in his big strong arms.

"You feeling okay?" he asks placing a soft kiss on my shoulder. I wish he'd stop asking me.

"I'm feeling wonderful. I've loved every minute of my time here with you," I tell him, turning my head and brushing my lips against his cheek.

"I'm happy to hear that," he smiles. "Does that mean you'll come back?" The hopeful look I see on his face melts my heart.

"If you'll have me, I'd love to come and stay with you again."

"Next week? I thought maybe we could stay in Sydney for the weekend, so you could spend time with your dad. I could bring you back with me Sunday night." I'm thrilled he wants me back here so soon.

"It sounds wonderful." I turn my body to face him, wrapping my legs around his waist. "But, I don't want to put you out. I don't want to disrupt your life any more than I already have. You've been so good to me."

"Hey," he says cupping my face. "Having you here hasn't disrupted my life at all. Only enhanced it." His words make me smile.

"I love you," I reply bringing my mouth down on his. I love him with every fibre of my being. He's been a wonderful distraction from what lies ahead, and has taken such good care of me. I hate that we have this illness looming over us, but just having him around helps more than he'll ever know.

"Please say you'll come back with me next week then," he whispers against my mouth as he grasps my hips, pulling me forward so our bodies are flush.

"Okay. I'd love that."

"That's my girl." I feel his lips curve into a smile against my mouth. *I love being his girl.* Threading my hands into his hair, I deepen the kiss. Carter groans as he slides his tongue into my mouth. "Jesus, I wanna fuck you so bad right now," he growls.

"Then do it," I say breathlessly.

"I can't, I don't have a condom."

"I'm on birth control, Carter," I say pulling back to look at him. "I've only ever been with one other person, and we never had unprotected sex. I want to experience that with you."

"I've never had unprotected sex either," he sighs, "but it's too risky. I can't take that chance." His words sting. Is the possibility of having a child with me so repulsive?

"Fine," I say trying hard to mask my hurt, but failing miserably. I lift myself off his lap and go to turn, but he holds me still.

"Don't," he growls. "Don't you dare pull away from me, Indi. You know about my past. You know I'd never want to bring an illegitimate child into this world, and risk him being tainted like I was."

"Carter," I say, wrapping my arms around his waist. "I'm sorry. It's just ..."

"Shhh," he whispers, brushing his lips with mine. "Don't think for a minute that I don't want to experience that with you, because I do. I just can't take that chance."

"You could always pull out before you come." I raise my eyebrows hopefully. I want this with him.

"Fuck," he groans taking me in his arms again. "You drive a hard bargain, babe." When his hands slip below the water and between my legs, I know I've won. Tilting my head back, I moan as his fingers circle my clit. "I've always wanted to feel what it was like to go bare back," he whispers against my neck as his tongue trails a path up to the sensitive part behind my ear. "Only with you. It will only ever be you, Indi," he breathes, gripping my hips, lifting me up slightly before pulling me back down and impaling me with his dick.

"Ohhhh, yes," I moan as he fills me completely.

"Sweet Jesus," he groans as his eyes roll back in his head. "You feel like fucking heaven."

Ditto Mr. Reynolds. Ditto.

••••

Carter ordered some takeout Chinese food when we got out of the bath. After we eat, we end up snuggling on the sofa; me between his legs, my back to his front with my head lying on his chest. His fingers make lazy circles against my temples. It feels amazing. I love how he cares for me.

"How are your headaches going today?" he asks.

"They're okay," I lie. "Manageable."

"Do you want me to get you some headache pills?"

"No. What you're doing with your fingers is fine. The pills don't really help anyway." My confession makes him exhale a loud breath.

"I know you've been putting it off, but we really need to go over that information the doctor gave you. We might have some questions for him tomorrow."

"I guess," I sigh. He's right. I have been avoiding it. I didn't want it to spoil my time here with him.

"Where is it?" he asks lifting me off his chest so he can stand.

"Bottom of my suitcase."

When he sits back beside me he opens the envelope, pulling out all the paperwork. He passes me half, keeping the rest for himself. I look over at him and smile. "What?" he asks shrugging. "I'm not letting you read them all on your own. I'll read these, and then we'll swap notes." God I love how invested he is in this.

"I just love you. That's all," I say leaning over and brushing my lips with his. "You're amazing."

"I love you too, Indi. *So much.*"

An hour later, I place my pile on the coffee table. All this reading is making my headache intensify. It's very daunting and way too much information to take in. "You okay?" he asks. His brow furrows as he studies me.

"Yeah. I just need to take a break. The reading is hurting my head."

"Come here," he says pulling my head down on his lap. "Close your eyes. I'll keep going." I sigh when he uses his free hand to massage my scalp.

"Mmmm. That feels nice."

I wake bathed in darkness. I'm in bed. Rolling over I reach out for Carter, but he isn't beside me. Looking at the bedside clock, I see it's 1:30am. Throwing back the covers, I go in search of him. When I enter the main room I smile. He's still sprawled out on the sofa reading. Papers strewed all around him, a pen between his teeth and a notepad on his lap. Guilt consumes me. I feel bad that he's still up doing this while I've been asleep.

"Hey," I say walking towards him. "Come to bed."

"I'm nearly done," he replies, looking up at me and smiling. He picks up the notepad off his lap and jots something down before placing it beside him. He opens his arms when I reach him, pulling me down onto his lap.

"How are you feeling now?"

"Better," I say snuggling into him. I look down at the notepad and see it's filled with writing. "What's all this?" I ask.

"Just some questions for the doctor and things I need to buy once the treatment starts."

"What things?"

"Just some special food you'll need ... stuff like that. You have to be careful what you eat during the treatment. They advise to eat healthy foods and stay away from sweet things, but not me, of course." I laugh at his comment.

"Just let them try and keep me away from you."

"I'd never let that happen, babe," he chuckles, placing his lips on my cheek. "Since the radiation will be going straight to your head, you'll have to be extra careful with your oral hygiene. It can affect your teeth and gums, so you can't eat anything too hot or too cold. I've made a list of all their suggestions for you to go through. We have an amazing Growers Market up here every Sunday. They sell all fresh produce. When the treatment starts we can go there and stock up on all your favourites." Tears rise to my eyes. What did I do to deserve someone so wonderful?

"Thank you," I sniffle as I wrap my arms around his waist. I can't even put into words how amazing he is. "Leave the rest, I'll go over them in the morning before we leave. I need you in bed with me."

"You don't have to ask me twice," he says, standing with me still in his arms. "There's no place I'd rather be, than beside you." Flicking off the light switch with his elbow as he passes, his lips capture mine as he carries me back to bed.

TWENTY-THREE

CARTER

one month later ...

WE'RE IN WEEK THREE OF THE RADIATION THERAPY. THE oncologist put Indiana on a course of radio-sensitising drugs the first week of treatment. They apparently make the cancer cells more sensitive to the radiation, helping to kill them off faster. She's going great guns, but it's been a tough few weeks.

The first week she seemed to breeze through it, with little or no side effects. These last two weeks, not so much. She's having small doses of radiation Monday through to Thursday, and having Friday, Saturday, and Sunday off as her rest days.

We've been driving down Monday morning and staying in Sydney until Thursday, then driving back to my place for the other days. I've been squeezing in as much work as I can, working until late Thursday night, and all day Friday and most of Saturday. I hate leaving her alone, but I need to work. She spends most of her time sleeping anyway.

Mum and Ross both offered to come and stay with her while I worked, but she wouldn't hear of it. I think she feels bad putting people out. She's forever apologising to me. Doesn't she realise how much we all love her? That there's nothing we wouldn't do to make this process easier or more comfortable for her?

I check on her between every client, and if it's a big job, I send Jacquie or Justine up to make sure she's okay and there's nothing she needs. It's killing me to see her so sick. I wasn't prepared for things to get this bad. She's nauseous all the time, so she's not eating as much as I'd like, and has subsequently lost some weight. There was already nothing of her, so it concerns me greatly.

She usually comes good by Sunday, but when the treatment starts up again Monday, she's back to where she started. I usually try and get as much food as I can into her on the good days. I know once this is all over she'll get back to where she was, but in the meantime, it's hard to watch. I'd give anything to change places with her.

Even LJ can tell things aren't right. He hasn't left her side. Follows her everywhere when she's up and about, and lays beside her when she's not. I'm glad he's here with her when I'm downstairs working.

I wish I could spend every second of my time with her, especially on her rest days, but being away from work three and a half days a week is really taking its toll on my clientele. Thankfully, they've been pretty understanding. I've lost a few of my regulars to the other artists, but most have been loyal and stuck by me. It's only for three more weeks, and hopefully we can then put this behind us and life will get back to normal.

To add to my already hectic schedule, the old man next door came over a few weeks back and told me he was planning to shut up shop at the end of the month. He wanted to know if I was still interested in buying his building, which of course I am. I have a few ideas up my sleeve that might help persuade Indi to stay up here permanently once the treatment is finished. Well that's my hope anyway.

So, now I have the added worry of organising finance, as well as getting the architect to draw up the plans to extend the apartment and refit the shop next door. I'd like to get started on the renovations as soon as the purchase is finalised. I'm going to use the same building company that fitted out my place when I first moved here. To be honest, I'm fucking exhausted, but if all goes to plan it's going to be worth it.

After finishing up the colour fill I'm working on, I walk my client out to the front desk, only to find my next job is already waiting for me. "Can you give me five minutes mate?" I ask when I walk over and shake his hand. I just have to duck upstairs quickly.

Only my staff know what's going on with Indiana. I'm a personal guy and don't like to talk about shit like that with my clients.

"Sure. No problem," he replies taking a seat again. I take the steps two at a time as I rush up to check on Indiana. I find her sound asleep in bed. When I see the sandwich I made her at lunchtime still sitting on the bedside table untouched, I exhale. I need her to fucking eat. She's so weak, and this no eating shit isn't helping.

"Indi," I whisper getting down on my knees beside the bed, and smoothing my hand over her hair. "Hey," I say smiling when her eyelids flutter open. She's so fucking pale and pasty, with dark circles under her eyes. It worries me to no end to see her like this.

She's been so courageous. Never once complaining. My heart hurts when her green eyes meet mine. They've lost their sparkle, and I fucking hate that. I just want this to be over with so she can be well again.

"Hi," she says forcing out a smile. I hate that she thinks she needs to be brave for me, because she doesn't.

"How are you feeling?" I ask, helping her when she tries to sit up.

"Okay." That's what she always says, even when I know damn well she isn't.

"You didn't eat your sandwich."

"I wasn't hungry," she replies shrugging her shoulders.

"You've gotta eat, babe," I say in a pleading tone as I tuck some loose strands of hair behind her ear. "You barely touched your breakfast." I pick up the plate off the bedside table and unwrap the sandwich.

"Can you take a bite for me, please? It would make me happy." She gives me a genuine smile when I say that.

"Okay. If it will make you happy," she answers, opening her mouth when I hold the food out in front of her. I watch as she slowly chews. I can tell she's really struggling. It brings a lump to my throat. I pick up the bottle of water, unscrewing the lid.

"Here, have a drink." She raises her hand to take it from me and I notice she's shaking. She's been doing a lot of that lately. She's probably got low blood sugars from the lack of food. "Let me," I offer as I move it towards her mouth. Seeing her lips wrap around the bottle, doesn't even make my dick stir.

We haven't been intimate for over two weeks. She's asked, no practically begged, but I can't do it. Don't get me wrong. I want to. I want to more than anything. I fucking miss that connection with her. But, she's so weak ... so fragile. Not only does she need to conserve her energy just to do menial things, like get around, I'm scared I'm gonna break her, or hurt her. I can't risk that at the moment.

We'll get back there. I have every confidence. The day I can sink my cock into that heavenly pussy of hers again, is gonna be one sweet day I can tell you. But for now, the most important thing is seeing her well again.

"How about I go to the fish market after work and get some of those fresh prawns you love? I can make you a nice prawn salad for dinner." My hopefully eyes search hers. I'm becoming desperate. I've noticed she can't really seem to stomach the stir-fries I've been making. Anything too saucy seems to make her nausea intensify.

"Sounds great," she answers reaching for my hand and giving it a weak squeeze. I know my client is waiting downstairs, but he's gonna have to wait. My girl comes first. I sit on the side of the bed until I get half the sandwich into her, and most of the water. When she tells me she's had enough, I lay her back down and tuck the sheets up around her neck. "I'll be back in about an hour." I gently place my lips against hers. "I love you."

"I love you too," she replies smiling. "Thanks for taking such good care of me."

"You don't have to thank me. I want to take care of you." I pick her phone up off the bedside table and place it on the pillow by her head. "Call me if you need anything in the meantime."

"Okay." I bend down and place a soft kiss on her forehead.

"Look after our girl while I'm gone, boy," I tell LJ, ruffling his fur before I turn and leave.

••••

We leave early Monday morning to be back in Sydney in time for Indi's next session of radiation. Sunday's have quickly become my favourite day. Not only do I get to spend the entire day with her, but it's the one day of the week that she's closest to being her old self and well enough to leave the house. Those few days rest from the radiation really seem to make a difference.

Last night I even rugged her up and carried her across the road to the beach. She tried to fight me, insisting she could walk, but I wouldn't hear of it. We ended up compromising on a piggyback instead. It's amazing how many stars you can see in the sky at night when you live close to the ocean. I'd never really noticed until I went back to Sydney and looked up at the sky. I guess the pollution from the city doesn't help.

I wanted her to experience it, so I laid a blanket on the sand and took an extra one to place over her so she was warm. Her immune system is so low right now. She can't afford to get sick.

We laid on the soft sand for hours, wrapped in each other's arms, looking up at the sky talking and laughing and even making out occasionally. It was just like old times.

Although the making out part was wonderful, it wasn't a great idea. The longer I go without having her, the harder I'm finding it to deny myself. She practically begged me to make love to her under the stars. Saying no was one of the hardest things I've ever done.

She was clearly upset by my knockback. *Doesn't she realise how hard this is for me? How much I want her?* I hate denying her of anything, so I eventually relented and slipped my hand down the front of her pants and brought her undone with my fingers.

Hearing her little whimpers and feeling her come against my hand almost had me caving. I wanted inside her so bad, but I held strong. As soon as she's well again, I'm gonna tie her to my bed and fuck her until we both pass out. That she can be certain of.

I couldn't stop smiling by the time we headed back to the apartment, neither could she. It was exactly what we both needed. My heart felt so much lighter.

Now we're back to where we started. I hate what this fucking radiation is doing to her. On our way back to Ross' house, I had to pull over to the side of the road twice so she could vomit. After I carried her into the house and placed her in bed, I laid down with her until she fell asleep before getting up and heading over to my mum's. I needed a little time out. Sadly though, what I found when I got there had me wishing I'd stayed in bed with Indiana.

As soon as I entered the house, I found my mum with her face buried in her hands, sobbing. *Christ.* I thought she was improving. I drop my keys onto the table by the entry, immediately making my way to her. "Mum," I say concerned, sitting beside her and draping my arm around her shoulder. "What's wrong? Are you okay?"

"Oh, Carter," she cries burying her face into my chest.

"What's going on?" I can't stand to see her like this.

"I just got off the phone with a private investigator. My father died." *What the fuck?* Her father died and she's crying? Why that pisses me off, I can't say. Yes I can. After the way he treated her, treated me ...

"And that upsets you? Why?" I ask a little angrier than anticipated.

"Despite everything, he was my father, Carter." Father my arse. That's the biggest crock of shit I've ever heard. Not only did he kick his daughter out of her home when she was nineteen, pregnant, and had nowhere else to go, he ruined my life. His only grandchild. "I just hoped that one day we'd be able to make amends. Now that's never going to happen."

"I'm sorry, Mum, but he was an arsehole. He treated us both like shit."

"I know," she sniffles wiping the tears from her eyes. "My mum wants me to get in contact with her. She hired an investigator after my father died, to track me down. He's given me her contact details."

"Are you going to contact her?" She doesn't even hesitate with her answer.

"Of course." It instantly gets my back up. "She was nothing like my father," she says in her defence.

"Well, where has she been for the last twenty-five years of your life?" I practically scream as I stand. I feel bad when I see her flinch, but I can't seem to control the anger that rages inside me. "If you want to do this, then you're on your own. I want nothing to do with her."

"Carter," she calls out to my retreating back as I storm towards my bedroom. I'm not sure why this has made me so angry. Maybe my nerves are just frazzled from everything I'm going through with Indi. Maybe it's something else.

As I sit on the side of my bed and bury my face in my hands, memories of that day flash through my mind. *Why did you bring that little bastard here? Get him out of here. Don't you ever bring him here again.* It's funny, it's been nineteen years, but it's still as fresh in my memory like it happened yesterday. I hate that motherfucker. I'm glad he's dead. He ruined my fucking life and broke my mother's heart. That may be harsh, but that's exactly how I feel.

"Carter," my mum says knocking on my bedroom door. "Can I come in?"

"Sure," I reply. I shouldn't be mad at her. She's the biggest victim in all of this. They were her parents. They let her down when she needed them most. "I'm sorry, Mum," I say, making eye contact with her when she comes and sits beside me on the bed.

"You have nothing to be sorry about sweetheart." Her voice is soft when she speaks. She raises her hand and gently rubs it over my back. "You're right. He did a number on both of us. My mother was nothing like him though. You need to understand he was very controlling. She had no say in any of this. She was devastated when he kicked me out. She tried to reason with him, but he wouldn't listen. He never did. He was very stubborn. The day I left the house, she broke down. She handed me an envelope that contained two thousand dollars. She'd been saving money over the years without my father's knowledge. She also gave me some of her jewellery to sell if I needed more money. It wasn't much, but it was all she had. It helped me get by until I could find a job. It gave me a place to stay and food to survive. Without that, I would've ended up on the street."

I sit and listen to everything she says, but I'm still not happy about this whole situation. She's had no contact from her mother in all these years. As far as I'm concerned, it's a little late to try and make up for it now.

"Things were different back then," she continues. "Having sex before marriage, having a baby out of wedlock … it was taboo, shunned upon. My father was very religious and old school. He was also a proud man. His reputation meant everything to him. Unfortunately, what people thought of him turned out to be more important than the welfare of his own daughter and grandchild. For that I can never forgive him. My mum, though? She was different, Carter. When you meet her, you'll see exactly what I mean."

"Like hell I'm meeting her," I snap. "If you want to, go right ahead, but I want nothing to do with this."

"Carter," she says in a shocked tone. "Please. I need you with me. I'm not sure if I can do this on my own. It's been nearly twenty-five years since I've seen her. I think this would be good for you, for both of us. It's time to let go of the past, sweetheart. It's time to heal." I exhale a defeated breath. I've never been able to say no to her, and that pleading look in her eyes tells me I'll be going to meet this fucking woman, whether I want to or not. *Fuck.*

••••

My mum called her mother later that afternoon. Apparently she was over the moon to hear from her and they talked and cried on the phone for over two hours. She wanted us both to come over straight away. There was no way I was going to drop everything and run to her, even if that's what my mum wanted. My first priority was Indi, and frankly, if I could put this unwanted reunion off, I was gonna delay it as much as I could.

As the days passed though, my mother's pleas became too much. I finally relented and agreed to go with her late Wednesday afternoon. I haven't discussed it with Indiana yet. I'll wait and see how the meeting goes first. I don't want to upset or worry her unnecessarily. I have no idea what to expect when I get there. Going by our visit all those years ago, I don't hold out much hope.

My mum has arranged for us to be at her mother's house at 3:00pm, for afternoon tea. Fuck that. I won't be eating shit when we get there, that's even if we make it through the front door. It's just after 2:00pm, so we're going to need to leave soon. It's a forty-minute drive to her parents' house.

Picking up the plate of fruit I've just chopped up for Indi, I head back into the lounge room where she's snuggled up on the sofa with LJ. Her gaze moves away from the television and locks with mine when I enter the room. I plaster a smile on my face to try and mask the inner turmoil that rages inside me. Thankfully she returns the smile. I've done a good job of hiding my worry and uncertainty from her all day.

Indi hasn't been that bad today. It's one of the rare good ones. She slept for a few hours after we arrived home from the hospital, but she's been awake ever since. She even managed to eat all her lunch and keep it down, which pleases me to no end.

"Here you go, beautiful," I say when I kneel down in front of her and place the plate on her lap. "Is there anything else I can get you before I leave?"

"Nope, but thank you," she replies as her shaky hand reaches out to caress my face.

"I'm gonna have to get going. Mum's appointment is at three. Your dad just called and he's on his way home. He's gonna sit with you until I get back."

"I don't need babysitting, Carter. I'll be fine until you get back," she says with an eye roll. I love her sass.

"I know, but I'd feel better knowing you're not alone." I lean forward and gently place my lips on hers. Ross knows where we're going, but I've asked him not to tell Indiana. He needed to know because with mum and I both being away, someone had to be here for Indi just in case. I was also interested to hear his take on this. Unlike me, he thinks this meeting is a good idea. It's easy for him to say, because he doesn't know what went down all those years ago. "I love you," I say as I stand.

"I love you too. I hope your mum's appointment goes well." *So do I.* I smile down at her as my stomach starts to churn again at the thought of what I'm about to face.

"Look after our girl," I tell LJ as I reach down and run my hand over his fur.

••••

No words are spoken on the drive to the house. My mum's leg has been bouncing with nervous anticipation most of the way. The huge smile planted on her face tells me she's excited for this reunion. Although I wish it wasn't taking place, I find myself hoping, for her sake, that everything goes okay.

I actually feel like I'm gonna be sick when we drive down the long circular driveway and come to a stop outside the house. It's funny, after all these years I still remember what it looks like. I guess it was a poignant moment in my life, so I'm not surprised it stuck with me all this time. It's the day my life changed forever. The day that cocksucker ruined me. I don't want to go anywhere near that house. I'm regretting agreeing to come here, but on the other hand, I don't want my mum to face this alone.

When I turn off the ignition I have a sudden moment of panic. *Fuck.* I can't do this. "Would you mind if I stayed in the car?" I say, turning my head to look at her.

"What? No. Please, Carter. After what happened last time when we were here, I can understand that you're apprehensive," she replies reaching for my hand. "Do you really think I'd bring you back if I thought we'd get the same reception? That day still haunts me too. Don't you think I saw how much you changed after that day? I'm your mother, Carter. Mother's notice things like that. Not a moment has passed that I haven't regretted putting you through that. I promise you things will be different this time. My mum is nothing like my father. She's really looking forward to meeting you." I exhale a large defeated breath.

Why can't I ever say no to this woman?

She needs this, so I have to put all my shit aside and do it for her. She gave up everything when she found out she was pregnant with me. She could've aborted me and continued on with her life, with her family in this house. But she didn't. If I can help her get a piece of her old self back, then I'd be a selfish fucker if I didn't do this for her.

Hesitantly, I get out of the car and walk around to open my mum's door. I count the same five motherfucking steps in my head, just like I did when I was a kid. Instead of the excitement that consumed me all those years ago, I'm filled with dread.

My stomach is churning when we stand in front of the big yellow door, except this time it doesn't look so big. It's just a regular door, and I fucking hate it. Hate *it*, and everything that lies behind it with a passion. So much so, I have to fight the urge to kick the living shit out of it. How can a person hate a damn door so much?

Because it's haunted my fucking dreams for the past nineteen years, that's why.

My mum's hand rises in the air before her knuckles connect with the wood. She knocks twice. Her hand reaches for mine before giving it a comforting squeeze, except this time it's anything but. Just like the previous time we were here, her head turns in my direction as she looks up at me and smiles. I'm no longer five, so now I tower over her tiny frame. This is déjà vu at its motherfucking worst. Christ, I feel like I'm going to be sick again.

Both our hands are trembling as we await our fate. We don't have to wait long. A minute later the door swings open. A frail, older version of my mum stands before us. I hold my breath as my heart pounds rapidly against my ribcage. I exhale when she briefly makes eye contact with my mum before launching herself into her arms.

"My baby," she cries. "I've waited way too long to see your beautiful face again." She starts to sob as my mum engulfs her in her arms and starts to cry as well. A lump forms in my throat as I stand here and watch them together. Although I still wish I wasn't here, my heart sings for my mum. This is the kind of reunion I guess she'd hope for when we came here all those years ago.

Why I'm still expecting this meeting to turn sour when my grandmother notices me, I'm not sure. A few minutes later they release each other, and my grandmother takes a step back, cupping my mum's face in her frail hands. "Let me look at you," she says smiling widely. I notice she has kind eyes. They're nothing like the mean ones my grandfather had. "You're still as beautiful as I remember. I've missed you so much, Lizzy." She leans forward and peppers tiny kisses all over her face.

"I've missed you too Mumma," my mum whispers as she wipes her tears away with the back of her hand. "This is Carter," she adds, and my grandmother's gaze moves to me. "Your grandson." I swear my heart stops beating when she tears her eyes away from my mum and looks up at me. Instead of the angry scowl my grandfather gave me when I was last here, she smiles a beautiful smile before wrapping her arms around my waist. I just stand there, unmoving. My arms are still planted by my side. I'm frozen.

"I've been waiting twenty-four years to meet you," she cries softly into my chest. "I've prayed for this day for so long. Not a day has passed that I haven't thought about you—haven't loved you." The lump in my throat grows, and I have to fight back the tears that threaten to fall. *She loves me.*

Although this is the kind of reunion I'd hoped for, *no, dreamt about*, for some reason I'm still sceptical. I'm still waiting for everything to turn ugly. "Let me look at you," she says stepping back. "Look how handsome you are," she smiles as her hand reaches up and gently caresses the side of my face. My mum was right ... she's nothing like my grandfather.

TWENTY-FOUR

INDIANA

ONCE I EAT AS MUCH FRUIT AS I CAN STOMACH, I HEAD TO THE bathroom to have a shower while my dad makes a start on dinner. I hate that I can't help, but my stupid body is so weak from the treatment. It's a struggle to stand on my feet for too long. I can't wait until this is over and I can get back to normal. On a positive note, my headaches seem to have lessened, so it gives me hope that the treatment is working. I pray it is, because I'm not sure how much more of this I can take.

I sit on the stupid plastic seat that my dad has placed in the shower recess. I fucking hate that I have to sit on this damn thing because I'm too weak to stand for that long. It makes me feel like some kind of invalid. In the beginning Carter helped me shower, but I soon put a stop to that. He's been doing so much. *So much.* He never stops. If I can lighten his load in any way, I will.

Don't get me wrong, he doesn't seem to mind, but he's taken on the world since offering to care for me during my treatment. He won't let anyone help. I love that he wants to do this, and I'll be forever grateful, but I can see it's starting to take its toll on him as well. It worries me.

As I let the warm water cascade over my tired, aching body, he's on my mind. He hasn't been himself the past few days. Sure he plasters on a smile whenever he's around me, but when he doesn't realise I'm watching him, I clearly see the worry etched on his handsome face. I'm gonna have a heart-to-heart with him when he gets home.

When I get out of the shower, I wrap myself in a towel and make my way into my bedroom. LJ follows close behind me. He was sitting outside the bathroom when I opened the door. He hasn't left my side since the treatment started. I guess he can sense things aren't right with me.

Opening my underwear drawer, the first thing I see is a note sitting on top. Ugh! I can already tell by the handwriting it's from Carter.

> I can and I will. YOU ARE MINE! If you want to get your rocks off, you know where to find me, beautiful!!!

I should be pissed with him, but I'm not. Instead, I laugh. I don't even need to look. I know my vibrator is gone. I miss being intimate with him so much. I know he thinks what he's doing is for the best, maybe he's right, but I need that connection with him again. I hate that we're wasting time apart. *We don't know how much time we have left.*

When I'm dressed, I lie down on the bed. It shits me that a simple shower has drained me of all the energy I had. I want the old me back. I want to be well again.

Cancer fucking sucks.

••••

My eyes slowly open when I feel the bed dip and two strong arms wrap around me. *He's home.* It brings a smile to my face. Rolling over to face him, I brush my lips against his when his beautiful chocolate eyes meet mine. "Hey, handsome," I say smiling.

"Hey, beautiful." The breathtaking smile he gives me melts my heart. I love seeing him happy like this. Reaching up, I run my hand gently down the side of his face.

"How did your mum's appointment go?"

"Well a lot better than I expected. I didn't tell you this before because I didn't want to worry you unnecessarily, but we actually went to see my grandmother." *What?*

"Shut up. You did not," I screech. It's not that I don't believe him; I'm just shocked that's all.

"We did," he chuckles. He goes to elaborate, but I cut him off.

"What? How? And why is this the first I'm hearing of it?" I inquire, reaching over and pinching his side. I can't believe he kept this from me.

"Ouch," he laughs, rubbing his ribcage. "If you let me get a word in, I'll tell you. He turns over on his side so we're facing each other, encircling his arm around my waist.

He tells me everything. From the private investigator, to the uncertainty of going there, and the joy he felt when he was greeted with open arms. He looks so happy and carefree, like a huge weight has been lifted from him. It warms my heart.

"My mum was right," he continues. "She's nothing like my grandfather. She had no idea that we'd come to the house all those years ago. My grandfather never told her. She was heartbroken when she found out." I don't say anything. I just listen. "I've never seen my mum so happy, Indi. She was beaming all the way home. You should've seen her." I don't need to. I bet it's the same look I'm seeing right now on his face.

"I'm so glad you all finally got to make peace with what happened," I say, cupping his cheek in my hand. "Are you going to see her again?"

"Of course," he replies without hesitation. "She wants to meet you too. You're going to love her, babe. She's just like an older version of my mum. She's so sweet." I smile as I lean forward and place my lips on his. The pure excitement in his voice is infectious. I'm thrilled this has happened. I know what his grandfather did, has haunted him for the last nineteen years. I hope this meeting has given him some kind of peace. He deserves that. He's carried the scars of that day around for too long.

"I can't wait to meet her too," I tell him, because I can't.

••••

By the time we arrive back at Newcastle Thursday afternoon, I'm feeling dreadful. Yesterday was a good day, but today is certainly making up for it. I usually sleep on my way up here, but we had to pull over seven times so I could be sick. Well, dry reach, because that's about all I did. I lost the contents of my stomach before we even left Sydney.

Carter is almost beside himself by the time we arrive. The worry he bears is clearly written all over his face. "I think I'm gonna get Justine to cancel all of my appointments for the rest of the afternoon," he says when he carries me into the bedroom. I hate that he has to carry me everywhere. Today I'm probably too weak to walk up those stairs, but even when I'm not he insists on doing it.

"No you're not," I snap in a tone that lets him know I mean business. It's time for a little tough love. "Stop being ridiculous. I'll be fine on my own. You've lost enough work because of me. I won't stand for ..." Before I get a chance to finish, he starts to laugh. "What's so funny?" I ask narrowing my eyes.

"You," he chuckles, leaning forward to plant a soft kiss on my nose. "I love your spunk. I've missed it." His light-heartedness softens me straight away.

"Please don't cancel your appointments," I plead, softening my voice. "Honestly, I'll be fine."

After he lies me down on the bed and fusses over me for a few minutes, he leaves to go downstairs. It doesn't take long for me to drift off to sleep.

I'm awoken a few hours later when he comes up to check on me. He brings me a plate of dry crackers and some juice, since that's all I'm going to be able to stomach. I manage to force a couple down while Carter takes LJ to the grass area out back to do his business.

"Please try and eat a little more than that," he says with a furrowed brow when he comes back upstairs. I roll my eyes. I know I shouldn't, but sometimes he makes me feel like a child. I wish I didn't feel so sick. Of course I'd eat more if I didn't. After sitting on the side of the bed, he forces a few more biscuits into me before he leaves.

When the nausea takes hold again, I lie back down, hoping my stomach will settle while I sleep. I'm not sure how long I'm out for, but when I wake the urge to vomit is strong. Dragging myself out of bed, I head towards the bathroom. I have to use the wall for support because I'm feeling dizzy and unsteady on my feet.

I hug the bowl for the longest time. What little food I managed to get down before is now gone. I use the vanity to help me stand. I feel dreadful. Going back to bed would be the wise thing to do, but a warm shower may help.

After brushing my teeth, I strip and make my way into the shower recess. Sitting on the damn chair that Carter and my dad insist I use, I turn on the taps. The warm water flowing over my skin feels wonderful. It's just what my aching muscles need.

I'm already feeling marginally better by the time I turn the water off. Somewhat human anyway. When I stand though, another wave of dizziness hits. The smart thing to do would be to sit back down, but all I want is to dry off and climb back into bed.

Stepping out of the shower, my shaky hand reaches for the towel. I barely get a chance to wrap it around me when the realisation that I'm going to pass out hits. Thinking fast, I turn with the intent of making my way towards the toilet so I can sit down. *I don't make it.* I fall forward, just as everything goes black.

TWENTY-FIVE

CARTER

I'M IN THE MIDDLE OF A JOB WHEN I HEAR THE FIRST BARK.
Occasionally LJ barks throughout the day, but not often. Sometimes it's
when he wants to go outside, which I know isn't the case because he
went out not so long ago. Other times, it's when he sees someone
walking down the street through the lounge room window, but today
the blinds are drawn. I did that because the bright light seems to make
Indiana's headaches worse.

Instantly it has me on edge. When the barking continues, I have to
excuse myself. "I'm sorry mate, but I just need to go and check on
something." Thankfully my client is a regular and doesn't seem to
mind.

In my gut, I have a feeling that something isn't right. Racing down
the corridor and out the side door, I take the steps two at a time.
"Indi," I call out as soon as I enter the apartment. *Nothing.* When I hear
LJ's bark grow more desperate, I head in that direction.

Rounding the corner I find him standing on his hind legs, frantically scratching on the bathroom door. My heart drops into the pit of my stomach. "Indi," I call out again as I rush forward. Still no answer. My hand reaches for the doorknob. Thank fuck it isn't locked.

I fling it open in a panic. "*Indiana*." I swear my heart stops beating and all the air leaves my body when I see her lying face down on the tiled floor. My knees buckle from beneath me. Immediately I think the worst for some reason. I guess because she has a life threatening illness. Quickly I approach.

Falling to my knees the first thing I do is feel for a pulse. *Thank fuck, she's alive.* "Indi," I say shaking her. I gently roll her over, placing her head on my lap. Instantly she starts to come to. Relief floods through me. That is until I see the blood trickling down her neck. Moving my head forward, I see a gash just under her chin. She must've hit it when she fell.

"Indi ... Indi, it's me ... Carter. Talk to me, babe."

"Carter," she moans as her eyes flutter open. *Thank Christ.*

"You're going to be okay," I say reassuringly as I lift her into my arms and stand. Walking briskly into the bedroom, I gently lay her on the bed.

"Carter," she moans again and tries to sit up.

"Don't move, baby. Everything is going to be alright." I gently stroke her hair trying and soothe her. Reaching for her phone on the bedside table, I dial downstairs. "Justine, it's Carter. Indi's had a fall. Call an ambulance."

"What? Fuck. Is she okay?" she asks in a panic. My employees have grown to love her over the last month. She's a pretty hard person not to love.

"She's fine. She has a nasty gash on her chin. Call them, and direct them up to my apartment when they get here. I need to get back to her," I say before ending the call. Justine's a good kid. I know she'll do exactly what I've asked.

Indi lifts her hand and brushes her fingers over her chin. "I'm bleeding," she exclaims when she lifts her hand away, moving it up towards her face.

"I know. You must've knocked it when you fell." I pull the towel out from underneath her body and bunch it up before pressing it to the wound. "Can you hold this against your chin for a minute? I need to get you dressed before the paramedics arrive."

"Sure." As usual, although dazed, she's as cool as a cucumber. I, on the other hand am not. I'm a fucking mess. My hands are shaking as I sift through the drawers trying to grab her something to put on. My nerves have been frazzled for weeks now. I don't know how much more I can take.

••••

"She's fine, Ross," I say in a reassuring voice as I pace the corridor at the John Hunter Hospital. The doctor asked me to leave the room while he examined her. She told us in the ambulance that she felt dizzy when she got out of the shower, and that's all she can remember.

"I'm gonna call work and let them know I won't be in. I'll be there in a few hours," he replies in a worried tone.

"No. You don't need to come up here. I can take care of her. I've got this, Ross." Well that's what I keep telling myself. I feel responsible for what happened. *I should've been there.* Does he think I'm not taking good enough care of her? Because apart from this, I think I am. Maybe that's just my paranoia. "As soon as the doctor's finished checking her over, I'll call you and let you know what he says."

"Fuck," he grates out as he exhales loudly. "Okay." This isn't easy for him, I get that.

"Ross. You know if I thought this was serious I'd tell you. The paramedic said she may need a stitch or two in her chin, but other than that her vitals were fine." Again guilt consumes me. *I should've fucking been there.*

"Call me as soon as you know what's going on."

"I will. I promise," I say before I end the call.

INDIANA

When I wake, I'm still in the hospital. It's dark outside, but there's a small light on behind me that illuminates the room enough for me to see Carter asleep in the chair beside my bed. After the X-ray to make sure nothing was broken or fractured, the doctor put a few stitches in my chin. They're keeping me in for overnight observation.

Honestly, I feel a lot better. They have me on a drip, which has helped immensely. Apparently I was severely dehydrated from all the vomiting.

Guilt consumes me as I lay here watching Carter. He looks so tired, so worn out. I wish he'd go home and get some decent sleep in a real bed, but when I asked him to earlier, he refused. I'm grateful to have him. He's been amazing. We've only been together for just over a month. The majority of that has been taken up by my illness. It's so unfair. This has really taken its toll on him.

I love how he's stepped up and taken on the role of caring for me, even though he never signed up for this. Most people in his position would've bailed weeks ago. Not him. He's a great guy and hasn't complained once, but it worries me. I hate that I'm putting through this.

"Carter ... Carter," I say, reaching my hand out to shake him. He stirs on the chair before opening his eyes.

"Shit. Is everything okay?" he asks, rubbing his hands over his face as he stands. He's on edge. That makes me feel worse.

"Everything is fine," I reply reaching for his hand. "Why don't you go home and get a good night sleep? That chair can't be comfortable."

"I'm not leaving you, Indi." I sigh at his stubbornness. After our earlier conversation, I know I'm not going to win this one. Shuffling over and tapping the bed beside me, I smile up at him.

"Come lie with me then." His lips turn up before he slips off his shoes and climbs into bed with me. I lift my head slightly so he can slide his arm underneath my neck. I roll onto my side and snuggle into his chest.

"I love you, Carter," I whisper.

"I love you too, babe," he replies as he kisses the top of my head.

I don't know what to do. I spoke with my dad on the phone earlier. He wanted to come up, but he said Carter didn't want that. I don't like that he feels so responsible for me, because he's not.

Maybe I need to go home. Even if it's just for a few weeks, until the treatment is complete. Carter needs his rest. He's been wonderful, but he's done more than his fair share. It's time I gave him a break. I've disrupted his life enough.

CARTER

"Are you okay, man?" Marcus asks as I prepare his arm for the tattoo. "You don't seem yourself today."

"Yeah," I admit, exhaling as my eyes briefly meet his. "I've just got some personal shit going on." I hate that I'm down here working and Indi's upstairs on her own. She insisted I work today. I made her promise me if she needed to get up, for whatever reason, she'd call me straight away. It's the only way I agreed to her demands.

"Sorry to hear that, mate," he replies giving me a sympathetic smile. "You're not gonna fuck up my tattoo are ya? I've never seen you like this. You keep spacing out ... and frankly, you look like shit man." I give him a half-hearted chuckle. I feel like shit too.

"I'm not gonna fuck up your tattoo," I snap. Well I fucking hope I don't. *Get yourself together Reynolds.* No more words are spoken as I start working on his arm. I'm not getting into my personal crap with my clients. That's not how I roll. I've always been a private person. I do need to pull my shit together though. This whole situation is taking its toll on me. On all of us.

It kills me to see her so sick. I know this treatment is going to make her better in the long run, but it still doesn't make it any easier. I even pulled the doctor aside at the hospital this morning and explained the situation to him while she was in the shower. He assured me that everything she is going through is normal.

Nothing about this seems normal to me.

Thankfully, I get through this job without fucking it up. When I follow Marcus out to the front desk, my phone rings in my pocket. My heart races for some reason. I'm on edge after everything that happened yesterday, I guess.

Pulling it out I see Ross' name flashing on the screen. He's probably just checking up to see how Indi is doing. "Hi, Ross," I say.

"Hi, son. I just got a call from Indi. She wants me to come and get her. What in the hell is going on?"

TWENTY-SIX

INDIANA

AFTER GETTING OFF THE PHONE WITH MY DAD, I GET MY suitcase out of the wardrobe and place it on the bed. My heart is heavy, but I know I'm doing the right thing. I hope Carter understands. It's going to take my dad a few hours to drive up here, but I want to be organised when he arrives. If I get it done now, it will give me extra time to spend with Carter before I leave.

As I open one of the drawers, I hear the front door slam before Carter comes barreling into the bedroom. "What the fuck do you think you're doing?" he screams, making me jump. *Shit he knows.* Turning to face him, I can clearly see he's hurt. My dad must've called him. *Damn him.* That's the last thing I wanted. I would've liked a chance to explain it to Carter myself. I'm furious with my dad for interfering.

"It's not what you think, Carter." I speak in a soft, calming voice as I walk towards him.

"You're leaving me?" is all he says, exhaling as his shoulders slump. The look on his face is one of complete devastation. It breaks my heart.

"I'm not leaving you, Carter. I'm just going home for a few days to give you a break. I'm worried about you. You're not eating or sleeping properly. I'm interrupting your work ... your life. I hate that you're constantly worrying about me. I'm responsible for everything you're going through. It would be selfish of me to stay under those circumstances." I'm trying to reassure him as I speak. My arms reach out to him, but he pushes them away and steps back.

"You think I'm gonna worry any less when you're two fucking hours away?" he yells, making me flinch. He's never spoken to me so harshly before. The anger is rolling off him. When his hands thread through his hair, tears rise to my eyes. This is not how I wanted this to go down.

"You don't need to do this, Carter. You didn't sign on for this, I get that. I know what type of man you are. I know you'd never walk away, even if you wanted to. I'm giving you an easy out here."

His hand reaches for me, roughly wrapping his fingers around the top of my arm as he forcefully tugs me towards him. "Listen to me," he snarls, getting up in my face. "I'm gonna say this once and once only. I fucking love you, Indiana. For better or for worse. I don't want a fucking out. Do you hear me? Don't you dare make decisions based on what you think is best for me. Don't you fucking dare."

"I ... I," is all I manage to get out. I can no longer hold the tears at bay as they freely flow down my cheeks. His face drops as soon as he notices them. He quickly lets go of my arm, pulling me into a crushing embrace.

"I'm sorry," he whispers in a much calmer voice, "but you're not fucking going anywhere, Indiana. That's final."

"I feel like I'm dragging you down with me. I don't want to do that," I cry into his chest. This whole situation is just too much. Pulling back from me, he cups my face in his hands. The anger that was in his eyes a few moments ago is now gone.

"You could never drag me down, babe. You're my sunshine. Don't you see that? Even with everything going on, you still brighten my day. I'd be fucking lost without you here." He pulls me into him again, practically crushing me. "I promised you right from the beginning that we were in this together, and I meant every word. Please don't leave. I need you here with me."

When he finally let's go, he grabs my hand and drags me towards the bed. He sits on the side of the mattress and pulls me down onto his lap, wrapping me in his arms. "We're not leaving here until we sort this shit out," he demands.

••••

We sat there for over an hour until everything was out in the open. I agreed to stay on the condition he pull back a bit, and stop letting my illness take over his life. Reluctantly he agreed. When I told him I needed to call my dad and tell him not to come, he said, "Don't bother. I've already told him you're staying." Ugh! Presumptuous arse. I called my dad anyway, reassuring him that everything was okay.

Carter begrudgingly ended up going back to work. Later that night, there was no mention of what happened. We'd both had our say and had put it behind us. After dinner, we snuggled on the sofa and fell into easy conversation. Nothing deep. Nothing about my illness. Just normal, everyday things. It was nice.

"I've been thinking," he says. *Okay, this could be dangerous.*

"About what?" I ask sceptically.

"Justine was talking about some girly spa place she goes to. Why don't you let me book you in for a pamper day? It will do you good." I tilt my head back and smile up at him, shrugging at the same time.

"I don't know. It sounds lovely, but that's something Meg and I always used to do together. It'll be no fun on my own."

"I could come with you." I start laughing as I roll onto my stomach to face him.

"You'd go and get a facial and a Mani/Pedi?" I ask in disbelief, because that's something I couldn't imagine him doing.

"What's a Mani/Pedi?"

"A manicure and pedicure."

"Oh," he deadpans, making me laugh again. "Yeah, maybe that's not my thing."

"It's definitely not your thing," I agree snuggling back into him.

••••

The following Friday, Carter takes me back to the John Hunter Hospital in New Lambton, to have my stitches removed from my chin. Yesterday I completed my second last week of the radiation therapy. Words can't express how happy I am that it's almost coming to an end.

Next week we have to stay for an extra day in Sydney, because Friday I'll be having another scan and some blood work to see how successful the treatment has been. My headaches have practically ceased, so I'm confident we're going to get good results. Well, I pray we do.

Things have been different between Carter and I this week. He's really stepped back, which makes me feel so much better. He still fusses over me like a mother hen, but he seems a lot more relaxed. I've had a pretty good week as far as the side effects go. I still feel dreadful, but my nausea isn't as bad so I've been able to keep most of my food down.

Mid-Saturday morning, Carter asked me to be showered, dressed, and ready by lunchtime. I didn't ask why, I just presumed we were going out to eat. We do that often when I'm feeling okay.

I'm wearing a new pair of jeans and a nice top when he comes upstairs just after midday. I bought some new clothes last week because I've lost a few kilos since treatment started. Most of my clothes I can still wear, although they're a little big on me now, but my jeans? No. I like them to be fitted.

"Grab your purse," he says when he enters the apartment. "I'm taking an extended lunch break."

"Where are we going?" I ask when he gives me a mischievous smile. He's up to something, I can tell.

"The Day Spa."

"What?"

"You said you didn't want to go alone, so I'm going with you." I can't help it. I start laughing. Carter Reynolds at a day spa. This I gotta see.

"I thought you said a Mani/Pedi wasn't your thing."

"It's not, but I want this for you, so I'm prepared to hand them my balls at the door. Don't worry, I'll collect them on my way out." We're both laughing as we walk down the stairs, heading for the car.

After parking down the street from the Day Spa, he walks around to my side to open my door. I'm still shocked that he's actually here with me. I love that he would go to any lengths to make me happy.

While Carter closes my door and locks the car, I stand on the sidewalk and tilt my head back letting the sun's rays hit my face, making my skin prickle. Although we're in the middle of winter, it's a beautiful sunny day. I feel my lips curve up after I inhale a large breath, taking the fresh air into my lungs. When I open my eyes, I find Carter staring down at me, with a sweet smile on his face.

"You okay?" he asks.

"Yeah. Just enjoying being outside."

"It's good to see," is all he says, leaning down to kiss the top of my head.

Lacing his fingers through mine, we make our way down the street. I can't tell you how good it feels to be out in the fresh air and sunshine again. I've been cooped up in that apartment way too much lately. A simple thing like being outdoors, was something I once took for granted. Not anymore. It's funny how you realise just how important the little things are once they've been taken away from you.

"You sure you want to do this?" I ask.

"Positive," he answers. "You need this, babe."

"Have I told you how much I love you today?"

"Yes, but I'll never get tired of hearing it," he admits as he pulls our linked hands up towards his face and places a kiss on my fingers. "So feel free to tell me again."

Carter pushes open the door of the spa, moving to the side so I can enter. I only make it a few steps before I'm stopped in my tracks. Tears instantly rise to my eyes. Oh. My. Fucking. God. Turning my head to look up at Carter, I find him gazing down at me with the biggest shit-eating grin on his face. "Surprise," he says. *Surprise is an understatement.* I can't believe he would do this for me.

Tears are now streaming down my cheeks as she rises from her seat in the foyer, closing the distance between us before engulfing me in her arms. I'm so overwhelmed. "Meg," I whisper as I wrap my arms around her waist and squeeze her tight. I can't believe she's actually here in the flesh.

"I fucking missed you," she cries, tightening her hold on me.

"I've missed you too. Like you wouldn't believe." I'm so overcome with joy right now.

She pulls back to make eye contact with me. Even though we're both crying, we have huge smiles on our faces. She hugs me to her once more. We hold each other for the longest time. I don't want to let her go.

Eventually, she takes a step back before reaching up and pinching my arm. "Ouch," I say, frowning at her. "What was that for?"

"I can't believe you've been sick and you didn't tell me, bitch." I can clearly hear the hurt in her voice.

"I didn't want to worry you." She takes me back into her arms and squeezes me again.

"I love you," she whispers. "I want to know this shit. Don't keep things from me."

"I love you too, Meg. I'm sorry I didn't tell you."

••••

I had the most amazing day ever. Just having my bestie here has lifted my spirits like you wouldn't believe. I couldn't thank Carter enough when we got home, for what he'd done.

Apparently, he had stolen Meg's number out of my phone and called her. She jumped on the first plane once she heard that I was sick. I'm not sure how long she's staying, but I'm going to enjoy my time with her while she's here.

Carter had booked us in for the full spa package. We were there for over four hours. We had a therapeutic Hydro Bath, exfoliating treatment, hot stone massage, a facial, and of course a manicure and pedicure. It even included lunch. It was just what my tired body needed. I felt revitalised when I walked out of there. As amazing as it was, just spending time catching up with Meg was the highlight for me.

••••

When Carter finishes his last job for the day, he finds Meg and I chatting on the sofa when he walks into the apartment. Making his way towards us he bends down, brushing his lips against mine.

"I'm gonna have a quick shower, then I'm taking you two out for dinner," he says smiling down at me.

"Okay," I reply returning the smile. My eyes are glued to his arse as he turns and makes his way towards our bedroom. He is still refusing to have sex with me. It's getting to the stage now that I'm tempted to tie him to the bed in his sleep, just so I can have my way with him.

I know the abstaining isn't easy on him either. Every time we've made out he's gotten hard, but has refused to let me do anything to relieve him. I hate it. I know how much I'm suffering, so I can only imagine how he feels.

We no longer shower together. Not only did it make me feel like an invalid that he felt the need to wash me, but the temptation of being naked together and not being able to take it further became too hard. Wednesday was the first time in weeks that we did. I was complaining about not being able to wash my hair because of the stitches in my chin, so he offered to wash it for me. He sat me on the stupid plastic chair and removed the showerhead from the cradle. After gently tilting my head back, he washed my hair from behind, careful not to wet my face.

When he was done, I stood and turned around to find his beautiful penis standing proud. He was hard as a rock. Enough was enough. I wrapped my fingers around his shaft, and even when he protested I refused to let go.

It only took a few strokes from my hand for his head to fall back and a loud groan to escape him before he relented. He needed it, and he knew it. It had been weeks since he'd had any relief. That didn't sit well with me. I know how important sex is to him, and I hated that he was going without. I trusted that he wouldn't go elsewhere because I know how much he loves me, but I wanted to do it for him.

With one of his arms wrapped around my waist holding me up, his lips met mine. His other hand moved down between my legs and his fingers circled my clit as I continued to work him over.

Within minutes our bodies were trembling as we moaned into each other's mouths, coming undone together. His grip tightened on my waist when my legs threatened to give way from the intensity of it. One thing is for sure; holding out seems to make those orgasms all the more sweeter. When we finally do get to go all the way again, it's going to be explosive.

Although it wasn't even close to what either of us really wanted to do to each other, it was enough to take the edge off.

Unbeknownst to him, I have big plans for tomorrow night. We *will* be having sex. That you can be sure of. I've taken all the necessary precautions to make sure that happens. He's not going to know what hit him.

TWENTY-SEVEN

CARTER

I SHOULD'VE CALLED MEGAN WEEKS AGO BECAUSE I CAN already see the improvement in Indi. Her spirits seem lifted. I love seeing that spark in her again. I took a chance calling Megan behind Indiana's back, but thankfully it all worked out. As soon as I told her what was going on with Indi she was not only shocked, but completely devastated. Before I even got the chance to ask her if she'd come home, she'd already said, "I'm gonna organise a flight. I'll be there as soon as I can." An hour later, she called me back to say she was on the way to the airport and would be flying out in a few hours.

It worked out perfect. Her plane was due to touch down in Sydney mid-morning the next day. I got Justine to organise a hire car to pick Megan up from the airport and bring her here, as well as book the appointment at the Day Spa. I told her I wanted the girls to have the works, to spare no expense.

I'll admit I had a lump in my throat when I observed their reunion. It was very touching. I was so glad I could do that for her. She needed that lift. She's at the tail end of her treatment now, and I can tell how much she's struggling. Hopefully this will give her the boost she needs to get over the last hurdle.

After showering and dressing in a pair of dark denim jeans and a nice dress shirt, I head back out to the girls. Indi whistles as I walk towards them. "You look good enough to eat," she whispers when she rises from the sofa, wrapping her arms around my waist. "Mmmm. You smell delicious," she sighs after placing her nose against my chest and inhaling. *Fuck me.*

Everything in me wants to pick her up, carry her into the bedroom and devour her. That thought has been consuming my thoughts every minute of every fucking day, but I can't do that. One more week, that's what I keep telling myself. Never in my life have I gone this long without sex. Do you have any idea how hard it is to lay next to the woman you love every night and not be able to connect with her in that way? It's fucking torture. I can't tell you how many times I've nearly caved when Indiana has all but begged for me to fuck her. I hate denying her of anything, especially sex, but it is for her own good. She's been too sick and too weak.

If all goes well, in one more week I'm gonna fuck her until she can't walk.

I end up taking the girls to a restaurant called the Surfhouse. It's situated on the shores of Merewether Beach. It was recommended to me by one of my clients, Kellie. I was told the food and the view were to die for, and she was right. It was.

For most of the night, I sat back and watched them talking and laughing. It warmed my heart to see Indiana like this again. I've missed her laugh, her smile, and her happy-go-lucky nature. The girls were tight back in high school, and it pleases me to see nothing has changed.

It's late when we arrive back at the apartment. I knew Indi wouldn't want Megan staying in a hotel, but because I only had the one bedroom, we pushed both sides of the sofa together to make a makeshift bed for her. It wasn't much, but she didn't seem to mind. We would be heading back to Sydney Monday morning to start the last course of radiation therapy anyway, so it was only going to be for two nights.

Sunday morning we rise early and head to the Growers Market. It has become our Sunday morning ritual since Indiana has been staying with me. After stocking up on fresh fruit, vegetables, and other local delicacies, we headed to the fish market to get some seafood to have with our lunch.

Late that afternoon, Jax turned up at the apartment unexpectedly. "Hey buddy," I say surprised when I answer the door. "What are you doing here?" To be honest, I've missed our catch-ups. We haven't been getting together for our card night since Indiana started her treatment. She was just too sick.

"Your woman called me," he answers. "She thought you needed an afternoon on the town with the boys." Looking over my shoulder at Indiana I find her smiling at me. Christ I love her. Even though the thought of leaving her initially worries me, she has Megan here, so I know she'll be fine.

Standing, she makes her way over to us. After greeting Jax with a kiss on the cheek, she wraps her arms around my waist. "I hope you don't mind, but you need this. A chance to unwind will do you good," she says smiling up at me. "Besides, if I'm lucky I might even get some drunk sex when you get home."

"Nice try," I reply laughing.

"He's not holding out on you is he?" Jax asks Indi.

"Yes, he is. I need you to get him shitfaced while you're out, so I can take advantage of him when he gets home." Jax and I both laugh at her comment. *Fuck.* I hate that she's feeling neglected in that department. We've had a long talk about this though. I know she understands my reasons for not sleeping with her.

••••

It's around 11:00pm when I stumble into the apartment. I'm alone. Jax ended up picking up two random chicks as we were leaving. Or should I say they tried to pick us up. They invited us back to their place. Of course I wasn't interested. The only woman I'll ever need or want was waiting for me at home. He ended up walking away with his arm around them both. Lucky bastard. *One more week* I chanted to myself, shaking my head as I turned in the other direction, making my way towards the apartment.

The lights are out when I arrive, but Indiana has left on the hall light that leads to our bedroom. I can see Megan is already asleep on the sofa. Quietly, so as not to wake her, I make my way towards my room. I've had a fair bit to drink, but I'm actually feeling pretty good. Very relaxed. Jax tried his best to get me shitfaced, but I need to drive back to Sydney in the morning, so as the night wore on I slowed down. It was a good night. Indi was right; it was just what I needed.

When I turn the bedroom light on, it wakes Indiana. *Shit.* Sitting up, she rubs her eyes. She's so sweet when she first wakes. The covers slide down revealing her spectacular tits. Fuck me, she's naked. My dick instantly stirs.

Throwing back the covers, she climbs out of bed. Sweet Jesus, I know exactly what she's up to. She stalks towards me. "Where are your pyjamas?" I ask, diverting my eyes. If I look at her I know I'm gonna fucking cave. The fact that I've been drinking doesn't help. My judgment is impaired. Burying my cock into that heavenly pussy of hers again is all I've thought about for weeks.

"I was hot," she says smirking as her arms snake around my waist. It's fucking winter. Bullshit she's fucking hot. I keep my hands by my side as my gaze moves up to the roof. I try not to think about the fact that I can feel her hard nipples pressed against my chest. Fuck she's a little vixen. My cock grows harder. "You're wearing too many clothes," she whispers, getting on the tips of her toes and placing a kiss on my neck.

At least I'm fucking wearing clothes.

She's playing dirty. I need to stay strong. Her hands reach up and start undoing my buttons one by one. "I can do that," I say looking down at her. Of course she's gazing up at me through her lashes, smiling. Yep, she's a vixen.

Christ she's fucking beautiful.

"I'm sure you can," she purrs. "But let me do it for you."

"You're not playing fair, babe."

"I have no idea what you're talking about." I can't help but chuckle at her reply. Does she think I'm fucking stupid? Like hell she doesn't know.

Once all the buttons are undone, she reaches up and slides her hands under my shirt before pushing it down my arms. It falls to the ground. Her eyes rake over my chest and down to my abs as she licks her lips. My cock grows harder. Her fingers skim over the scrolled script tattooed across my chest.

"What's does *'Mi Vida Loca'* mean?" she whispers.

"My crazy life." I see the corners of her mouth curve up at my response.

"I'm glad your crazy life led you to me," she says.

"Me too baby," I reply as the back of my hand traces a line down the side of her face. She makes everything I went through, growing up, worth it. *Every damn thing.*

Next she reaches for the button of my jeans. "Oh no you don't," I say taking a step back. She ignores me, closing the distance between us again and reaching for the waistband of my jeans. My refrain is slipping by the second.

As she works feverishly at my button and zipper, she places a few kisses on my abdomen before her tongue darts out, licking a line up my chest. Fuck me. "Mmmm. You taste delicious," she breathes.

"Are you alright there?" I chuckle. I fucking love her mouth on me, and she knows it.

"What? I'm hungry," she purrs again, making me growl. *Seductress.* "Hungry for your cock." That's it. *I'm a fucking goner.* If that sexy mouth of hers goes anywhere near my cock, there's no way in hell I'm gonna be able to stop her.

She finally gets my jeans undone before pulling them down my legs. Everything in me wants to help her, but I refuse to be an enabler.

When she falls down to her knees, a loud growl rumbles in the back of my throat. She looks up at me through her lashes again and smiles sweetly. Right in this moment, she's anything but fucking sweet.

She's taking advantage of me. She knows quite well my inhibitions are impaired from the alcohol I've been drinking. That was her plan all along. I'd be a damn liar if I said I didn't secretly love that she's doing this. It's fucking hot—she's hot, and all mine.

I'm one lucky bastard.

I continue to stand there as she lifts my legs one by one, removing my shoes, socks and then slides my feet out of my jeans. I know I could easily stop this, but all the fight has gone out of me. I want this more than I need my next breath.

Once she has me completely naked, her fingers run lightly up the front of my legs. Her eyes are fixed on my hard, aching cock. She moistens her lips with her tongue as the pad of her thumb spreads the bead of pre-cum over the tip of my head. *Sweet Jesus.*

She wraps her tiny hand around the girth of my cock and strokes it once. I groan loudly as my head tilts back and my eyes close. *Yep, I'm a fucking goner.* I open my eyes again and look down at her, just as her lips part widely and she draws my cock into her mouth.

"Mmmm," she moans. It vibrates down the length of my shaft and I already feel like I'm gonna blow.

"Sweet Jesus, Indi," I groan when her tongue swirls around my dick while the rest is buried deep in her mouth. My hands move down to thread through her hair as she continues to work me over. I fucking love it when she sucks my cock.

She moans again when my hips begin to move, slowly pumping into her mouth. When I see her hand slip down between her legs, I fucking lose it. I need to touch her pussy too. No I need to fuck it. She's won. My little vixen has won. She's gonna get her way.

My need to be inside her takes over as my hands move from her hair to under her arms. I lift her in one swoop and carry her over to the bed. "I give up," I admit as I lay her down and climb on top of her. "I need to be inside you, babe." She grins when she realises she's going to get her way.

"Thank God," she whimpers, smiling triumphantly. It makes me chuckle.

"I'm gonna fuck you now," I whisper before my mouth covers hers.

She opens her legs wide and I settle in between them. I'm so desperate for this that I don't even take the time to feel if she's ready for me. I know damn well she will be. As soon as I grab my cock and slide it against her pussy, I groan. I was right. She's fucking dripping.

My body starts to shake with anticipation as I line myself up with her opening. I've been dying to sink into her heaven for weeks. It's all I've been thinking about. She consumes me.

As soon as I slip the head inside her she whimpers. When I push all the way in, we moan in unison. *Home.* That's what it feels like— fucking home. As much as I want to pound into her tight pussy right now, I don't. She's still so fragile and the last thing I want to do is hurt her.

She, of course, has other ideas. Her hands slide down the length of my back before resting on my arse. Her fingers dig into my cheeks, pushing me further inside her. "Fuck me, Carter," she begs. "Don't hold back. I need this."

I can't resist her. How can I deny her? I've denied her long enough. My hand moves to grasp her hip. "Okay," I say hesitantly. "Don't move though. Let me do all the work."

"Just fuck me," she begs as her fingers dig deeper into my flesh. If my girl wants me to fuck her, then that's exactly what I'm gonna do. I start to pump into her in short, fast, and hard strokes. Fuck she feels amazing. I'm not sure how much longer I'm gonna last.

Within minutes she starts to moan loudly as her orgasm takes hold. As soon as I feel her pussy clench around my cock, I lose it. I drive into her a few more times before I still. My body trembles as I spill my seed deep inside her.

When I open my eyes again, I see her smiling up at me. It's a smile lined with pure bliss, but I also see a hint of gloating. She fucking played me. She played me good. "Are you okay?" I ask as my hand brushes the hair back off her face.

"I'm wonderful," she replies. That makes two of us. It's not until I pull out of her that I realise I didn't wrap my cock. *Fuck.* I came inside her. "Are you okay, Carter?" she asks when she notices the panic on my face.

"I didn't wear a condom. Shit." I can't believe I was so fucking stupid.

"Hey," she says reaching up to stroke my face. "I'm on the pill. Don't worry. It'll be okay." It's easy for her to say. I know she's probably right, but it doesn't stop the churning in my gut. *What if it's not?*

●●●●

The three of us headed back to Sydney Monday morning for Indiana's last bout of treatment. I pray the radiation has been successful. I can't stand to see her sick like this anymore.

Megan is staying with her parents while we're in Sydney, but has been coming with us daily to the hospital. It's been nice to have someone sit with me while we wait for Indi to get done.

The first morning, Megan asked me if I wanted to go for coffee while we waited for Indiana. I said no. Technically I know there's nothing I can do while she's in there, but if this is the closest I can get to her while she's having the treatment, then this is exactly where I'm gonna stay.

She ended up disappearing for a few minutes, coming back with a coffee for both of us before taking a seat beside me. That became our ritual for the next four days. We'd both hugged and kissed Indi, and wished her luck before she disappeared through the doors. Meg would then go and get our coffees, and we'd sit in silence until she re-emerged.

I could clearly see the worry on Megan's face as the week progressed and Indi became sicker. I'd like to think I'm used to it by now, but truth is, I'm not.

Thursday morning, when Megan and I are alone outside the

treatment room, she asks, "Has she been this sick throughout the whole treatment?"

"Pretty much," I reply. She goes quiet. When I look over at her, I see the silent tears streaming down her face. I don't know what to do, or what to say, so I just reach over and grasp my hand around hers. I love that she cares about my girl as much as I do.

When we leave the hospital I want to take the girls out to celebrate her last day of treatment, but Indiana is too sick. We had to pull over a few times on the way home for her to vomit. It fucking kills me inside to see her like that. Hopefully today will be the last time I have to witness it, and the last time she has to endure it.

The oncologist got pathology to take a round of blood tests and perform another scan before we left the hospital. Megan laid down in the bed with Indi when we got home, so I headed over to my mum's house. I wanted it to be me lying with her, but Megan will be heading back overseas soon, so I didn't want to be selfish. They need their time together. If I have my way, I'll have the rest of my life to spend with Indiana.

Tomorrow is D-day. We have an appointment in the morning to see if the radiation therapy has been successful. I'm in two minds about it. I'm both excited and scared to hear the results. I can only imagine how Indiana feels. If this radiation hasn't cured her, I don't know what I'll do.

••••

Friday morning, the five of us pile into Ross' car: our parents, as well as Megan. We're all going with her today for moral support. Let's hope she doesn't need it. Indiana has been quiet ever since she woke. I can't really blame her. She has a lot riding on today. Even though I have been through the treatment every step of the way, I wasn't the one who was sick. I'm not the one whose very future is relying on a good outcome. Regardless of what happens, I do know that I will remain by her side no matter what.

As we sit in the waiting room waiting for her to be called for her appointment, she turns to me, clutching my hand in hers. "Carter. I know you've come in to hold my hand for every appointment, and I appreciate it more than you know." Okay, I don't like where this is heading. "Would you mind if I went in alone today?"

There it is. *Yes I fucking would.* Hurt consumes me that she wouldn't want me in there with her. Even though from the beginning, I did force that upon her. I want to be her rock. I don't want her to have to face what the doctor has to say alone. What if the prognosis isn't good?

"Is that what you really want?" I ask, trying hard not to let her see I'm hurt. I have to put my wants and needs aside. Ultimately, this is about her. This is her life, her future. If it's something she really wants, then I need to respect that. Nobody says I have to like it, because frankly I don't. Not one bit.

When the nurse calls her name, we both rise. "Are you sure?" I ask again wrapping her in my arms.

"I'm sure." I tighten my embrace briefly before kissing the top of her head.

Pulling back, I cup her pretty face in my hands, making eye contact with her. I can see the uncertainty on her face. It tugs at my heart. "Okay. Good luck," I whisper with all the confidence I can muster.

"Thank you. Just so you know, I wouldn't have been able to do this without you." A lump rises to my throat as I briefly wrap her in my arms again. She's got this. I know it.

I sit back down. My heart is beating furiously against my ribcage. My eyes are on her as she follows the nurse towards the door. I watch as she briefly stops before entering. Holding her head high, I see her inhale a large breath before squaring her shoulders. I'm in awe of her. The lump in my throat grows. She's so strong, so kick-arse. I'm so damn proud. *She's got this in the bag.*

Once she disappears, my eyes move to Megan's legs that are bouncing nervously beside me. Then my gaze moves towards my mum's hand clenched around Ross'. It brings a brief smile to my face.

For some reason, seeing them together makes me happy. I know they're just friends, but they have become so close over the past few months. This is going to sound really pathetic, but sometimes I imagine in my head that they're married. That they are my parents. I know it's just wishful thinking on my part, but fuck me if I don't want that.

Eventually, I stand and start to pace. It seems like it is taking forever for her to come out, when in reality, only fifteen minutes have passed. My eyes are firmly trained on the door she went through earlier.

A few minutes later it opens. My heart skips a beat. When she walks out, she stops. Her eyes go to our parents, then Megan. When they lock with mine I hold my breath. I release it when a huge smile forms on her face. Pure fucking relief floods through me when she says the three words I've been praying for. "I'm cancer free."

Quickly closing the distance between us, I pull her into my arms, swinging her around. I'm so fucking happy right now. When I place her back on her feet, her arms snake around my waist before she does something she hasn't done since her diagnosis. She sobs into my chest. Tears of joy rise to my eyes.

Thank fuck. My girl is going to be okay.

TWENTY-EIGHT

CARTER

INDIANA HAS TO CONTINUE TO HAVE THREE MONTHLY CHECK-
ups, just to make sure the cancer doesn't return. Fuck, I hope it
doesn't. Nevertheless, we're all buzzing on the drive home from the
hospital.

Ross took us all out to celebrate that night. Her news definitely
called for a celebration. We had a great time. I think we all feel like a
huge weight has been lifted off our shoulders. It's been a long time
since I've seen Indiana or her father smile so much.

There is a small cloud hanging over my head. There's something I
need to discuss with Indi, and I'm worried how she's going to take it.
I've been putting it off the last few days for that very reason.

Later that night when we're lying in bed, I decide to bring it up. I'm
leaving in the morning, so it's now or never. "I need to talk to you
about something," I say to her as she lies in my arms, drawing lazy
circles on my chest with her finger. We not long ago finished making
love. Fuck it's good to be back to normal again.

"About what?" she asks, her finger stilling.

"Well, you know I have to go back home tomorrow morning. Jax is coming up to help me move all the furniture in the apartment, ready for the builders to start the renovations on Monday."

"And?"

"And, I was thinking maybe it would be better if you stayed down here."

"What? Why?" she asks, raising her head to make eye contact with me. I can clearly see the hurt on her face.

"It's not what you think," I immediately answer, stroking her hair as I try to reassure her. "It's just going to be chaotic up there this week with the builders and everything. Plus you have Megan here. I thought you might want to spend some quality time with her before she goes home."

"Oh. I guess," she says in a disappointed tone as she rests the side of her face against my chest again. "I suppose I need to start looking for a job anyway. Are we still going to see each other on the weekends?" Fuck. Is she crazy? I knew she'd take it the wrong way.

"Indi." Placing my finger under her chin, I lift her face. "If you let me finish, I was going to say, once the renovations are complete I was wondering if you'd consider moving up to Newcastle permanently."

"Really?" she squeals as her beautiful green eyes widen in surprise.

"Yes. Really. I'm sure you can find work up there. If not, you can always come and work for me."

"In the tattoo parlour?" she asks giggling. "That's sweet, but I love working with animals. I'd really like to get into something like that again."

"I was thinking more like hiring you as my sex slave," I joke. She slaps my chest, narrowing her eyes at me.

"Ha ha. Although it does sound like a job I'd enjoy," she laughs. Of course she would, she's an insatiable vixen. *My* insatiable vixen. "Jokes aside, are you sure you're ready for a commitment like that?" I don't even need to think about it. Of course I am. She's it for me. I couldn't imagine my life without her in it now.

"Couldn't be surer."

"Well then I'd love to," she says beaming. I know my face mirrors hers. She has just made me the happiest man on this earth. There was a part of me that worried she'd say no, that's why I've been putting it off. I brought it up with Ross yesterday. I wanted to make sure he was alright with it before I asked her. He said he was going to miss her like crazy, but seemed happy that our relationship was heading to the next level.

••••

My week has been fucking crazy. Not only do I have my normal job during the day, but I've been working late into the night on the renovations as well. My apartment is a chaotic mess, but it's finally all coming together. The builders have been working their arses off to try and get it finished for me.

As busy as I've been, I'm missing Indiana like crazy. The nights when I finally fall into bed are the worst. Even though I'm fucking exhausted, I find it hard to fall asleep without her beside me. Thankfully, she's missing me too. That's why I've been busting my arse to get everything completed. The sooner it's done, the sooner I can bring her home.

Tomorrow, mum's coming up for the day. She's bringing my grand-mother with her. I'm looking forward to seeing her again. They're going to help with all the girly shit like the finishing touches and decorating.

Late Friday afternoon, Jax arrives. He's going to stay for the week-end. Instead of our usual card night we're going to be painting. We head down to the pub for dinner and a quick beer before we get started.

While he's filling the paint trays for us to use with the rollers, I give Indiana a quick call. "Hey, babe," I say when she picks up.

"Hey. How're the renovations going?"

"Getting there. I've been busting my arse to get it finished. I need you up here. I fucking miss you," I tell her. I hear Jax chuckle at my comment so I flip him off.

"I miss you too. So much." Her reply has me smiling.

"How are you feeling?" I ask. I know I shouldn't keep asking, but it's all still so fresh in my mind. Even with the good news she got from the doctor, it's hard not to worry.

"Great. I haven't stopped eating all day. I've certainly been making up for all the food I couldn't stomach during treatment." That pleases me no end.

"I'm glad, babe. You need to rebuild your strength. How's the packing going?"

"I'm nearly done. You might need to bring a trailer down when you come and get me," she says laughing. Fuck.

"How much stuff are you bringing?"

"Oh the trailer's not for my stuff, it's for me. If I keep eating like this, I'm not gonna be able to fit in your car." I chuckle. *Hardly.* She's so cute.

"Well you could do with gaining a few kilos. Anything more, I'll be sure to work it off you in the bedroom when you get up here," I tell her.

"Oh, I like the sound of that." So do I. Just thinking about it makes my cock twitch. We talk for a few more minutes before Jax clears his throat. He has everything set up, and he's waiting for me so we can start.

"I've gotta get going, babe. I'll try to call back before you go to bed."

"Okay. Love you," she says making me smile again. I look over at Jax. He's standing there listening to my every word. I know he's going to rib me for this.

"Love you too." I flip him off again when he smirks. Fucker.

••••

We were up until 2:00am painting, but we got most of it done. I feel like I've been dragging my arse all day at work. I'm exhausted. Jax has the job of driving my mum and grandma around town so they can get everything they need to decorate the apartment. I want it to be perfect for when Indi comes home.

I head upstairs around lunchtime. My grandmother has made a huge plate of sandwiches for us. It's great having her here, and in my life. Even my mum seems different. I can see it in her eyes. She's finally at peace.

I took them both for a tour of my shop when they arrived this morning. They both told me how proud they are of me, and all my accomplishments. It was nice to hear.

Before they left for their shopping spree, my grandmother pulled me aside. "I have something I'd like to give you," she said, taking an envelope out of her purse and holding it out to me.

"What is it?" I asked.

"Open it." I was shocked when I did. There was a cheque for five hundred thousand dollars inside.

"I can't accept this," I told her, placing it back inside the envelope and passing it to her.

"You can, and you will," she replied pushing my hand away. "Think of it as twenty-four years of missed birthday and Christmas gifts." It was a sweet offer, but I couldn't accept it.

"I appreciate the sentiment behind it, but I couldn't take this from you. It's too much."

"Yes you can," she said folding her frail hand around mine. "When I pass, everything I own will be left to you and your mother. Consider it an early inheritance. Please let me do this for you, Carter. You can invest it, or use it to expand your business. The money is just sitting there. I'd rather see it go to good use. I can afford this. I always knew we were pretty well-off, but my husband handled all the finances when he was alive, so I had no idea how much money we had. As it turns out, I'm worth millions," she whispered, winking at me. It made me smile. "Please." The pleading look in her eyes almost had me saying yes.

"I don't know if I can," I admitted.

"Please say you'll accept it. It will make an old lady very happy." I chuckled at her words. She drives a hard bargain.

"Okay. Thank you," I eventually said wrapping my arms around her. I didn't know what else to say. I was lost for words.

"You're welcome. It makes me happy to know I'm in a position to help you. I'm sure life wasn't easy for you growing up. I only wish I could've been there for you back then." She pulled back and ran her hand down the side of my face.

"I wish that too," I replied smiling. Because I do.

"I'll be checking with my bank to make sure you've cashed it by the way." She shook her finger at me when she said that part. We both laughed before I took her in my arms again.

It's taken twenty-four years for everything to come full circle, but looking back now, it was worth the wait. I couldn't be happier with the direction my life has taken.

TWENTY-NINE

INDIANA

MEG HAS SPENT THE WHOLE WEEK AT MY HOUSE, ONLY GOING home to her parents' at night to sleep. I'm worried about her. The last few days she seems withdrawn. I've asked her if she's okay, but she keeps telling me she's fine. She's not fine, and I intend to get to the bottom of it when she comes over this morning.

I have all my things packed up for the move. I only have the last-minute things to do tomorrow morning. Carter is coming down, so I'll have his car. Dad is driving mine and Elizabeth is going to follow us in hers, so it should only take one trip. I didn't think I'd have so many boxes, but I do.

As much as I'm looking forward to moving in with Carter, I'm gonna miss my dad. He's taken the next few days off work so we can spend some quality time together. I know I'll only be two hours away, but I'm going to worry about him being here on his own. Sure he has Elizabeth living next door, but it's not the same. It's the only thing I'm struggling with. The only dampener on my big move.

I'm taping up yet another box containing more of my shoes when Meg arrives. Instantly I can tell she's been crying. She looks like shit. "Hey," I say standing and going to her. "What's wrong?"

"Nothing," she replies, forcing out a fake smile. *Nothing my arse.* Grabbing her arm and leading her over towards my bed, we sit.

"Spill." Instead of telling me what's going on, she places her hands over her face and starts sobbing. "Hey," I say softly, wrapping her in my arms. "Talk to me."

"I'm okay," she eventually replies, pulling away and wiping her eyes. *Lying bitch.* I raise my hand and pinch her arm. "Ouch," she whines, a small smile tugging at her lips.

"You've got three seconds to tell me what the hell is going on." It hurts me to see her like this. She's usually so happy-go-lucky. I raise my hand, ready to pinch her again. "One." God, I'm counting. I sound like friggin' Carter. "Two."

"I'm just sad, that's all," she answers, pushing my hand down.

"No shit. Why?" I ask, grasping my fingers around hers. "Are you homesick?"

"Huh," she scoffs. "What home? I've had over fifteen in the past two years." I squeeze her hand. I know moving around has been hard for her.

"Do you miss Drew?"

"Of course I miss him," she says, tears rising to her eyes again.

"Well go to him. As much as I've loved having you home, you belong with your husband."

"I told him last night I'm not coming back," she admits as the tears stream down her face. *Far out.*

"What? Why?" I ask concerned and extremely shocked. I had no idea she was feeling like this. I wrap her in my arms.

"As much as I love him, Indi, I can't live like that anymore. Coming home to Australia has made me see just how unhappy I am living over there. Every time we get settled, we up and move again. I can't even leave the damn house without a friggin' interpreter, because most of the countries we've lived in don't speak English. I'm lonely. He's gone most of the time. I just can't do it anymore." My embrace on her tightens when she starts to sob again. I've never seen her this upset before.

"Have you thought about starting a family? Maybe that will help fill in some of your time. Maybe then you won't feel so lonely."

"Drew said the same thing, but it wouldn't be fair to bring a child into the world when we don't even have a stable home."

"Oh, Meg," I say, sadness lining my voice. "Are you really prepared to throw away everything you have with Drew?"

"I can't go back, Indi. I just can't."

"What did Drew say? Can he find another job?" I ask. I understand how she feels, but I can't help feeling that she's making a huge mistake.

"He was devastated. But he loves his job, I'd never ask him to leave it for me." I continue to hold her while she cries. I don't know what else I can do. Running may not be the answer, but I need to support her on this. I'm sure it wasn't an easy decision for her to make. I pray that they can come to some agreement. They're perfect for each other.

A while later, my dad takes us both out for lunch. Neither of us are great company though. Megan is clearly broken by her decision, and I'm not only worried, but I'm hurting for her too. I'm not sure if I can leave her when she's like this. I may need to call Carter and put the move off for a few more days. She needs me.

"Wanna stay over tonight?" I ask later that night when we're lying on my bed. "We could have a slumber party like old times." I don't want her to be alone.

"I guess," she shrugs.

"Things have a way of working themselves out, Meg," I say reassuringly, reaching for her hand as we lie side by side on my bed staring up at the roof. "Look at Carter and I. Who would've thought we'd be where we are today?"

"I'm glad things worked out for you both," she replies.

"Things will work out for you and Drew too, you wait and see."

"Thanks, babe. I hope so."

And I was right. We didn't have to wait long at all. Five minutes after I said that to her, my dad knocks on my bedroom door.

"Megan," he says, popping his head around the door. "You have a visitor." We both sit up just as the door pushes open all the way, and Drew waltzes in. *Yes,* I silently chant.

"Oh my God," Meg squeals, leaping off the bed and into his arms. "What are you doing here?"

"I quit my job," he replies, pulling her into a crushing embrace. I can tell by the dark circles under his eyes he's been suffering too. My heart goes out to both of them.

"What? No!" Stepping back to make eye contact with him, she continues, "You loved that job."

"I love you more," is all he says.

"But—"

"No buts," he interrupts, cutting her off. "I can always find another job, but you my love, are irreplaceable." He tenderly caresses the back of his hand down the side of Meg's face before placing his lips against hers. *Awww.* Tears well in my eyes as I watch them together. I'm so glad things worked themselves out.

••••

Carter arrives early Sunday morning. He was originally going to come Saturday night, but he still had some last-minute work to do at the apartment. God, I've missed him. As soon as I hear his car pull up in the driveway, I run outside to greet him. I'm still in my pyjamas, but I don't care.

I jump off the front porch and bolt across the lawn as he's getting out of the car. As soon as I'm close enough, I launch myself into his arms. "Fuck I've missed you," he breathes into the crook of my neck as he wraps his arms around me tight.

"I've missed you too."

"Let me look at you?" he asks placing me back on the ground. I smile up at him as he cups my face in his hands. "There's my girl. I've missed your pretty face. It's so good to see you've got your colour back." My dad said the same thing yesterday. I even noticed how pale my skin was during treatment.

Before I get a chance to reply, his mouth covers mine. I've missed his kisses. He groans into my mouth when I deepen the kiss. When we finally come up for air, he rests his forehead against mine. "I can't wait to get you home."

That makes two of us.

••••

A few hours later we're on the road. Well, Carter and I are. My dad and Elizabeth are going to leave in a few hours to give Carter and I a little alone time. They're picking up Carter's grandmother on the way. I can't wait to meet her. We're expecting them around midday, so Carter is going to take us all out for lunch when they arrive. The three of them are going to stay over tonight, and since my car will be staying up here, my dad will travel home with Elizabeth tomorrow.

Carter and I talk the whole drive. It's so good to be together again. I fill him in on everything that happened with Meg, and he tells me all about the renovations. I can't wait to see the new apartment. "I was thinking, while I look around for a job, I might see if there are any animal shelters in the area. I could volunteer." Carter reaches for my hand, bringing it up to his lips.

"That's sweet, but I don't think you'll have trouble finding a job," he says smiling. I'm glad he's so confident. I've been so busy with Meg and packing I never got a chance to research how many veterinarian clinics there are in the area.

I'm excited to go upstairs when we pull up outside the tattoo parlour. As usual, Carter comes around to open my door. I love how sweet he is. After helping me out, he pulls me into his arms, planting a soft kiss on my lips.

"I need you to close your eyes," he says.

"What, now? Shouldn't I wait until we get upstairs?"

"Just close them. I need to show you something down here first."

What is he up to? He has that smug look on his face that has me instantly suspicious. Fine. I'll go along with it. I close my eyes as he reaches for my arm and places his other hand on the small of my back, guiding me onto the sidewalk. "No peeking." Peeking at what? I presume he wants to show me something inside the tattoo parlour, but he leads me in the opposite direction. Suddenly he stops walking. Moving around behind me, he tilts my head back so my face is looking up. What in the hell is he up to? "Open your eyes," he whispers.

I do as he asks. When I see what he wants to show me, I gasp. "Oh. My. God. Carter, you didn't," I say turning to face him.

"I did," he replies. "I was right when I said you wouldn't have any trouble finding a job." Throwing myself into his arms I bury my face in his chest and start to cry; tears of shock, tears of happiness, tears for Lassie. "Don't you like it?"

"I friggin' love it." I stand back to look up at him. I smile widely through my tears. "I'm just overwhelmed." He kisses my forehead before turning me in his arms so I'm facing the shopfront again. There's a sign in the window that says 'opening soon'. His hands wrap around my waist as his chin rests on my shoulder. I can't believe he would do this for me. Again, I look up at the large sign that's spread across the whole front of the building. 'Lassie's Veterinarian Clinic'. It even has a picture of him on the side.

"Do you want to take a look inside?" he asks. Do I ever.

"Please. I'd love to." He laces his fingers through mine as we walk towards the door.

"Here you go," he says passing the keys to me. "It's yours, so you should do the honours." After I take the keys from him, I slink my arms around his neck and pull his face down towards mine.

"What did I ever do to deserve someone so wonderful?" I ask, brushing my lips against his. He chuckles at my question.

"You annoyed the crap out of me until I fell in love with you."

"I did not," I screech, pinching his arm.

"Ouch," he says laughing, rubbing his bicep. "Your fingers are lethal."

"I'm sorry," I reply, planting a soft kiss where I'd pinched him.

"My dick hurts too, will you kiss that better?" I narrow my eyes at him when he grabs hold of his crotch, and we both laugh.

"Nice try."

"Well you've gotta give me ten points for trying," he says putting his hand on the small of my back and leading me inside. I'll gladly kiss his dick after the tour, but I'm not telling him that.

You can smell the fresh paint when we enter. The walls are painted in a soft lemon. The floor tiles are white. There's a long white reception counter on one side, and a row of white chairs along the floor to ceiling window at the front of the reception area. A green indoor palm tree sits in one corner in a tall white ceramic pot. It looks so clean, so fresh. I love it.

My eyes dart everywhere while Carter moves to disable the alarm. "The code is two thousand and ten," he says coming to stand beside me again. "Just like my shop. It was a very important year."

"It was?" My mind starts to race. What was so important in two thousand and ten?

"It was the year my life changed for the better. It was the year I met you," he says leaning down to kiss the top of my head. *Awww.* He says the sweetest things sometimes.

Grabbing hold of my trembling hand, he leads me through to the back. There are two large examination rooms. They're both identical. It makes me think of the pissy little room I had when I worked for Mark. This place shits all over his. Both rooms are complete with stainless steel examination tables in the centre of the room, and white custom-made benchtops running the whole length of the far wall. It has drawers and cupboards for storing supplies and equipment in.

"I know the walls are bare, but I wanted you to be able to add your own touch. I've just set you up with the basics."

"It's perfect," I say squeezing his hand. I'm still in shock that he has done this for me, but I'm beaming as he shows me around. We move further down the corridor until we come to a larger room. It's completely decked out for surgery, with two large stainless steel operating tables in the centre of the room. I'm flabbergasted. Lost for words. This would've cost him a fortune to set up. How he managed to do this in a little over a week amazes me. "I love you," I tell him, sliding my hand around his waist and resting my head on his arm.

Eventually leaving his side I walk around the room, skimming my hands over everything. I can't wait to get this place up and running. Adjacent to the room is a door that leads to the recovery area. There are cages stacked three high, lining both walls. This will be not only for the animals that have to stay after surgery, but any sick animals that need to be here for observation or treatment overnight. Living upstairs is going to make keeping an eye on them so much easier.

"Oh, Carter," I say, throwing my arms around him when the tour is complete. "I don't know what to say."

"You don't have to say anything, babe. I'm glad I could do this for you. I probably should confess. I did have an ulterior motive."

"You did?" I ask.

"Yes. This was my way of guaranteeing you'd stay up here with me," he says smiling sheepishly.

"Well I hate to tell you, but you wasted your money because I would've stayed regardless. You're stuck with me Mr. Reynolds."

"Damn," he says, and we both laugh. "I've organised a rep to come meet with you on Wednesday so you can stock up on the supplies you're gonna need before you open."

"You're amazing," I reply placing my lips on his.

"I know."

"And extremely modest," I add, kissing him again.

"That too," he chuckles.

"And all mine."

"You better believe it, baby," he says.

Next we head upstairs so I can see the renovations he's made to the apartment. "Wow," is all I say when we first enter. I can't believe how much bigger it looks. They've knocked down the majority of the wall that divided both buildings, opening the space right up.

"We have three bedrooms now. Our room has moved. I've even

added an en-suite so our guest can use the main bathroom. Come, let me show you." I can hear the excitement in his voice as he pulls me along. It's infectious. I'm still on a high from downstairs. Of course he leads us straight to our new room.

"Wow," I say when we walk in. The bedroom is now in what was the building next door. Carter has installed floor to ceiling windows in this part as well. Our new bedroom now has the same view of the ocean, like the lounge room does. It's breathtaking. I'm not sure what is going to be better, waking up to Carter's handsome face everyday, or the ocean.

As pretty as the ocean view is, I think Carter would have to win that one.

"As you can see I bought us a new bedroom suite. I put the old one in the spare room. Your drawers are over there," he says pointing to the ones on the left. "Come look at the walk-in-robe I had built for you." I'm smiling as he drags me across the room. I look back over my shoulder at my new room, trying to take it all in.

The suite he bought is so nice. There are two large, matching timber chest of drawers that are painted white, but the drawer fronts are finished in a dark timber stain with white handles to tie it all together. The bedside tables are the same. The bed is ginormous, so much bigger than the last one. The room is painted in a deep, musky, sky blue colour, still keeping its masculinity, but the large white mirror hanging on the far wall, the sheer white curtains, and white covers on the bed, soften the room. There is a large oval blue and white rug on the floor, and a few blue cushions on the bed that blend in with the wall colour. Honestly, I love it. He must've had some help decorating this room. Although masculine, it definitely has a feminine touch.

"Holy crap," I screech when we round the corner to the walk-in-robe. "I think I've died and gone to heaven." He chuckles at my comment.

"I knew you'd like this. Look, it even has little shelves for the ridiculous amount of shoes you own."

"It's not ridiculous," I say, playfully elbowing him. "I'm a girl. Girls need a lot of shoes. It's in our genetic makeup." He rolls his eyes, but doesn't respond. My eyes dart everywhere. This is one mother of a walk-in-robe. Carter already has some of his clothes hanging. "This is absolutely breathtaking." I open my arms wide and twirl around in a circle. "I could seriously live in this space." He laughs at my craziness.

"As long as you're in bed with me every night, I don't care how long you spend in here." When I finish my little twirl I saunter over to him, reaching for the button of his jeans. "What are you doing?" he asks, raising his eyebrows.

"Kissing your dick better. You said when we were downstairs it was hurting." He growls when I say that.

"It only hurts because it's been missing you."

"Well maybe we need to get reacquainted," I say, falling to my knees.

"Fuck, yes," he hisses out through a clenched jaw as soon as I set his dick free. "First you need to reacquaint me with your mouth, then your pussy. I've missed your fucking pussy, babe."

He groans when I slide his shaft between my lips. His fingers thread through my hair as he tilts his head back making a feral sound. I only get to work on him for a minute or so before he puts his hands under my arms and lifts me to my feet. "I need to be inside you now." We don't even make it back into the room. He has me stripped of my clothes in seconds before pinning me up against the wall. "Wrap your legs around me," he commands, lifting me. In one swift move he impales me.

"Yes," I moan when he pushes all the way in. I love the way he makes me feel when we're connected like this. It's like we become one. "I've missed you so much."

"I've missed you too, baby," he says before his mouth covers mine.

THIRTY

CARTER

three months later ...

OUR FIRST CHRISTMAS IS ALMOST UPON US. I'VE NEVER CARED about celebrating that day, but this year is going to be different. This year I have Indiana. She's my new beginning. Having her living here has been incredible. I never knew life could be this good. The person I was before meeting her has gone. I actually love waking up every day now. I look forward to it because I get to be with her.

Last week we even went shopping and bought a Christmas tree for the apartment. We decorated it together. It was nice. Yesterday I put the first present underneath it. I busted her shaking it this morning, trying to guess what's inside. She'll never guess. I knew she'd snoop, so I put the smaller box inside a larger one.

It's something special. Something I've wanted to give her since she moved in with me. I actually bought it a few months ago, but I've been waiting for the right time. Christmas is the perfect opportunity.

I love having her working next door to me. Her clinic is going great guns. She's even hired another veterinarian because she was run off her feet. Her name is Sarah-Jane. Indi's really happy with her.

Megan is working for her as well. She's Indi's receptionist. Drew ended up getting a new IT job up this way, so they bought a house not far from us. Indiana was so excited when she found out Megan was going to be living in Newcastle. Drew and I have become good friends. He's a nice guy. The four of us do a lot together.

Indiana had her three-month check-up two weeks ago. We drove down to Sydney Friday morning for her appointment and spent the weekend with our parents. The oncologist called her later that day to say her test results came back negative. She's still cancer free. It was a huge relief. Even though she seems fine, it's still lingering in the back of my mind. I still worry that it may come back. He wants to see her again in three months' time. If all goes well then her appointments will change to six monthly.

••••

A week before Christmas, we're both flat out. We're going to close for a week over the holidays, so we can spend some quality time together. Indi hasn't been getting much sleep the last few nights. She has a sick dog staying at the clinic. He was brought in with paralysis, caused by a tick. She medicated him and has him on a drip, but it's still touch and go. She's been getting up during the night to go check on him. She's going to be devastated if he doesn't make it, I know it.

I love how much she cares, but in her line of business she has to have a certain amount of detachment or she'll never survive it. She's even gotten involved with a local animal shelter. She does all the immunisations and procedures on the strays, for free. She has a board set up in the waiting room of her clinic, with pictures and stories of all the animals on death row. She has helped find the majority of them new homes. She amazes me. I'm sure if our yard wasn't so small, she'd adopt the ones she can't help place. It's sad, but a part of life I'm afraid.

Last night I offered to go and check on the dog, but she wouldn't hear of it. I'd noticed the dark circles under her eyes during the day, and it worried me. I knew it was from lack of sleep. Well, that's what I thought until I found her with her head in the toilet bowl, vomiting, this morning. It brought all my worries to the forefront, so even though she protested, I hauled her arse straight to the doctors.

He took some blood and a urine sample, and we sat there waiting for two hours for the results to come back. I wasn't leaving until we had answers. She kept telling me she was fine, but until I knew for sure, we weren't going anywhere.

"Stubborn arse," she sneers after I refuse her demands to go home. It brings a smile to my face. I'll never get sick of her sass. I fucking love it too much.

"Takes one to know one," I retort like a child. She folds her arms over her chest and narrow's her eyes at me. Our little standoff is interrupted when the nurse calls out her name.

"The doctor will see you now, Ms. Montgomery." I stand and reach for her hand. She gives me a brief smile when I lace our fingers together. She can't stay mad at me for long. I'm too damn irresistible.

"Take a seat," the doctor says when we enter his room. Fuck I hate that we're here. It brings back too many bad memories. I hope he has good news for us. "So, I have your results back Indiana. I'm not sure if this is planned, but congratulations. You're pregnant." *What the fuck!* I feel all the air leave my body. Did I just hear him right? She can't be pregnant. We're not married. I refuse to put my child through what I went through. There must be some mistake.

"Are you sure?" I ask. I can hear the shock and disbelief in my voice when I speak.

"Yes. Both the blood and urine tests confirm it." His words are like a sucker punch to my gut.

INDIANA

THE DEVASTATION I SEE ON CARTER'S FACE HURTS. A LOT. SURE
this wasn't planned. To be honest I'm not sure how I feel about it, but
the look on his face pisses me off. I'm not sure if I want to cry or punch
him. He hasn't said a word to me all the way home.

"Carter. I'm sorry," is all I say reaching for his hand. This wasn't
planned he's got to know that.

"We have to get married," he replies, taking his eyes off the road to
glance at me. Umm, no.

"I'm not marrying you just because I'm pregnant, Carter," I snap.
That's ridiculous. He pulls the car immediately over to the curb,
screeching to a stop.

"You don't want to marry me?" he asks in a whisper as the colour
drains from his face.

"Eventually maybe, but not now."

"What? Why?" I can see the hurt etched into his features and it
makes me feel bad. Of course I'd hoped one day we would get married,

but I'm not going to force him into marrying me just because we're going to have a baby.

"Because it's ludicrous to get married just because of this," I state.

"Bullshit," he snaps. I take a deep breath and try to calm myself. Turning my body in my seat, I face him and reach for his hand again.

"Look, Carter. I'm not going to force you into marrying me just because I'm pregnant. That's wrong. I want you to marry me because you want to, not because you feel you have to."

"For fuck sake, Indiana. I want to marry you," he says raising his voice.

"Eventually maybe, but not now. You only said it because I'm pregnant."

"We're getting married, Indiana, and that's final." He lets go of my hand and starts the car again before pulling into the traffic. God he's infuriating sometimes.

"Like hell we are," I spit. I turn my face to look out the passenger side window when I see his head snap in my direction. This conversation is over.

When we pull up outside the tattoo parlour, I immediately get out of the car and start walking towards the clinic. "Where are you going?" he calls out.

"To work," I reply without turning around. He made me sit at that damn doctor's surgery for over two hours. I'm behind now.

••••

My head is all over the place as I try and concentrate on the job. I feel awful about what happened with Carter. I've been tempted to go next door for the past few hours, but it's probably best we both calm down first. We can hash it out tonight. One thing is for sure; he will not be forcing me into marrying him.

When Mrs. Kennedy and her cat, Felix, leave, Meg knocks on my door. "Are you gonna tell me what's going on?" she asks placing her hands on her hips. She's been trying to get it out of me since I came back from the doctors.

"I'm pregnant," I blurt out. She's going to find out soon enough anyway.

"What? Oh. My. God," she squeals throwing her arms around me. "Why are you in such a mood then? Aren't you happy?"

"I'm happy, but shocked. It wasn't planned."

"So, who cares? You and Carter love each other. You'll make great parents. You've only gotta look at the way you guys treat LJ to know that."

"He wants to get married now," I say sighing.

"No fucking way. He proposed?"

"More like demanded. I'm not marrying him just because I'm pregnant," I snap.

"Why?" she asks, giving me a strange look.

"Because it's preposterous."

"It is not. It makes perfect sense," she says, rolling her eyes like I'm being ridiculous. "You know why he's doing this right? The bastard thing."

"I know," I reply. "People have children out of wedlock all the time these days. It's no big deal."

"It's a big deal to him. You know how he is, Indi. He's not going to let you win this." That's what I'm afraid of. I don't want him to feel like he has to marry me.

When Meg leaves, her words play on my mind. The thought of being married to Carter excites me, but I don't want to rush into things. I don't want to get married for all the wrong reasons.

Not even ten minutes pass before she's knocking on my door again. "A delivery just arrived for you," she says smirking. I roll my eyes because I can tell by the look on her face it has something to do with Carter.

I follow her out to the reception area where I find an older man holding a huge bouquet of white roses. "Sign here," he says before passing them to me.

When he leaves, I place them on the counter and remove the card.

To my fiancée, Indiana,

I love you.

I love our baby.

I can't wait to marry you.

Love your fiancé, Carter.

As sweet as that card is, it pisses me off to no end. I can't help but laugh at his brazenness. Meg was right; he's not going to give up without a fight. I pull my phone out of my coat pocket, and send him a text.

> Thank you for the flowers. They're beautiful. I'm sorry about before. I hate fighting with you. I love you, but I haven't agreed to marry you, so technically I'm not your fiancée!

A few seconds later he replies.

> I love you too, babe. But you're wrong. You ARE my fiancée, Indiana, and we ARE getting married!!!

I message him straight back.

> No we're not!!!

I stand there waiting for his reply, but it doesn't come. Just as I turn to head back down the corridor, the front door flies open. It's him. He grabs hold of my elbow, dragging me towards my room before closing the door and locking us in.

"We are getting married, Indiana," he snaps. "Look." He holds up his wedding finger. "This just proves it. You're mine and you *will* be my wife as soon as I can organise it." I grab hold of his hand, bringing it towards my face. Ugh! He's gone and tattooed Indiana on his wedding finger where the band sits.

"That proves nothing," I reply dropping his hand. Doesn't he get it? If he'd proposed to me before I found out I was pregnant, I would've said yes. I would've been over the moon. But now he's being forced to do it, it doesn't sit well with me.

"It proves everything," he says, pulling me into his arms and covering his mouth with mine before I have a chance to respond. I try to push him away for all of a second, but my body melts into him and I deepen the kiss. I hate fighting with him. Eventually pulling back, he cups my face in his hands. "I love you, babe, and you love me. Why shouldn't we get married? It makes perfect sense." When I try to respond, he places his finger on my lips. "Just think about it."

That's exactly what I do for the next hour before I finally relent and call Justine. She manages to shuffle Carter's appointments around for me, so when it's time, I head over to see him. "Come in," he says when I knock on his door. His face lights up when he sees it's me. It instantly brings a smile to my face. I love how he always does that. "Indi." He stands and makes his way towards me. "Is everything okay?"

"I'm your next appointment," I tell him and he wraps me in his arms.

"You are?" he asks pulling back to look at me, surprised.

"Yes. I want to get my fiancé's name tattooed on my wedding finger."

"Then you're going to marry me?" he asks beaming.

"Yes, I'm going to marry you." He exhales before pulling me into a crushing hug.

"Thank fuck," he breathes.

After he seats me in the chair, he prepares my finger, wiping it over with an alcohol strip. "Is it safe to get a tattoo while you're pregnant?" I ask suddenly.

"It is if you use sterilised equipment and a new needle. I researched it a few years ago when a heavily pregnant lady asked me for a tattoo. You know I'd never do anything that would jeopardise you or our child." He leans forward, brushing his lips against mine. "I love you both too much." His words not only make me smile, they melt my heart. He's going to make a wonderful husband, and father.

•••

Christmas morning comes around fast. We sit in the lounge room and exchange gifts. There's been no more talk of weddings, but we have agreed to get married before the baby comes along. I hate that he feels our child would be tainted if it was born out of wedlock, but if this is all I need to do to make him not feel that way, then I'd be selfish not to marry him.

Smiling over at my sexy-as-hell fiancé, I pass him his present. I had a diecast replica car made for him. It's identical to his Monaro. I sent the guy who made it, photos of the exterior and interior of his car, and he copied it from that. It turned out great. It wasn't cheap to have it custom-made, but I knew Carter would love it. He loves that car just as much, if not more than he loves me. Okay, not as much as me, but a lot.

Boys and their toys.

"Fuck me," he says beaming when he opens it. "How?"

"I found a guy online. I sent him photos and he made it from them."

"I love it, babe." I smile as I watch him look over it. The doors, hood and trunk all open. He's even matched the motor and interior of the car identical to Carter's. It took months for him to order all the parts and put it together, but thankfully it was ready in time.

Ten minutes later he's still holding it in his hand, opening and closing the doors whilst smiling like a little boy. It's very amusing to watch. I'm glad he loves it as much as I thought he would.

"Umm ... can I get my present now?" I ask, raising an eyebrow at him. He chuckles before finally putting the car down and grabbing the box I've been dying to open from under the tree. I'm all smiles when he passes it to me. I've been shaking it when he's not around, trying to figure out what it is, but I have no clue. All I know is it rattles and it's light.

Undoing the bow, I peel off the card that's taped to the box. I know I should really open the card first, but I'm dying to see what's inside.

Opening the lid, I find a smaller box inside. That explains the rattling. He played me. My eyes move up to him. He's smiling as he watches me.

Pulling the smaller box out, I unwrap it to find a black velvet jewellery box inside. I gasp when I open the lid. Inside sits a ring. An exquisite, large, princess cut diamond engagement ring. My eyes move back to his again. I'm pretty sure my mouth is hanging open. "Open the card," is all he says. So I do just that.

To my dearest Indiana,

Once upon a time, right in the middle of my fucked up life, love gave me a fairy-tale. You. A second chance. You're my fairy-tale, Indi. My sunshine. My air. The reason I look forward to waking up every morning. My life, without you in it, would be meaningless. I don't want what we have to ever end. This is our first Christmas together, and I wanted to make it a memorable one that neither of us will ever forget. I love you completely, babe. With every fibre of my being. I want to spend the rest of my life with you by my side. Please say you'll marry me!

Merry first Christmas.
Love Carter.
P.S. Please say yes!!!

Tears cloud my eyes when I close the card and make eye contact with him. He was right. He did want to marry me before we found out about the baby. This present has been sitting under the tree for weeks. I clutch the card to my chest as he crawls across the floor towards me.

"Well, I'm waiting," he says smirking. Saying yes is kind of mute now since I've already agreed to marry him. Nevertheless, I throw my arms around his neck.

"Of course I'll marry you. Nothing would make me happier." I cry into his chest when he wraps his arms around my waist and pulls me into him. These damn baby hormones are making me so emotional.

He pulls back, cupping my face in his hands and wiping my tears away with the pads of his thumbs. "I love you so much, Indiana," he says exhaling a large breath. "So fucking much."

"I love you too, Carter." Letting go of my face, he picks up the jewellery box off my lap and pulls out the ring, slipping it onto my finger. It covers my Carter tattoo, but I don't care. I'm inked for life. Looking down at the ring on my finger, I smile.

I love it. I love him.

"You have one more present to open," he says, crawling back over to the tree and picking up a long white box wrapped in a red ribbon. I didn't see that present there before. He must've put it under the tree last night. He smiles when he hands it to me. Untying the ribbon, I remove the lid. When I lift the tissue paper I find a white silk dress inside. It's simple, but very elegant. "I want you to wear this today when we go out for lunch with our parents."

"Okay. It's beautiful. Thank you," I reply, smiling as I hold the dress up in front of me. Our parents and Carter's grandmother are coming up to have Christmas lunch with us today. Carter has booked the restaurant on Merewether Beach. The one we took Meg to after our day of pampering. Carter and I have been back a few times since that day. It's kind of become our place.

"Oh, I almost forgot. There's one more present." Once he retrieves it he passes it to me. The package is tiny. I squeeze it between my fingers. Whatever is inside is soft. I tear open the wrapping. Inside I find a tiny white baby jumpsuit. Tears rise to my eyes. "Hold it up," he says. When I do, I start laughing. It has *'My daddy is seriously hot'* embroidered on it.

"Yes he is hot," I say in agreement. Fisting my hand in the front of his T-shirt, I pull him into me so I can kiss his lips. His hand moves behind my knees as he scoops me into his arms before standing.

"We have a few hours until our parents arrive, so if you don't mind, I'm going to take my fiancée back to bed so I can show her how much I love her."

"I don't mind at all," I reply.

"Merry Christmas, Indiana."

"Merry Christmas, Carter."

••••

Turning the blow dryer off, I run the brush through my hair. When I look up I find Carter standing in the doorway of the bathroom, watching me. He smiles at me through the mirror. He's already dressed in a white button up shirt and a pair of grey slacks. He looks delicious.

"You look nice," I say turning and walking towards him.

"So do you." His comment makes me laugh.

"I'm wrapped in a towel," I reply dryly.

"You're still beautiful," he says, pulling me into his arms and brushing his lips against mine. "Even more so without the towel." I roll my eyes. Of course he'd say that.

"I just got a call from the Surfhouse. There's a problem with our reservation. I'm gonna head over there now, but our parents are going to swing past here and pick you up on the way. I'll meet you guys there."

"Oh really?" I ask in a disappointed tone.

"It's nothing I can't fix. I'll call you if there's a problem," he says reassuring me as he kisses my forehead. I hope so. I love that place.

After he leaves I slip into the dress he bought me. It fits like a glove. He has wonderful taste. I had my first ultrasound last week. I'm only seven weeks pregnant, so I'm not showing yet. I've had a few off mornings, but basically I've been pretty lucky with the morning sickness.

Half an hour later my dad arrives. He's on his own. "Where's Elizabeth and Evelyn?" I ask.

"I've already dropped them off at the restaurant. Carter called and said he was already there, so it made sense. Plus it gives me the chance to have some alone time with my little girl." He leans forward and kisses my forehead. "I have a special gift for you. I wanted to give it to you when we were alone."

"Thanks, Dad," I reply, kissing his cheek when he passes it to me. "Merry Christmas."

"Merry Christmas, Pumpkin."

"I have your gift under the tree, but I'll give it to you when Carter's here."

"Okay. Open it," he says looking down at the small parcel in my hand. Ripping open the wrapper, I do as he asks.

"Oh, Daddy. It's beautiful," I tell him when I open the pouch. It's a necklace with a heart shaped locket on it. There's a diamond set into the heart."

"That diamond is from your mother's engagement ring. I wanted to make it into something special for you." Tears rise to my eyes when he says that.

"I love it," I breathe, wrapping my arms around him.

"Open the locket." When I do, I find a picture of my mother inside. It was from their wedding day. I clutch it to my chest.

"Thank you. I'll treasure it forever."

"She'll always be in your heart, Pumpkin, but this way you can wear a piece of her every day as well." When I make eye contact with him I see tears glistening his eyes, so I wrap him in my arms and hold him tight. It's special times like Christmas, Mother's Day and my birthday, that I miss her most. I wish she were alive to meet Carter and her grandchild when it comes along.

We haven't told our parents about the baby yet. Carter and I had copies of the ultrasound images framed. We've wrapped them up with their Christmas presents.

"I love you," I whisper as he fastens the necklace around my neck.

"I love you too, baby girl."

••••

When we pull up outside the restaurant I'm surprised to see Meg standing there. "What are you doing here?" I ask getting out of the car. "I thought you and Drew were heading back to Sydney for Christmas with your parents."

"I lied," she replies giving me a sheepish smile. What's she up to? "I am spending Christmas with them, but up here."

"Why?"

"Because if you think I'm going to miss your wedding day, you've got rocks in your head. Besides I'm the maid of honour, I have to be here. My mum didn't want to miss your wedding either. You're her adopted daughter after all."

"What? My wedding day?" I ask dumbfounded.

"Yes. You, my friend, are getting married today." That's news to me. My eyes move to my dad searching for confirmation.

"She's right," is all he says.

"Come," Meg says, linking arms with me and dragging me around the side of the building. "See." When I follow the line of her finger, I see Carter and Jax standing side by side down near the shore. Some old dude in a suit is standing in front of them. Then I notice LJ sitting by Carter's feet. I feel my lips curve up. My eyes then move to his mother, grandmother, Meg's parents and Drew sitting on five of the six chairs that are positioned behind them. Excitement broils inside me.

My dad slinks his arm around my shoulder. "Congratulations, Pumpkin," he says, kissing the top of my head. "That's why I wanted to give you the necklace now. I wanted your mother to be part of your special day. I know if she was still alive, she would've been just as proud of you as I am."

"Oh, Daddy." I'm struggling to hold in the tears as I wrap my arms around his waist.

"We need to get you ready," Meg chimes in breaking our moment.

She walks over towards Drew's car and retrieves a box off the back seat. Making her way back towards us, she pulls out a large white silk rose that's attached to a clip. She pins it in my hair just above my ear. "Beautiful," she whispers.

Next she pulls out a small leather pouch. When she tips it upside down, shaking the blue Sapphire bracelet into her palm, I smile. I recognise it straight away. It belonged to her grandmother. Meg wore it on her wedding day. My something borrowed, something blue.

"Thanks, Meg," I say hugging her.

"I'm your maid of honour, it's my job." I smile. Even though I definitely would've had her as my maid of honour, I find it amusing that she's given herself that title. "Here's your bouquet." It's a beautiful arrangement of white rosebuds. She pulls out a matching pink arrangement for herself. It matches her pink dress.

"You hate pink," I say.

"I know, but it's your favourite colour. I knew if you had a choice it's what you would've wanted." I love her so much. I couldn't ask for a better best friend.

My dad links his arm through mine. "You look beautiful. Are you ready to marry the man of your dreams?"

"I am."

Far out. I'm getting married today.

••••

The ceremony was perfect. Carter and I both got a little teary eyed when we exchanged our vows. The whole day was a little overwhelming to be honest. In a good way though. The highlight for me was seeing Carter so happy. The smile didn't leave his face once.

When the celebrant pronounced us husband and wife, Carter didn't even wait for him to say, 'You may now kiss the bride'. He took matters into his own hands, pulling me into his arms and locking his lips with mine. It was a scorching hot kiss too. Not the kind of kiss to give me in front of my dad, that's for sure. When he eventually came up for air, he tenderly brushed the back of his hand down the side of my face.

"I love you so much, Mrs. Reynolds," he whispered, sending my heart into a flutter. I'll admit Mrs. Reynolds has a nice ring to it.

Our reception was held in the Surfhouse. Well, it was more like an extended three course luncheon with our loved ones, but it was perfect. I couldn't have planned it better myself. Carter had even organised a wedding cake. I had to laugh when I saw it.

It was only a one-layered cake, since there were only ten of us in attendance. It had been baked into a large heart shape, covered in white icing. The base was wrapped in a thick red ribbon, but the sweetest part was the icing decorations sitting on top. A miniature replica of Carter's red Monaro was sitting towards the back of the cake. In front of it stood small figurines; Carter with his arm draped around my shoulder, and LJ laying at our feet. Not your traditional wedding cake, but perfect for us. It's hard to believe we are now a real family, and in just over seven months we'll be parents.

Later that night back at the apartment, we exchanged Christmas gifts with our parents. Elizabeth burst into tears when she saw the ultrasound picture. My dad was over the moon as well. It was the perfect end to a perfect day.

The next morning, Carter and I flew to the Gold Coast in Queensland for our honeymoon. He had booked us into the Sheraton Mirage Resort and Spa. It was a magical five days. We even had a relaxing one-hour hot stone massage at the Day Spa the day before we left to fly home. After the crazy few months we'd had prior to the wedding, it was just what we both needed to unwind. The only downfall was it had to end. I know we have our whole lives ahead of us though, and I look forward to spending the rest of my life with Carter.

I have the most amazing husband ever!

THIRTY-TWO

CARTER

seven months later ...

"CARTER," I HEAR INDIANA SCREECH FROM BESIDE ME, SHAKING me out of my sleep.

"What?" I whine, opening one eye. I'm fucking tired. She better not want sex again, she's worn me the hell out. Normal Indiana was insatiable, but pregnant Indiana, fuck me. As much as I love having sex with my beautiful wife, my dick's exhausted. It needs a few hours break at least.

The last few months she's even been sneaking into my work for a quickie between clients. Even our lunch breaks are spent in bed fucking each other's brains out, and then we have to scoff down our food before going back to work. Honestly, I fucking love it, but if I'm gonna keep this up, I need rest. Time to replenish my stamina.

"My water just broke," she says as cool as a fucking cucumber.

"What?" I practically yell in a panic as I bolt upright.

"My water just broke," she repeats, like I didn't hear her the first time. *I fucking heard her.* My gut starts to churn. I thought I'd prepared myself for this moment. Wrong. I'm not even out of bed yet and I'm already a bundle of nerves.

"I can do this," I mumble to myself as I try to calm the fuck down. Jumping out of bed I make my way around to her side, extending my hand.

"Stop panicking, Carter," she says.

"I'm not panicking," I lie. *I'm fucking panicking.*

"It's okay," she says in a calm voice. How can she remain so composed? Helping her up, she wraps me in her arms. "It's going to be okay. Take a deep breath," she says trying to reassure me. It's not working. I'm a fucking mess. Shit. We've practised this a hundred times. Why was I so cool and calm then? *Get your shit together Reynolds.* Your wife needs you. I should be supporting her, not the other way around. When she lets go of me and doubles over in pain, I almost lose it.

"Let's go," I say leading her towards the door.

"We need to get changed first. We can't go in our pyjamas." Shit. She's right. Okay. I can do this. Who am I kidding? I fist my hair in my hands. "Clothes."

"Look. Get yourself dressed. I can dress myself," she says heading towards her drawers and rifling through them. I do the same. I throw a T-shirt over my head and strip out of my pyjama bottoms and slip into a pair of sweats. See, I can do this. I look over at Indiana as she struggles to slide on her pants. Who am I kidding? I can't do this.

Moving towards her, I help her get dressed. When she doubles over again, I clutch my head in my hands. Running over towards the bedside table, I retrieve my phone. I search Ross' number. He picks up almost immediately. It's 4:00am. I guess he knows it's important. We've all been waiting for this day to come.

"It's time," is all I say. I don't even give him a chance to talk. "We need you to come. We're leaving for the hospital now."

"I'm on my way," he replies. Thank fuck for that. I don't even take into consideration he's a two-hour drive away. I'm on my own. It's up to me to get her to the hospital safely. *Shit.*

Finally we make it down to the car. "My hospital bag," Indiana says once I have her seated in the passenger side. Fuck me. I had the routine down pat. What the hell is wrong with me? This is the real deal, I guess. I need to pull myself together if I'm going to get either of them to the hospital in one piece.

I run back upstairs and grab it. Throwing it in the back of the car, I get seated. "How are you feeling, babe?" I ask as I turn the keys in the ignition.

"Apart from the contractions, surprisingly okay." Of course she is. I reach the end of the street and put my left indicator on. "The hospital's that way," she says laughing, pointing to the right. I've driven this route twenty times in the past few weeks, doing my practice runs and now I can't even remember which way to go.

Following Indi's instructions, I turn right. "Are you still alright?" I ask, briefly turning my head in her direction. She has a huge smile on her face.

"I'm faring a lot better than you by the looks of it." I'm glad she finds this amusing. "Take some deep breaths. Like they taught us in the birthing classes." I look at her like she's lost her mind. I remember thinking when we went over the breathing techniques in class, how ridiculous it was. "Just do it," she says rolling her eyes. "It will help."

I follow her lead as she starts panting and doing those stupid-arse breaths. I feel like a dick, but I copy her. Within minutes I start feeling myself relax. Surprisingly it does help. Who knew?

••••

Three hours have passed and still no baby. Poor Indi is in so much pain. I've been rubbing her back for the past half hour. I wish I could trade places with her. I hate that she has to go through this. Our parents and my grandmother arrived ten minutes ago. They've been in to see her, but are now outside in the waiting room with Meg and Jax. I called them to let them know Indi was in labour, and they both came straight here.

We're waiting for the doctor to come back in to check on her. She wasn't fully dilated earlier, but I'm hoping by now she is. I want this to be over for her as soon as possible. I want to meet my child. We've been waiting a long time for this day to arrive.

I stand when the doctor enters the room. I help Indi roll over onto her back. She's been crouched on all fours while I've been trying my best to relieve her back pain. She clutches her hand in mine while the doctor checks her over.

"It's time," he says making eye contact with her. "As soon as your next contraction hits, I'm going to ask you to start pushing." She nods her head at him before making eye contact with me. She looks exhausted the poor thing, but manages to give me a brief smile.

A few seconds later I see her face screw up in pain. This contraction hits hard as she moans loudly. Up until now she's been pretty quiet. She's so fucking amazing. So brave. I've heard the lady in the delivery suite next door practically screaming the damn hospital down for the past hour, so I know Indiana is playing this down.

Her grip on my hand tightens as the midwife moves into place next to the doctor. "Push," he says. My girl does exactly as he asks. Another loud moan escapes her and a lump rises to my throat.

"You're doing great, babe," I encourage, wiping the sweat off her brow with the cool cloth the nurse gave me earlier. She's had no drugs whatsoever. She refused them. I'll admit I've taken a few pulls of the happy gas when she hasn't been looking. That's some good shit, that is.

When her next contraction hits, the doctor tells her to push again. This time she screams, and fuck me I almost lose it. "You're doing great, Indiana," he says. "I can see the head." His gaze moves up to me. "Come take a look." I don't want to leave Indi's side, so without letting go of her hand I lean forward and look between her legs.

The baby's tiny head is turned to the side, giving me a glimpse of the most angelic profile I've ever seen. A magical feeling hits me right in the chest. Tears brim my eyes. That's my child.

"You're almost there, babe," I say, moving back beside her and leaning down to kiss her forehead. "I'm so proud of you," I whisper. She starts to do her breathing exercises when the next contraction comes. When she bears down again, she lets out a loud moaning sound. She's in fucking agony. It's so hard to watch her go through this. It tugs at my heart. I wasn't prepared for this shit. I knew it wasn't going to be a walk in the park, I'm not that naive, but to see the woman you love with all your heart in so much pain, it's fucking heartbreaking.

"One more push," the doctor says. It's her last one. The baby slips out and into the doctor's hands. Relief floods through me. *It's finally over.* We decided not to find out the sex of the baby. Although every time we went in for an ultrasound, I think we were both tempted, but we held strong. "It's a boy," the doctor announces. Leaning down, I press my lips to Indiana's mouth.

"Thank you," I whisper against her lips. I have so much to thank her for. She saved me. Saved me from myself. She gave my life meaning. She gave me her, and now a son. A chance to right all the wrongs that were committed against me all those years ago.

Fuck me, I have a son. I'm a dad.

Words cannot describe how incredible I feel right now. After I cut the cord, the doctor places our boy on Indi's chest. Tears fill my eyes as I look at the perfect picture in front of me. My wife. My son. *My whole life.* Indiana has tears streaming down her face as she lifts her head slightly and places a kiss on his forehead.

"Hello little man," she whispers. "I've been waiting a long time to meet you." Raising my hand towards my face, I wipe away my own tears. I thought the day Indi became my wife was the best day of my life, but this moment definitely tops it. I have a family. My son has a father who's going to love him and be there for him every second of every fucking day. He'll never experience what I had to as a child. He'll never know what it feels like not to be wanted.

Indi is going to be a fantastic mother. I only have to look at the love and affection she showers on me to know that. Her tearful eyes meet mine as her hand extends out to me. I lace our fingers together as she pulls me closer to the bed. "I love you," she says as I lean down and place my lips on hers.

"I love you too," I say against her mouth. Pulling back, I brush her hair back off her face before cupping her cheek in one of my hands. "I'm so proud of you. Thank you for giving me a son. For giving me a family. For loving me unconditionally."

Because she always has.

Once Indi is cleaned up and we have a little time alone with our boy, I head out to the waiting room to tell the others. My mum and Meg both cry. Even Ross gets a little teary eyed when he shakes my hand and pulls me into a hug. "Congratulations, son," he whispers.

They follow me back into the room. After our parents have a hold of their grandson, my mum sits my grandmother on a chair and passes the baby to her. I watch on from the other side of the bed. It's such a bittersweet moment. It reminds me of everything I missed out on when I was a kid. When I see a tear fall down her cheek as she looks down at my son, a lump rises to my throat.

It makes me wonder if that was the same reaction my grandmother would've had if she wasn't denied from seeing me when I was born. Her head suddenly lifts as her eyes seek out mine. She gives me the most amazing smile as another few tears leak from her eyes. I get the feeling she was thinking the same thing I was.

My little guy's future already looks promising. He has so much more than I did the day I was born; two parents, grandparents, and a great grandmother that not only love him, but I know are going to make him the centre of their world. I want that for my children, because that's all I ever wanted for myself when I was a child.

EPILOGUE

INDIANA

eight weeks later ...

I CAN'T BELIEVE HOW EXCITED I FEEL ON THE DRIVE BACK home to see our parents. Well, technically it's no longer my home, but my dad and Carter's mum are still living in Sydney, so it will always hold a special place in my heart. My home now, is wherever my husband and son, Jaxson, reside. We named our son Jaxson after his Uncle Jax.

Sydney was where I was born, where my mum took her last breath, where Lassie lived, played and unfortunately died, where I met Meg, and then Carter. Although growing up in my hometown came with incredible highs, and lows, I can't regret any of it. Ultimately, it led me to where I am today. It has shaped me into the person I've become. It's given me the incredible fulfilling life I lead. My boys are my world.

My six monthly check-ups have now turned into yearly ones. The doctor is pretty confident that the cancer won't come back. Nobody knows for sure I guess, but it looks promising. All I can do is keep going to each examination, and pray that I keep getting good results. I do experience the occasional headaches, just like everyone does I suppose. I will admit when they first come, it worries me. I don't think that feeling will ever go away. The cancer is always going to be in the back of my mind. As soon as the headache is gone though, I know that's all it was. *A headache.*

When we pull into the driveway of my dad's place, excitement broils in the pit of my stomach. It's only been three weeks since we've seen each other, but I miss him. He and Elizabeth have been coming up to Newcastle every few weeks since the birth of their grandson. Every visit is special. This is our first big trip away from Newcastle as a family.

Although my dad worked such long hours whilst I lived here, meaning we didn't get to see each other as much as we would've liked, he was still close by if I needed him. Now that he lives hours away, I struggle sometimes. I hate that he's all alone. Before I moved away with Carter, it was just the two of us.

Well, he has Elizabeth next door, I suppose, which gives me some comfort. They've bonded since her husband's death. They've become great friends. Nothing romantic, just companions you could say. They occasionally have dinner together or go to the movies. When they come down to visit, they usually travel together. *That kind of thing.* It makes being so far away a little easier for me.

"You excited?" Carter asks as he brings my hand to his lips, planting a soft kiss on my knuckles.

"I am. Our parents are going to be so happy to see Jaxson, and surprised to see how much he's grown in the last three weeks."

"They will," he says smiling before turning his head to look at our son in the back seat. I love the look Carter gets when he looks at Jaxson. He rarely frowns nowadays. He's come so far. He's an amazing father.

"Can we quickly go and see if dad's awake before we go over to your mum's house?" Our parents weren't expecting us until next week, but we thought we'd surprise them.

"Of course," he replies, giving my hand a light squeeze before getting out of the car. I watch my gorgeous husband as he walks around the front of the vehicle towards my door. I traded my car in for an SUV. We needed something bigger now we're a growing family. Carter still has his Monaro. He'll never get rid of that, but when we go out as a family, this is the car we use.

I smile at my handsome husband when he extends his hand to me, helping me out of the car. He's such a gentleman and treats me the way any girl would dream of being treated; like a princess, like I'm the centre of his universe, his existence. That's exactly how I feel towards him as well. I can't put into words just how happy we both are. We're perfect for each other. A marriage made in heaven.

There's no doubt about that.

Sure, growing up he did some pretty horrible things to me, but I'm grateful I had the sense to see straight through him, grateful that I was given the opportunity to see the real Carter Reynolds. The one he did a good job of hiding from the rest of the world. From the second I met him, I suspected deep down it was all a facade. Like a protective armour to save himself from getting hurt. I was right.

I still occasionally see his insecure side, but it no longer upsets me like it used to. Thankfully, with some help from me, he's embraced who he is. He now sees in the grand scheme of things, it's just a silly, meaningless word. A word that only has the power to define you if you let it. Technically he may be a bastard, but to me he's a *beautiful, kind, sweet, caring, incredibly loyal, and loveable bastard*. His list of qualities are endless. Despite the life he's led, I'm proud of the man he has become. I wouldn't have him any other way. I know I make him happy, just like he makes me.

After Carter lets LJ out of the car, he leads him down the side of the house, letting him loose in the back yard. He's such a great dog, and so protective of the baby. When Carter makes his way back towards me, he slides his arms around my waist. Pulling me against him, he plants a soft kiss on my lips. I don't think I'll ever lose this feeling I get being in his arms. He still has the power to send my heart into a flutter.

"You okay?" he asks smiling down at me.

"Couldn't be better," I reply. Tightening his embrace, he presses his lips to my forehead.

"Yeah, me too, baby." Letting go, he opens the back door and grabs our little man out of the baby capsule. Carter immediately buries his lips into the soft, chubby cheeks of Jaxson's face. It warms my heart watching them together. "Are you ready to see your grandparents again, little champ?" he whispers to our son.

That's what he calls him, 'little champ'. He's amazing. He strives to be everything he dreamt of having when he was a young boy. We're already talking about trying for another one.

Smiling over at my boys, I fish my keys out of my bag as we walk up the front steps. I don't knock just in case my dad's still asleep. The house is very quiet when we walk through the front door. I presume he's still in bed. Walking quietly, I lead Carter towards the kitchen. I can feed Jaxson while we wait for him to wake.

When I round the corner, I'm stopped in my tracks. Carter walks straight into my back, nearly bowling me over. I hear him chuckle from behind me when he sees what I see. I'm sure my chin is now resting on the floor. I softly elbow him in the stomach to quiet him.

I can't believe what I'm seeing.

Right in front of us, is our parents. Let's just say in a very compromising position. My father has Elizabeth sprawled out over the surface of the kitchen table. *Holy fucking crap.* I suddenly feel the need to bleach my eyes. I guess their friendship has grown into something more. *Friends with benefits.* By the way they're gazing into each other's eyes, I'd say it was a little more than that though. They look pretty smitten to me.

Shit, Carter. I'm waiting for him to shove me out of the way and attack my dad for what he's doing to his mum. Hesitantly looking over my shoulder at him, I'm surprised to find him smiling. Not a small one either. He's beaming. I guess he's okay with this.

As horrified as I am at the sight before us, it brings a smile to my face as well. Truthfully, I like the idea of them together. In my heart,

I've secretly wished for this. They're perfect for each other. Reaching up, my hand instinctively covers our son's face. He's just a baby, but I still don't want him to see what his grandparents are up to.

They're so lost in each other that they don't even notice we're standing here. I flick my head at Carter gesturing for us to leave. I don't want to disturb them. Carter being Carter though, has other ideas. He clears his throat loudly. Both our parents swing their heads in our direction in unison. Elizabeth's face turns bright red. My father on the other hand, looks absolutely horrified. It's priceless. "Busted," Carter says, and we both laugh.

Oh. My. God. *Busted is an understatement.*

CARTER
eleven months later ...

Stepping out of the car, I head inside. "You look lovely," I say leaning forward and placing my lips on her cheek when she greets me at the door.

"And you look very handsome," she replies, placing her frail hand on the side of my face. "Doesn't my grandson look handsome," my grandmother says, turning her head towards the cute carer who's making her bed.

"Yes he does," she says smiling at me. She gives me a look that says she'd like to rip this suit off me with her teeth. I give her a look that hopefully says, sorry love, I'm taken. I have the only woman I'll ever need waiting for me at home. My soulmate, my wife, my baby's mumma.

"Ready to go Grandma?" I ask smiling down at her. I can't describe the feeling I get having her in my life. I only wish it had been for my whole life, not just the past few years. She's such an amazing woman. My grandfather robbed us all of so much with his stubborn, pig headed, narrow-mindedness. I hate him for that.

But today is a day for new beginnings, a time for looking forward, not backwards. Today my life takes a turn for the better, because my mum is marrying Ross. In a little over an hour, he'll officially become my dad. The dad I feel like I've waited my whole life for. I couldn't be happier for me, and my mum. She'll finally get the man she deserves, and I'll get the father figure I've always wanted.

They both had huge reservations about getting married. Only because Indi and I were already together, so they thought if they tied the knot it would be taboo. What a crock of shit. Indi and I discussed it for all of a minute. We wanted this for them. They're perfect for each other. I'd grown up my whole life without a father, and Indi only had her mother for a few short years, so this was a win-win for all of us. They get to live out their days happy, in love and together. Indi and I both get to have two parents. How could that be taboo?

"I'll just grab my purse," my grandmother says. When she comes back to me, she links her arm through mine as we walk towards the door. My grandmother now lives in a retirement village. Well actually it's more like a luxury apartment building for people over sixty. She has a two bedroom fully self-contained unit. It has a community dining area and a staff of carers that live on site to look after the residents. She got tired of living in that big-arse house all on her own.

She still has her independence here, but also plenty of company from people her own age. To be honest, I never felt comfortable visiting her in that *other* house. Here, I have no qualms whatsoever.

As we make our way down the corridor, an older man walking towards us smiles widely when his eyes land on my grandma. "Well don't you look lovely, Evelyn," he says stopping in front of us. He reaches for her hand, bringing it to his mouth, and my grandmother giggles like a schoolgirl. Looking down at her I find her blushing. I feel my lips turn up into a smile. This old dude is very suave, a real ladies man, I can tell. My grandmother seems very taken with him.

"Thank you, Arthur," she replies with a flutter of her eyelashes. Fuck me. Do women still do that shit at this age? Standing in awkward silence, I watch on as these two make googly eyes at each other. I hate to break up their moment, but we need to get going.

"We really should get going, Grandma," I interrupt clearing my throat.

"Will you be back in time for dinner?" Arthur asks, his hopeful eyes locked with hers.

"No. I'm afraid not. I'm going to my daughter's wedding. I won't be back until later tonight." I have to hold back my laugh when his face drops. He definitely has a thing for her. I'm not sure how I feel about that. "I'll be here for breakfast in the morning though." Okay, now he's smiling again. It's kind of nice, and kind of creepy. Aren't they too old for this shit?

"I'll save you a seat," he says as I guide her away. I have to refrain from rolling my eyes at them, but it's nice she has company when we aren't around I suppose. She seems to be extremely happy living here. When I look down at her, I find her smiling happily to herself. Seeing her like this makes me so happy. I know firsthand how wonderful it feels to be in love.

"Do I need to bring my shotgun back here, Grandma?" I ask as we head towards the front entrance where the car is waiting. Not that I even have one, but I know she understands the meaning behind my words when she playfully swats my arm and laughs.

"Don't be silly. Arthur is a lovely man. A real gentleman. He's always looking out for me." That may be the case, but I'm still going to be keeping my eye on him from now on. Looking over my shoulder, I see he's whistling as he shuffles away from us. I smile, shaking my head.

Arthur, you're officially on my radar, buddy.

••••

When we arrive back at the house, I help my grandmother out of the car and lead her down towards the back of the property.

Indi is my mum's bridesmaid today, and Ross asked me to be his best man. This morning Ross and I erected a large marquee in the back yard for the reception later on today. They've hired caterers that are already in the house preparing the food for the reception that will follow the ceremony.

We also set up a white gazebo by the lake. That's where they're exchanging their vows. Megan came over while mum and Indiana were at the hairdressers, to help decorate it. She lined the outside edges with white tulle and a long garland of white silk roses to make it look more wedding-ish, I guess.

Every time I'm down by the lake near the dock, it brings back so many memories for me. It was the place that Indiana gave me her greatest gift—her virginity. In return I gave her my heart. It's also the night things changed for me, forever. Thinking back now, me leaving was the best thing that could've happened to us.

If I had stayed, I'm not sure we would've lasted. My head was in a bad place, and I was consumed with anger. Moving away gave me the chance to grow. The chance to see just how much I needed her. By the time I came back, I was ready. I was a better man—more worthy.

My mum sold Fuckwit's house six months ago and moved in with Ross. I wasn't the least bit sad to see that place go. At least when Indi and I come home to stay now, I no longer have to feel uncomfortable. Ross even packed up the room that he used to share with Indiana's mother. It's been converted into a nursery for his grandchildren.

Well it's Jaxson's room for now, but he'll be sharing it with his baby brother, Levi, when he's born.

If I have my way they'll have to extend the house with all the grandchildren I plan on giving them. Jaxson was only a few months old when I knocked Indiana up again. I can't explain the feeling I get seeing her carrying my child, but I fucking love it.

"Dad-da," Jaxson squeals from Ross' arms when he sees me. When Ross places him down, I extend my hands to him as he walks unsteadily towards me. He's still trying to find his feet. He only started walking a few weeks ago.

Ross grabs hold of my grandmother's hand, leading her towards the chairs that are set up near the gazebo. "Thanks, Dad," I say smiling at him. He asked me if I'd call him dad the day Indiana and I got married. I didn't hesitate. It's one of those poignant moments in your life that you never forget; like the day Indiana became my wife, the day my son was born, and the day my grandmother welcomed me with open arms. It's right up there with them.

"Hey, champ," I say as I scoop my little boy into my arms and bury my lips in his soft, chubby cheek. I love this little guy, so hard. My real dad doesn't know what he missed out on when he walked away from my mum when she was pregnant. Nothing beats the feeling of being a parent. *Nothing.*

Jaxson looks so cute in the little suit my mum had made for him today. I'm smiling as I stare down into his big green eyes. They're exactly like Indi's. "No," he squeals, tugging at his tie in frustration. I hear ya buddy. I fucking hate them too.

"You have to leave it on until Nanna and Pa get married," I say calmly, removing his chubby little hand from the death grip he has on it.

"No," he snaps, scrunching up his face and frowning at me. It makes me chuckle. Not only did he inherit his mother's looks, he also inherited her temper and stubbornness. It's close to his nap time, so that doesn't help his mood either. I pull his dummy out of my pocket, remove the cover and stick it in his mouth. I always carry one with me. It's a fucking godsend sometimes. Walking towards the chair, I pick up his teddy bear and hand it to him. He cuddles it into his chest. Hopefully that will distract him until the ceremony is over.

"They're ready," Meg calls out as she walks towards us before taking Jaxson out of my arms. She blows a raspberry on his neck to distract him when he tries to protest. I watch as she walks towards Drew, who's holding their daughter Isabella. She was born four weeks after Jaxson. Indiana cried tears of joy when Megan named their little girl after Indi's mum. It was very touching.

"You ready, Dad?" I ask as I grasp his shoulder.

"Never been readier," he smiles as we both walk over and stand by the marriage celebrant. There's only about thirty guests here today;

mainly the guys from Ross' work and a few neighbours. They wanted to keep it small and intimate.

When the music starts to play, my eyes move to Indiana as she waddles towards us. She still takes my breath away after all this time. Her hair is pulled into an up-do on top of her head, with a few loose curls falling down over her pretty face. She's wearing a soft pink strapless dress, accentuating her spectacular rack. It then falls loosely to her knees accommodating her large stomach. Levi is due to come into this world sometime next week.

We're both looking forward to his birth. Her smile widens when her eyes lock with mine. "I love you," I mouth when she gets closer. It's not until she's standing opposite us that my gaze then moves to my mother. She's wearing an ivory dress that's covered with lace. She looks beautiful, and so happy. It warms my heart to see her like this. I turn to look at Ross, whose teary eyes are glued to my mother as she walks towards him.

The love he has for her is radiating off him. It brings a lump to my throat. I love this man so much. I think I've been looking forward to this wedding just as much as I was my own. Finally, my mum not only got the wedding day she deserved, but the man as well.

••••

Once the vows are exchanged, calmness settles over me. I know I'm right where I should be, where I was destined to be. Everything I've endured over my life was meant to happen. It helped mould me into the man I am today. It makes me appreciate everything I have now, so much more.

For the majority of my life, I only knew the love of one person, my mother. Now I'm surrounded by it. I feel like the richest man in the world. *Finally I'm whole.* It's taken twenty-six years to get here, but I've finally arrived. From this day forward I no longer consider myself a bastard. I have a mother and a father who love me just as much as I love them. I have the woman of my dreams by my side, my son Jaxson whom I adore, and our second child on the way. Life couldn't be sweeter. My heart is so full, there's no longer any room for the darkness that once consumed me. Thanks to my sunshine, Indiana, I'm filled with light ...

Right down to the very depths of my soul.

••••

After we eat, our parents head to the dance floor for the bridal waltz. They're dancing to 'Only you', sung by The Platters. Indi and I stand beside the dance floor and watch them. They look so happy. I snake my arms around my wife's waist from behind, resting my chin on her shoulder as I gently rub her belly.

"Are you happy?" I ask, turning my head slightly to place a soft kiss on her cheek.

"Extremely," she sighs, lacing her fingers over the top of mine.

"Same." My smile grows, because fuck me, I am. Indiana suddenly tilts her body to the right, as her gaze moves down to the floor.

"Shit," I hear her mumble.

"What's wrong, babe?" I ask following her line of sight. She doesn't even need to answer because I can see it for myself. Panic rises within me. *Here we fucking go again.*

"My water just broke."

Oh fuck ...

If you enjoyed *Bastard*, you'll devour

LUCKIEST BASTARD: THE NOVELLA

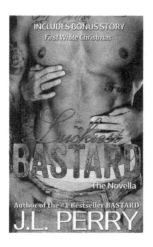

Available now in ebook!

It's been two years since reformed bastard Carter and his treasured wife, Indi, had their happy-ever-after in the #1 bestselling *Bastard* . . .

Contains:
Luckiest Bastard, a novella with a HEA
First White Christmas, a bonus story

Two years and two children after their happy ending in *Bastard*, **Carter** and **Indiana** have settled into married life after their tumultuous pasts. But a shocking event will threaten everything they hold dear.

From the author of the #1 bestseller *Bastard*:

HOOKER

**One night of passion with a sinfully hot stranger will
change everything.**

Jade's young life was tough. She grew up feeling unloved and unwanted as she was passed around from one screwed up foster home to the next. Things began to look up for her when she was adopted by a wealthy socialite at the age of eleven. Jade didn't know it at the time, but her new adoptive mother had big plans for her . . .

Brock grew up with everything going for him. Money, looks and an endless array of beautiful women. He wasn't interested in commitment. Then he met Jade. Their one night together ignited a burning desire to own her, possess her. But Jade had other plans. Nobody says no to Brock Weston, nobody.

When fate brings them together again, will Brock get what he wants? Or will Jade's secrets ruin everything?

ACKNOWLEDGEMENTS

I'm going to start off my acknowledgements by telling you a story. It was a poignant moment in the life of my writing career, and therefore I believe it needs to be acknowledged. Although it was a negative experience, I quickly turned it into a positive. I could've easy let it beat me, but I didn't. I know in my heart that this moment is part of the reason I am where I am today.

A little over two years ago, I sat down to write my debut novel, My Destiny. Writing is something I've always wanted to do, but to be honest, I wasn't sure if it was something I was capable of doing. In saying that though, I'm the type of person that likes to challenge myself. I like to prove to myself that I can do something, even if I doubt that I can. I'm not afraid to give anything a go, even if it falls into the too hard basket.

When I wrote My Destiny, I had no intentions of publishing it. As I said, it was merely something I wanted to do, to prove to myself that I could do it. Only the people close to me knew I was writing. They were all extremely encouraging, except one. This particular person told me, "You're wasting your time. You can't do this. This will never amount to anything." I'm not going to lie, hearing those words from someone I care about stung. It hurt me a lot. But, instead of using them to discourage me, I used them to drive me. If you tell me I can't do something, you can be sure as hell I'm gonna do it, just to prove you wrong. *Or die trying.* LOL.

So that's exactly what I did. Not only did I finish the book, I wrote part 2, My Forever, which was followed by Damaged, and Against All Odds. Bastard is my fifth published work. I'm already working on my sixth.

I'm not a vindictive or revengeful person, but I can tell you I got great pleasure in tactfully serving up this person, who shall forever remain nameless, a huge slice of humble pie, served with a delicious side of fuck you. Their reply, "No one will buy it." Seriously! *Again they were wrong.*

So the moral of this story is, don't be afraid to dream big. Don't let negativity sway you to give up. Like me, use it to inspire you, to spur you on. Even if people don't believe in you, believe in yourself. *I believe in you, you can do this.* My parting words to this person are, "*I* can, *I* will and *I* did." I am living proof that with a bit of hard work and a lot of determination, dreams can come true, because mine did.

••••

To my family and friends: Thank you for always encouraging and believing in me. You have no idea how much the support you give me means to me. I love you guys with all my heart. My life is so much richer because I have you all in it.

To my readers: Thank you for taking a chance on me and for reading my stories. You all inspire me to keep going. To keep doing what I love—that is writing. Writing about real life situations. Things we can all relate to. About people who've had a tough life. I may torture them a little further, but in the end I do turn their lives around to give them the happily ever after they deserve. LOL. As the old saying goes, what doesn't kill us makes us stronger.

To my street team: I love you guys. Thank you for everything you girls do for me. For making me laugh when I'm down, picking me up when I'm deflated and supporting me no matter what. I would be lost without you all.

I'd like to give a special mention to Jacquie, Sophia, Cheryl, Candy, Charmaine, Vicki, Elaine, Justine, Nicola, Rachel, Sarah-Jane, Jeanette, Nadine, Beth, Kristy, Jamie, Sam, Lisa, Sandra, Yulanda, Amanda, Christie, Erika, Jennifer, Jules, Rebecca, Stephanie and Kris. You girls go above and beyond. From the bottom of my heart, thank you for all the time you put into me. I couldn't do this without you.

To Karen Mandeville-Steer: Thank you for filling in all the gaps for me. You have a wonderful talent for seeing the little things I missed. I loved working with you.

To Candy Ross: Thank you for all the time and effort you have put into going over the rough draft of this book, and for helping me make it the best it can be.

To my Editor Nicola: As always, thank you for being so wonderful. I'd be lost without you. You're not only my editor, you're my friend.

To Stephanie Smith and Kristine Barakat: Thank you for taking the time to read the finished draft of this story, and for giving me your insight and honest opinion. I really appreciate that you both did this for me.

To Kylie McDermott from Give Me Books: Thank you for all the time and effort you and your team put into organising my release day blitz. You do a magnificent job. I love working with you.

To the wonderful Bloggers: Thank you for everything you guys so selflessly do for me on a regular basis. I'd be lost without your support. To everyone that signed up for the blitz, thank you for taking the time to read and promote my work. I appreciate it.

To Soxie: Thank you for the wonderful job you did on making the incredibly hot 'Bastard' cover, and for all the other things you do for me on a regular basis. I know we've been through a lot of ups and downs with this cover and I'm so grateful you stuck by me throughout it all. You are an amazing person and have an incredible talent.

To Max Henry: Thank you for the wonderful job you do, as always, on the formatting of my books. I love your work. You rock!

To Kelly Donaldson: Thank you for giving me the information I needed for your beautiful hometown of Newcastle. I hope I did it justice.

To Melissa McDonald: Thank you for the most amazing drawing you did of my boy, Carter Reynolds. You brought him to life. There are no words for your incredible talent. You have a special gift, my friend.

J.L. PERRY

J.L. Perry is a mother and a wife. She was born in Sydney, Australia in 1972, and has lived there her whole life. Her other titles include *My Destiny*, *My Forever*, *Damaged*, *Against All Odds* and the novella *Luckiest Bastard*, which follows *Bastard*. J.L. Perry is currently writing three novels: *Hooker*, *Jax* and *Nineteen Letters*.

For updates and teasers on all my future books,
you can follow or friend me on:

Facebook Profile
www.facebook.com/JLPerryAuthor

Facebook Page
www.facebook.com/pages/J-L-Perry-Author/216320021889204

Goodreads
www.goodreads.com/author/show/7825921.J_L_Perry

Twitter
www.twitter.com/JLPerryAuthor

Amazon Author Page
www.amazon.com/author/jlperry

Destiny's Divas Street Team
www.facebook.com/groups/323178884496533/

JL Perry Fan Page
www.facebook.com/groups/667079023424941/